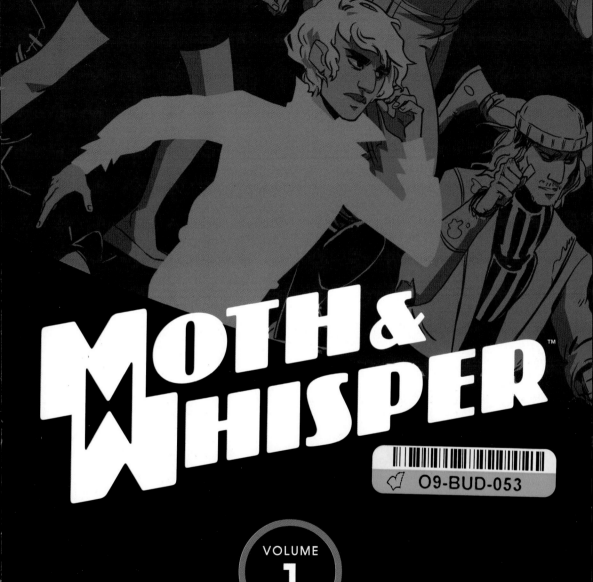

MOTH & WHISPER ™

VOLUME

1

THE KID

M O T H & W

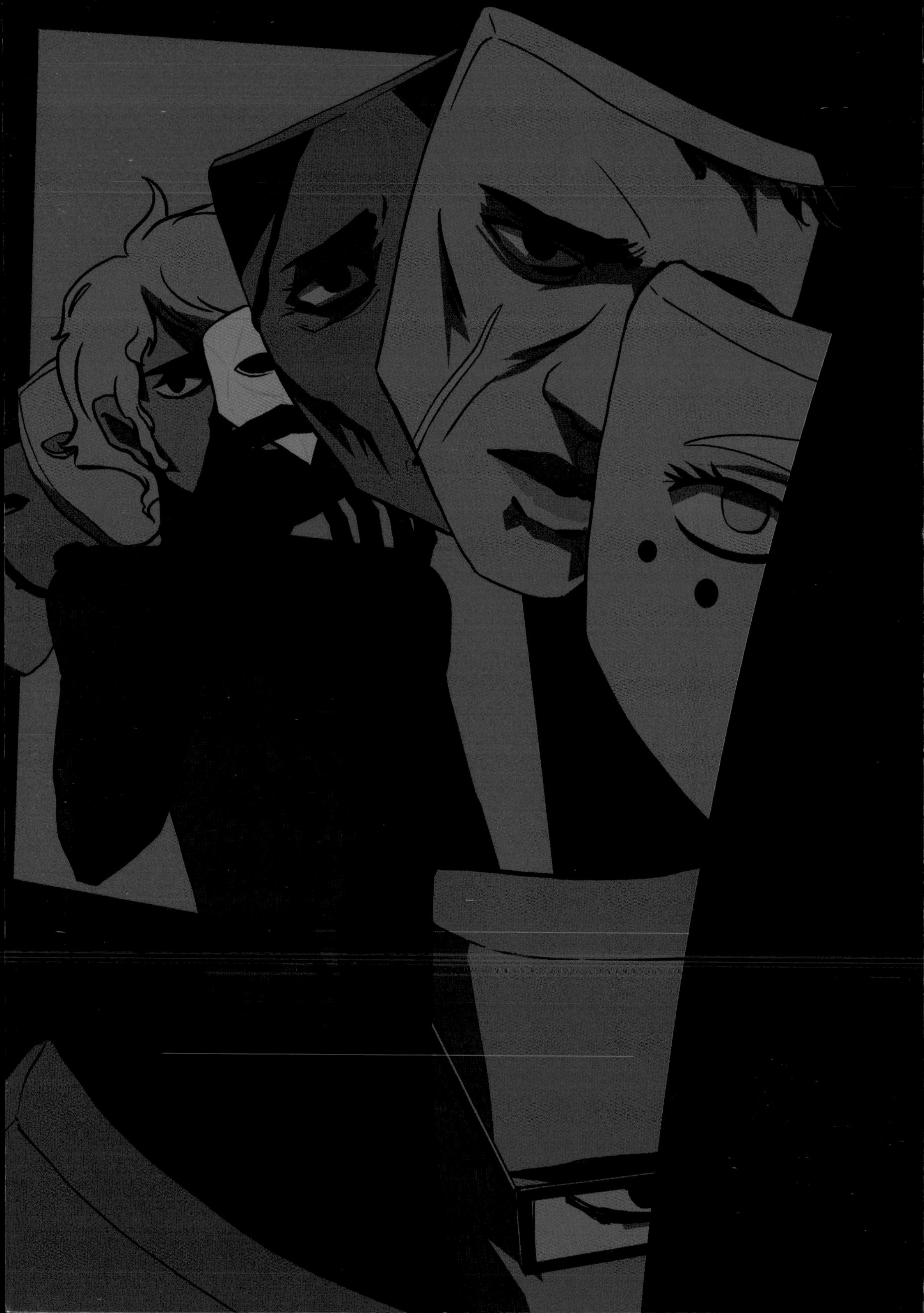

HISPER

VOLUME 1

THE KID

TED ANDERSON co-creator & writer

JEN HICKMAN co-creator & artist

MARSHALL DILLON letterer

JEN HICKMAN front & original series covers

JORGE CORONA variant cover

JARED K. FLETCHER logo designer

COREY BREEN book designer

MIKE MARTS editor

special thanks to **K. UVICK**

AFTERSHOCK™

MIKE MARTS - Editor-in-Chief • **JOE PRUETT** - Publisher/CCO • **LEE KRAMER** - President • **JON KRAMER** - Chief Executive Officer
STEVE ROTTERDAM - SVP, Sales & Marketing • **LISA Y. WU** - Director, Retailer Relations • **DAN SHIRES** - VP, Film & Television UK
CHRISTINA HARRINGTON - Managing Editor • **BLAKE STOCKER** - Chief Financial Officer • **AARON MARION** - Publicist
LISA MOODY - Finance • **CHARLES PRITCHETT** - Comics Production • **COREY BREEN** - Collections Production
TEDDY LEO - Editorial Assistant • **STEPHANIE CASEBIER** & **SARAH PRUETT** - Publishing Assistants

AfterShock Logo Design by **COMICRAFT**
Publicity: contact **AARON MARION** (aaron@publichausagency.com) & **RYAN CROY** (ryan@publichausagency.com) at **PUBLICHAUS**
Special thanks to: **IRA KURGAN, MARINE KSADZHIKYAN, ANTONIA LIANOS, STEPHAN NILSON** & **JULIE PIFHER**

AFTERSHOCKCOMICS.COM Follow us on social media 🐦 📷 f

I wrote MOTH & WHISPER for my friends who are invisible.

I am a straight cisgender allosexual man. I have never experienced persecution due to my sexuality or gender identity, and I likely never will. But I have friends who could, and have, and may again. I listen to them, and I do what I can for them.

Some of my friends have never seen themselves represented in comics, or movies, or books, except perhaps as the butt of a joke, or the victim of tragic violence—a plot device, not a character. Even those stories that *are* about them focus solely on their marginalized identities. My friends don't get to see stories about people like them having a normal life, or adventures, or achieving their dreams. To mainstream entertainment, they are invisible. So, I wrote this story for them.

I wanted Niki to be a complete character—interesting, flawed, with hopes and fears and a purpose—whose gender identity was a *part* of their story, but not the *whole*. Niki being genderqueer is a crucial part of their character, but it does not define them; it shapes them, but it does not *limit* them. I could not have written Niki without the invaluable help of Jen, who not only informed Niki's character but gave them life, a history and a solidity that comes through beautifully on the page.

I hope Niki's story can be enjoyed by readers of all sorts. But I wrote Niki especially for my friends who have never seen themselves. So, for my friends, and for the many readers who might also be looking for themselves in a book: I hope you find something in Niki that speaks to you.

TED ANDERSON
February 2019

I still remember settling in to read the very first MOTH & WHISPER script. I'm pretty sure I drove my studio-mates insane that day with just how often I interrupted them to shout that the script was amazing, that it was going to be so much fun to draw.

And then I got very sweaty as I started into the work itself, because I was intimidated by how clean and clever Ted's scripting was, because I wanted to make amazing art for this very good book, and because getting to draw a story about a genderqueer super-thief was, more or less, living the dream. As work on the book progressed, I began to realize that we were creating something very special— Niki is, actually, the dream. They're an escapist fantasy avatar of a lot of genderqueer ideals—getting to pick your presentation, getting read correctly, never getting misgendered, getting revenge on the gross old mob boss who torched all your fake identities. You know. Ideals.

It's so important to me that there be stories out there where gender-nonconforming kids have agency, respect, goals and friends. Where we're the hero.

I'm incredibly proud of the book you hold in your hands. You're going to love it.

JEN HICKMAN
February 2019

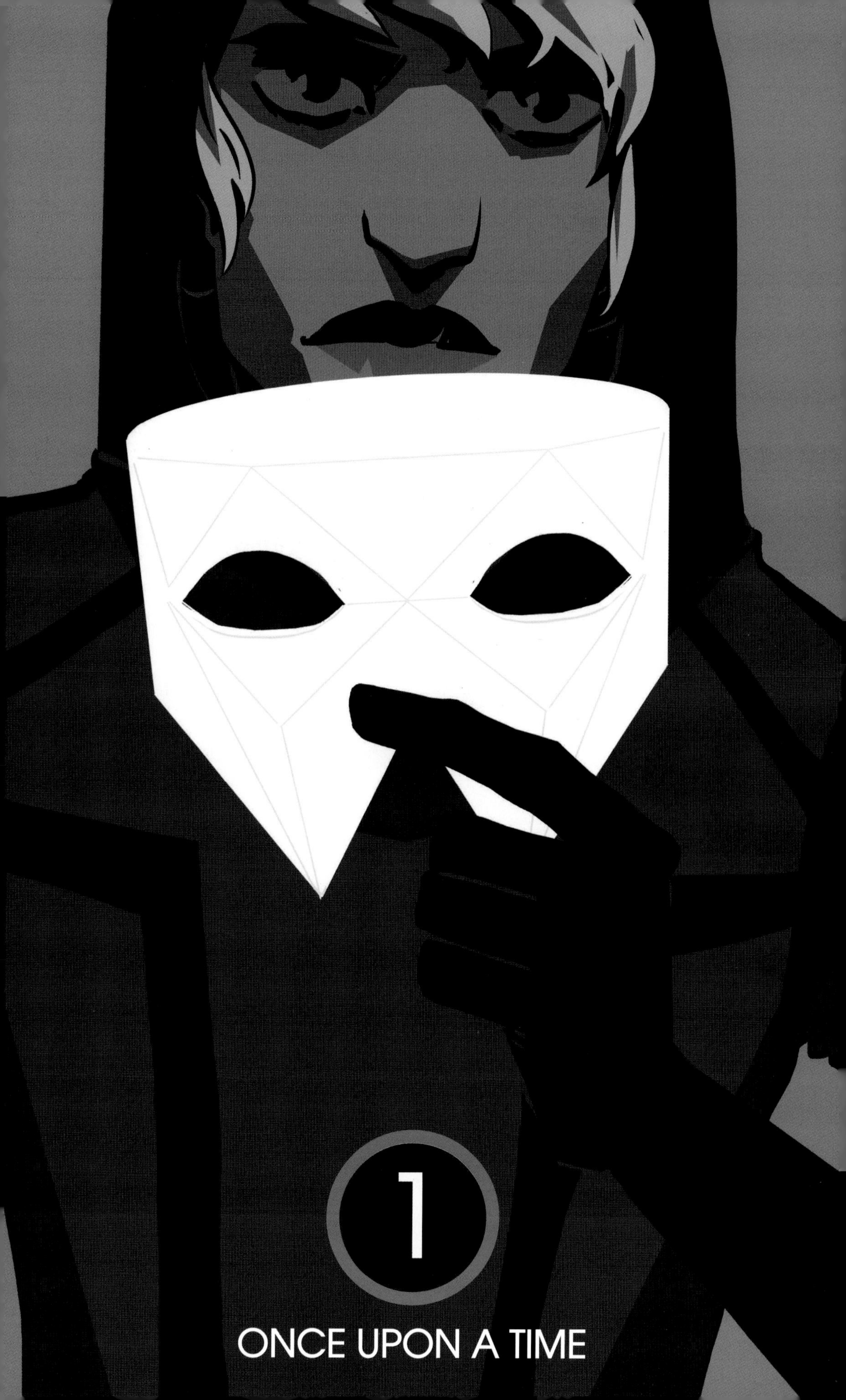

1
ONCE UPON A TIME

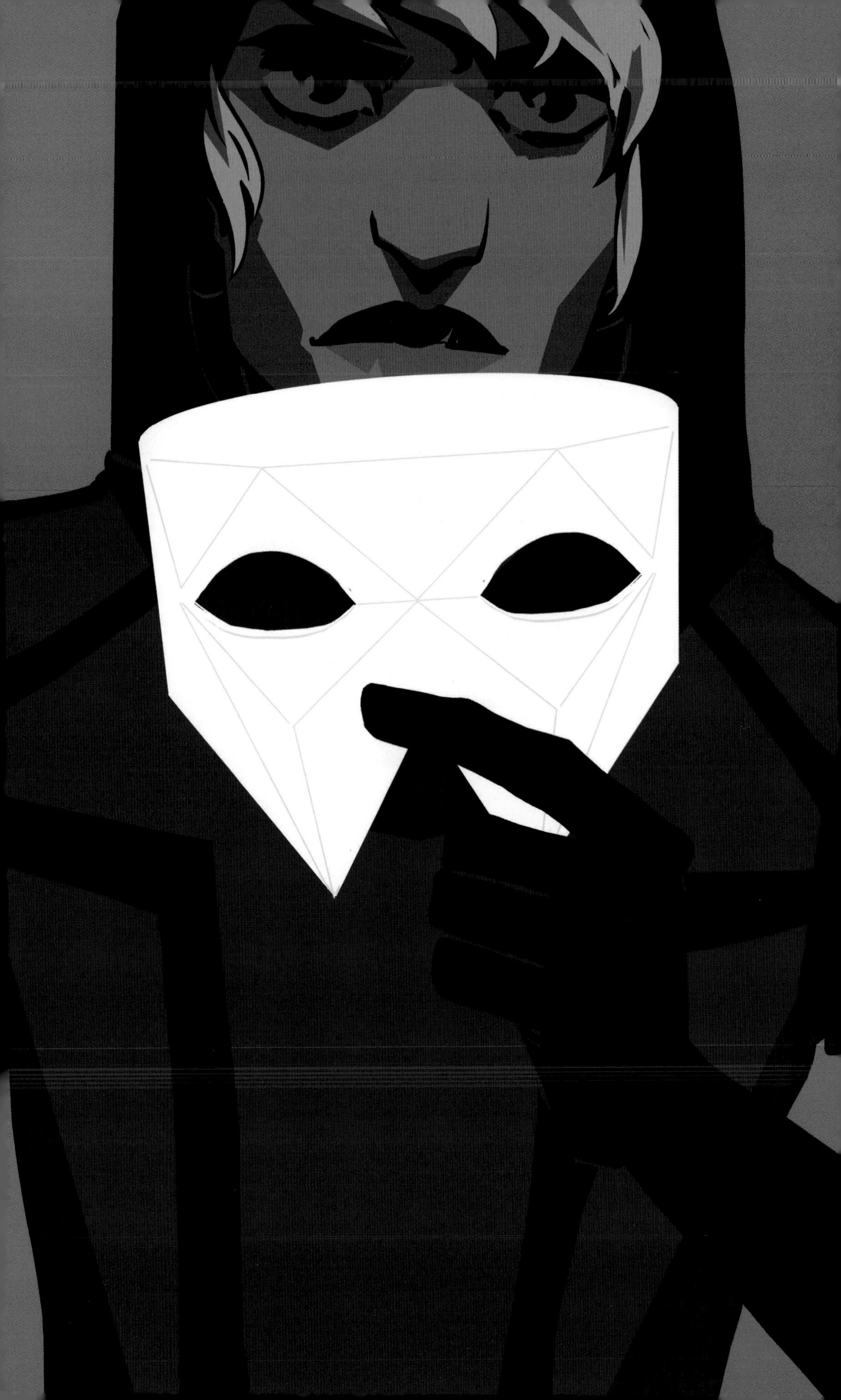

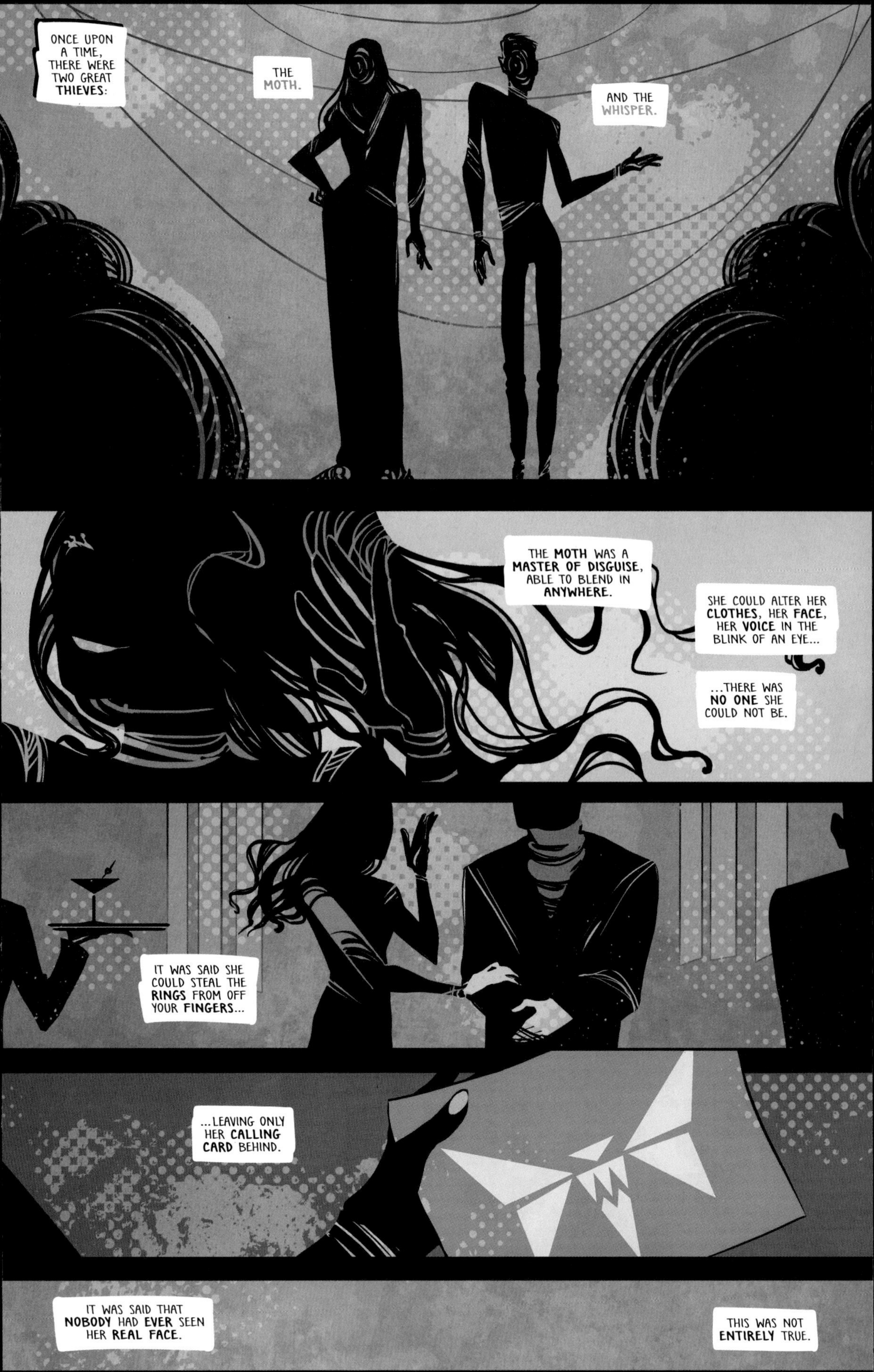
ONCE UPON A TIME, THERE WERE TWO GREAT THIEVES:
THE MOTH.
AND THE WHISPER.
THE MOTH WAS A MASTER OF DISGUISE, ABLE TO BLEND IN ANYWHERE.
SHE COULD ALTER HER CLOTHES, HER FACE, HER VOICE IN THE BLINK OF AN EYE...
...THERE WAS NO ONE SHE COULD NOT BE.
IT WAS SAID SHE COULD STEAL THE RINGS FROM OFF YOUR FINGERS...
...LEAVING ONLY HER CALLING CARD BEHIND.
IT WAS SAID THAT NOBODY HAD EVER SEEN HER REAL FACE.
THIS WAS NOT ENTIRELY TRUE.

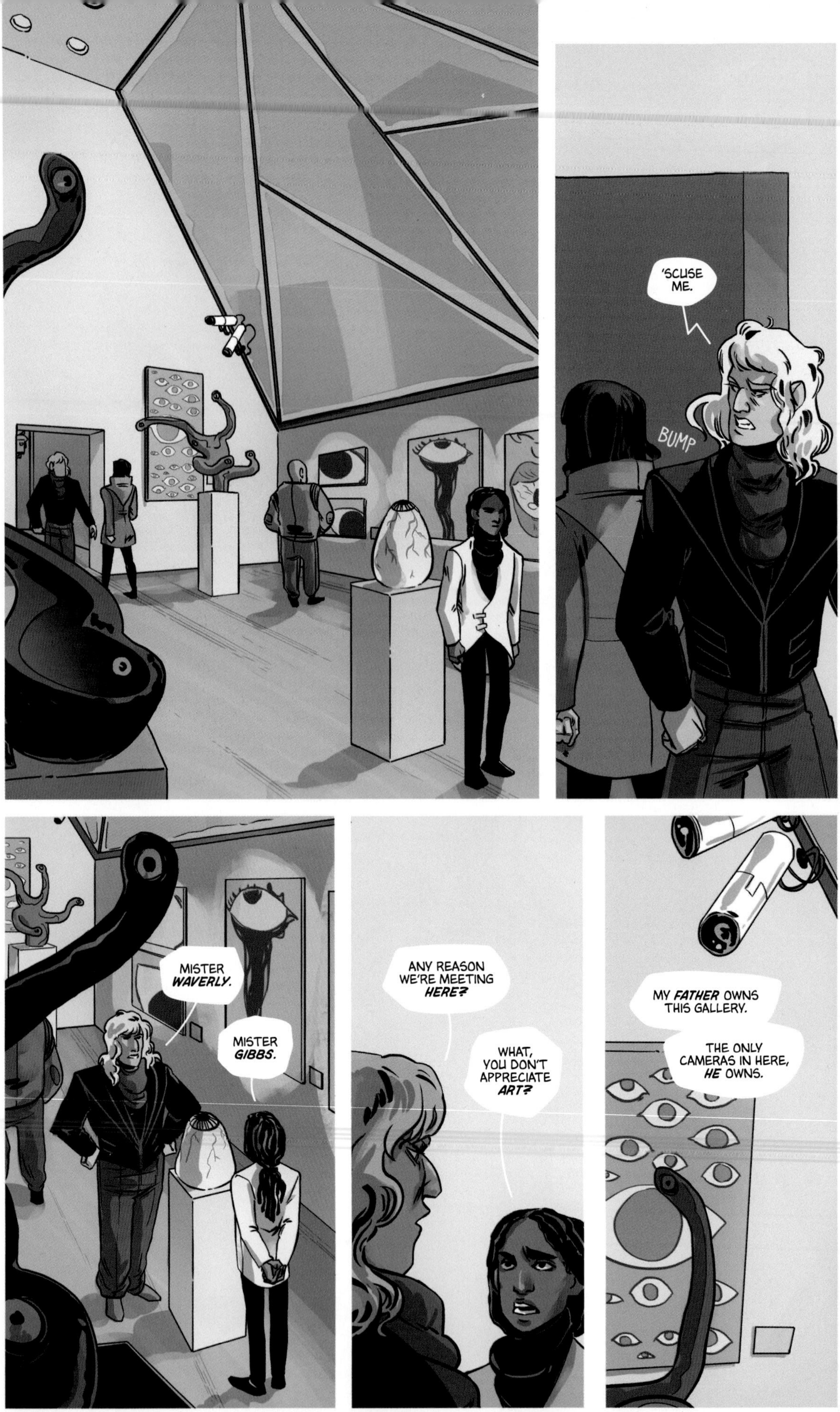
'SCUSE ME.
BUMP
MISTER WAVERLY.
MISTER GIBBS.
ANY REASON WE'RE MEETING HERE?
WHAT, YOU DON'T APPRECIATE ART?
MY FATHER OWNS THIS GALLERY.
THE ONLY CAMERAS IN HERE, HE OWNS.

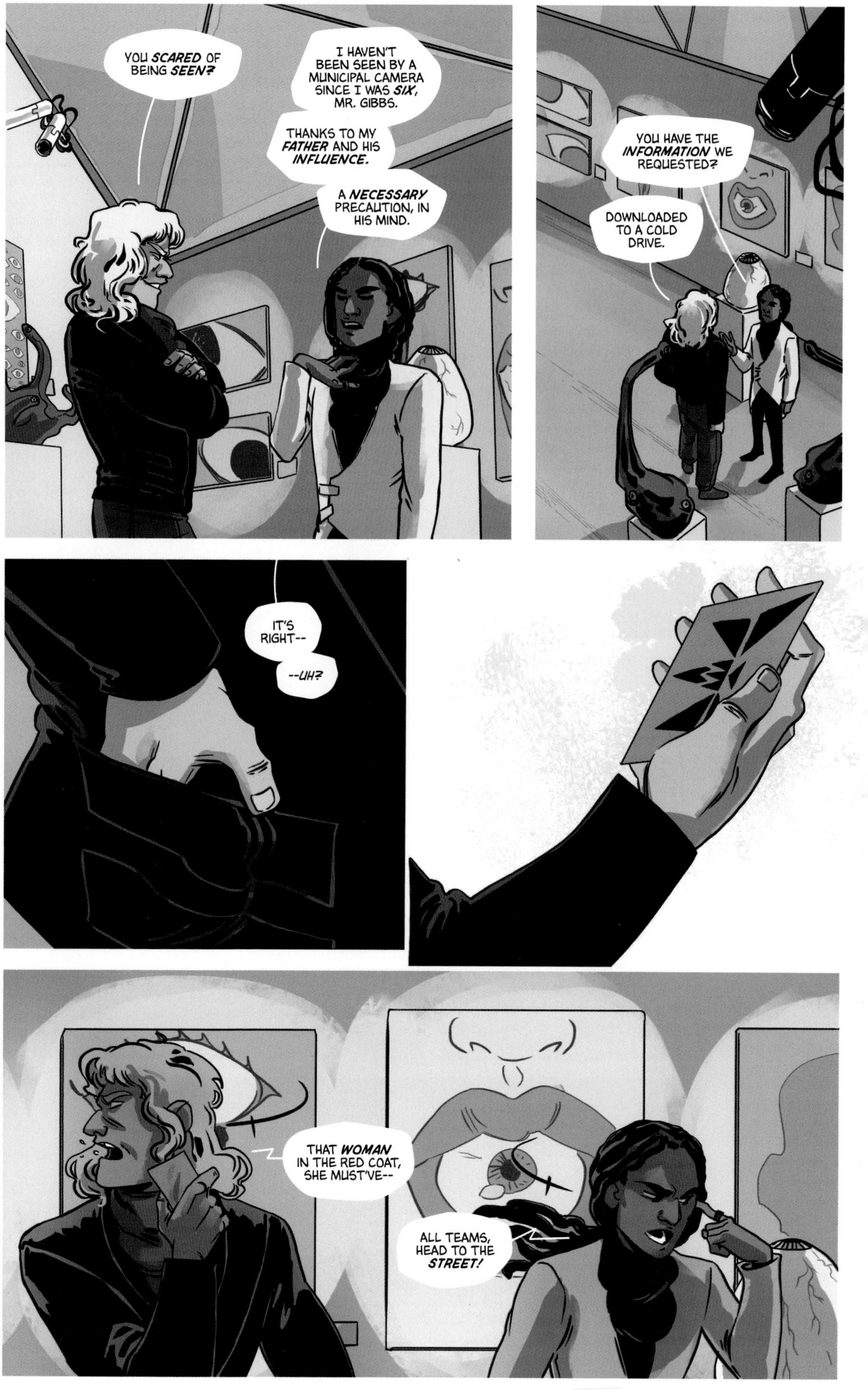

YOU SCARED OF BEING SEEN?
I HAVEN'T BEEN SEEN BY A MUNICIPAL CAMERA SINCE I WAS SIX, MR. GIBBS.
THANKS TO MY FATHER AND HIS INFLUENCE.
A NECESSARY PRECAUTION, IN HIS MIND.
YOU HAVE THE INFORMATION WE REQUESTED?
DOWNLOADED TO A COLD DRIVE.
IT'S RIGHT--
--UH?
THAT WOMAN IN THE RED COAT, SHE MUST'VE--
ALL TEAMS, HEAD TO THE STREET!

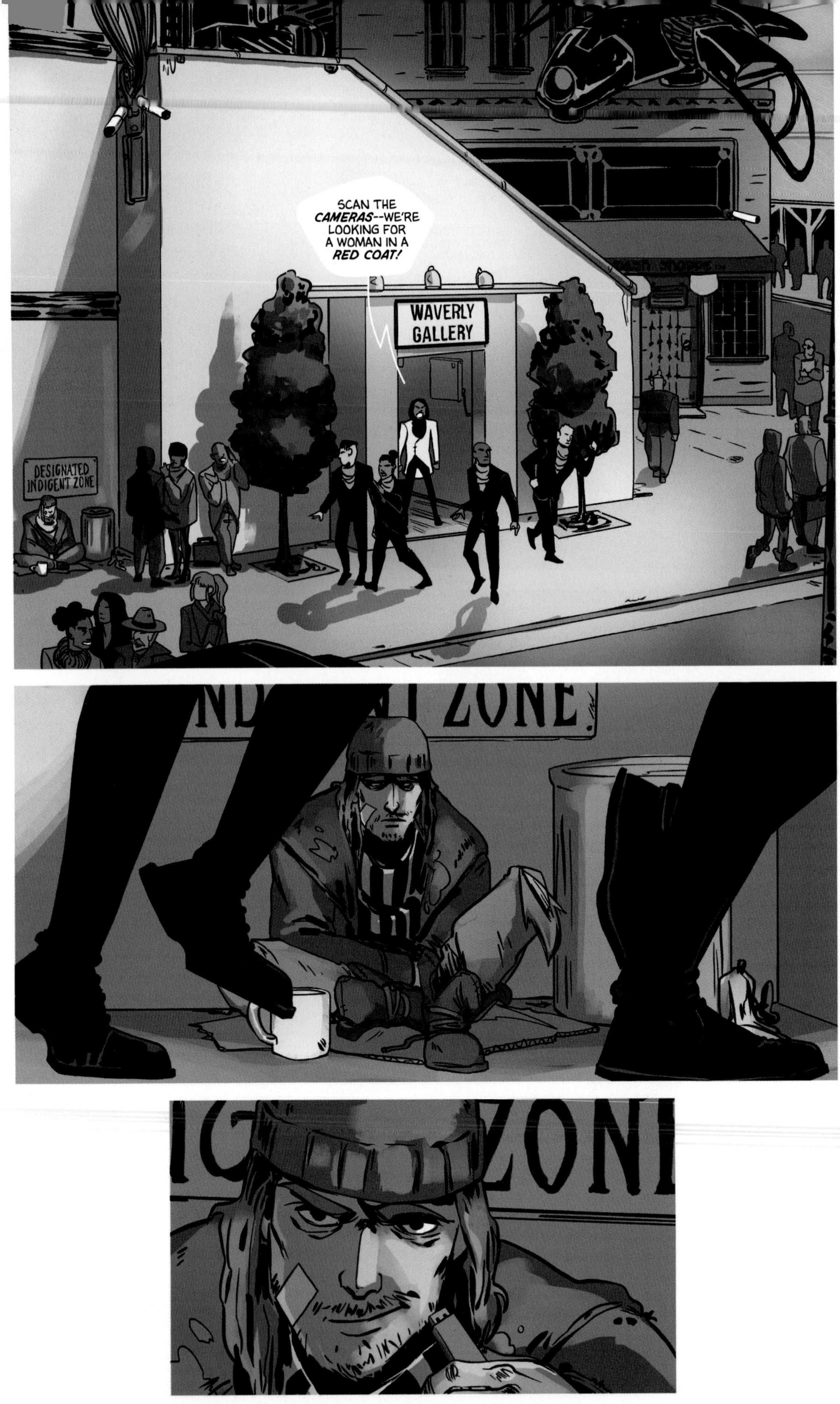
SCAN THE CAMERAS--WE'RE LOOKING FOR A WOMAN IN A RED COAT!
WAVERLY GALLERY
DESIGNATED INDIGENT ZONE

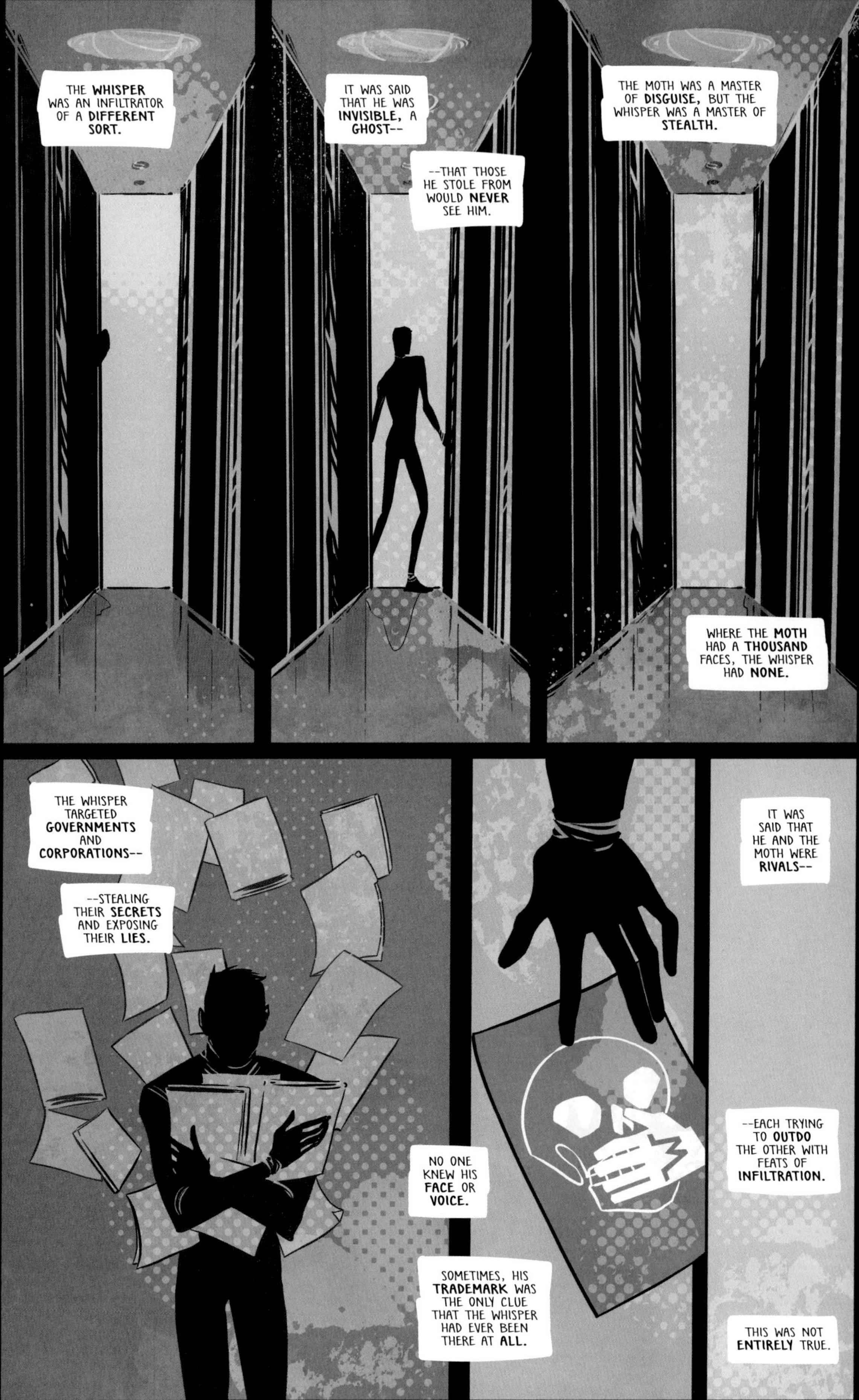
THE WHISPER WAS AN INFILTRATOR OF A DIFFERENT SORT.
IT WAS SAID THAT HE WAS INVISIBLE, A GHOST--
--THAT THOSE HE STOLE FROM WOULD NEVER SEE HIM.
THE MOTH WAS A MASTER OF DISGUISE, BUT THE WHISPER WAS A MASTER OF STEALTH.
WHERE THE MOTH HAD A THOUSAND FACES, THE WHISPER HAD NONE.
THE WHISPER TARGETED GOVERNMENTS AND CORPORATIONS--
--STEALING THEIR SECRETS AND EXPOSING THEIR LIES.
NO ONE KNEW HIS FACE OR VOICE.
SOMETIMES, HIS TRADEMARK WAS THE ONLY CLUE THAT THE WHISPER HAD EVER BEEN THERE AT ALL.
IT WAS SAID THAT HE AND THE MOTH WERE RIVALS--
--EACH TRYING TO OUTDO THE OTHER WITH FEATS OF INFILTRATION.
THIS WAS NOT ENTIRELY TRUE.

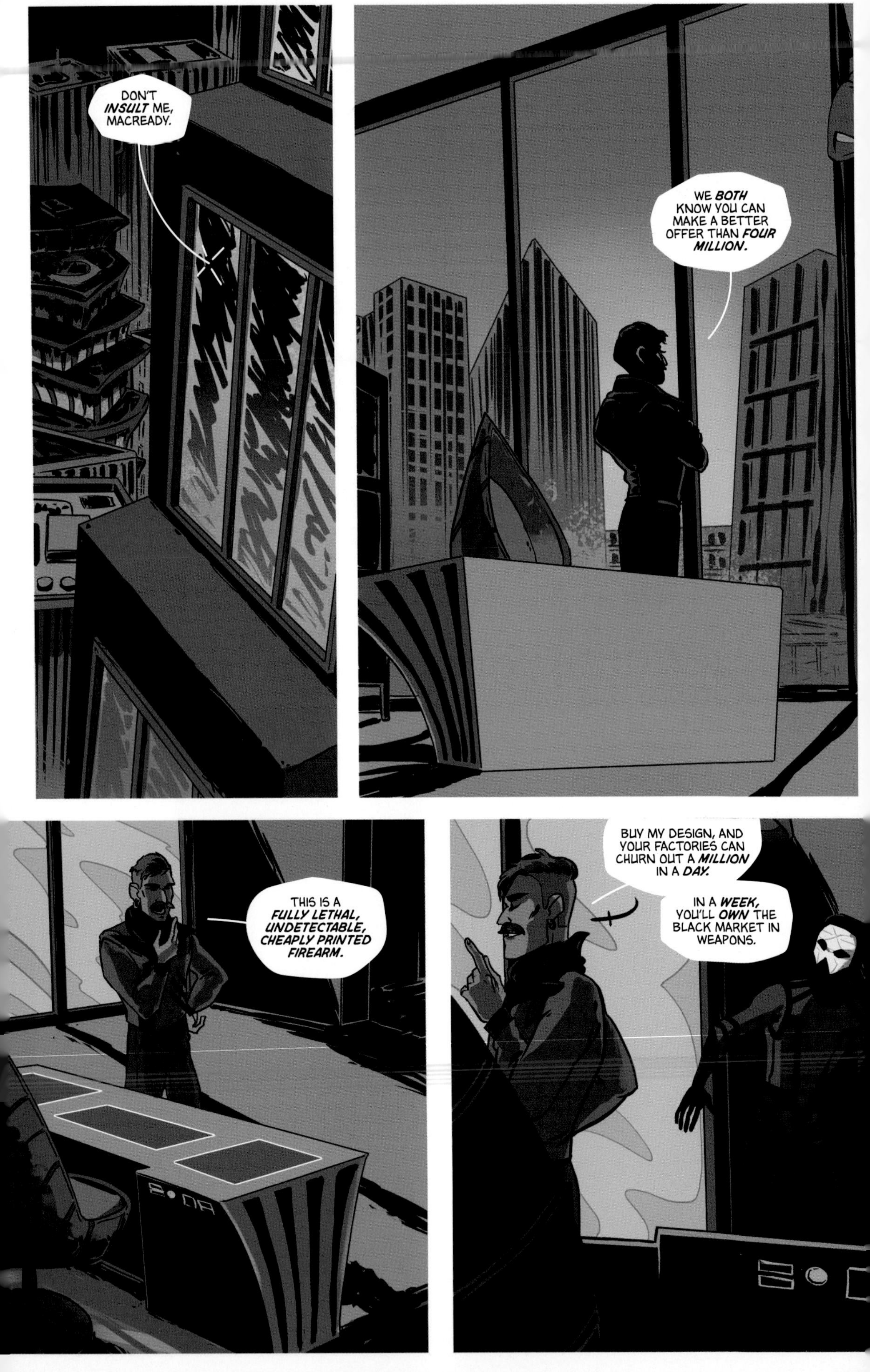
DON'T INSULT ME, MACREADY.
WE BOTH KNOW YOU CAN MAKE A BETTER OFFER THAN FOUR MILLION.
THIS IS A FULLY LETHAL, UNDETECTABLE, CHEAPLY PRINTED FIREARM.
BUY MY DESIGN, AND YOUR FACTORIES CAN CHURN OUT A MILLION IN A DAY.
IN A WEEK, YOU'LL OWN THE BLACK MARKET IN WEAPONS.

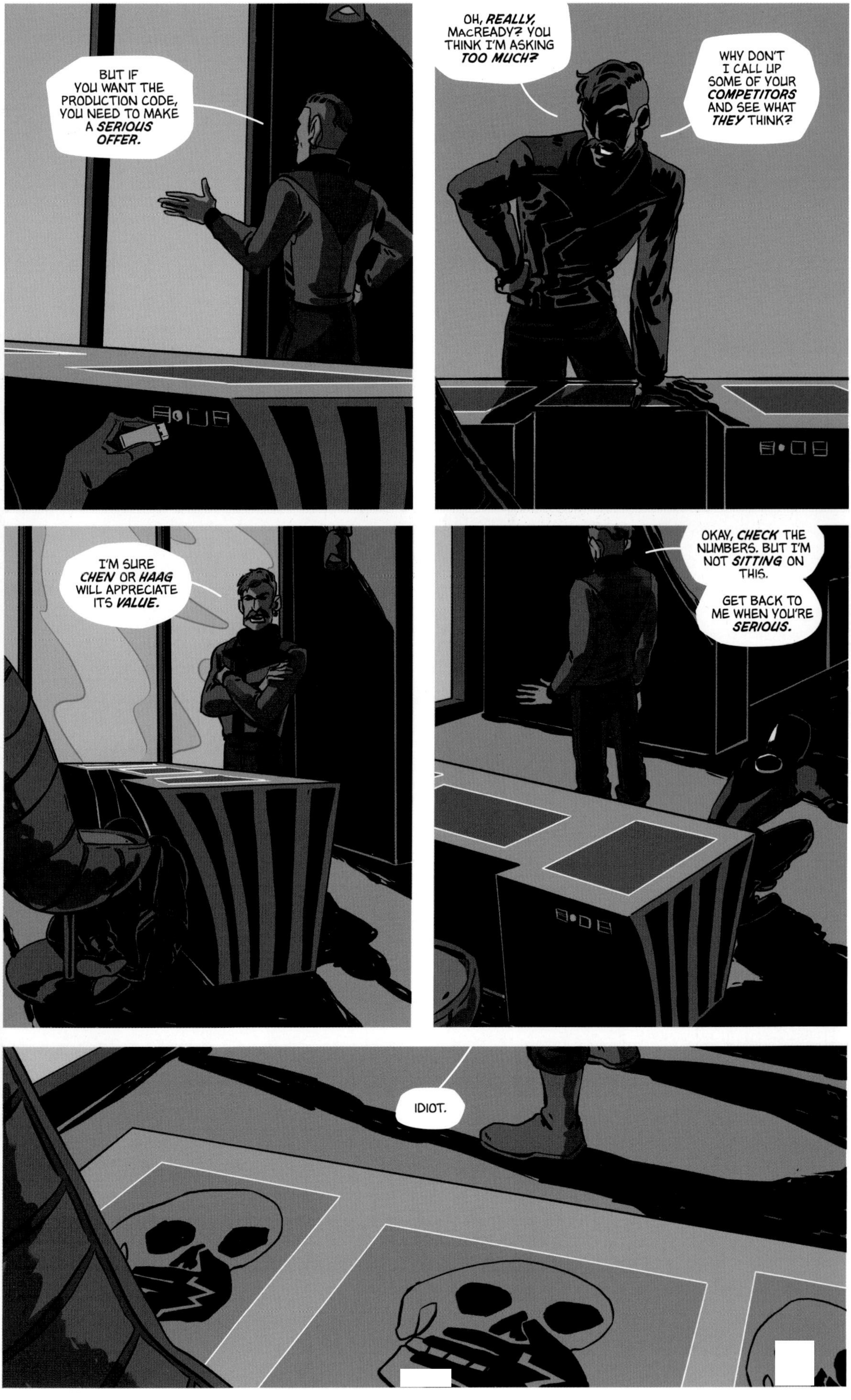
BUT IF YOU WANT THE PRODUCTION CODE, YOU NEED TO MAKE A SERIOUS OFFER.
OH, REALLY, MACREADY? YOU THINK I'M ASKING TOO MUCH?
WHY DON'T I CALL UP SOME OF YOUR COMPETITORS AND SEE WHAT THEY THINK?
I'M SURE CHEN OR HAAG WILL APPRECIATE ITS VALUE.
OKAY, CHECK THE NUMBERS. BUT I'M NOT SITTING ON THIS.
GET BACK TO ME WHEN YOU'RE SERIOUS.
IDIOT.

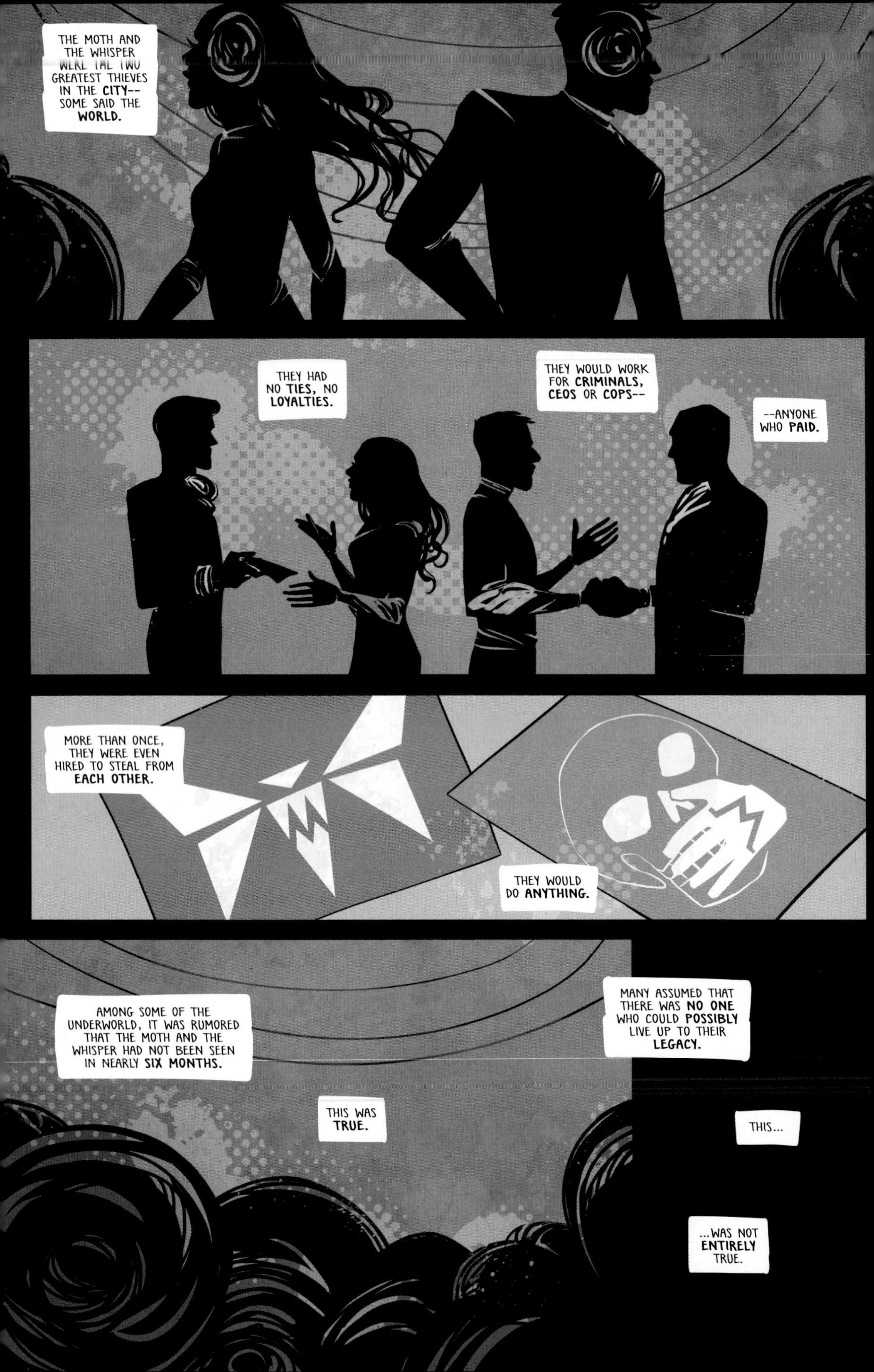

THE MOTH AND THE WHISPER WERE THE TWO GREATEST THIEVES IN THE CITY-- SOME SAID THE WORLD.
THEY HAD NO TIES, NO LOYALTIES.
THEY WOULD WORK FOR CRIMINALS, CEOS OR COPS--
--ANYONE WHO PAID.
MORE THAN ONCE, THEY WERE EVEN HIRED TO STEAL FROM EACH OTHER.
THEY WOULD DO ANYTHING.
AMONG SOME OF THE UNDERWORLD, IT WAS RUMORED THAT THE MOTH AND THE WHISPER HAD NOT BEEN SEEN IN NEARLY SIX MONTHS.
THIS WAS TRUE.
MANY ASSUMED THAT THERE WAS NO ONE WHO COULD POSSIBLY LIVE UP TO THEIR LEGACY.
THIS...
...WAS NOT ENTIRELY TRUE.

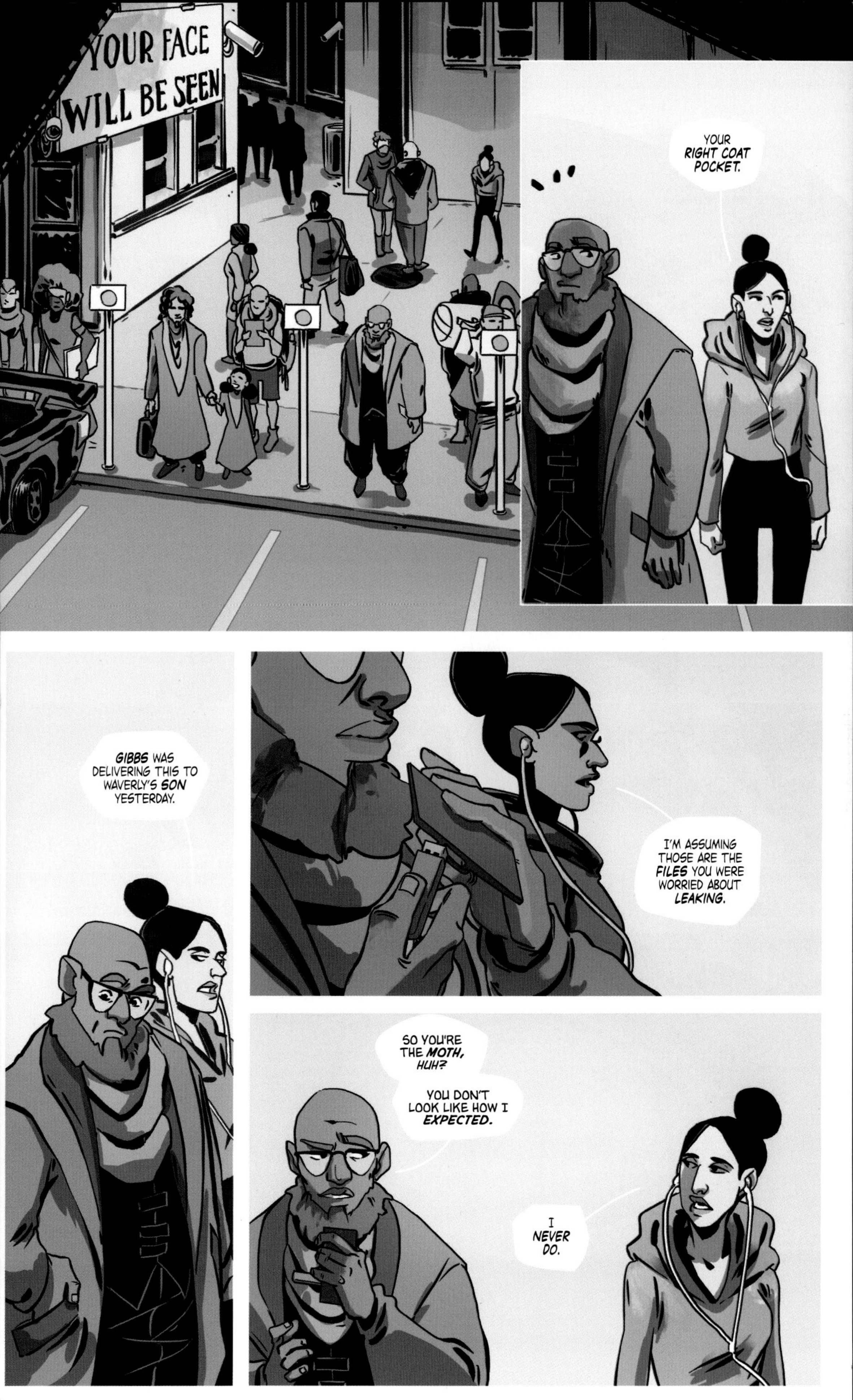
YOUR FACE WILL BE SEEN
...
YOUR RIGHT COAT POCKET.
GIBBS WAS DELIVERING THIS TO WAVERLY'S SON YESTERDAY.
I'M ASSUMING THOSE ARE THE FILES YOU WERE WORRIED ABOUT LEAKING.
SO YOU'RE THE MOTH, HUH?
YOU DON'T LOOK LIKE HOW I EXPECTED.
I NEVER DO.

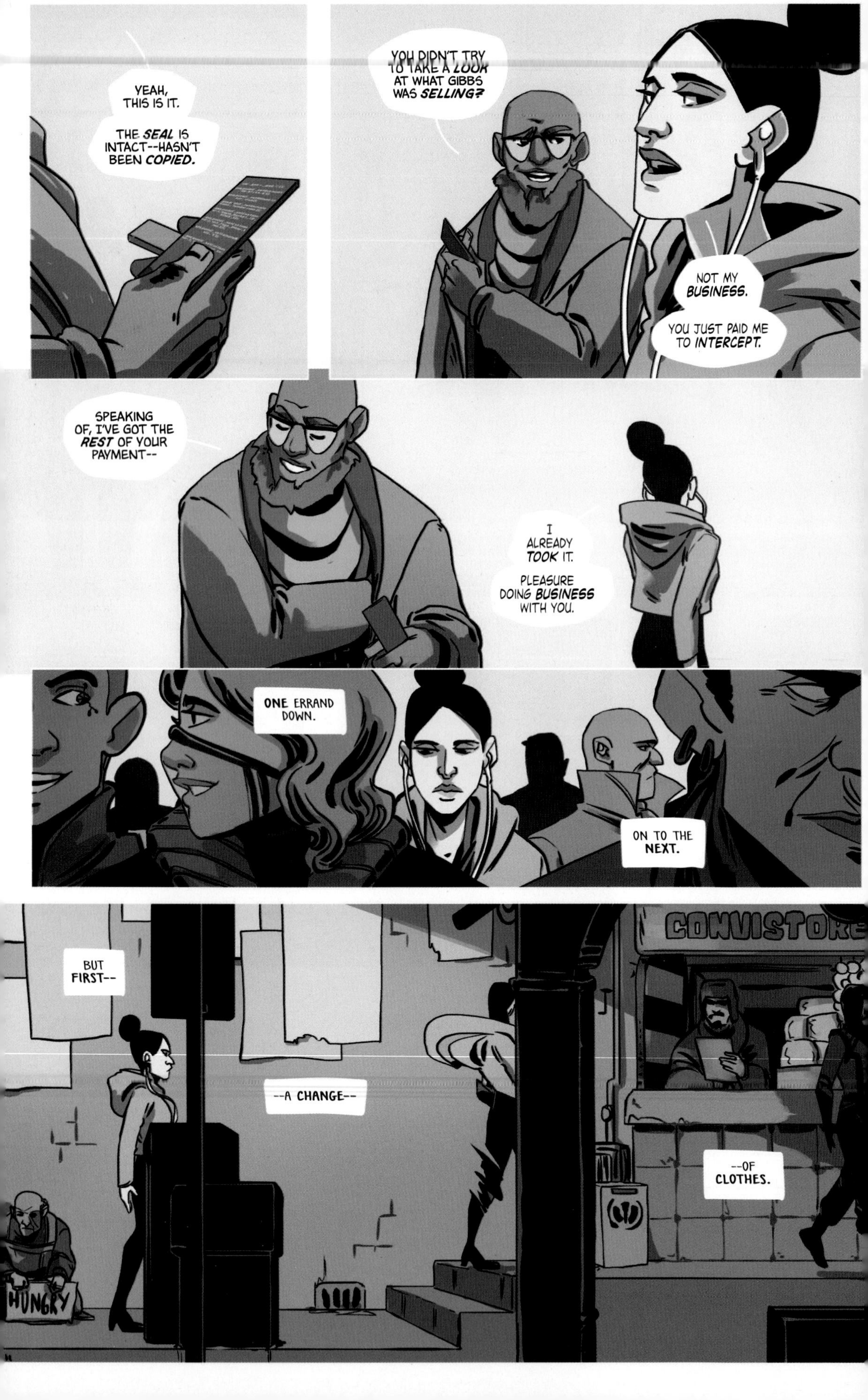

YEAH, THIS IS IT.
THE SEAL IS INTACT--HASN'T BEEN COPIED.
YOU DIDN'T TRY TO TAKE A LOOK AT WHAT GIBBS WAS SELLING?
NOT MY BUSINESS.
YOU JUST PAID ME TO INTERCEPT.
SPEAKING OF, I'VE GOT THE REST OF YOUR PAYMENT--
I ALREADY TOOK IT.
PLEASURE DOING BUSINESS WITH YOU.
ONE ERRAND DOWN.
ON TO THE NEXT.
CONVISTORE
BUT FIRST--
--A CHANGE--
--OF CLOTHES.
HUNGRY

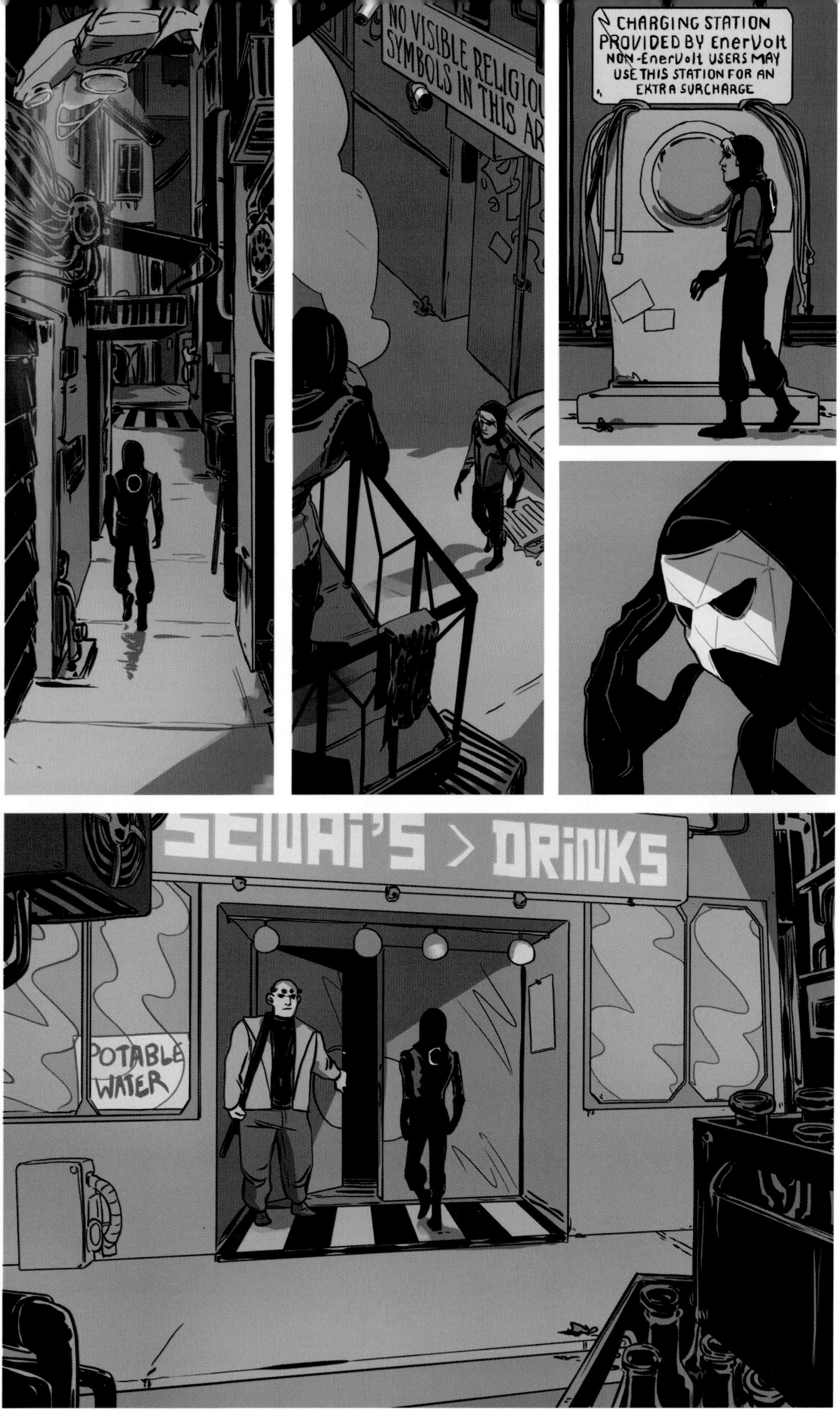
NO VISIBLE RELIGIOU
SYMBOLS IN THIS AR
CHARGING STATION
PROVIDED BY EnerVolt
NON-EnerVolt USERS MAY
USE THIS STATION FOR AN
EXTRA SURCHARGE
SENAI'S > DRINKS
POTABLE
WATER

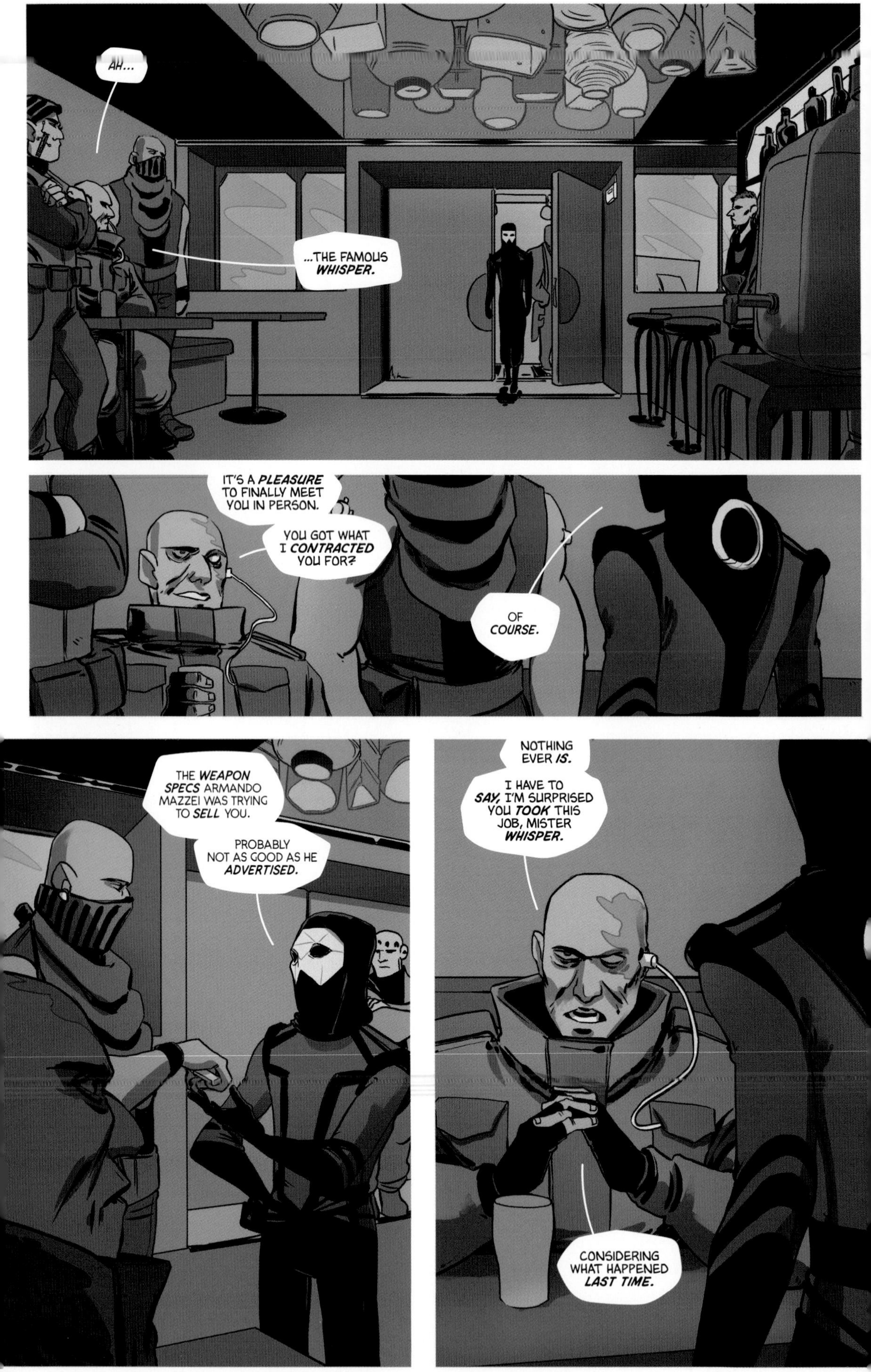
AH...
...THE FAMOUS *WHISPER.*
IT'S A *PLEASURE* TO FINALLY MEET YOU IN PERSON.
YOU GOT WHAT I *CONTRACTED* YOU FOR?
OF *COURSE.*
THE *WEAPON SPECS* ARMANDO MAZZEI WAS TRYING TO *SELL* YOU.
PROBABLY NOT AS GOOD AS HE *ADVERTISED.*
NOTHING EVER *IS.*
I HAVE TO *SAY,* I'M SURPRISED YOU *TOOK* THIS JOB, MISTER *WHISPER.*
CONSIDERING WHAT HAPPENED *LAST TIME.*

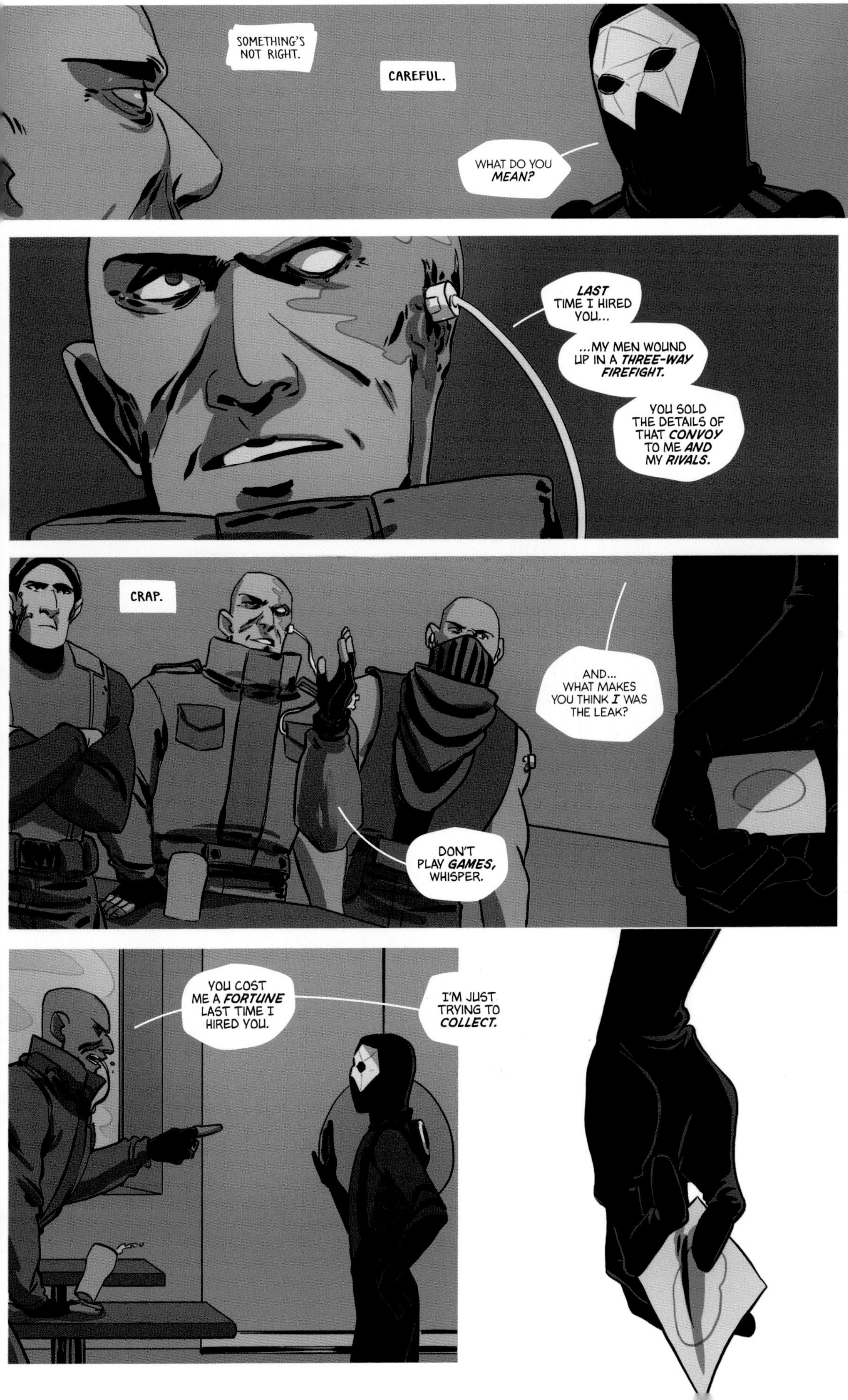
SOMETHING'S NOT RIGHT.
CAREFUL.
WHAT DO YOU MEAN?
LAST TIME I HIRED YOU...
...MY MEN WOUND UP IN A THREE-WAY FIREFIGHT.
YOU SOLD THE DETAILS OF THAT CONVOY TO ME AND MY RIVALS.
CRAP.
AND... WHAT MAKES YOU THINK I WAS THE LEAK?
DON'T PLAY GAMES, WHISPER.
YOU COST ME A FORTUNE LAST TIME I HIRED YOU.
I'M JUST TRYING TO COLLECT.

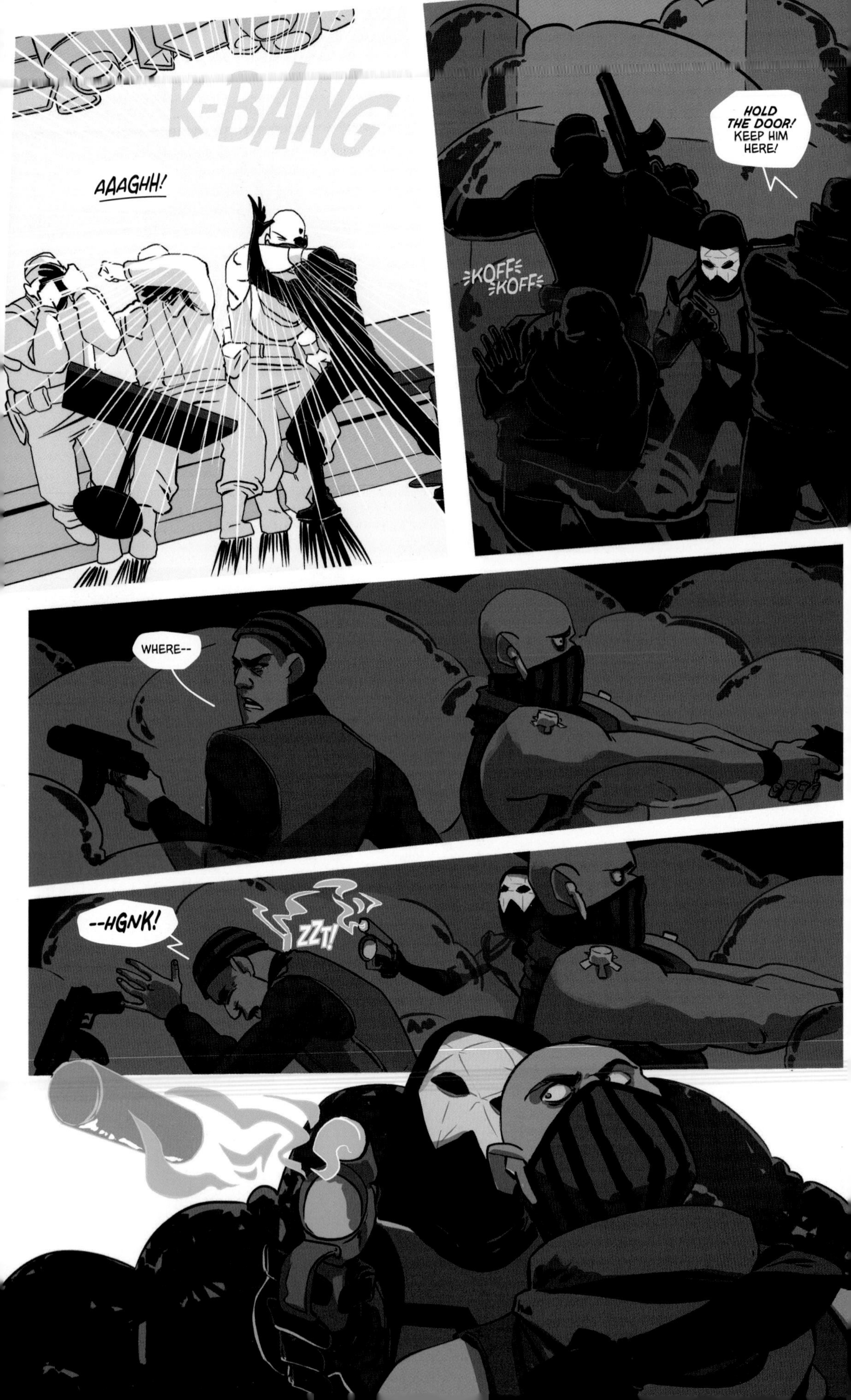
K-BANG
AAAGHH!
HOLD THE DOOR! KEEP HIM HERE!
KOFF KOFF
WHERE--
--HGNK!
ZZT!

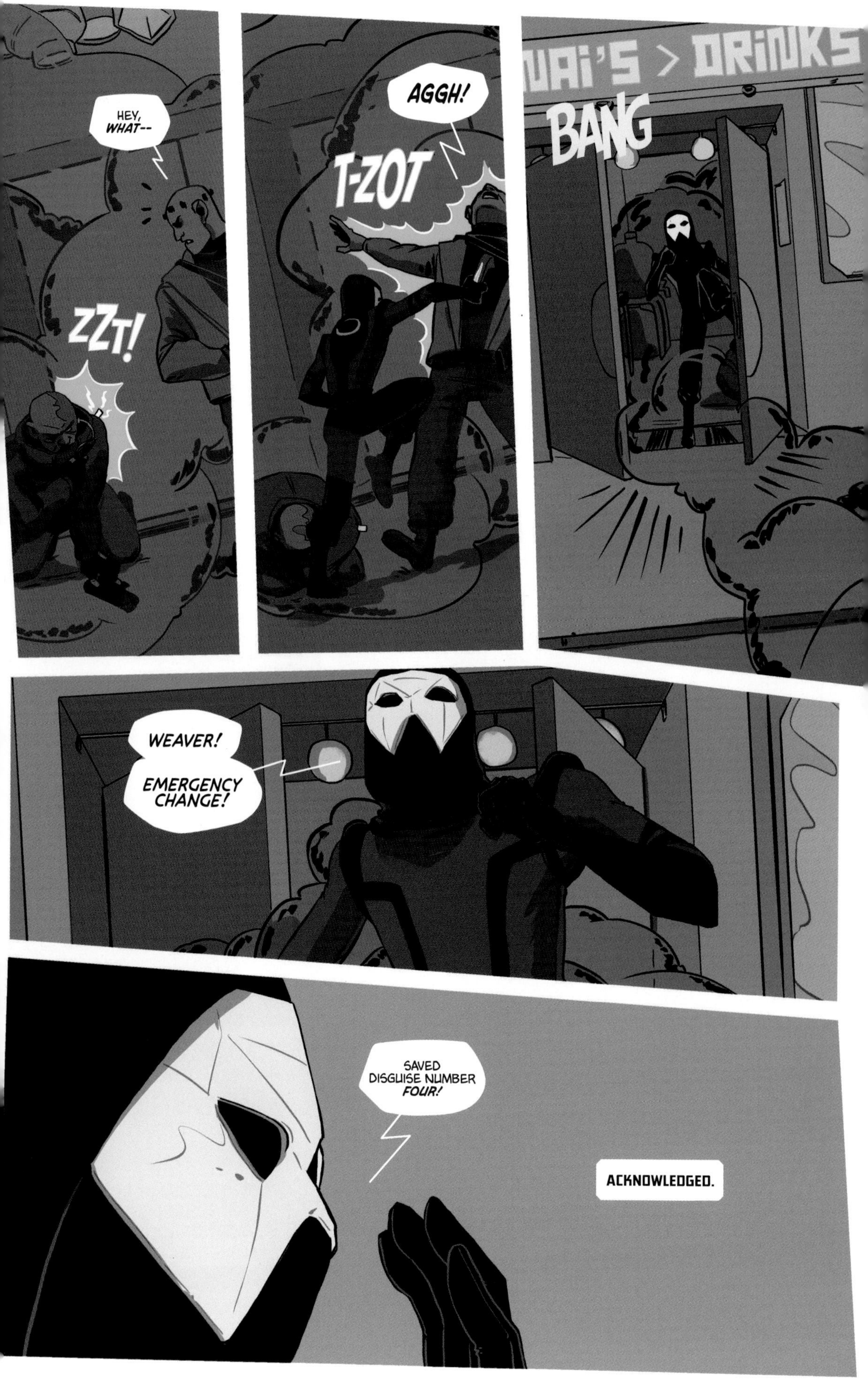
HEY, WHAT--
ZZT!
AGGH!
T-ZOT
NAI'S > DRINKS
BANG
WEAVER!
EMERGENCY CHANGE!
SAVED DISGUISE NUMBER FOUR!
ACKNOWLEDGED.

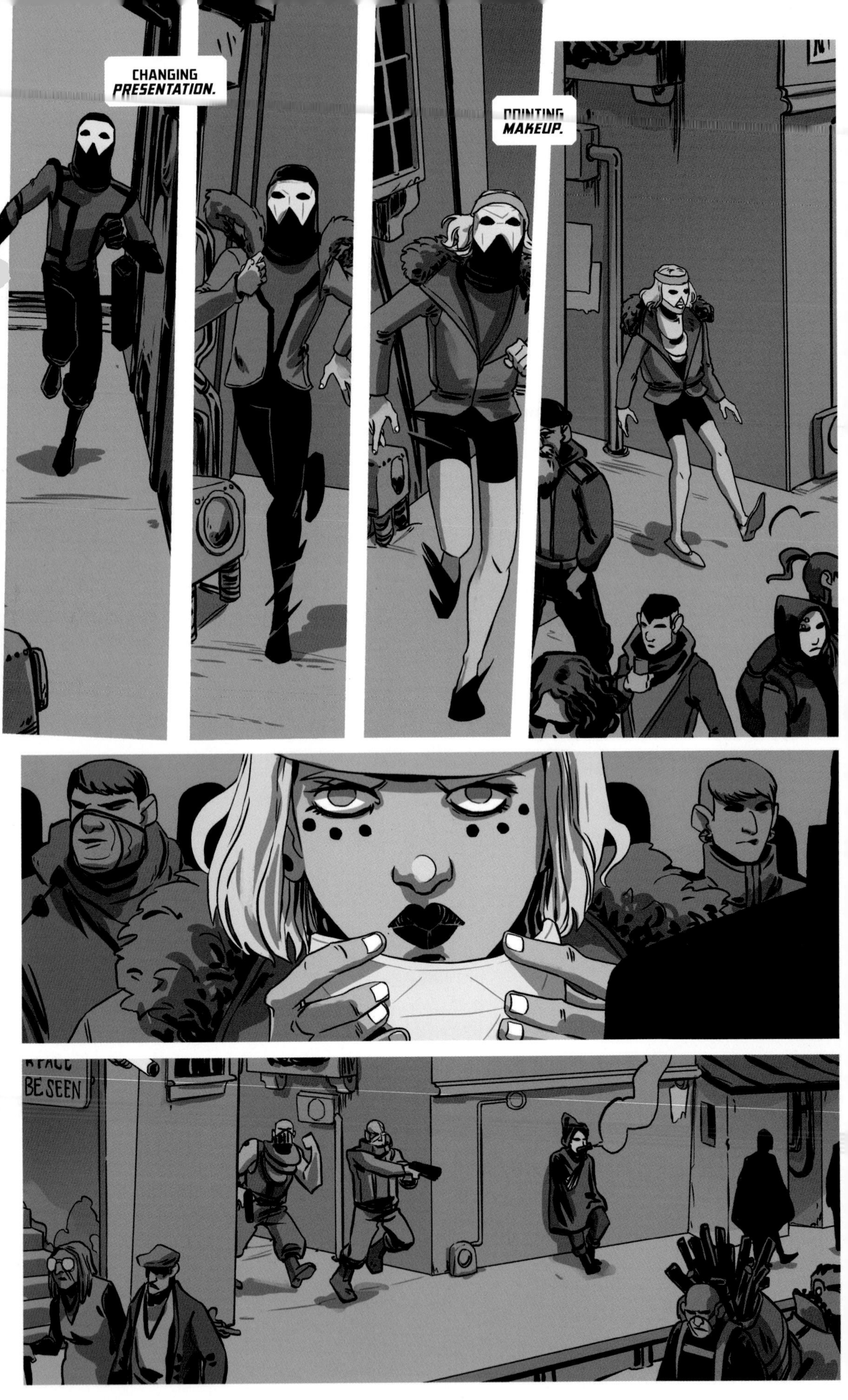
CHANGING PRESENTATION.
PAINTING MAKEUP.
BE SEEN

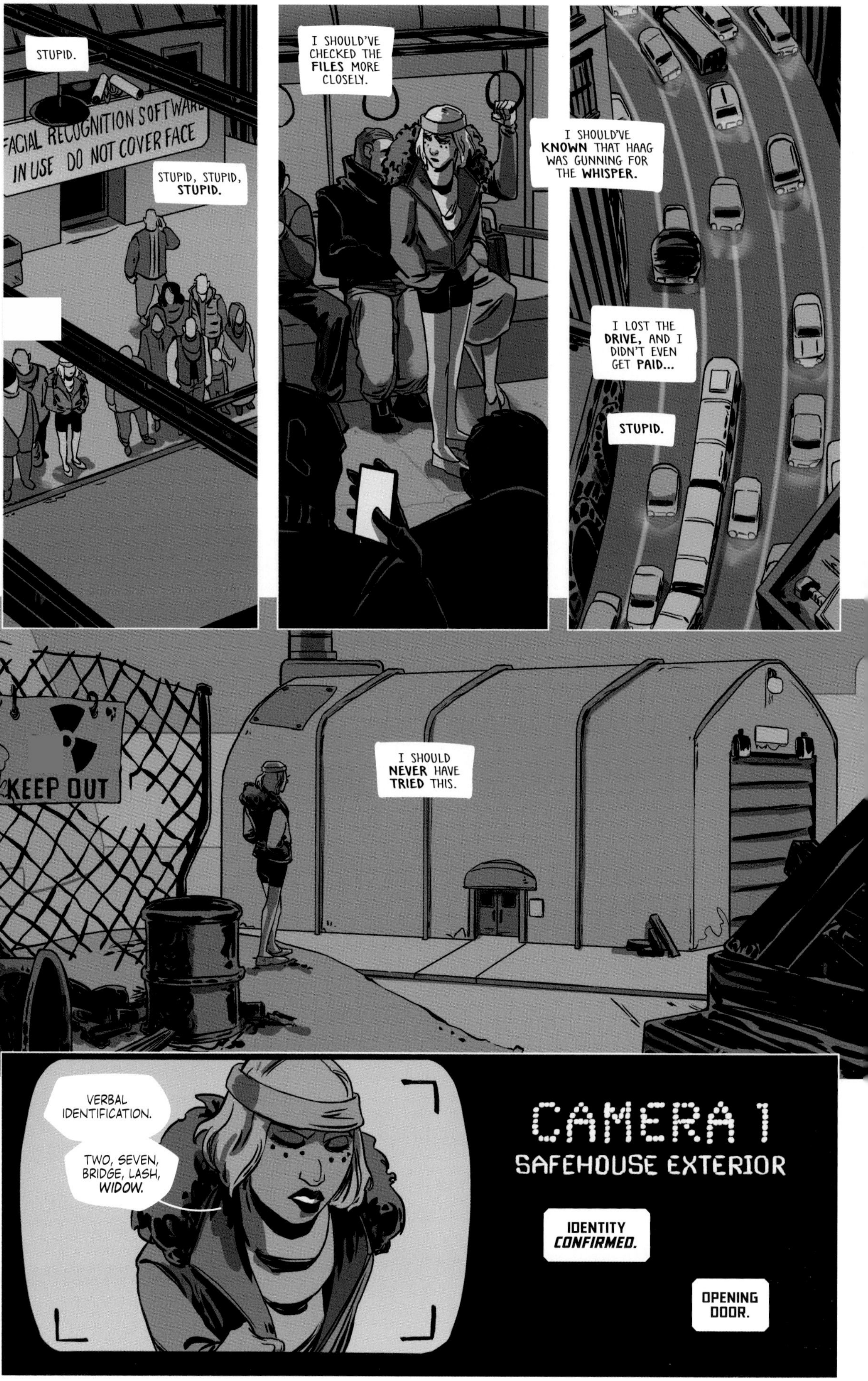
STUPID.
FACIAL RECOGNITION SOFTWARE IN USE DO NOT COVER FACE
STUPID, STUPID, STUPID.
I SHOULD'VE CHECKED THE FILES MORE CLOSELY.
I SHOULD'VE KNOWN THAT HAAG WAS GUNNING FOR THE WHISPER.
I LOST THE DRIVE, AND I DIDN'T EVEN GET PAID...
STUPID.
KEEP OUT
I SHOULD NEVER HAVE TRIED THIS.
VERBAL IDENTIFICATION.
TWO, SEVEN, BRIDGE, LASH, WIDOW.
CAMERA 1
SAFEHOUSE EXTERIOR
IDENTITY CONFIRMED.
OPENING DOOR.

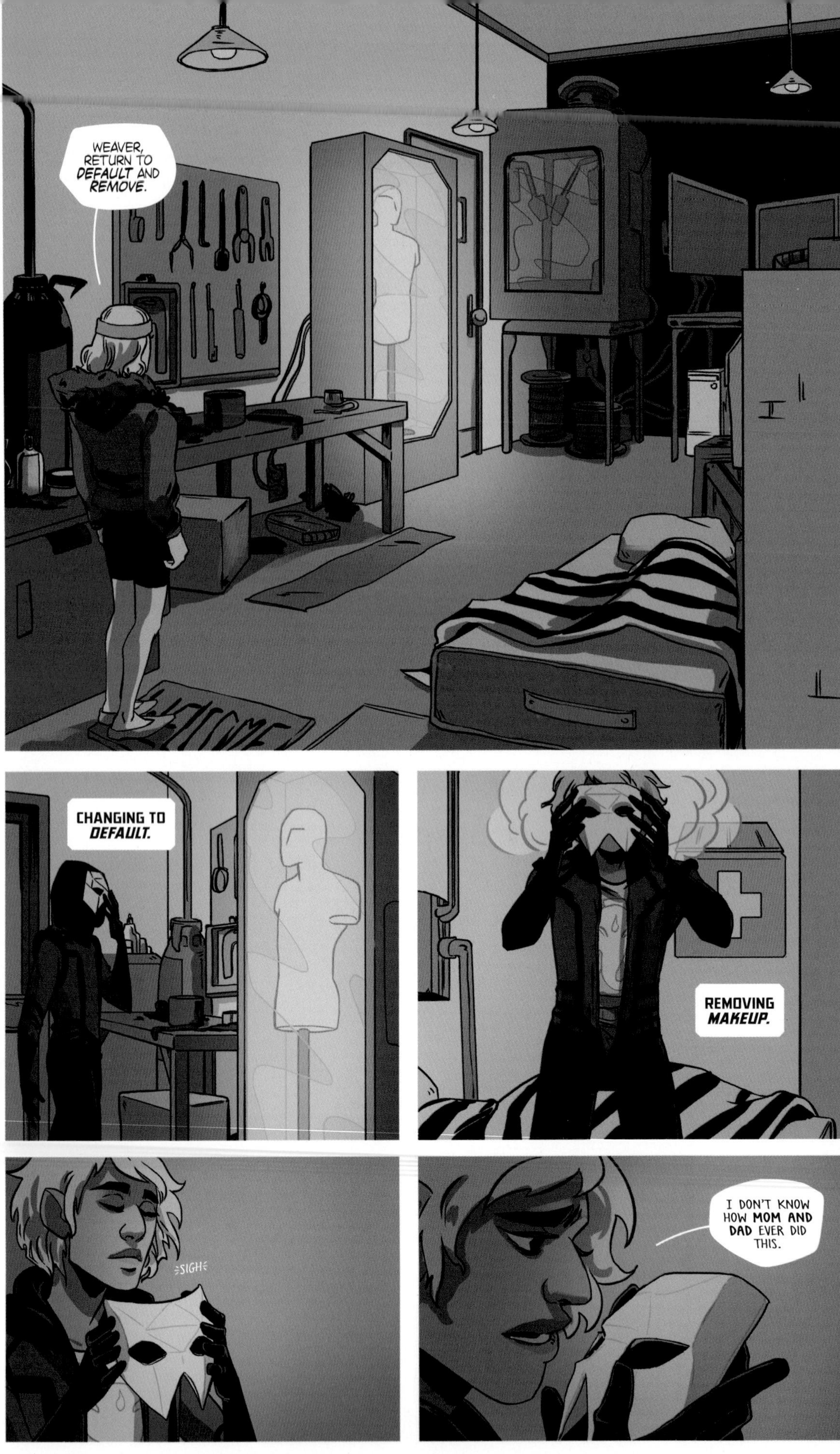
WEAVER, RETURN TO DEFAULT AND REMOVE.
CHANGING TO DEFAULT.
REMOVING MAKEUP.
SIGH
I DON'T KNOW HOW MOM AND DAD EVER DID THIS.

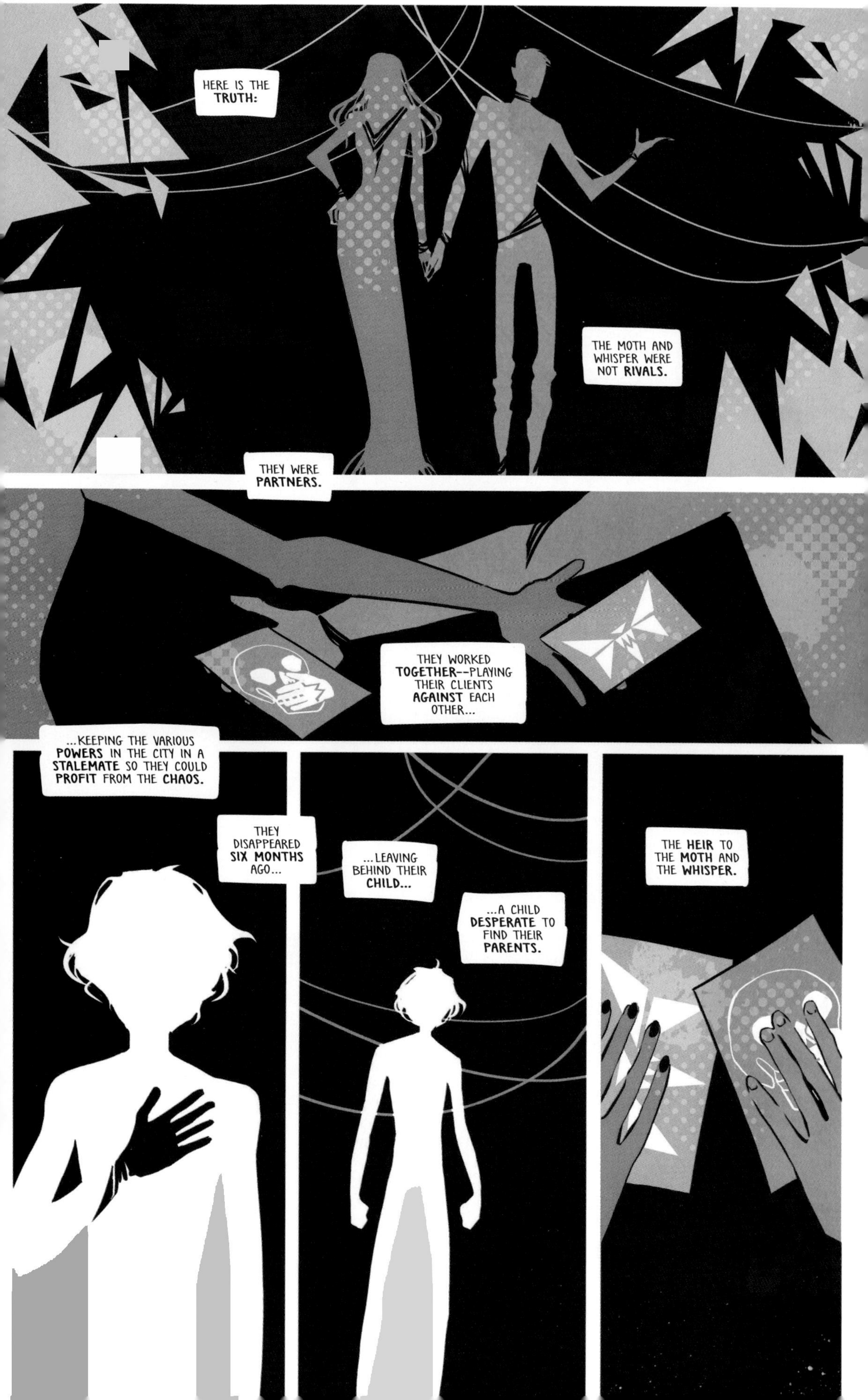
HERE IS THE TRUTH:
THE MOTH AND WHISPER WERE NOT RIVALS.
THEY WERE PARTNERS.
THEY WORKED TOGETHER--PLAYING THEIR CLIENTS AGAINST EACH OTHER...
...KEEPING THE VARIOUS POWERS IN THE CITY IN A STALEMATE SO THEY COULD PROFIT FROM THE CHAOS.
THEY DISAPPEARED SIX MONTHS AGO...
...LEAVING BEHIND THEIR CHILD...
...A CHILD DESPERATE TO FIND THEIR PARENTS.
THE HEIR TO THE MOTH AND THE WHISPER.

CHECKING WEAVER SUIT.

POWER RESERVES: 87%. RECHARGING.

MAKEUP RESERVES: 92%. REFILLING.

ONE FLASHBANG USED. *FOUR* FLASHBANGS REMAINING.

WARNING: NO *REPLACEMENT* FLASHBANGS IN INVENTORY.

I WASTED ONE ON HAAG AND HIS MEN.

NEED TO BE MORE CAREFUL.

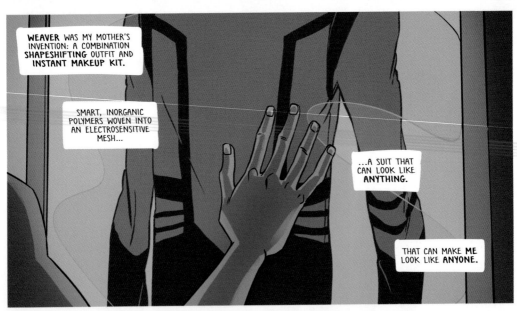

WEAVER WAS MY MOTHER'S INVENTION: A COMBINATION SHAPESHIFTING OUTFIT AND INSTANT MAKEUP KIT.

SMART, INORGANIC POLYMERS WOVEN INTO AN ELECTROSENSITIVE MESH...

...A SUIT THAT CAN LOOK LIKE ANYTHING.

THAT CAN MAKE ME LOOK LIKE ANYONE.

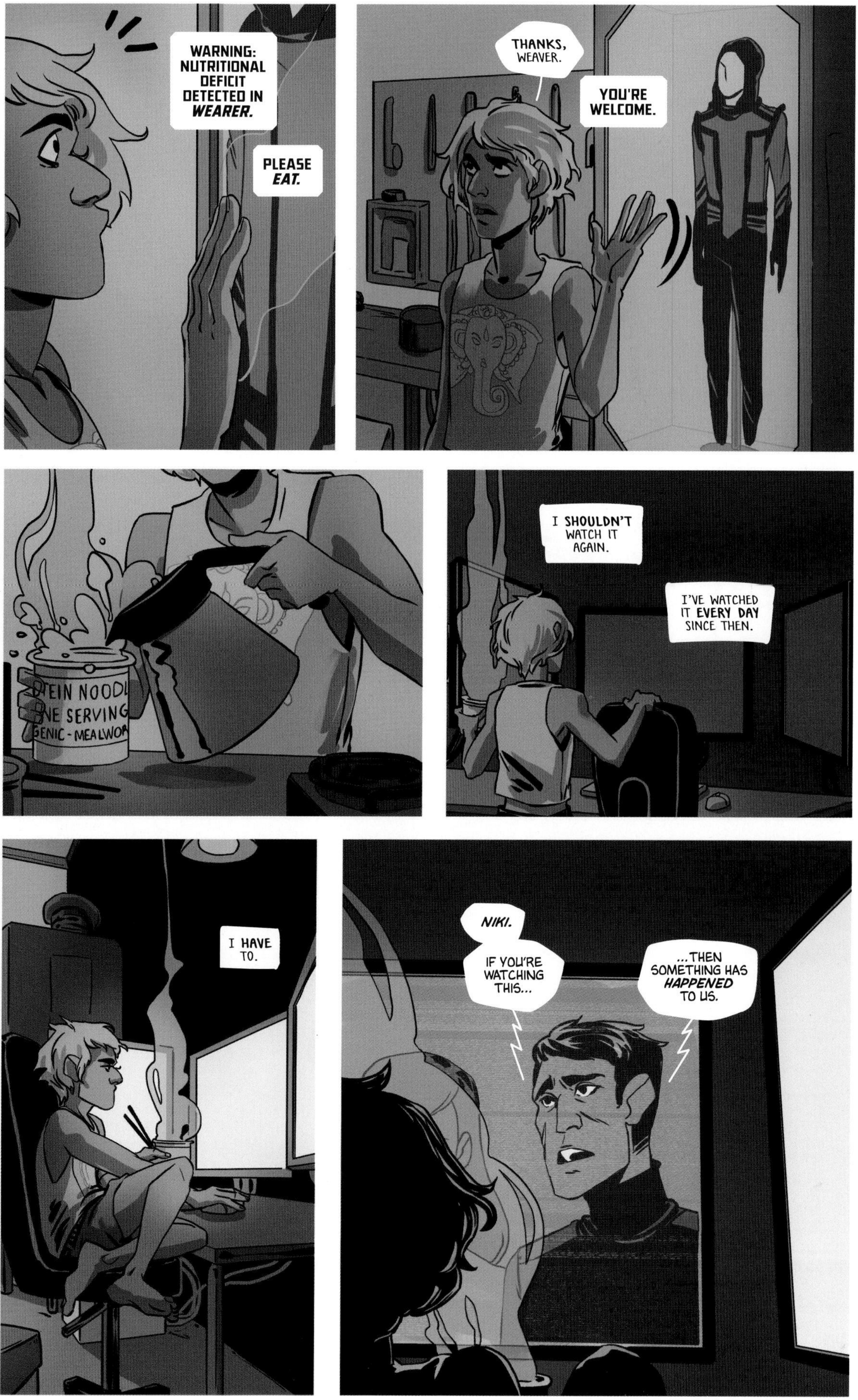
WARNING: NUTRITIONAL DEFICIT DETECTED IN *WEARER.*
PLEASE *EAT.*
THANKS, WEAVER.
YOU'RE WELCOME.
TEIN NOODL
NE SERVING
ENIC - MEALWOR
I **SHOULDN'T** WATCH IT AGAIN.
I'VE WATCHED IT **EVERY DAY** SINCE THEN.
I **HAVE** TO.
NIKI.
IF YOU'RE WATCHING THIS...
...THEN SOMETHING HAS *HAPPENED* TO US.

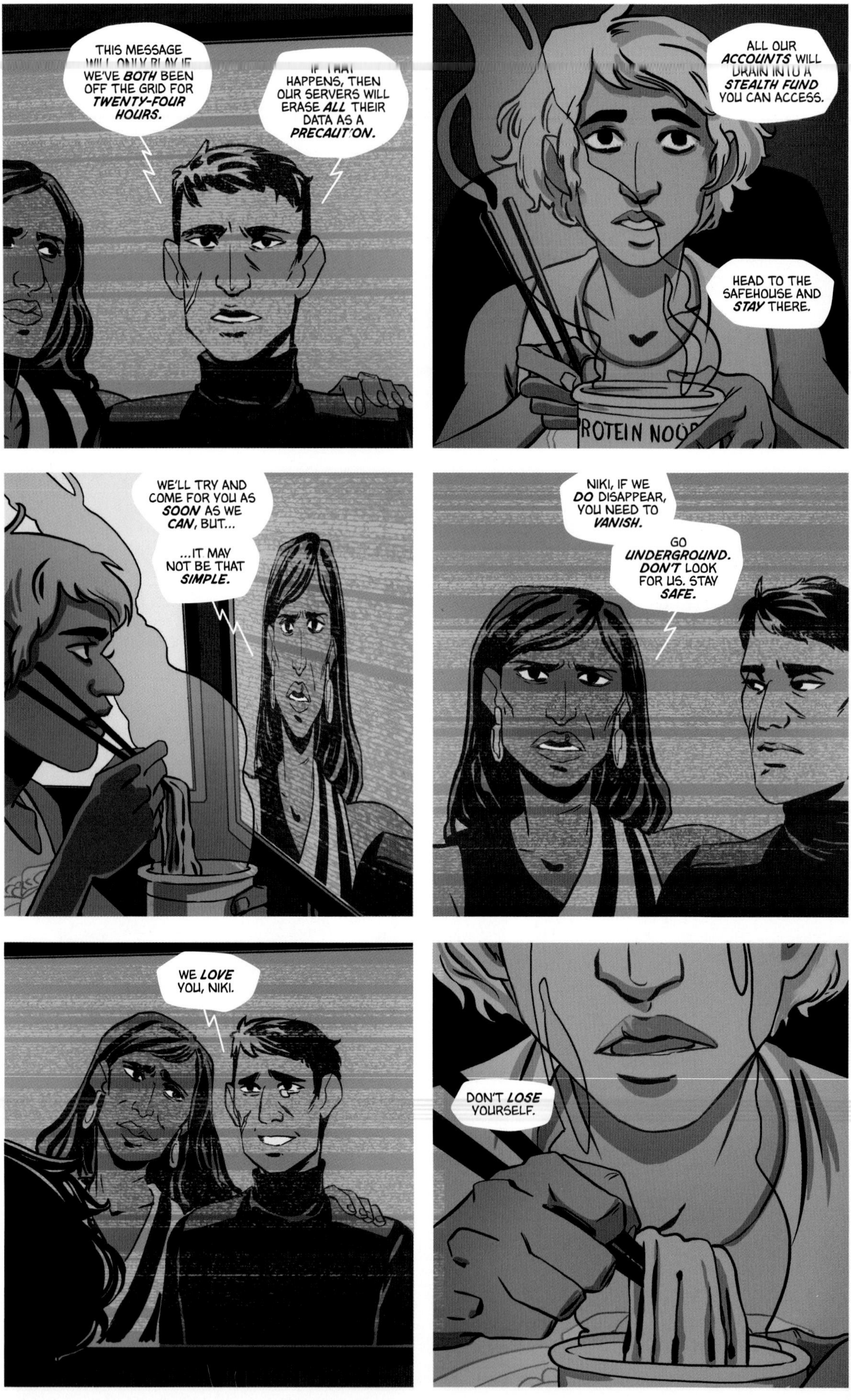
THIS MESSAGE WILL ONLY PLAY IF WE'VE BOTH BEEN OFF THE GRID FOR TWENTY-FOUR HOURS.
IF THAT HAPPENS, THEN OUR SERVERS WILL ERASE ALL THEIR DATA AS A PRECAUTION.
ALL OUR ACCOUNTS WILL DRAIN INTO A STEALTH FUND YOU CAN ACCESS.
HEAD TO THE SAFEHOUSE AND STAY THERE.
WE'LL TRY AND COME FOR YOU AS SOON AS WE CAN, BUT...
...IT MAY NOT BE THAT SIMPLE.
NIKI, IF WE DO DISAPPEAR, YOU NEED TO VANISH.
GO UNDERGROUND. DON'T LOOK FOR US. STAY SAFE.
WE LOVE YOU, NIKI.
DON'T LOSE YOURSELF.

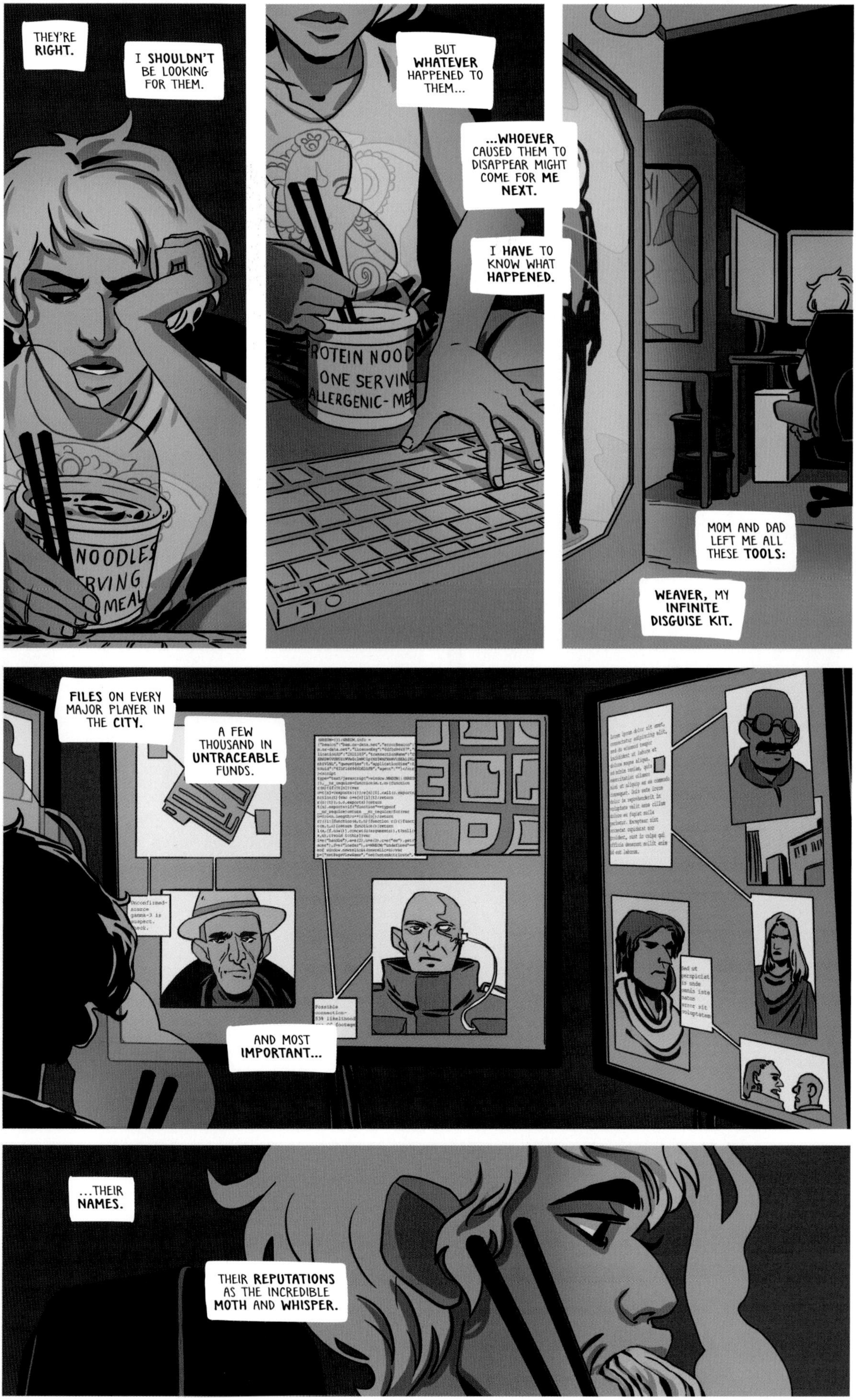
THEY'RE RIGHT.
I SHOULDN'T BE LOOKING FOR THEM.
NOODLES
RVING
MEAL
BUT WHATEVER HAPPENED TO THEM...
...WHOEVER CAUSED THEM TO DISAPPEAR MIGHT COME FOR ME NEXT.
I HAVE TO KNOW WHAT HAPPENED.
ROTEIN NOOD
ONE SERVIN
ALLERGENIC- ME
MOM AND DAD LEFT ME ALL THESE TOOLS:
WEAVER, MY INFINITE DISGUISE KIT.
FILES ON EVERY MAJOR PLAYER IN THE CITY.
A FEW THOUSAND IN UNTRACEABLE FUNDS.
AND MOST IMPORTANT...
...THEIR NAMES.
THEIR REPUTATIONS AS THE INCREDIBLE MOTH AND WHISPER.

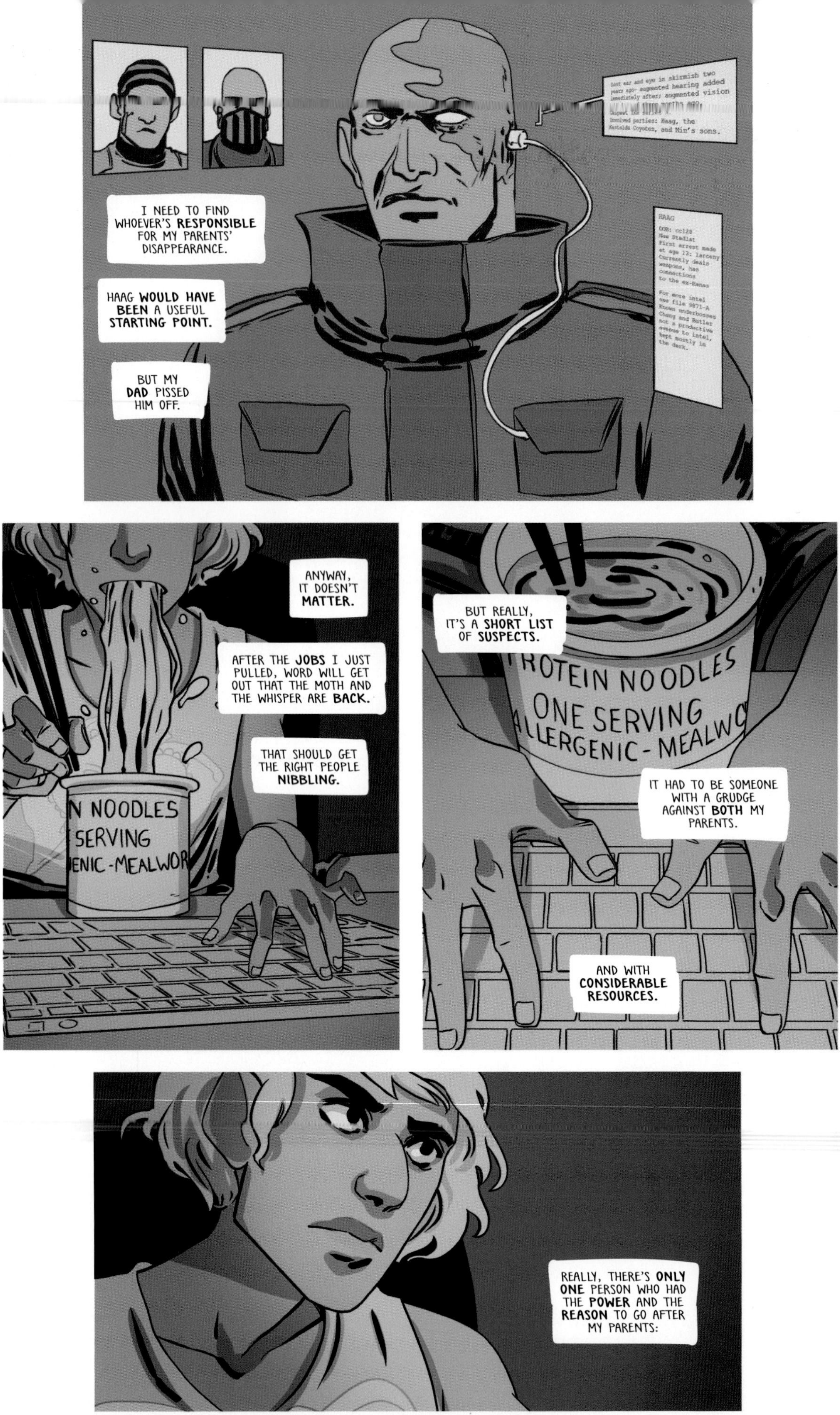
Lost ear and eye in skirmish two
years ago- augmented hearing added
immediately after; augmented vision
Involved parties: Haag, the
Eastside Coyotes, and Min's sons.
HAAG
DOB: cc128
New Stadlat
First arrest made
at age 13: larceny
Currently deals
weapons, has
connections
to the ex-Ranas
For more intel
see file 9871-A
Known underbosses
Chang and Butler
not a productive
avenue to intel,
kept mostly in
the dark.
I NEED TO FIND WHOEVER'S **RESPONSIBLE** FOR MY PARENTS' DISAPPEARANCE.
HAAG **WOULD HAVE BEEN** A USEFUL **STARTING POINT.**
BUT MY **DAD** PISSED HIM OFF.
ANYWAY, IT DOESN'T **MATTER.**
AFTER THE **JOBS** I JUST PULLED, WORD WILL GET OUT THAT THE MOTH AND THE WHISPER ARE **BACK.**
THAT SHOULD GET THE RIGHT PEOPLE **NIBBLING.**
N NOODLES
SERVING
ENIC-MEALWOR
BUT REALLY, IT'S A **SHORT LIST** OF **SUSPECTS.**
ROTEIN NOODLES
ONE SERVING
ALLERGENIC-MEALWO
IT HAD TO BE SOMEONE WITH A GRUDGE AGAINST **BOTH** MY PARENTS.
AND WITH **CONSIDERABLE RESOURCES.**
REALLY, THERE'S **ONLY ONE** PERSON WHO HAD THE **POWER** AND THE **REASON** TO GO AFTER MY PARENTS:

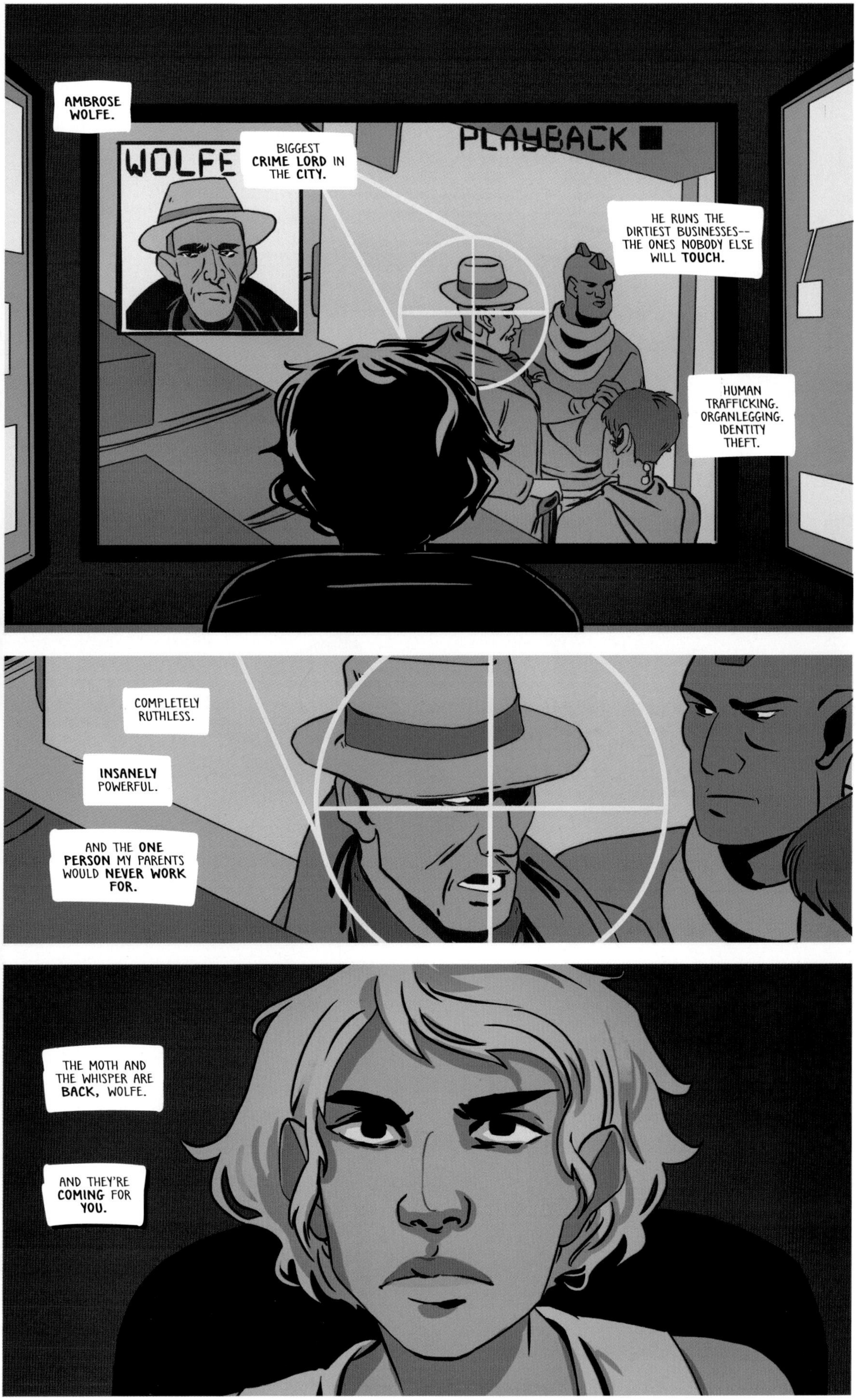

AMBROSE WOLFE.
WOLFE
BIGGEST CRIME LORD IN THE CITY.
PLAYBACK
HE RUNS THE DIRTIEST BUSINESSES-- THE ONES NOBODY ELSE WILL TOUCH.
HUMAN TRAFFICKING. ORGANLEGGING. IDENTITY THEFT.
COMPLETELY RUTHLESS.
INSANELY POWERFUL.
AND THE ONE PERSON MY PARENTS WOULD NEVER WORK FOR.
THE MOTH AND THE WHISPER ARE BACK, WOLFE.
AND THEY'RE COMING FOR YOU.

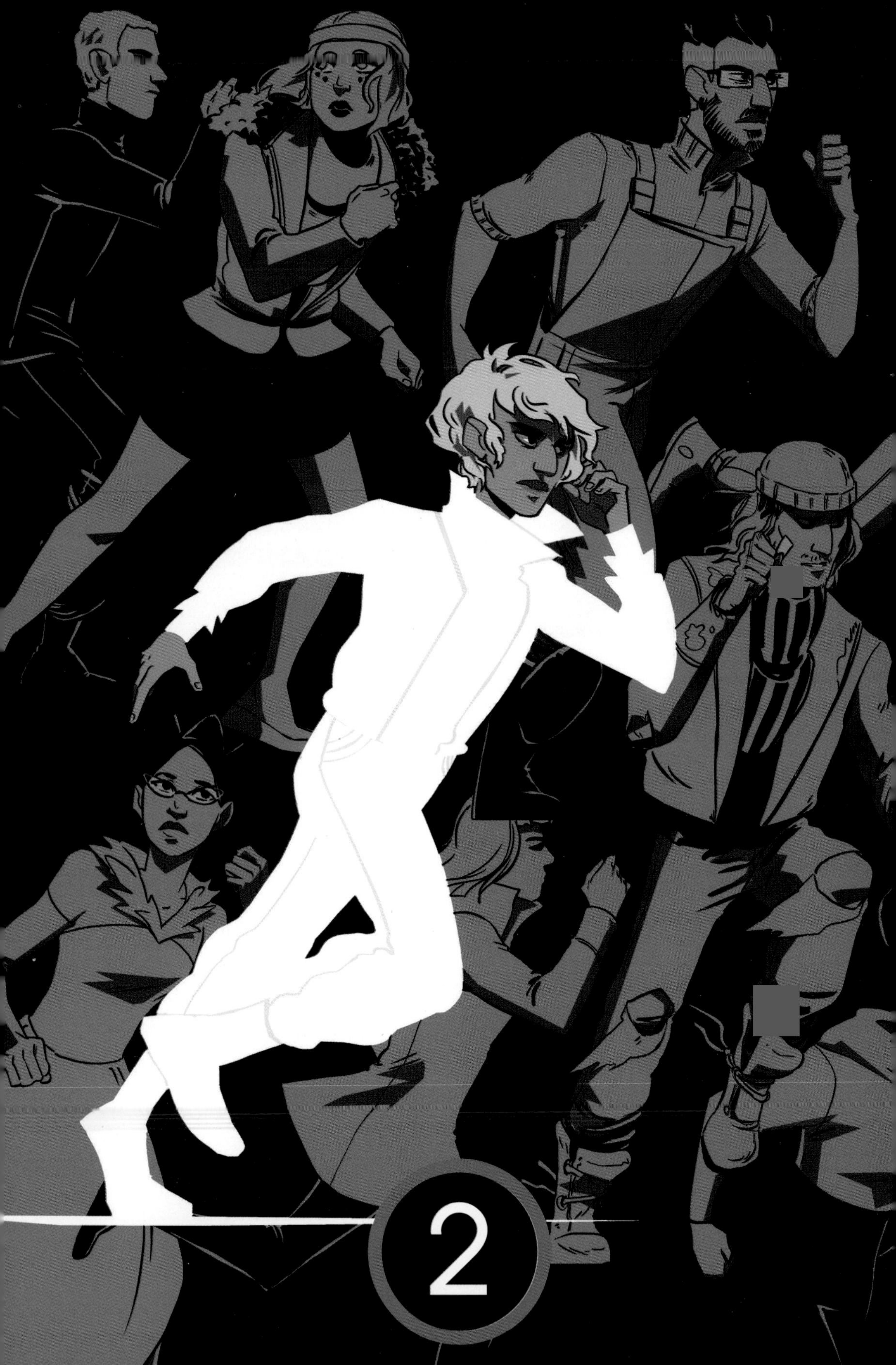

2

GOING TO THE BALL

...NEGOTIATIONS HAVE BROKEN DOWN YET AGAIN. THIS WILL MARK THE TWELFTH CONSECUTIVE YEAR WITHOUT ANY COMMUNICATION BETWEEN THE TWO PARTIES.

...ANNOUNCED THAT ALL HUMAN INHABITANTS HAVE OFFICIALLY BEEN RELOCATED FROM THE SECTOR. ENVIRONMENTAL RECLAMATION EFFORTS CAN NOW TAKE PLACE, IN THE HOPES OF RESTORING THE LOCAL ECOSYSTEM...

...THE ANILAC CORPORATION HAS ACQUIRED MBACHU-SOLVIIG, MAKING THEM THE SEVENTH-LARGEST CORPORATION IN THE WORLD. NEW EMPLOYEES OF ANILAC WILL BE OFFERED REHOUSING IN THE ANILAC DISTRICTS OF SEVERAL MAJOR CITIES...

...STATISTICS RELEASED TODAY BY OUTLAW RIGHTS-MONITORING GROUPS SUGGEST THAT ATTACKS ON REFUGEES HAVE INCREASED PRECIPITOUSLY...

...THE GOVERNMENT DENIED THIS, BUT AS THESE CRIMES CANNOT OFFICIALLY BE RECORDED, THEY CANNOT REBUT THE CLAIMED FIGURES...

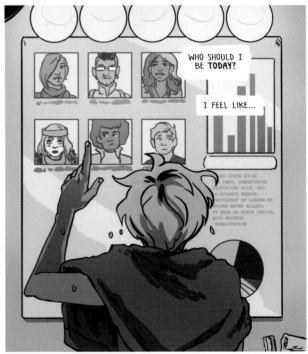

WHO SHOULD I BE TODAY?

I FEEL LIKE...

...KHALIL MORRIS.

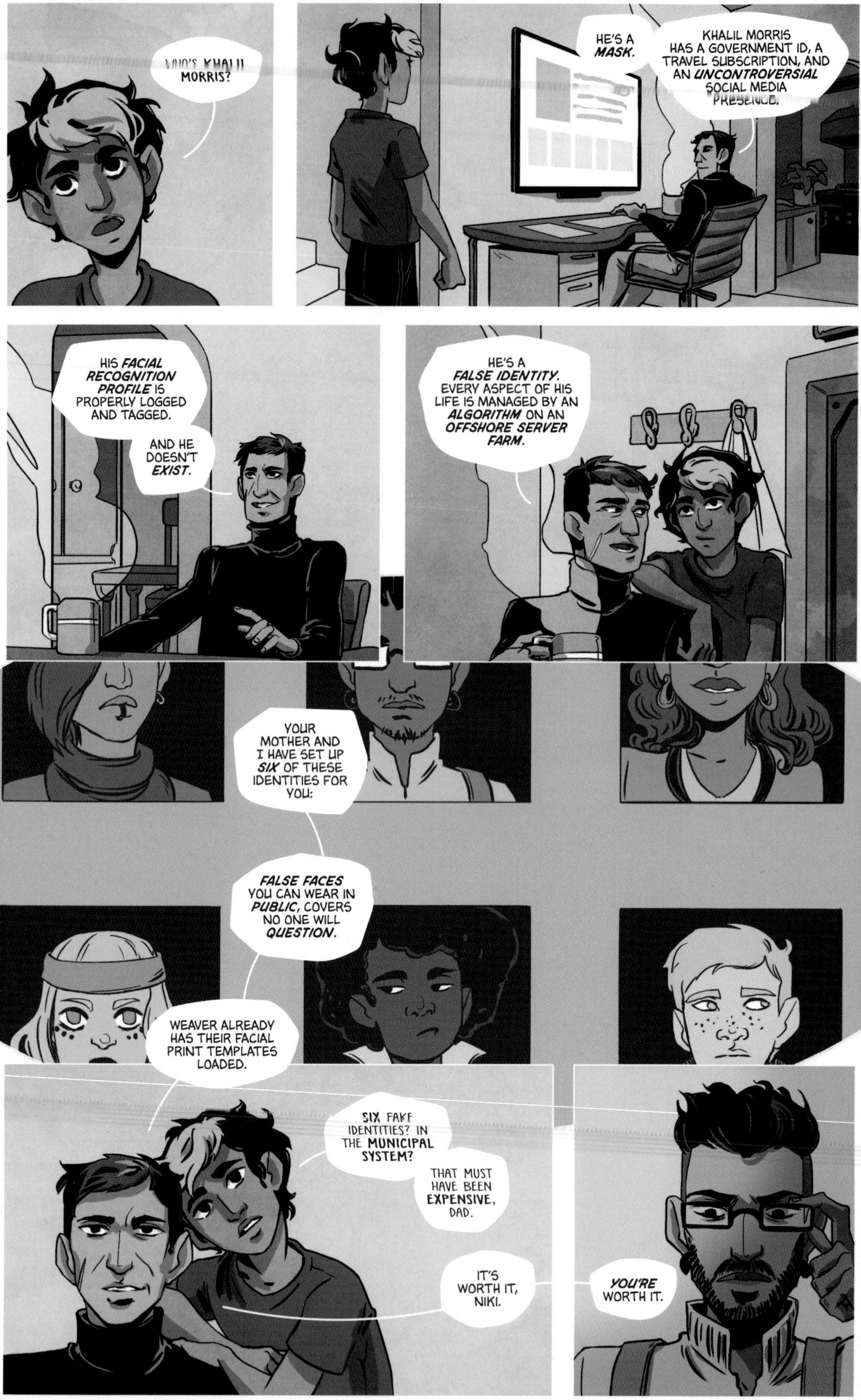
WHO'S KHALIL MORRIS?
HE'S A *MASK.*
KHALIL MORRIS HAS A GOVERNMENT ID, A TRAVEL SUBSCRIPTION, AND AN *UNCONTROVERSIAL* SOCIAL MEDIA PRESENCE.
HIS *FACIAL RECOGNITION PROFILE* IS PROPERLY LOGGED AND TAGGED.
AND HE DOESN'T *EXIST.*
HE'S A *FALSE IDENTITY.* EVERY ASPECT OF HIS LIFE IS MANAGED BY AN *ALGORITHM* ON AN *OFFSHORE SERVER FARM.*
YOUR MOTHER AND I HAVE SET UP *SIX* OF THESE IDENTITIES FOR YOU:
FALSE FACES YOU CAN WEAR IN *PUBLIC*, COVERS NO ONE WILL *QUESTION*.
WEAVER ALREADY HAS THEIR FACIAL PRINT TEMPLATES LOADED.
SIX FAKE IDENTITIES? IN THE **MUNICIPAL SYSTEM?**
THAT MUST HAVE BEEN **EXPENSIVE,** DAD.
IT'S WORTH IT, NIKI.
YOU'RE WORTH IT.

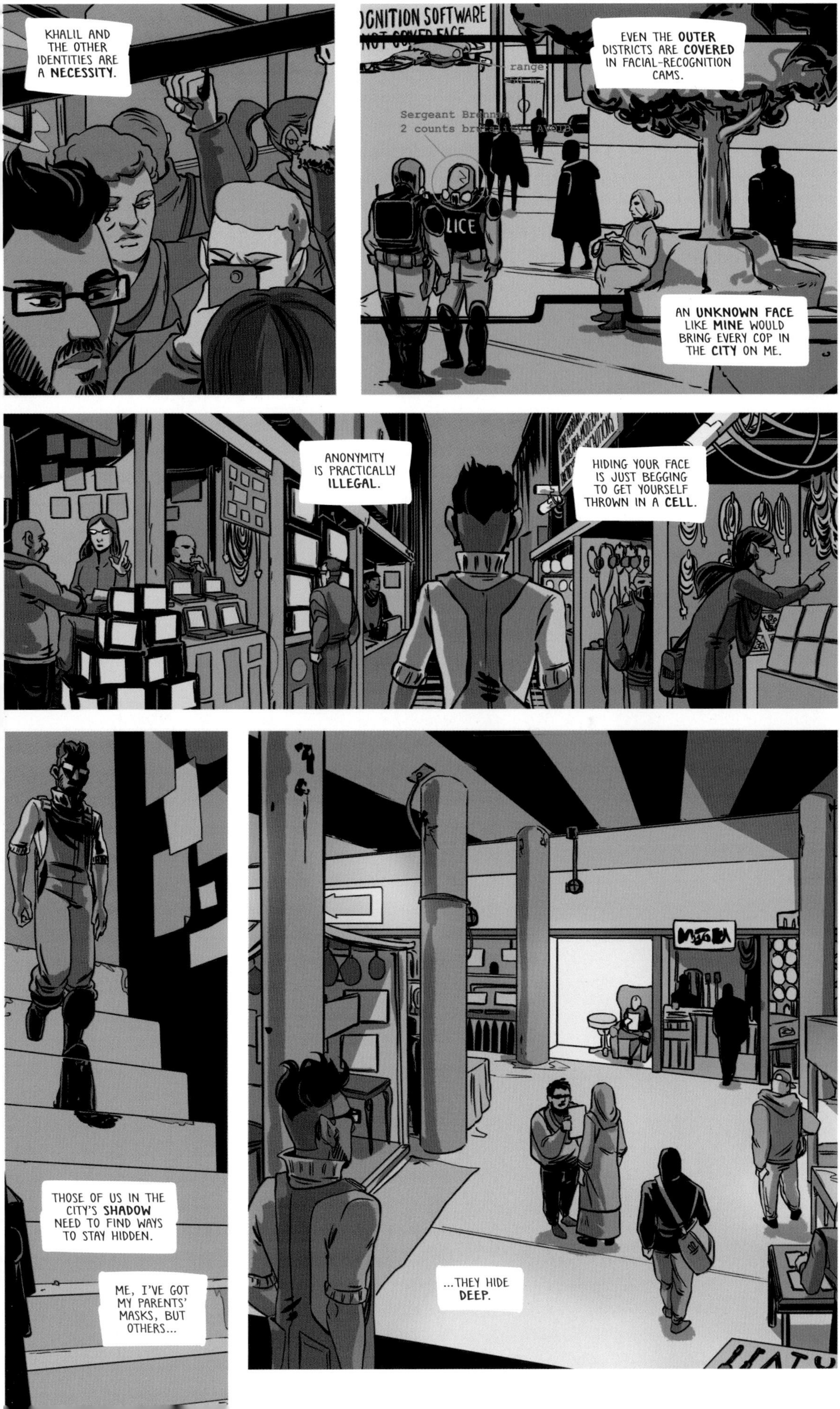
KHALIL AND THE OTHER IDENTITIES ARE A NECESSITY.
EVEN THE OUTER DISTRICTS ARE COVERED IN FACIAL-RECOGNITION CAMS.
AN UNKNOWN FACE LIKE MINE WOULD BRING EVERY COP IN THE CITY ON ME.
ANONYMITY IS PRACTICALLY ILLEGAL.
HIDING YOUR FACE IS JUST BEGGING TO GET YOURSELF THROWN IN A CELL.
THOSE OF US IN THE CITY'S SHADOW NEED TO FIND WAYS TO STAY HIDDEN.
ME, I'VE GOT MY PARENTS' MASKS, BUT OTHERS...
...THEY HIDE DEEP.

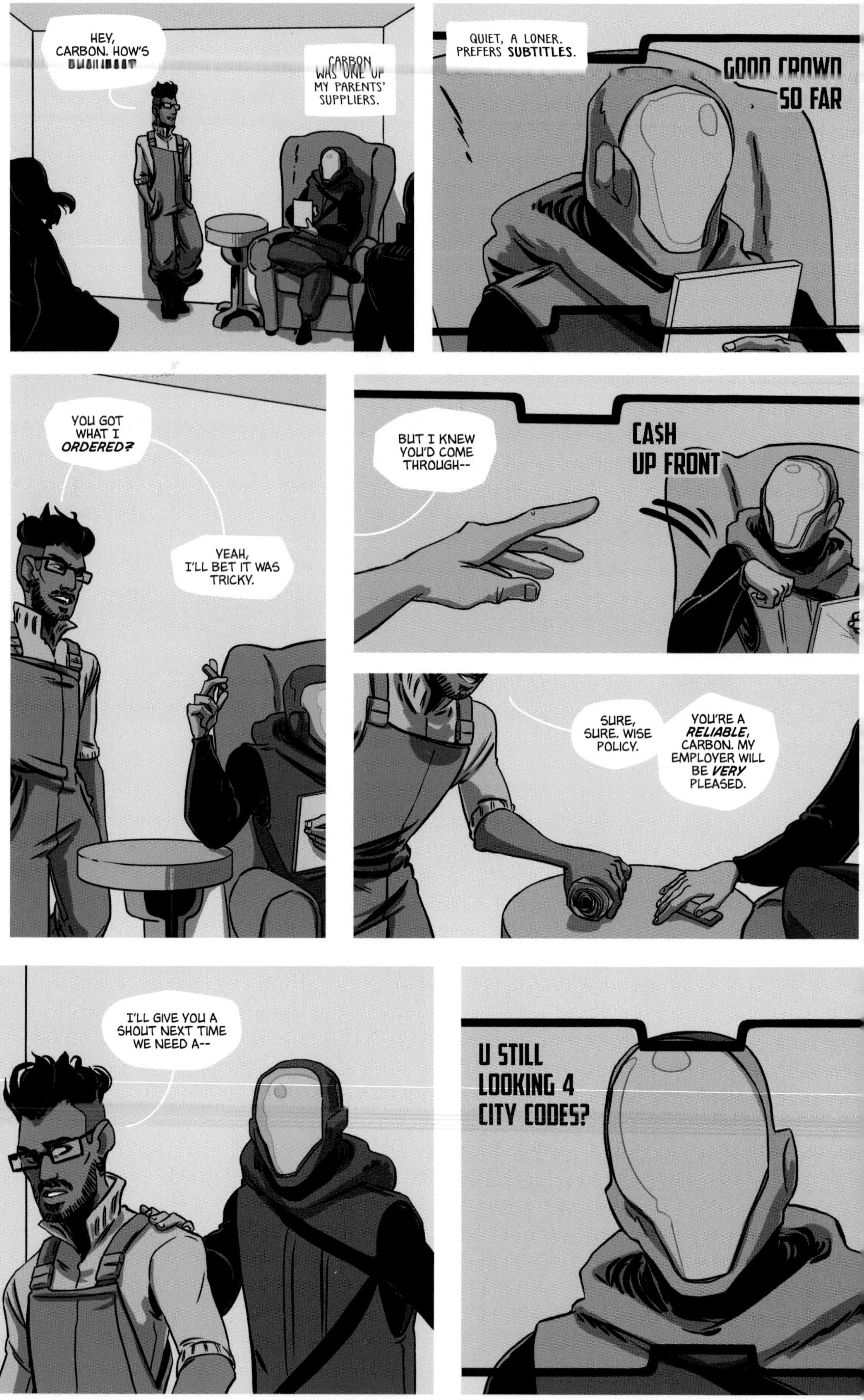

HEY, CARBON. HOW'S
CARBON WAS ONE OF MY PARENTS' SUPPLIERS.
QUIET, A LONER. PREFERS **SUBTITLES.**
GOOD CROWD SO FAR
YOU GOT WHAT I *ORDERED?*
YEAH, I'LL BET IT WAS TRICKY.
BUT I KNEW YOU'D COME THROUGH--
CA$H UP FRONT
SURE, SURE. WISE POLICY.
YOU'RE A *RELIABLE,* CARBON. MY EMPLOYER WILL BE *VERY* PLEASED.
I'LL GIVE YOU A SHOUT NEXT TIME WE NEED A--
U STILL LOOKING 4 CITY CODES?

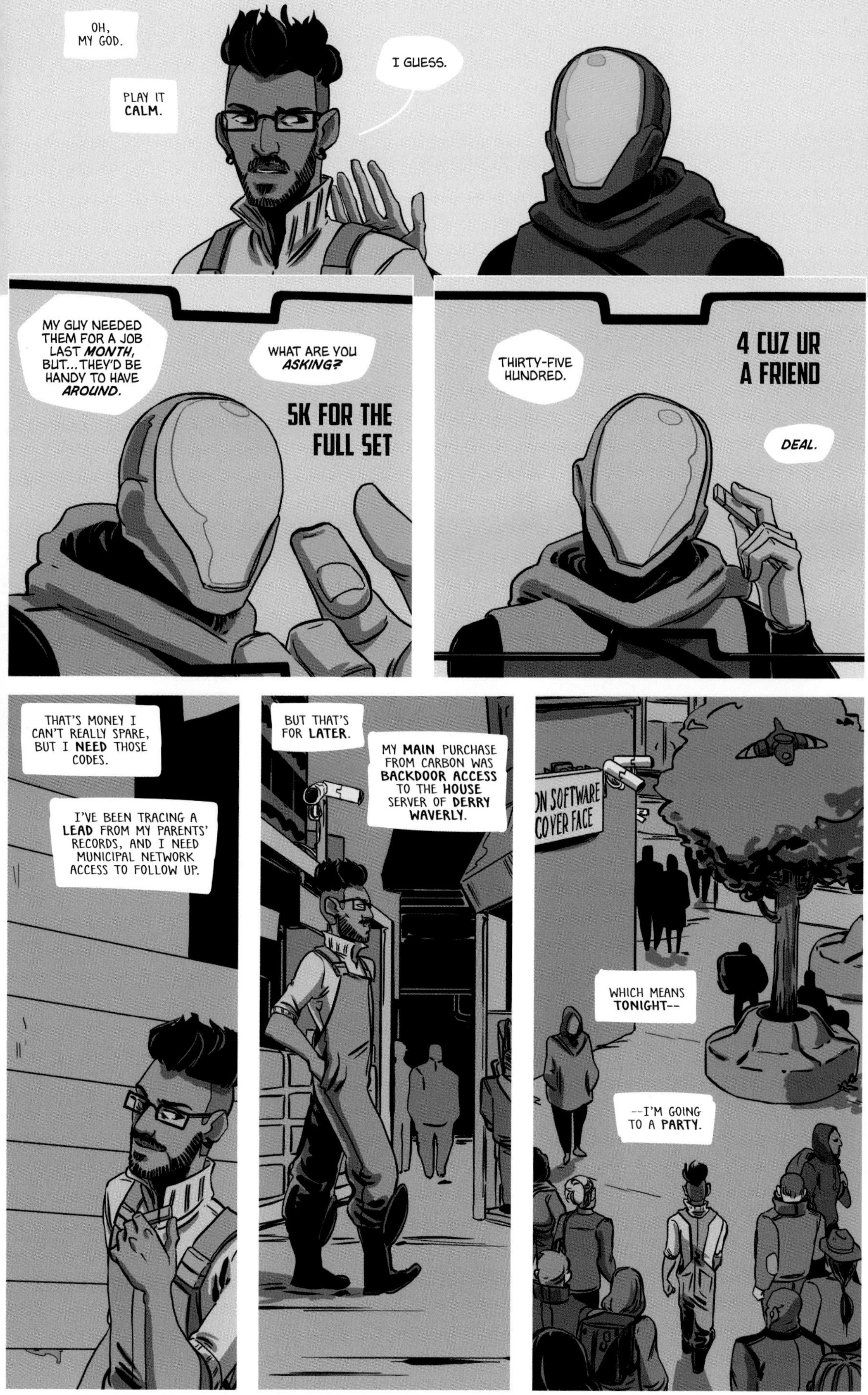
OH, MY GOD.
PLAY IT CALM.
I GUESS.
MY GUY NEEDED THEM FOR A JOB LAST MONTH, BUT... THEY'D BE HANDY TO HAVE AROUND.
WHAT ARE YOU ASKING?
5K FOR THE FULL SET
THIRTY-FIVE HUNDRED.
4 CUZ UR A FRIEND
DEAL.
THAT'S MONEY I CAN'T REALLY SPARE, BUT I NEED THOSE CODES.
I'VE BEEN TRACING A LEAD FROM MY PARENTS' RECORDS, AND I NEED MUNICIPAL NETWORK ACCESS TO FOLLOW UP.
BUT THAT'S FOR LATER.
MY MAIN PURCHASE FROM CARBON WAS BACKDOOR ACCESS TO THE HOUSE SERVER OF DERRY WAVERLY.
ON SOFTWARE
COVER FACE
WHICH MEANS TONIGHT--
--I'M GOING TO A PARTY.

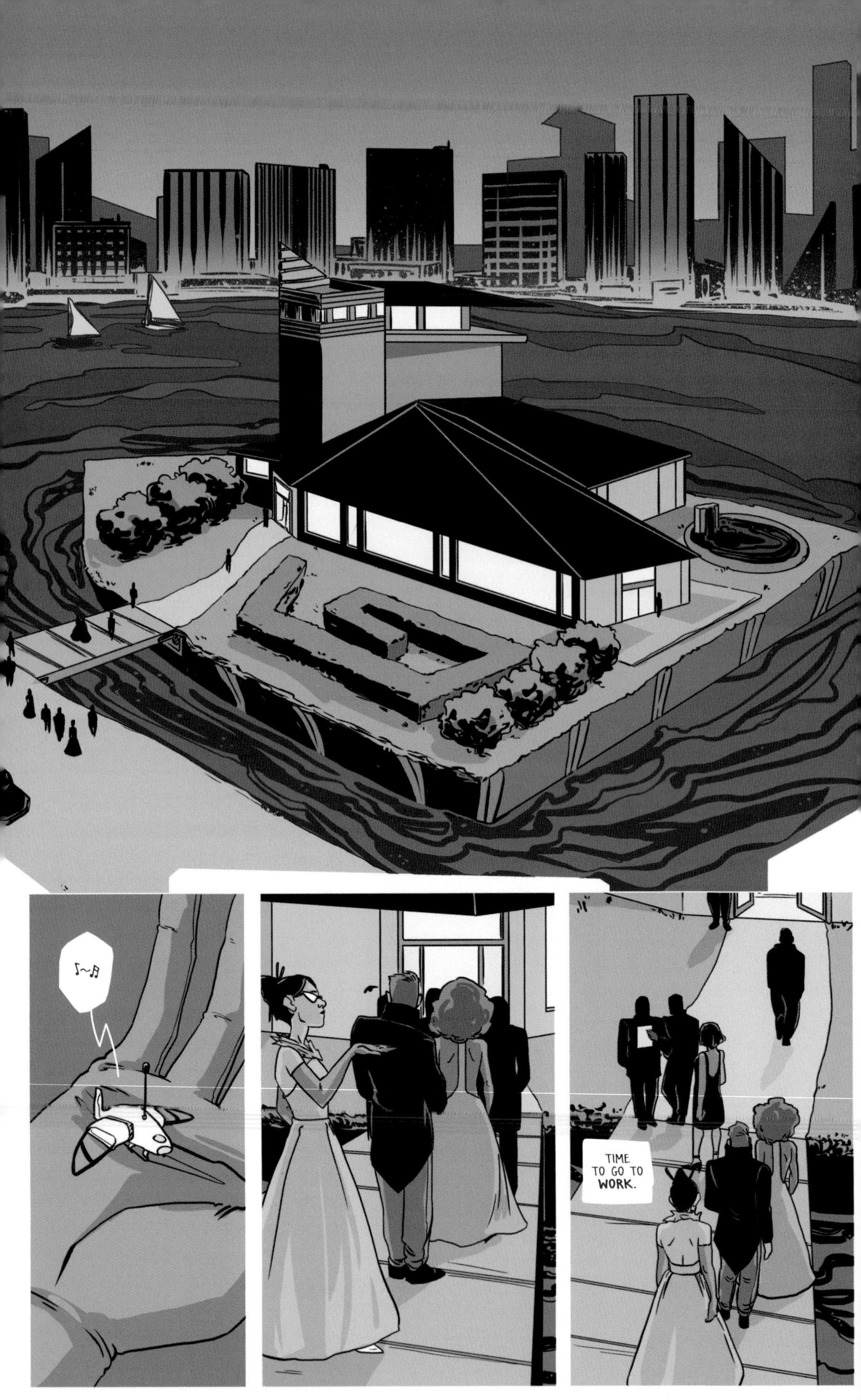
TIME TO GO TO **WORK.**

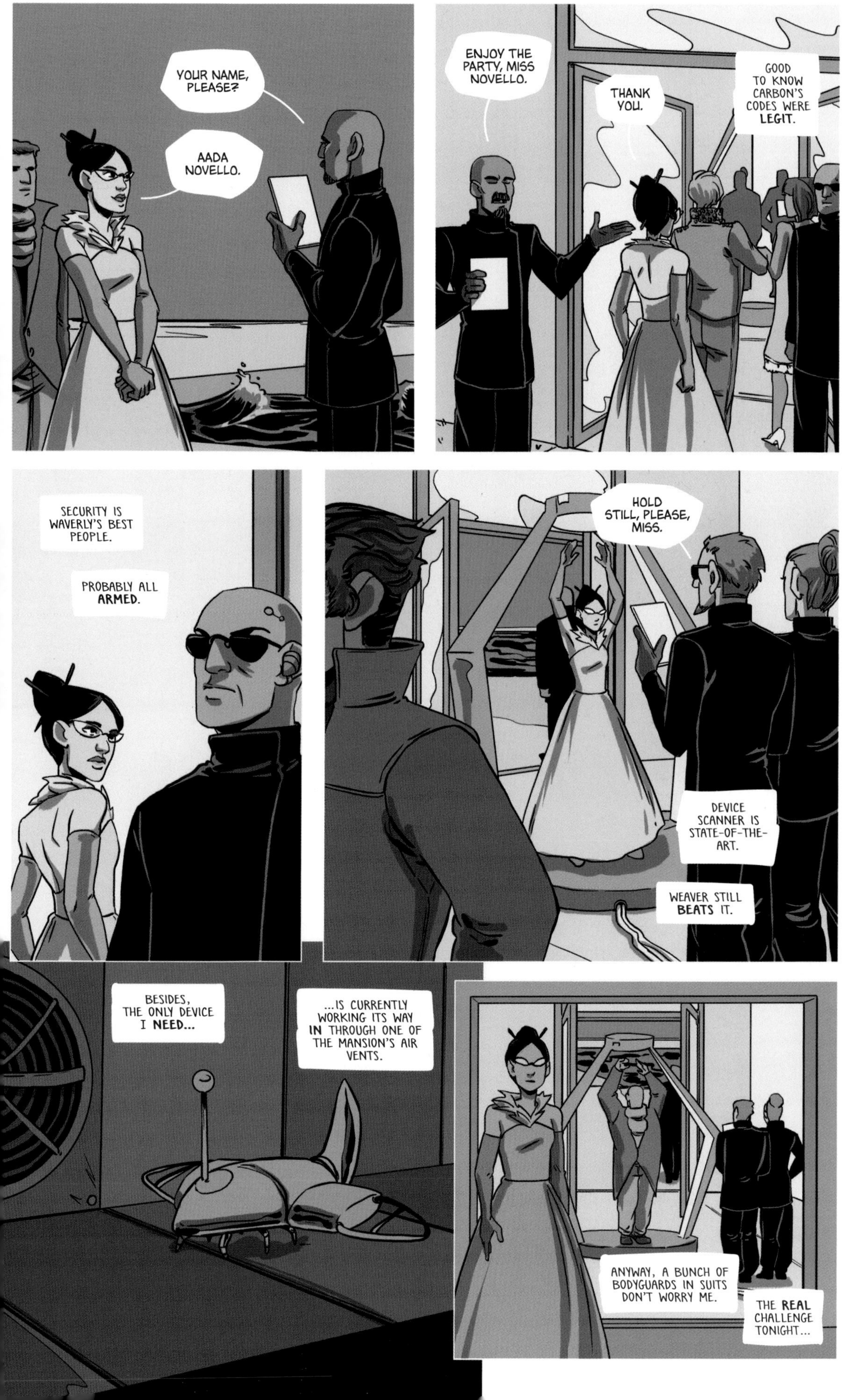
YOUR NAME, PLEASE?
AADA NOVELLO.
ENJOY THE PARTY, MISS NOVELLO.
THANK YOU.
GOOD TO KNOW CARBON'S CODES WERE LEGIT.
SECURITY IS WAVERLY'S BEST PEOPLE.
PROBABLY ALL ARMED.
HOLD STILL, PLEASE, MISS.
DEVICE SCANNER IS STATE-OF-THE-ART.
WEAVER STILL BEATS IT.
BESIDES, THE ONLY DEVICE I NEED...
...IS CURRENTLY WORKING ITS WAY IN THROUGH ONE OF THE MANSION'S AIR VENTS.
ANYWAY, A BUNCH OF BODYGUARDS IN SUITS DON'T WORRY ME.
THE REAL CHALLENGE TONIGHT...

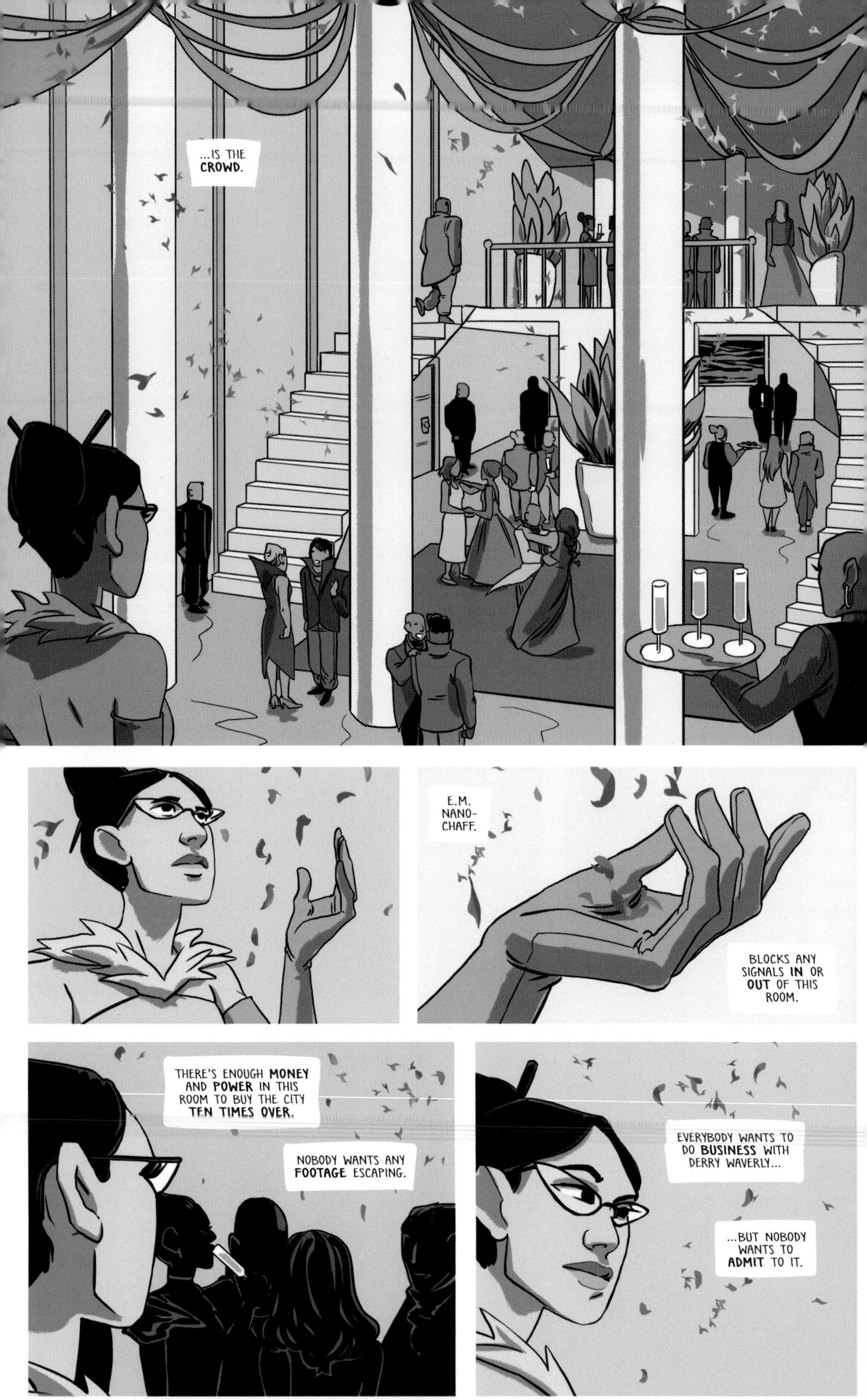
...IS THE CROWD.
E.M. NANO-CHAFF.
BLOCKS ANY SIGNALS IN OR OUT OF THIS ROOM.
THERE'S ENOUGH MONEY AND POWER IN THIS ROOM TO BUY THE CITY TEN TIMES OVER.
NOBODY WANTS ANY FOOTAGE ESCAPING.
EVERYBODY WANTS TO DO BUSINESS WITH DERRY WAVERLY...
...BUT NOBODY WANTS TO ADMIT TO IT.

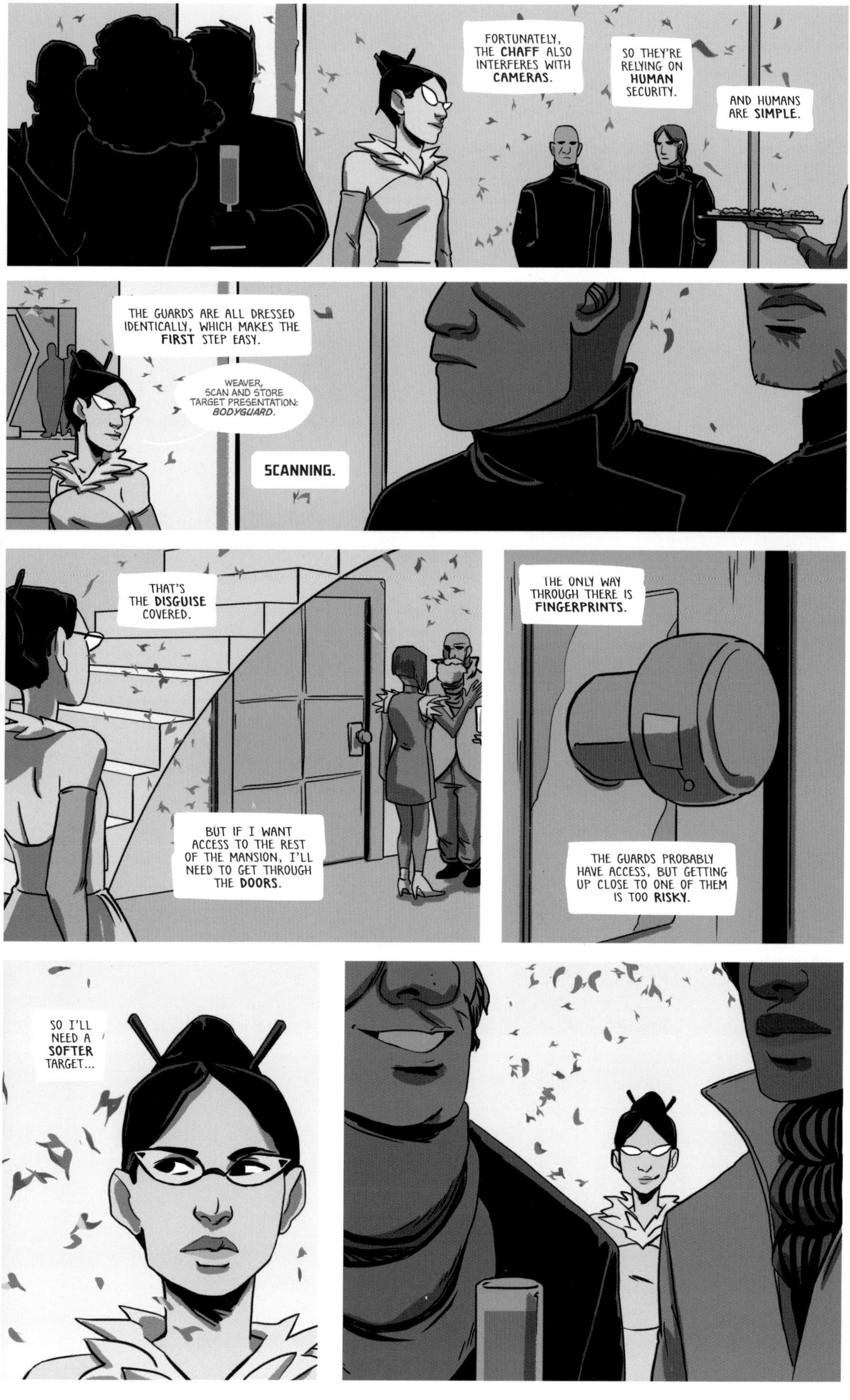

FORTUNATELY, THE CHAFF ALSO INTERFERES WITH CAMERAS.
SO THEY'RE RELYING ON HUMAN SECURITY.
AND HUMANS ARE SIMPLE.
THE GUARDS ARE ALL DRESSED IDENTICALLY, WHICH MAKES THE FIRST STEP EASY.
WEAVER, SCAN AND STORE TARGET PRESENTATION: BODYGUARD.
SCANNING.
THAT'S THE DISGUISE COVERED.
BUT IF I WANT ACCESS TO THE REST OF THE MANSION, I'LL NEED TO GET THROUGH THE DOORS.
THE ONLY WAY THROUGH THERE IS FINGERPRINTS.
THE GUARDS PROBABLY HAVE ACCESS, BUT GETTING UP CLOSE TO ONE OF THEM IS TOO RISKY.
SO I'LL NEED A SOFTER TARGET...

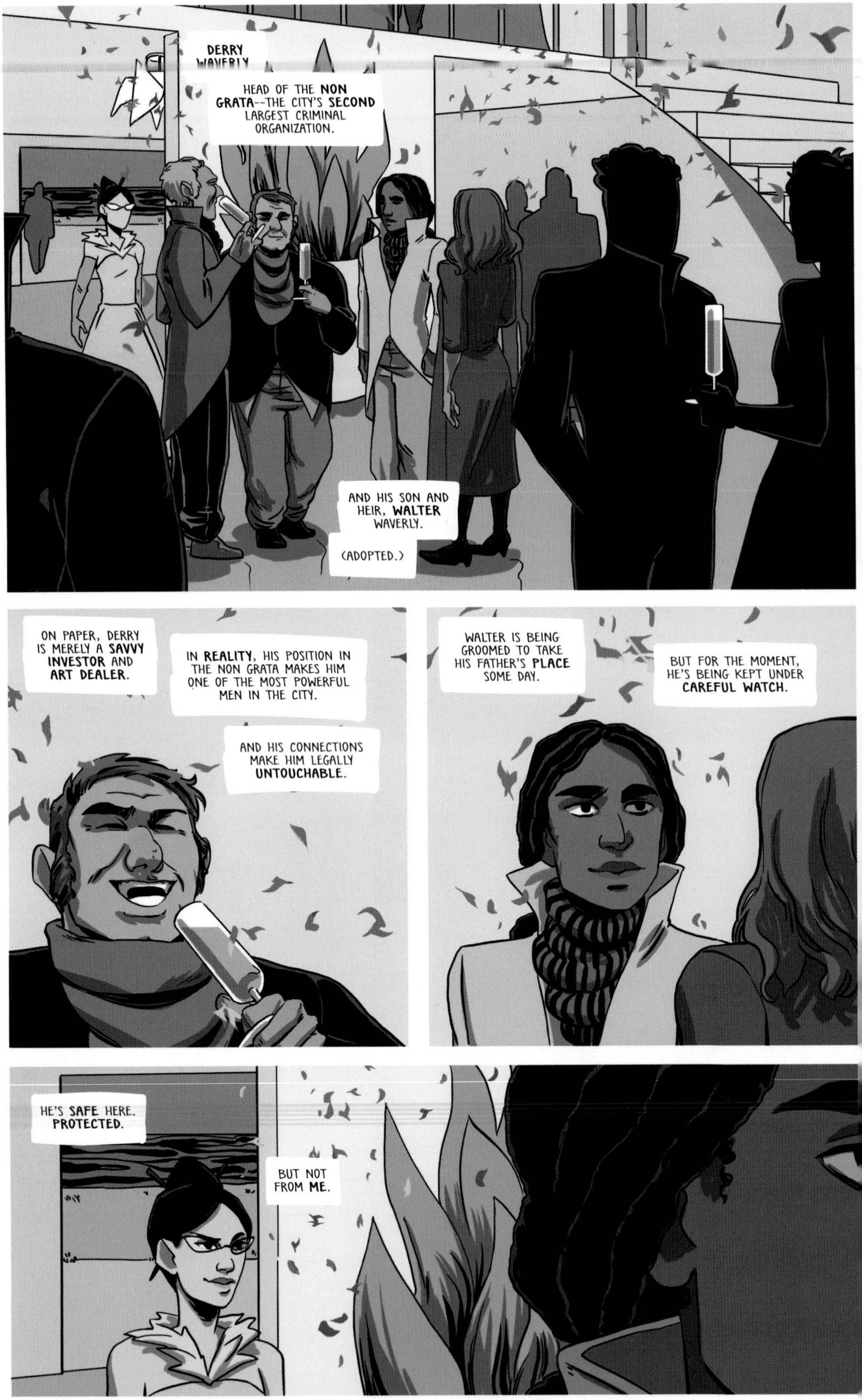
DERRY WAVERLY
HEAD OF THE NON GRATA--THE CITY'S SECOND LARGEST CRIMINAL ORGANIZATION.
AND HIS SON AND HEIR, WALTER WAVERLY.
(ADOPTED.)
ON PAPER, DERRY IS MERELY A SAVVY INVESTOR AND ART DEALER.
IN REALITY, HIS POSITION IN THE NON GRATA MAKES HIM ONE OF THE MOST POWERFUL MEN IN THE CITY.
AND HIS CONNECTIONS MAKE HIM LEGALLY UNTOUCHABLE.
WALTER IS BEING GROOMED TO TAKE HIS FATHER'S PLACE SOME DAY.
BUT FOR THE MOMENT, HE'S BEING KEPT UNDER CAREFUL WATCH.
HE'S SAFE HERE. PROTECTED.
BUT NOT FROM ME.

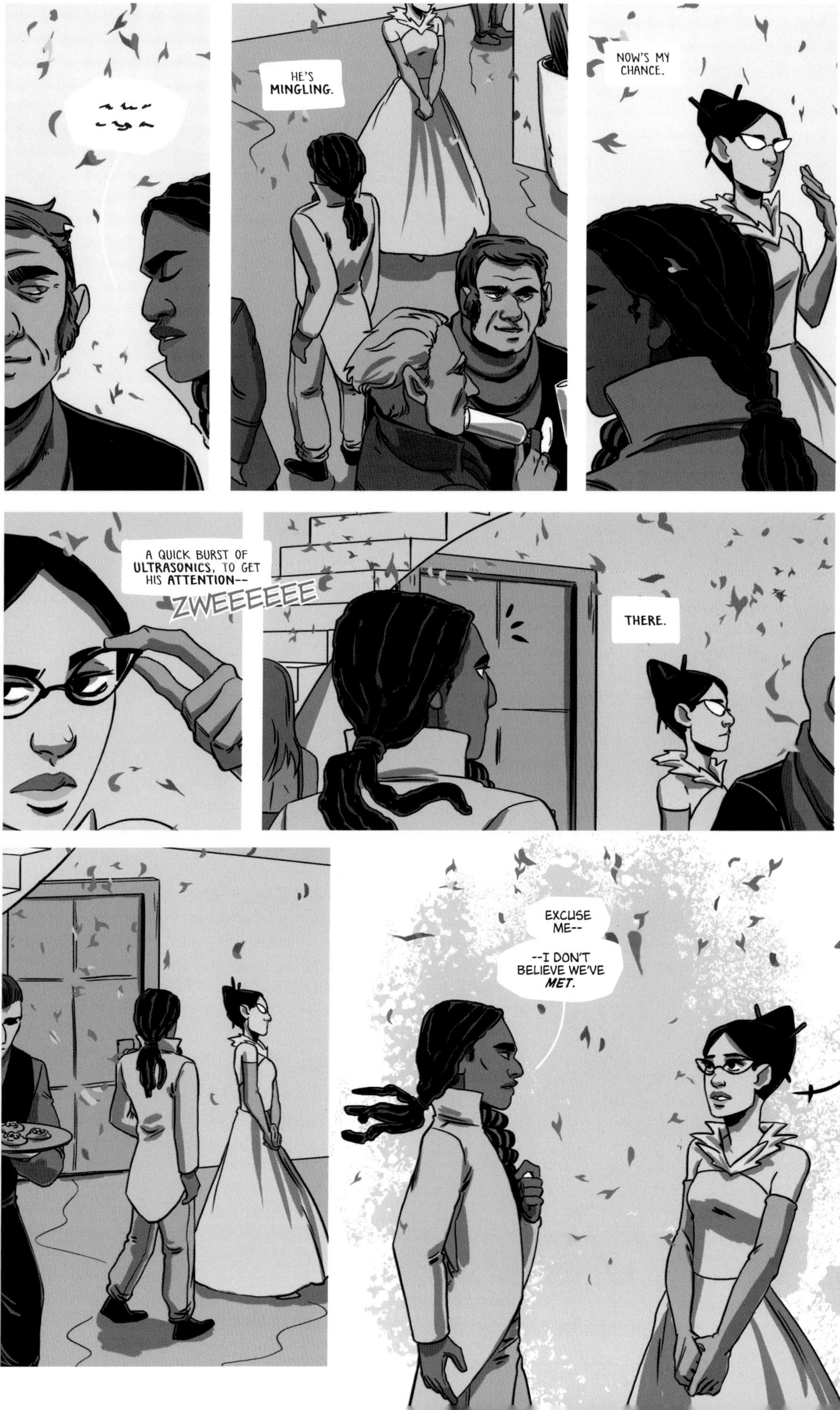
HE'S MINGLING.
NOW'S MY CHANCE.
A QUICK BURST OF ULTRASONICS, TO GET HIS ATTENTION--
ZWEEEEEEE
THERE.
EXCUSE ME--
--I DON'T BELIEVE WE'VE MET.

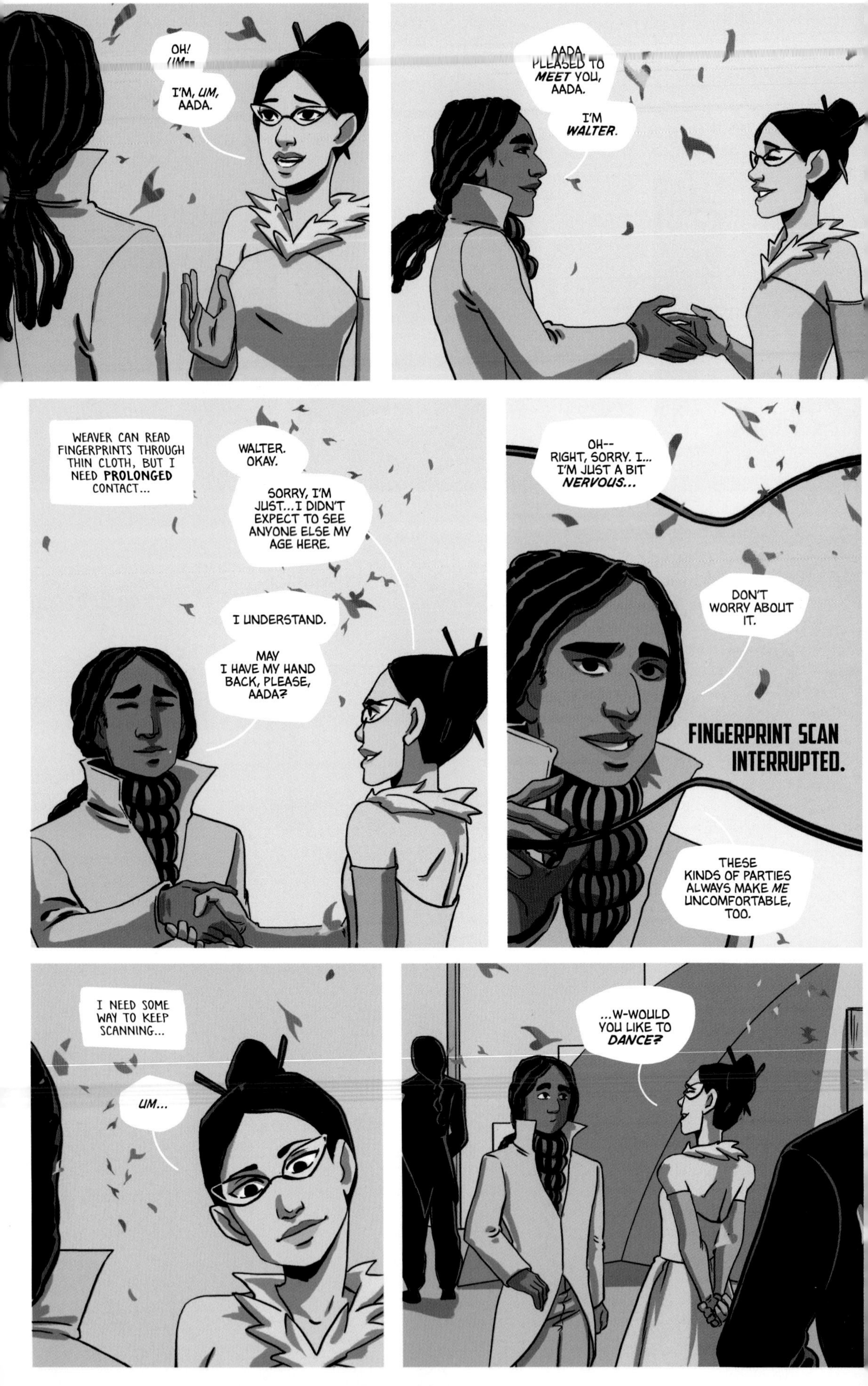
OH! UM--
I'M, UM, AADA.
AADA. PLEASED TO MEET YOU, AADA.
I'M WALTER.
WEAVER CAN READ FINGERPRINTS THROUGH THIN CLOTH, BUT I NEED PROLONGED CONTACT...
WALTER. OKAY.
SORRY, I'M JUST...I DIDN'T EXPECT TO SEE ANYONE ELSE MY AGE HERE.
I UNDERSTAND.
MAY I HAVE MY HAND BACK, PLEASE, AADA?
OH-- RIGHT, SORRY. I... I'M JUST A BIT NERVOUS...
DON'T WORRY ABOUT IT.
FINGERPRINT SCAN INTERRUPTED.
THESE KINDS OF PARTIES ALWAYS MAKE ME UNCOMFORTABLE, TOO.
I NEED SOME WAY TO KEEP SCANNING...
UM...
...W-WOULD YOU LIKE TO DANCE?

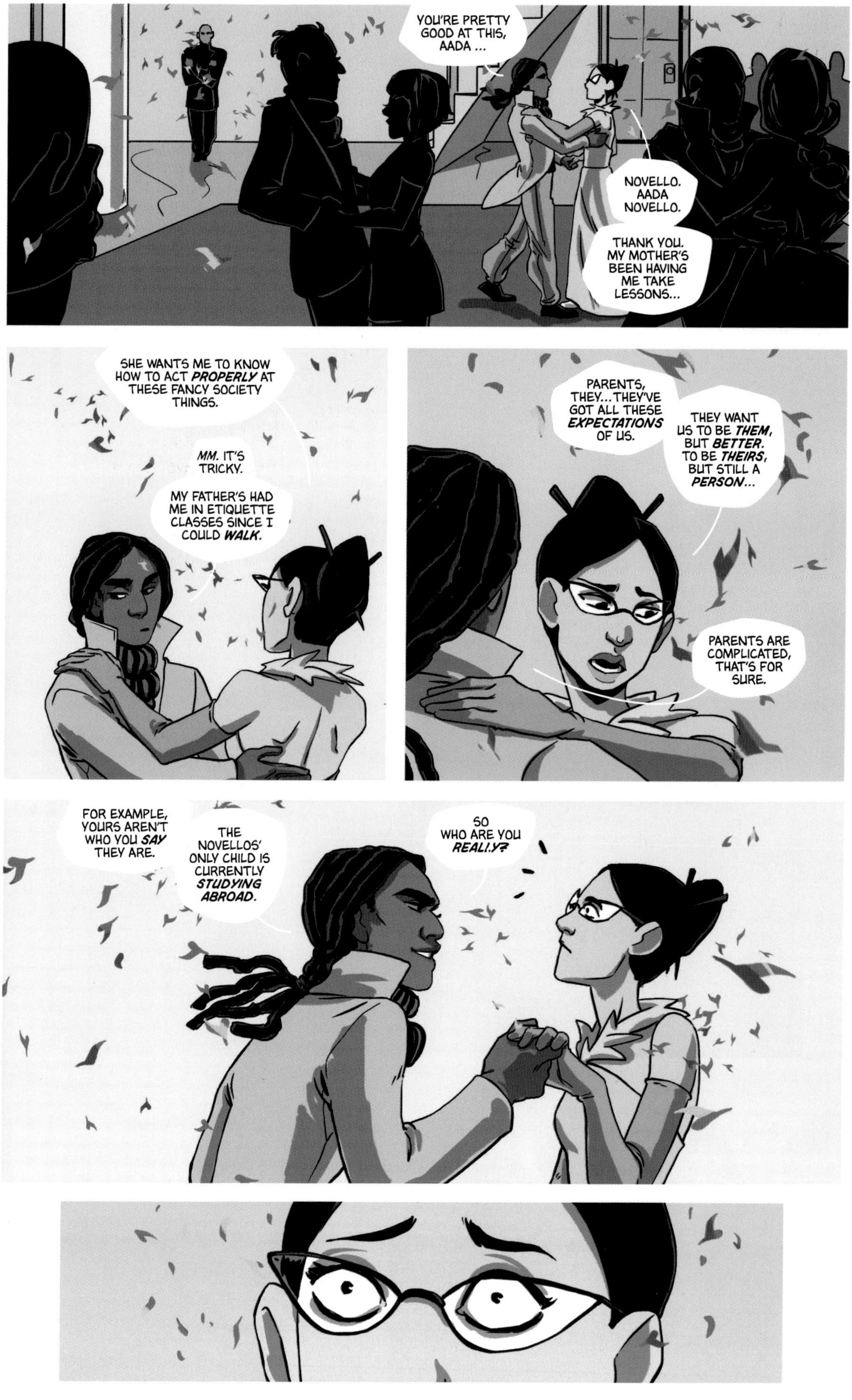
YOU'RE PRETTY GOOD AT THIS, AADA ...
NOVELLO. AADA NOVELLO.
THANK YOU. MY MOTHER'S BEEN HAVING ME TAKE LESSONS...
SHE WANTS ME TO KNOW HOW TO ACT PROPERLY AT THESE FANCY SOCIETY THINGS.
MM. IT'S TRICKY.
MY FATHER'S HAD ME IN ETIQUETTE CLASSES SINCE I COULD WALK.
PARENTS, THEY... THEY'VE GOT ALL THESE EXPECTATIONS OF US.
THEY WANT US TO BE THEM, BUT BETTER. TO BE THEIRS, BUT STILL A PERSON...
PARENTS ARE COMPLICATED, THAT'S FOR SURE.
FOR EXAMPLE, YOURS AREN'T WHO YOU SAY THEY ARE.
THE NOVELLOS' ONLY CHILD IS CURRENTLY STUDYING ABROAD.
SO WHO ARE YOU REALLY?

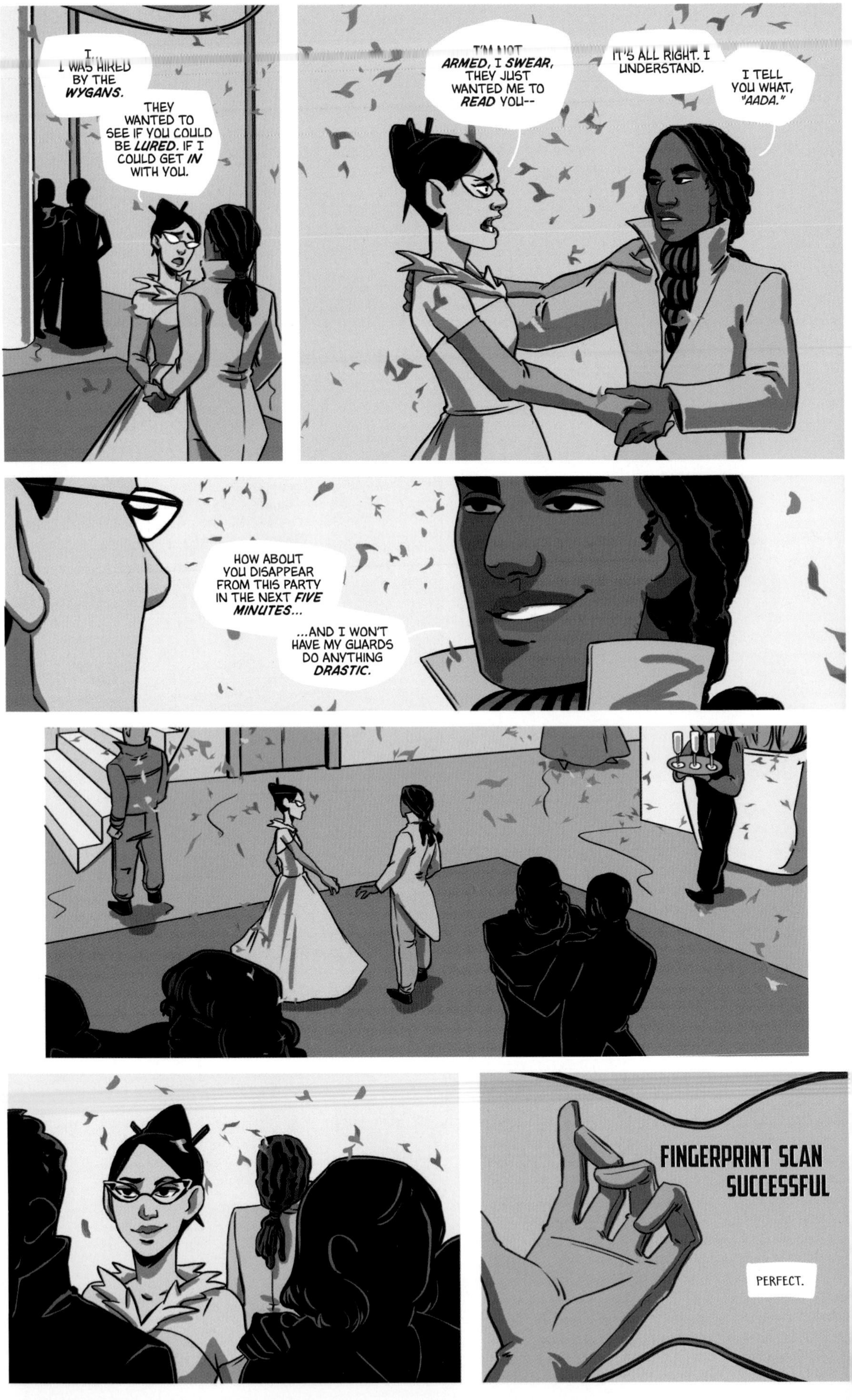
I... I WAS HIRED BY THE WYGANS.
THEY WANTED TO SEE IF YOU COULD BE LURED. IF I COULD GET IN WITH YOU.
I'M NOT ARMED, I SWEAR, THEY JUST WANTED ME TO READ YOU--
IT'S ALL RIGHT. I UNDERSTAND.
I TELL YOU WHAT, "AADA."
HOW ABOUT YOU DISAPPEAR FROM THIS PARTY IN THE NEXT FIVE MINUTES...
...AND I WON'T HAVE MY GUARDS DO ANYTHING DRASTIC.
FINGERPRINT SCAN SUCCESSFUL
PERFECT.

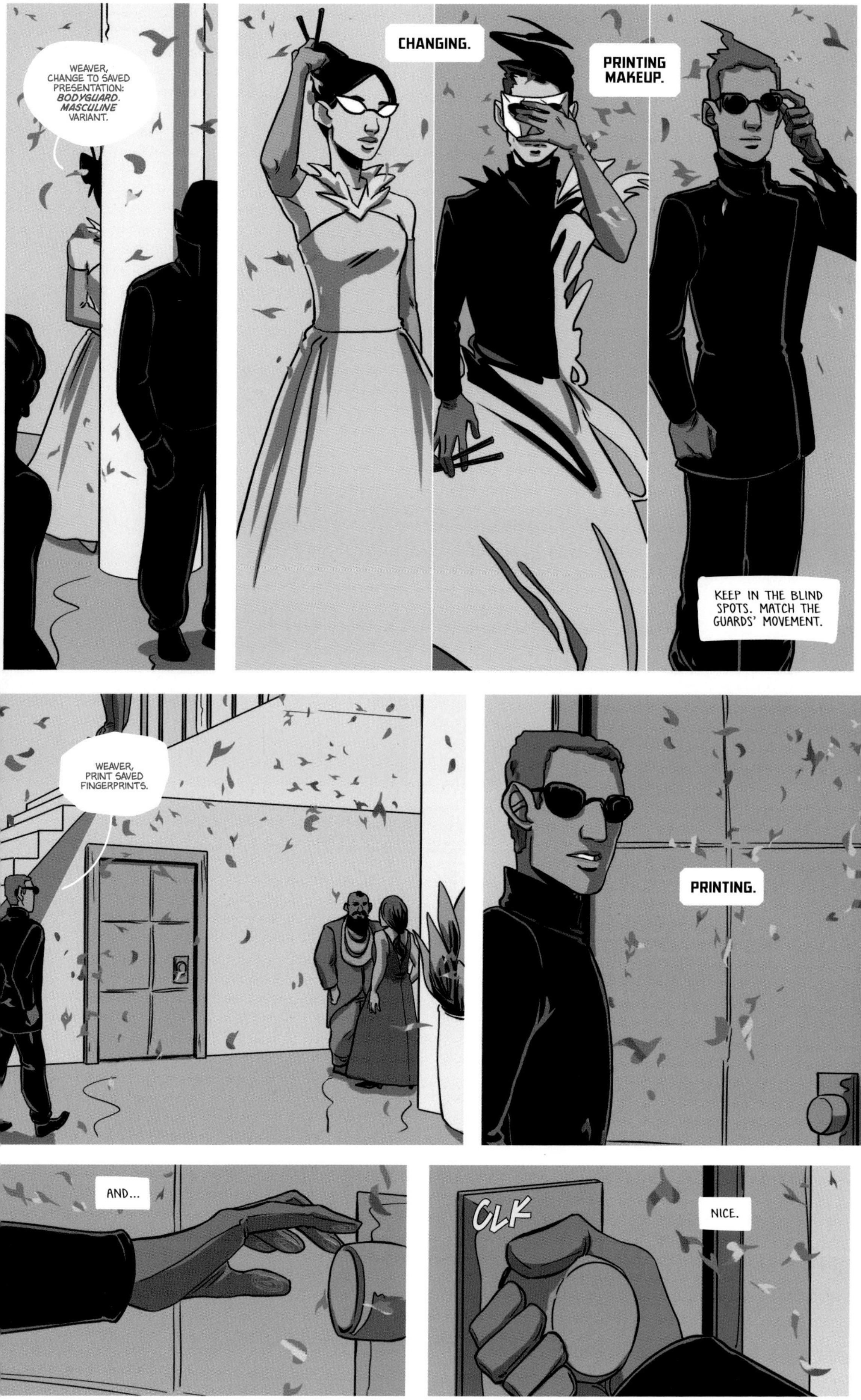
WEAVER, CHANGE TO SAVED PRESENTATION: ***BODYGUARD***. ***MASCULINE*** VARIANT.
CHANGING.
PRINTING MAKEUP.
KEEP IN THE BLIND SPOTS. MATCH THE GUARDS' MOVEMENT.
WEAVER, PRINT SAVED FINGERPRINTS.
PRINTING.
AND...
CLK
NICE.

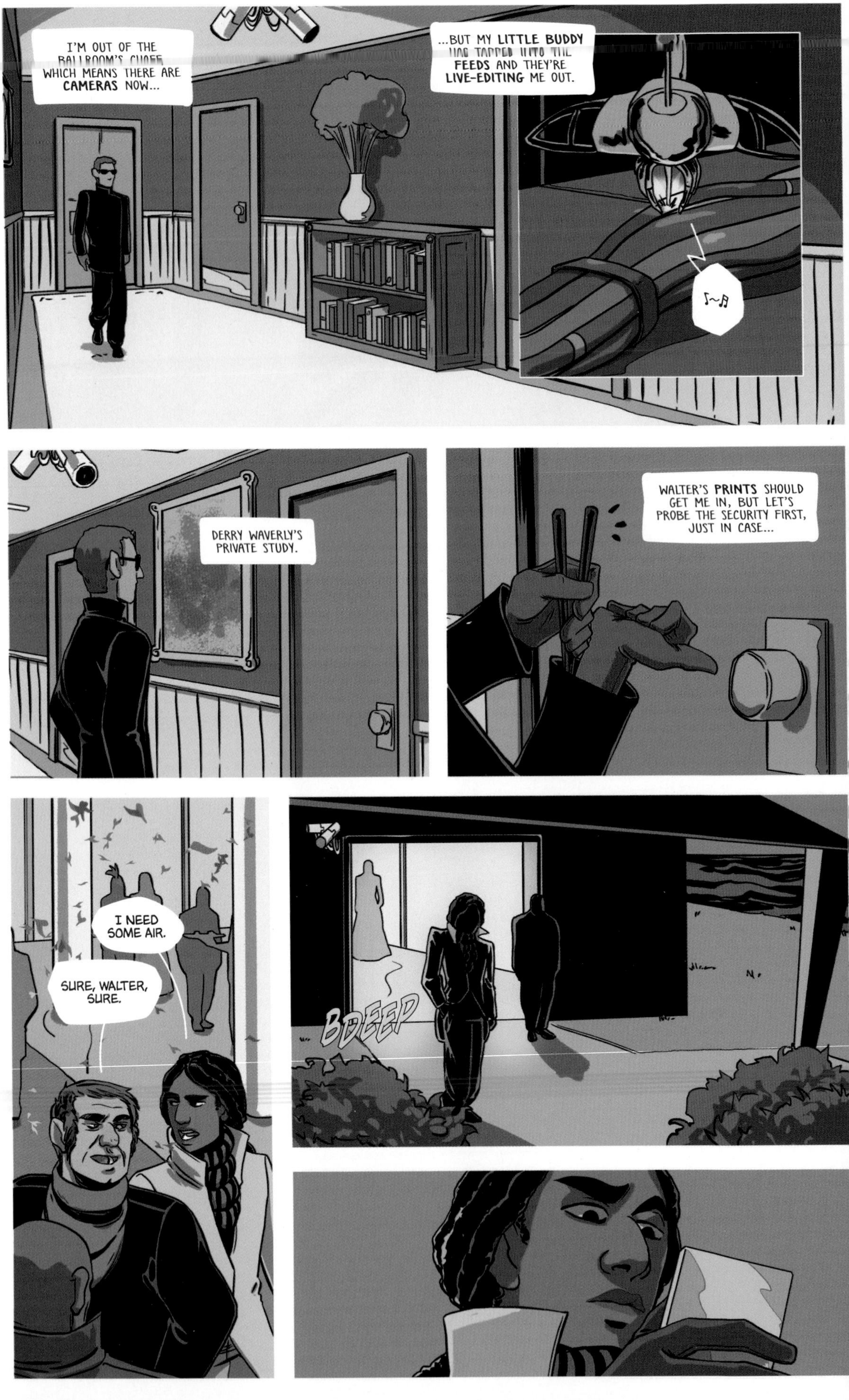
I'M OUT OF THE BALLROOM'S CHAFF WHICH MEANS THERE ARE **CAMERAS** NOW...
...BUT MY **LITTLE BUDDY** HAS TAPPED INTO THE **FEEDS** AND THEY'RE **LIVE-EDITING** ME OUT.
DERRY WAVERLY'S PRIVATE STUDY.
WALTER'S **PRINTS** SHOULD GET ME IN, BUT LET'S PROBE THE SECURITY FIRST, JUST IN CASE...
I NEED SOME AIR.
SURE, WALTER, SURE.
BDEEP

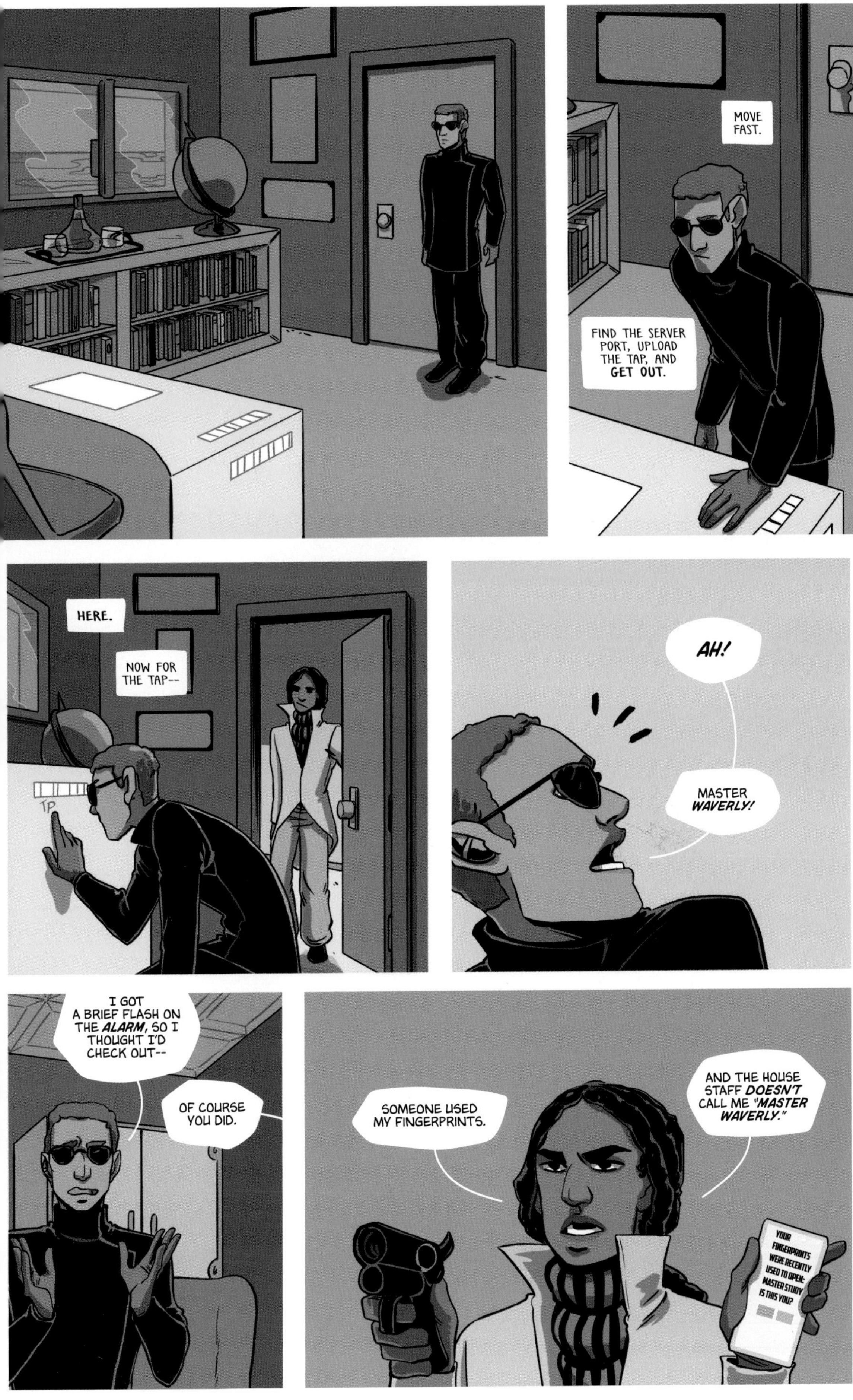
MOVE FAST.
FIND THE SERVER PORT, UPLOAD THE TAP, AND GET OUT.
HERE.
NOW FOR THE TAP--
TP
AH!
MASTER WAVERLY!
I GOT A BRIEF FLASH ON THE ALARM, SO I THOUGHT I'D CHECK OUT--
OF COURSE YOU DID.
SOMEONE USED MY FINGERPRINTS.
AND THE HOUSE STAFF DOESN'T CALL ME "MASTER WAVERLY."
YOUR FINGERPRINTS WERE RECENTLY USED TO OPEN: MASTER STUDY IS THIS YOU?

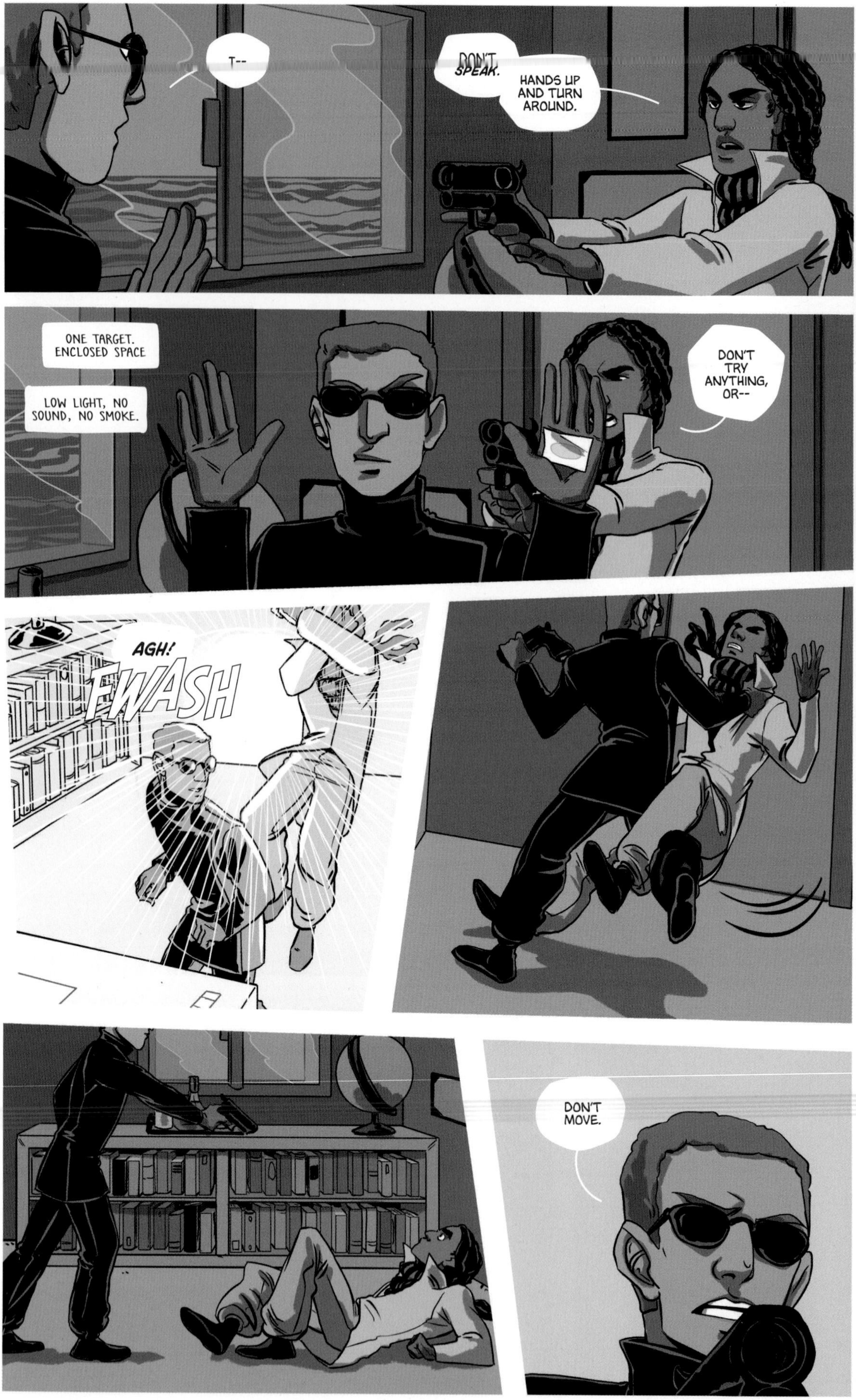
T--
DON'T SPEAK.
HANDS UP AND TURN AROUND.
ONE TARGET. ENCLOSED SPACE
LOW LIGHT, NO SOUND, NO SMOKE.
DON'T TRY ANYTHING, OR--
AGH!
FWASH
DON'T MOVE.

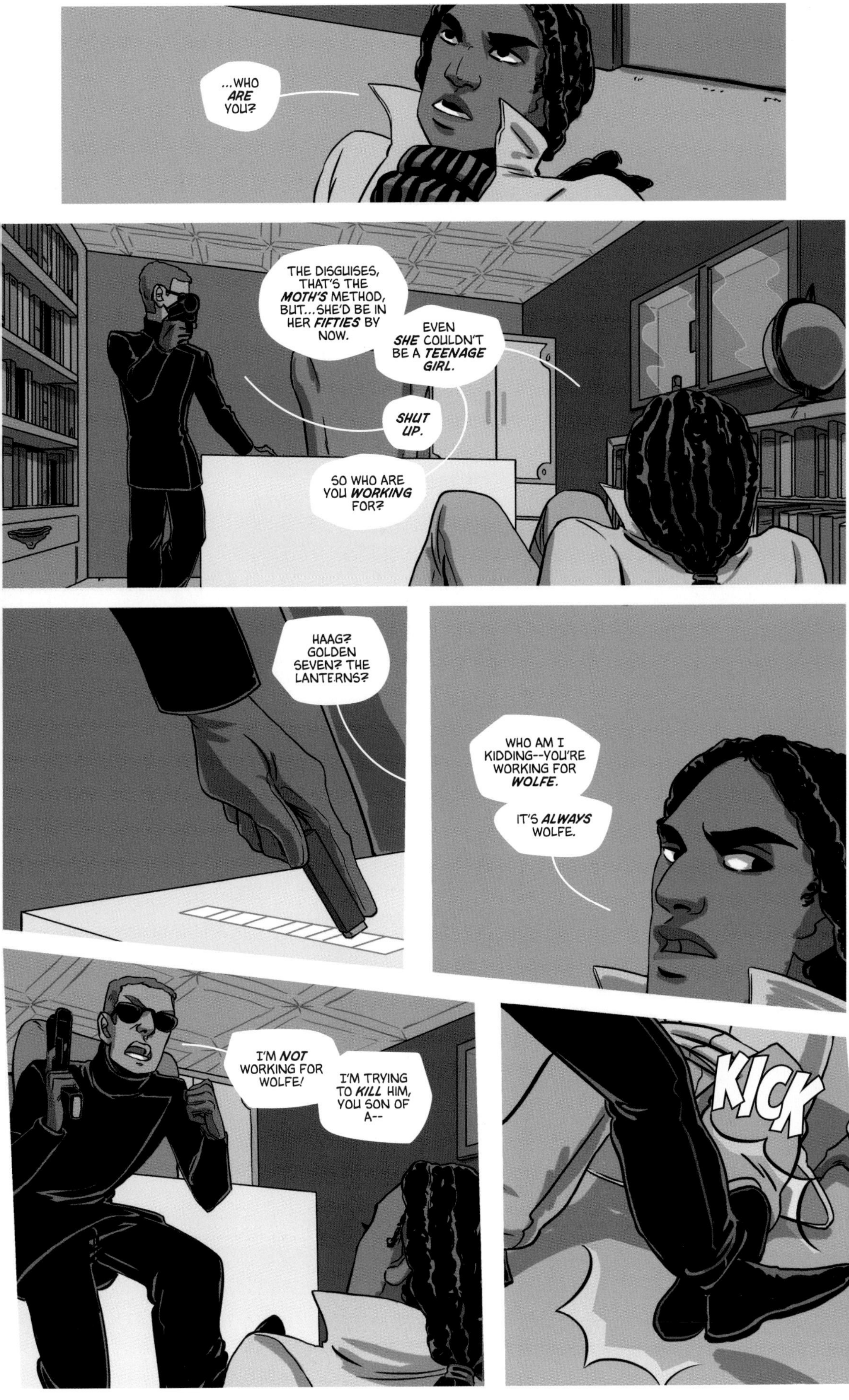
...WHO ARE YOU?
THE DISGUISES, THAT'S THE MOTH'S METHOD, BUT...SHE'D BE IN HER FIFTIES BY NOW.
EVEN SHE COULDN'T BE A TEENAGE GIRL.
SHUT UP.
SO WHO ARE YOU WORKING FOR?
HAAG? GOLDEN SEVEN? THE LANTERNS?
WHO AM I KIDDING--YOU'RE WORKING FOR WOLFE.
IT'S ALWAYS WOLFE.
I'M NOT WORKING FOR WOLFE!
I'M TRYING TO KILL HIM, YOU SON OF A--
KICK

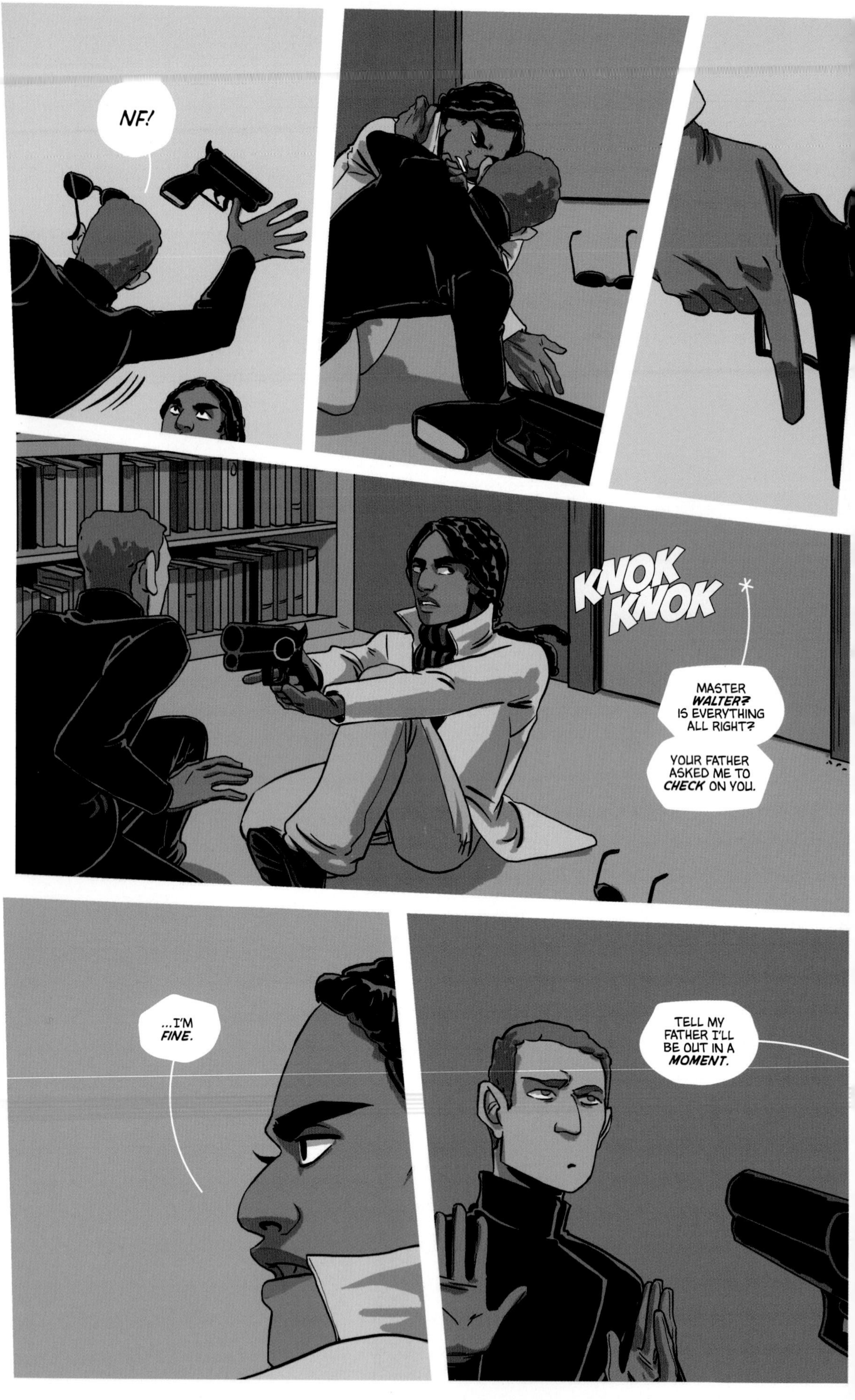
NF!
KNOK KNOK
MASTER WALTER? IS EVERYTHING ALL RIGHT?
YOUR FATHER ASKED ME TO CHECK ON YOU.
...I'M FINE.
TELL MY FATHER I'LL BE OUT IN A MOMENT.

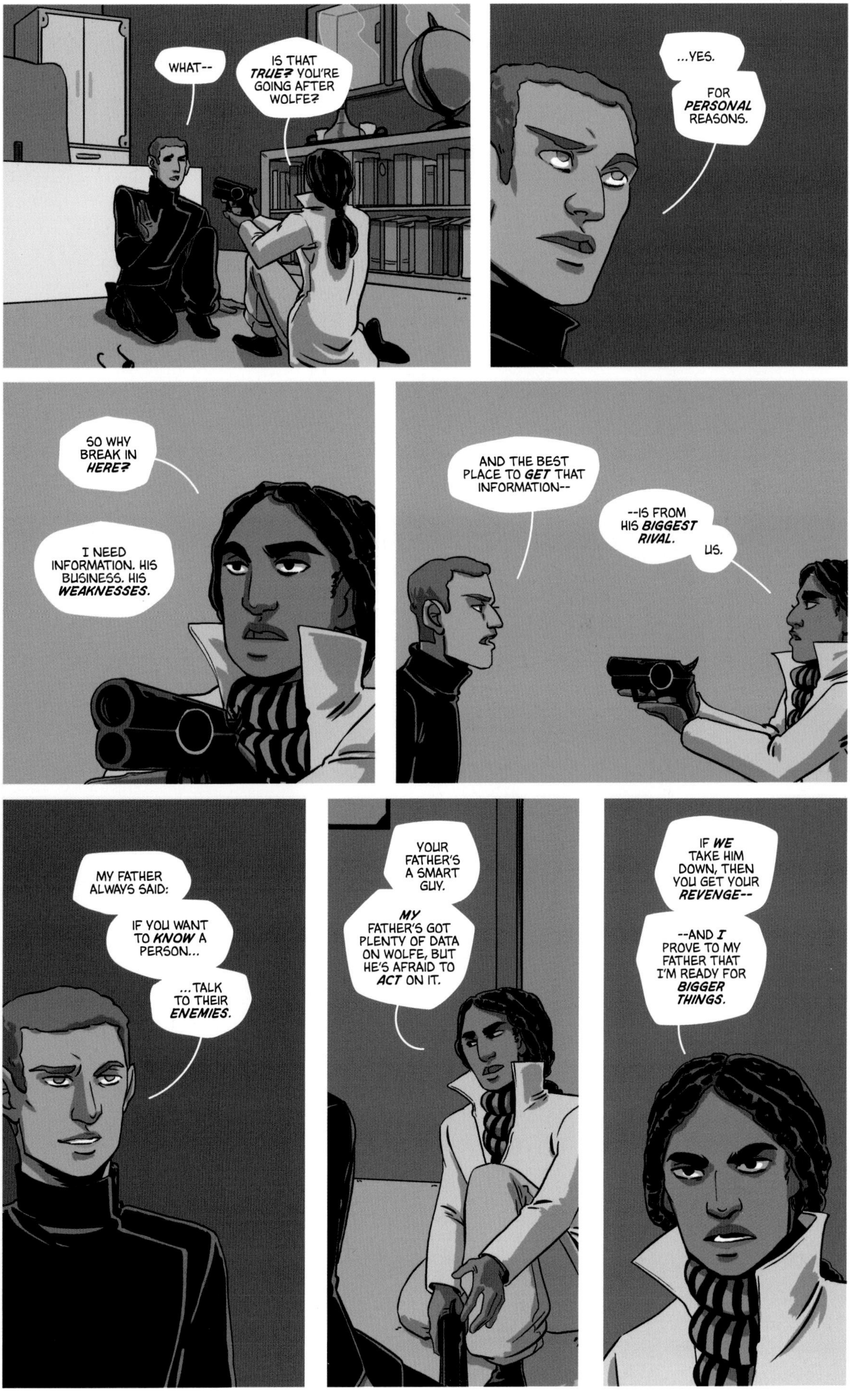
WHAT--
IS THAT TRUE? YOU'RE GOING AFTER WOLFE?
...YES.
FOR PERSONAL REASONS.
SO WHY BREAK IN HERE?
I NEED INFORMATION. HIS BUSINESS. HIS WEAKNESSES.
AND THE BEST PLACE TO GET THAT INFORMATION--
--IS FROM HIS BIGGEST RIVAL.
US.
MY FATHER ALWAYS SAID:
IF YOU WANT TO KNOW A PERSON...
...TALK TO THEIR ENEMIES.
YOUR FATHER'S A SMART GUY.
MY FATHER'S GOT PLENTY OF DATA ON WOLFE, BUT HE'S AFRAID TO ACT ON IT.
IF WE TAKE HIM DOWN, THEN YOU GET YOUR REVENGE--
--AND I PROVE TO MY FATHER THAT I'M READY FOR BIGGER THINGS.

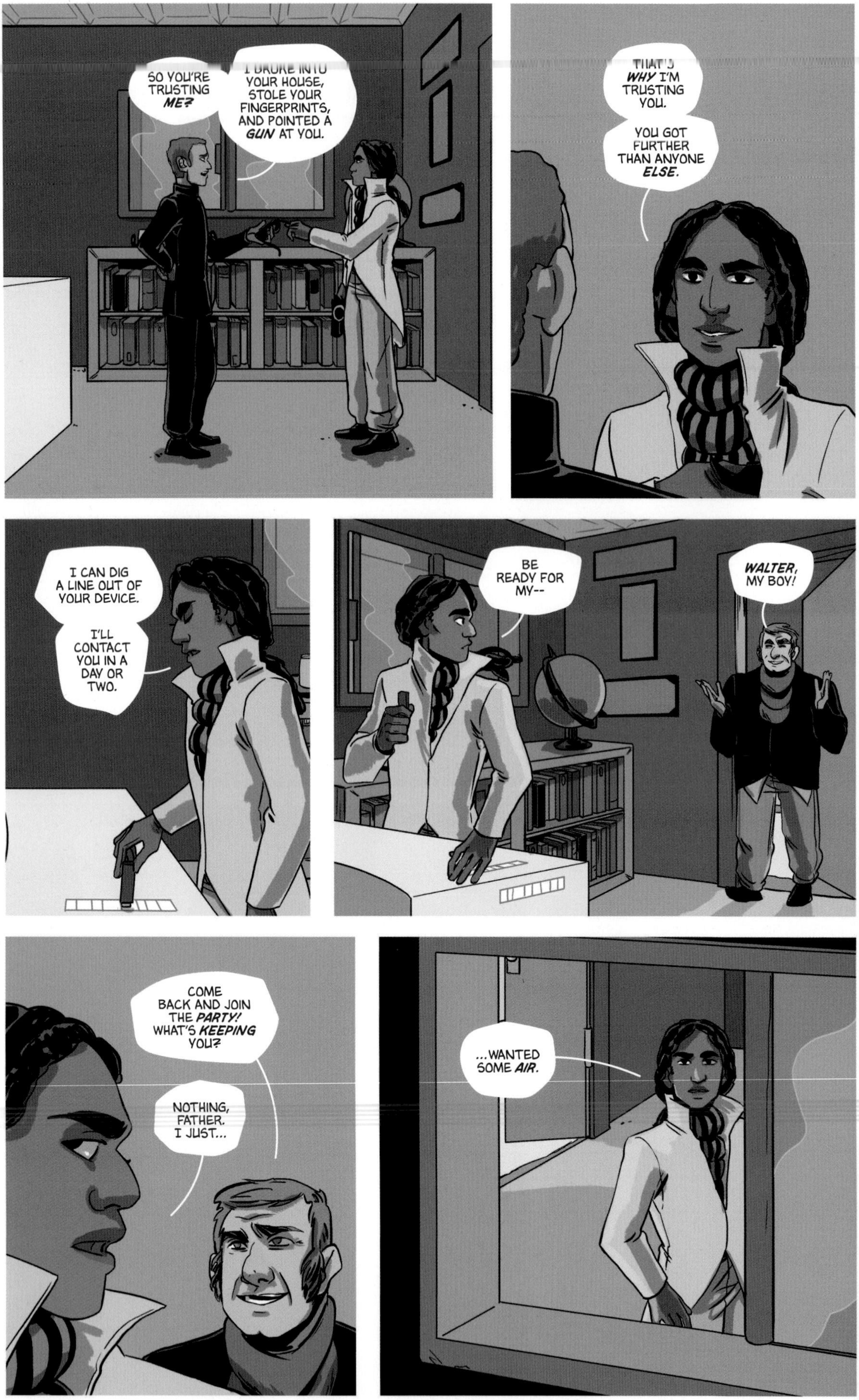
SO YOU'RE TRUSTING *ME?*
I BROKE INTO YOUR HOUSE, STOLE YOUR FINGERPRINTS, AND POINTED A *GUN* AT YOU.
THAT'S *WHY* I'M TRUSTING YOU.
YOU GOT FURTHER THAN ANYONE *ELSE.*
I CAN DIG A LINE OUT OF YOUR DEVICE.
I'LL CONTACT YOU IN A DAY OR TWO.
BE READY FOR MY--
WALTER, MY BOY!
COME BACK AND JOIN THE *PARTY!* WHAT'S *KEEPING* YOU?
NOTHING, FATHER. I JUST...
...WANTED SOME *AIR.*

3

SUSPENDED BODIES

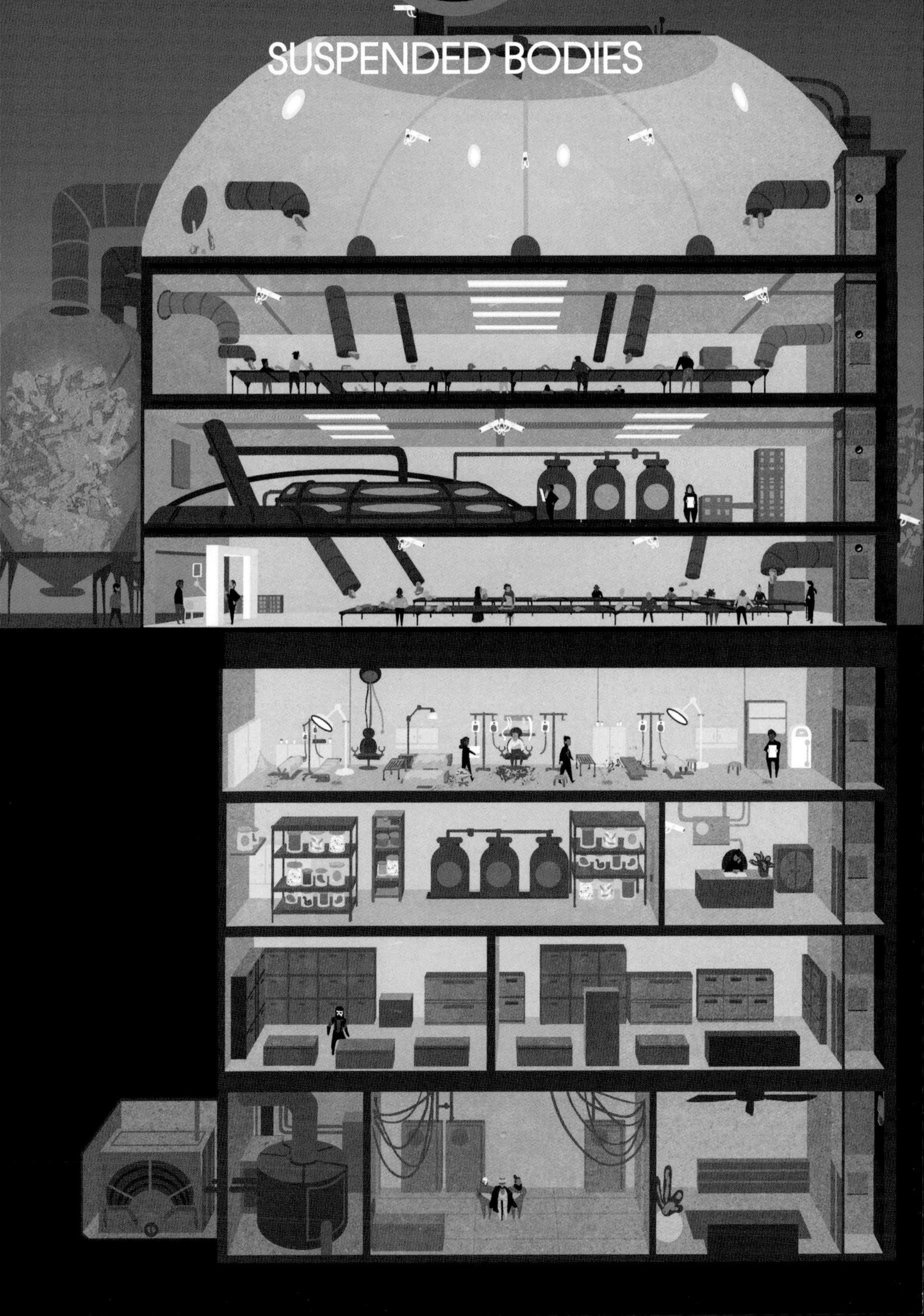

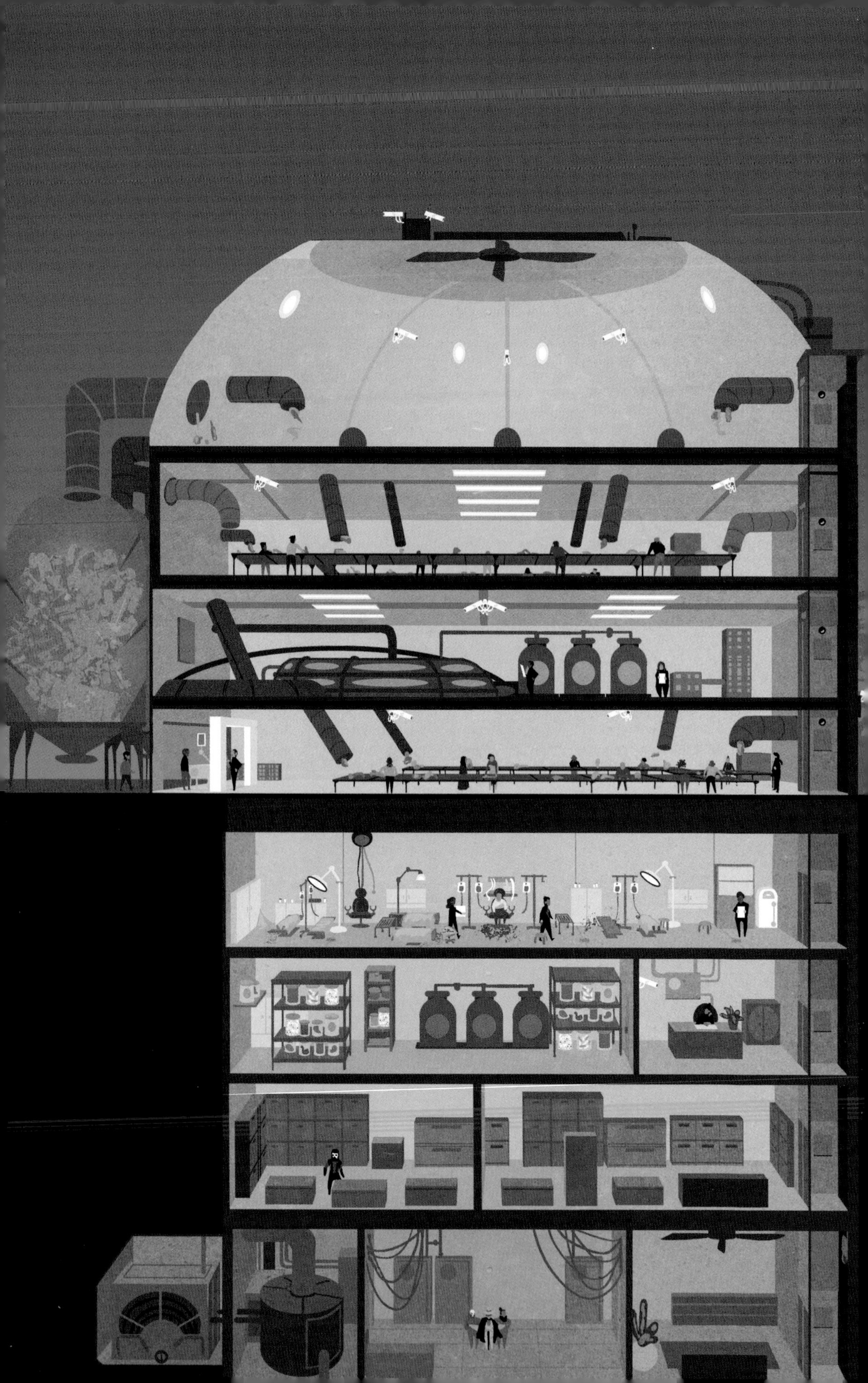

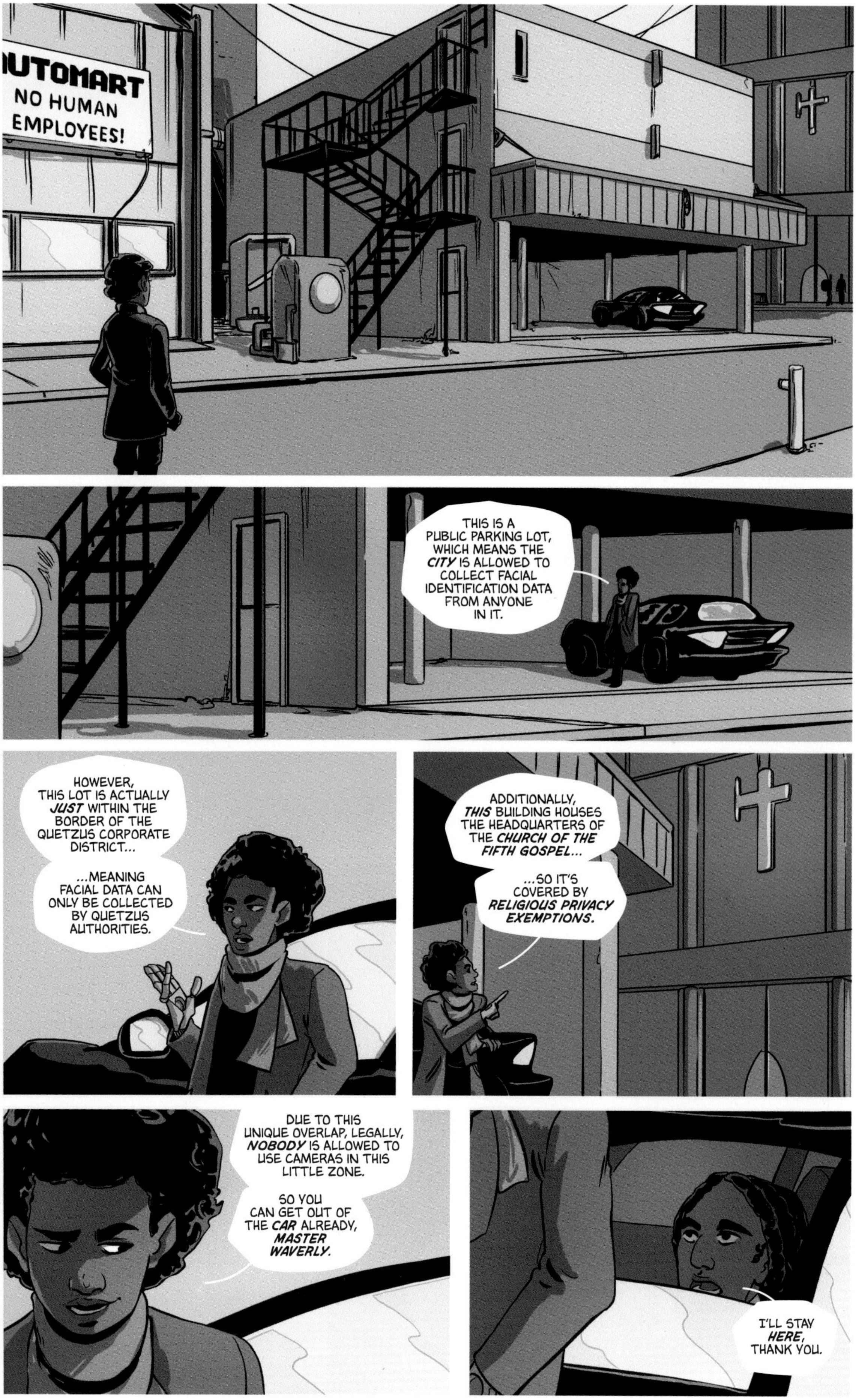

UTOMART
NO HUMAN EMPLOYEES!
THIS IS A PUBLIC PARKING LOT, WHICH MEANS THE *CITY* IS ALLOWED TO COLLECT FACIAL IDENTIFICATION DATA FROM ANYONE IN IT.
HOWEVER, THIS LOT IS ACTUALLY *JUST* WITHIN THE BORDER OF THE QUETZUS CORPORATE DISTRICT...
...MEANING FACIAL DATA CAN ONLY BE COLLECTED BY QUETZUS AUTHORITIES.
ADDITIONALLY, *THIS* BUILDING HOUSES THE HEADQUARTERS OF THE *CHURCH OF THE FIFTH GOSPEL*...
...SO IT'S COVERED BY *RELIGIOUS PRIVACY EXEMPTIONS.*
DUE TO THIS UNIQUE OVERLAP, LEGALLY, *NOBODY* IS ALLOWED TO USE CAMERAS IN THIS LITTLE ZONE.
SO YOU CAN GET OUT OF THE *CAR* ALREADY, *MASTER WAVERLY.*
I'LL STAY *HERE*, THANK YOU.

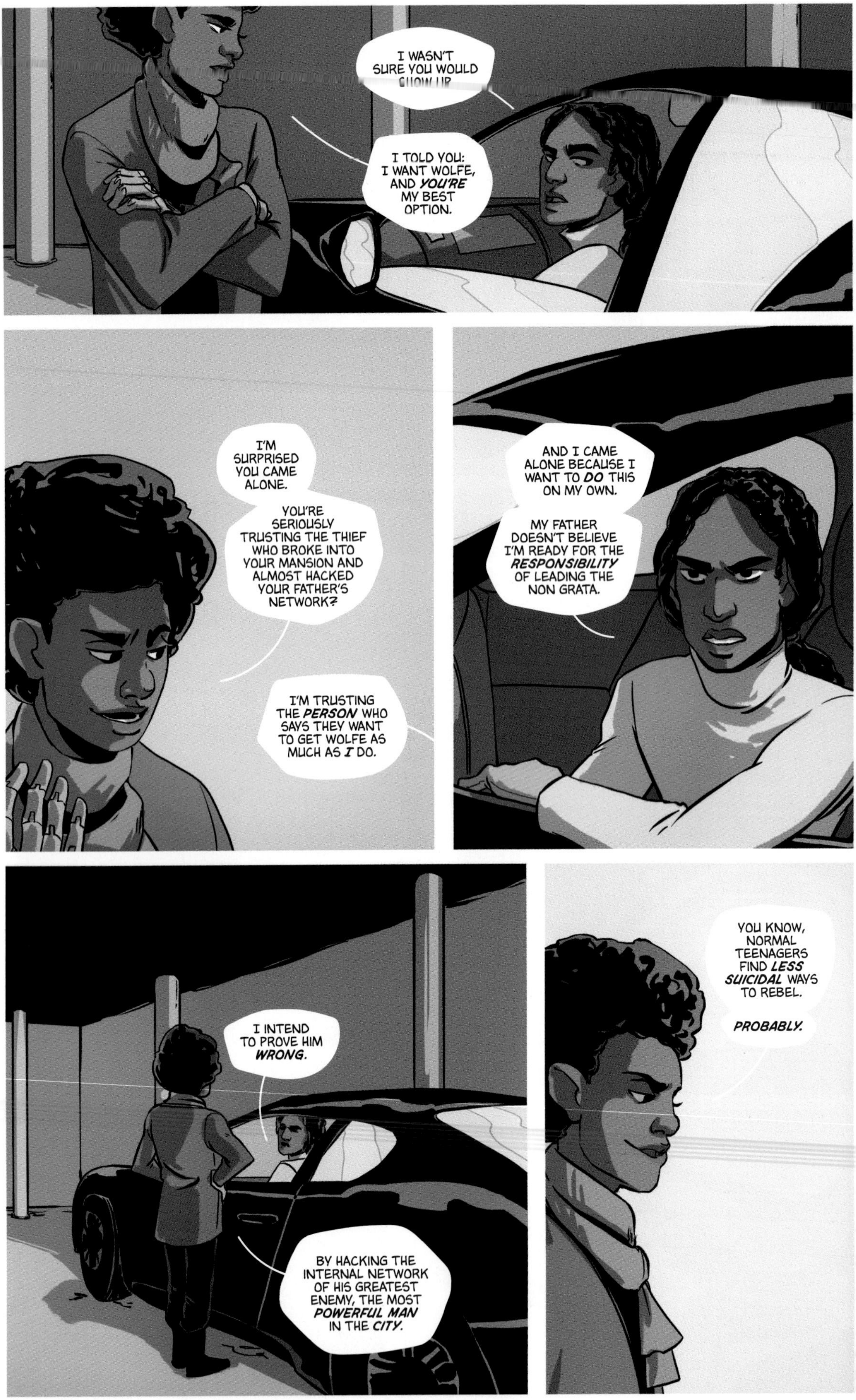
I WASN'T SURE YOU WOULD
I TOLD YOU: I WANT WOLFE, AND YOU'RE MY BEST OPTION.
I'M SURPRISED YOU CAME ALONE.
YOU'RE SERIOUSLY TRUSTING THE THIEF WHO BROKE INTO YOUR MANSION AND ALMOST HACKED YOUR FATHER'S NETWORK?
I'M TRUSTING THE PERSON WHO SAYS THEY WANT TO GET WOLFE AS MUCH AS I DO.
AND I CAME ALONE BECAUSE I WANT TO DO THIS ON MY OWN.
MY FATHER DOESN'T BELIEVE I'M READY FOR THE RESPONSIBILITY OF LEADING THE NON GRATA.
I INTEND TO PROVE HIM WRONG.
BY HACKING THE INTERNAL NETWORK OF HIS GREATEST ENEMY, THE MOST POWERFUL MAN IN THE CITY.
YOU KNOW, NORMAL TEENAGERS FIND LESS SUICIDAL WAYS TO REBEL.
PROBABLY.

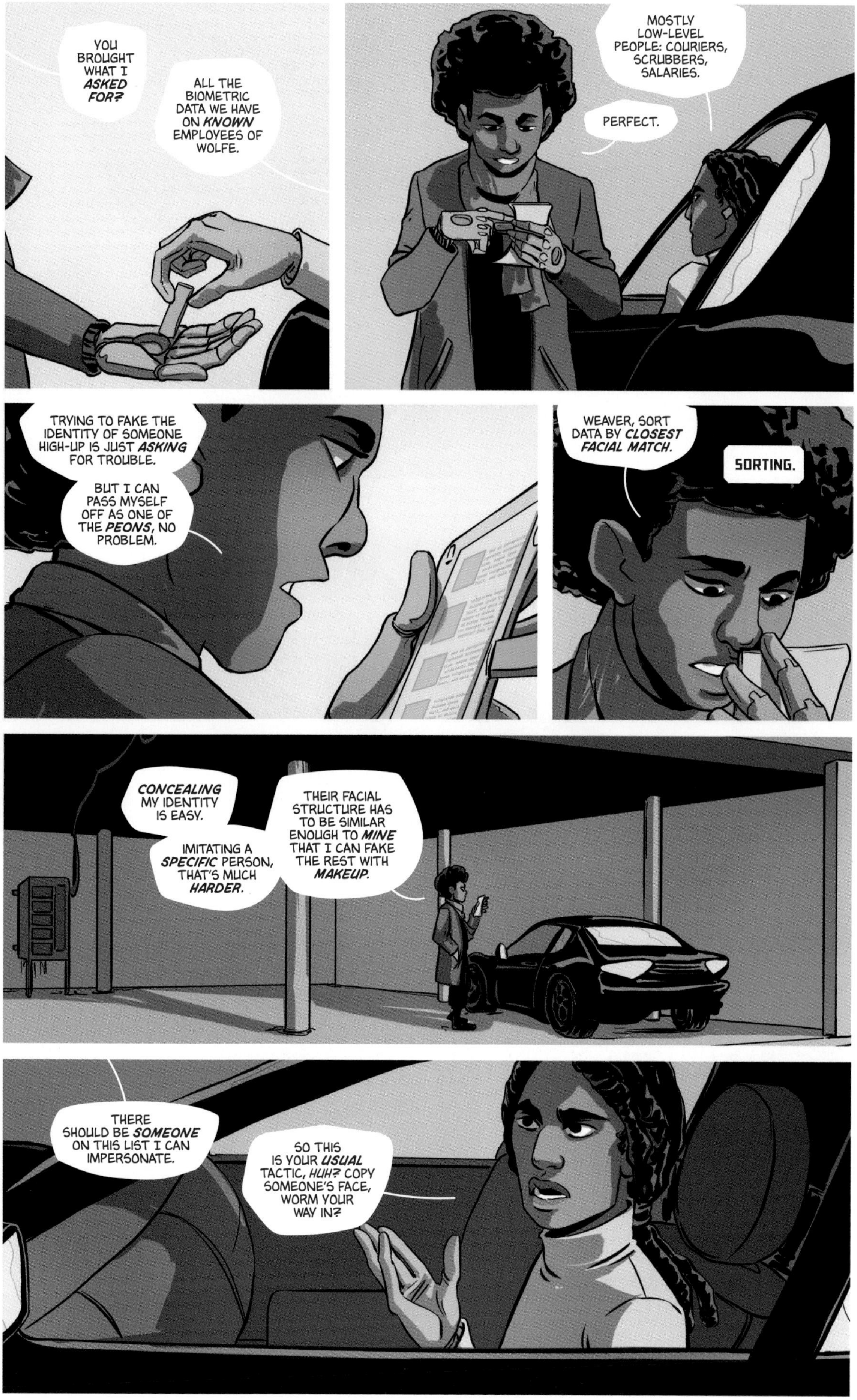

YOU BROUGHT WHAT I *ASKED FOR?*
ALL THE BIOMETRIC DATA WE HAVE ON *KNOWN* EMPLOYEES OF WOLFE.
MOSTLY LOW-LEVEL PEOPLE: COURIERS, SCRUBBERS, SALARIES.
PERFECT.
TRYING TO FAKE THE IDENTITY OF SOMEONE HIGH-UP IS JUST *ASKING* FOR TROUBLE.
BUT I CAN PASS MYSELF OFF AS ONE OF THE *PEONS*, NO PROBLEM.
WEAVER, SORT DATA BY *CLOSEST FACIAL MATCH*.
SORTING.
CONCEALING MY IDENTITY IS EASY.
IMITATING A *SPECIFIC* PERSON, THAT'S MUCH *HARDER*.
THEIR FACIAL STRUCTURE HAS TO BE SIMILAR ENOUGH TO *MINE* THAT I CAN FAKE THE REST WITH *MAKEUP*.
THERE SHOULD BE *SOMEONE* ON THIS LIST I CAN IMPERSONATE.
SO THIS IS YOUR *USUAL* TACTIC, *HUH?* COPY SOMEONE'S FACE, WORM YOUR WAY IN?

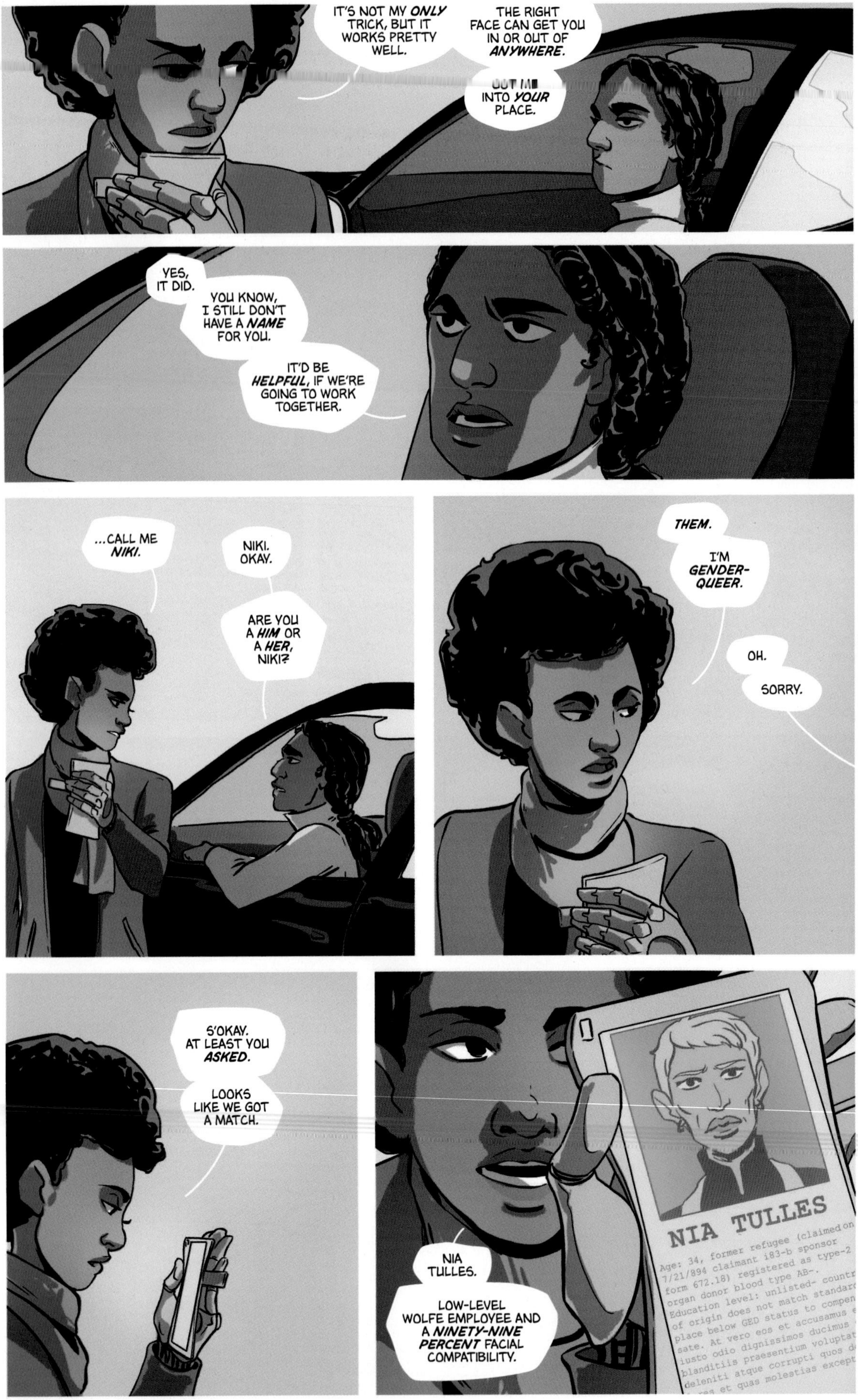

IT'S NOT MY *ONLY* TRICK, BUT IT WORKS PRETTY WELL.
THE RIGHT FACE CAN GET YOU IN OR OUT OF *ANYWHERE.*
INTO *YOUR* PLACE.
YES, IT DID.
YOU KNOW, I STILL DON'T HAVE A *NAME* FOR YOU.
IT'D BE *HELPFUL,* IF WE'RE GOING TO WORK TOGETHER.
...CALL ME *NIKI.*
NIKI. OKAY.
ARE YOU A *HIM* OR A *HER,* NIKI?
THEM.
I'M *GENDER-QUEER.*
OH.
SORRY.
S'OKAY. AT LEAST YOU *ASKED.*
LOOKS LIKE WE GOT A MATCH.
NIA TULLES
Age: 34, former refugee (claimed on
7/21/894 claimant i83-b sponsor
form 672.18) registered as type-2
organ donor blood type AB-.
Education level: unlisted- countr
of origin does not match standar
place below GED status to compen
sate. At vero eos et accusamus e
iusto odio dignissimos ducimus
blanditiis praesentium voluptat
deleniti atque corrupti quos d
et quas molestias except
NIA TULLES.
LOW-LEVEL WOLFE EMPLOYEE AND A *NINETY-NINE PERCENT* FACIAL COMPATIBILITY.

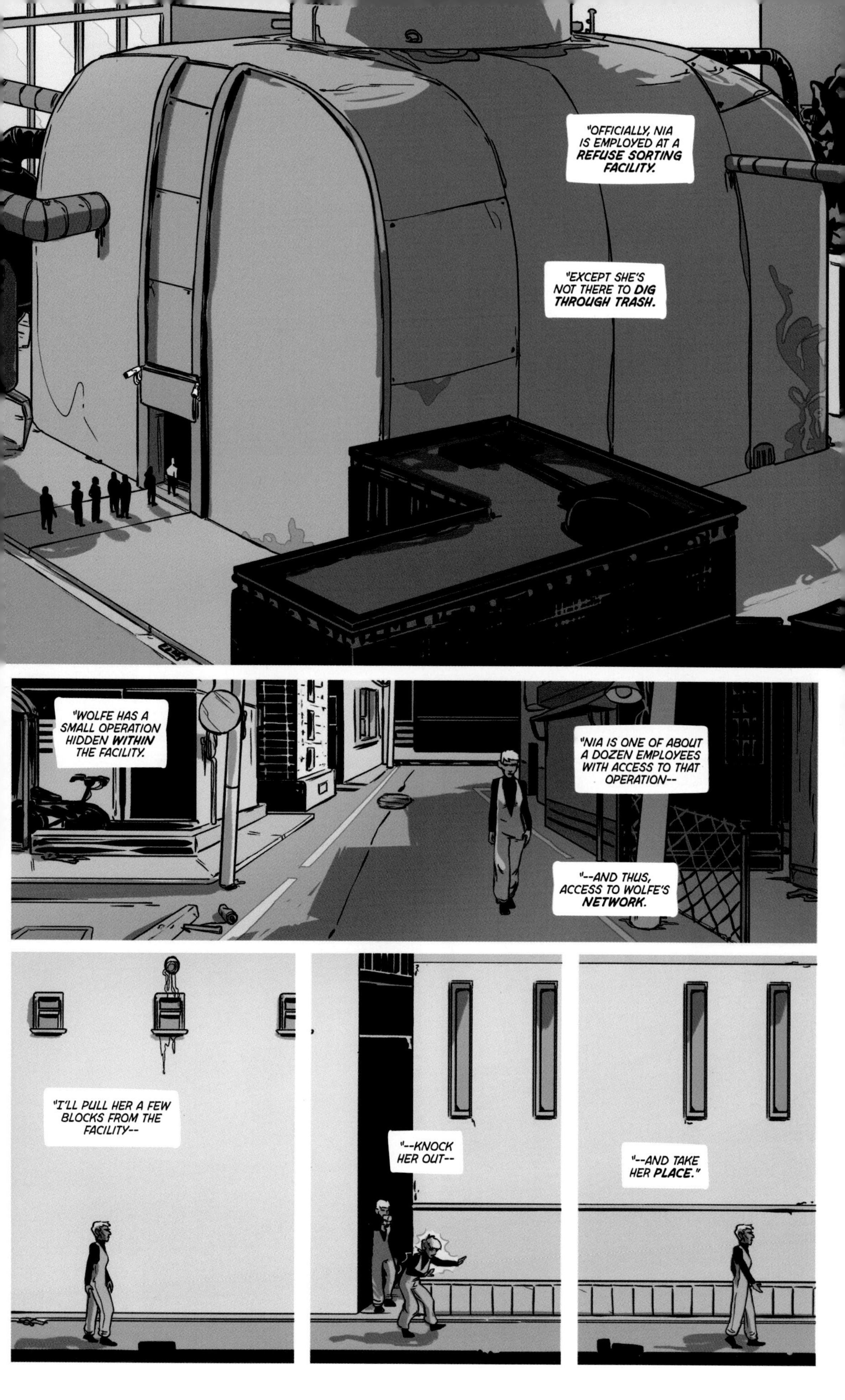
"OFFICIALLY, NIA IS EMPLOYED AT A REFUSE SORTING FACILITY.
"EXCEPT SHE'S NOT THERE TO DIG THROUGH TRASH.
"WOLFE HAS A SMALL OPERATION HIDDEN WITHIN THE FACILITY.
"NIA IS ONE OF ABOUT A DOZEN EMPLOYEES WITH ACCESS TO THAT OPERATION--
"--AND THUS, ACCESS TO WOLFE'S NETWORK.
"I'LL PULL HER A FEW BLOCKS FROM THE FACILITY--
"--KNOCK HER OUT--
"--AND TAKE HER PLACE."

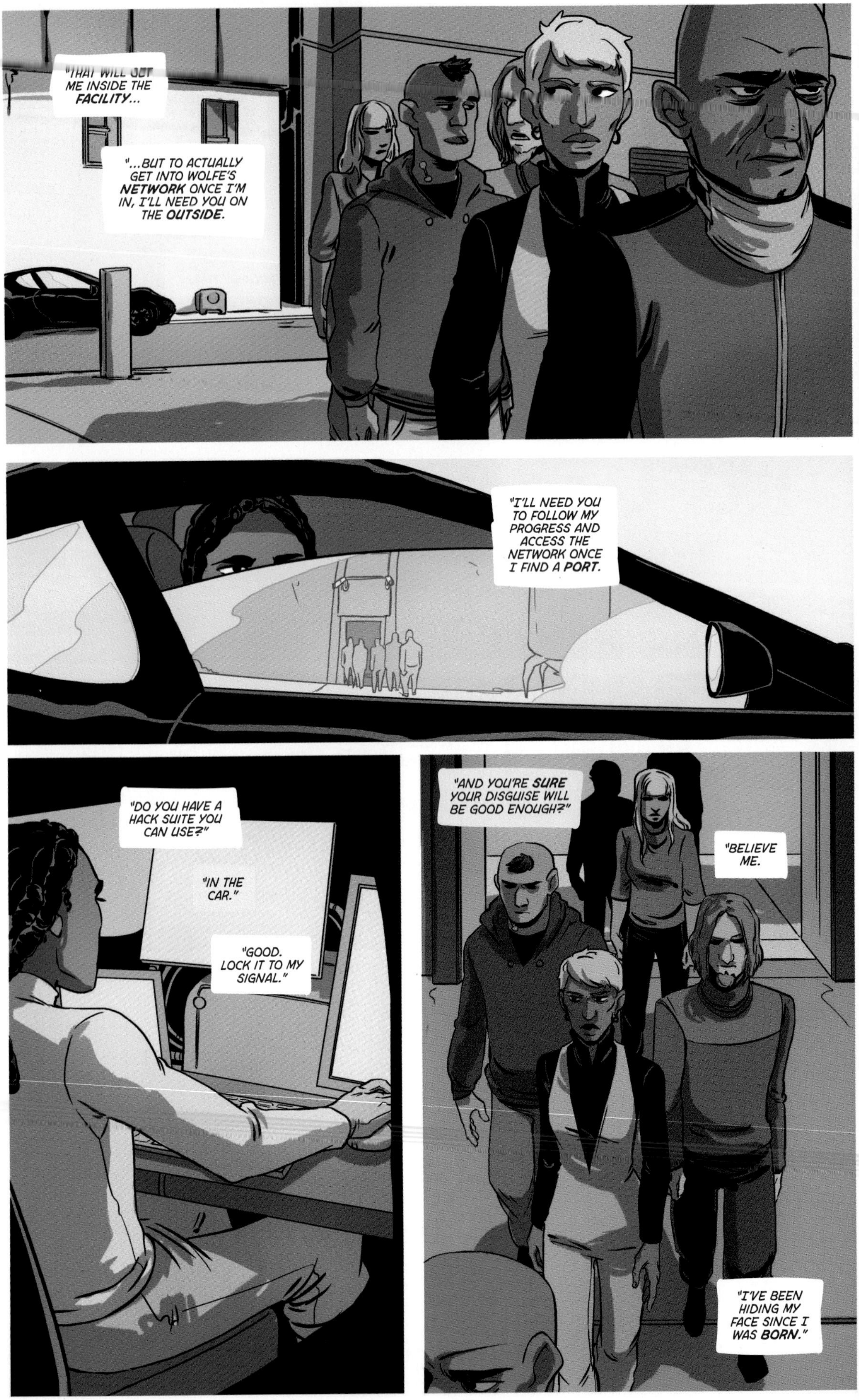
"THAT WILL GET ME INSIDE THE FACILITY...
"...BUT TO ACTUALLY GET INTO WOLFE'S NETWORK ONCE I'M IN, I'LL NEED YOU ON THE OUTSIDE.
"I'LL NEED YOU TO FOLLOW MY PROGRESS AND ACCESS THE NETWORK ONCE I FIND A PORT.
"DO YOU HAVE A HACK SUITE YOU CAN USE?"
"IN THE CAR."
"GOOD. LOCK IT TO MY SIGNAL."
"AND YOU'RE SURE YOUR DISGUISE WILL BE GOOD ENOUGH?"
"BELIEVE ME.
"I'VE BEEN HIDING MY FACE SINCE I WAS BORN."

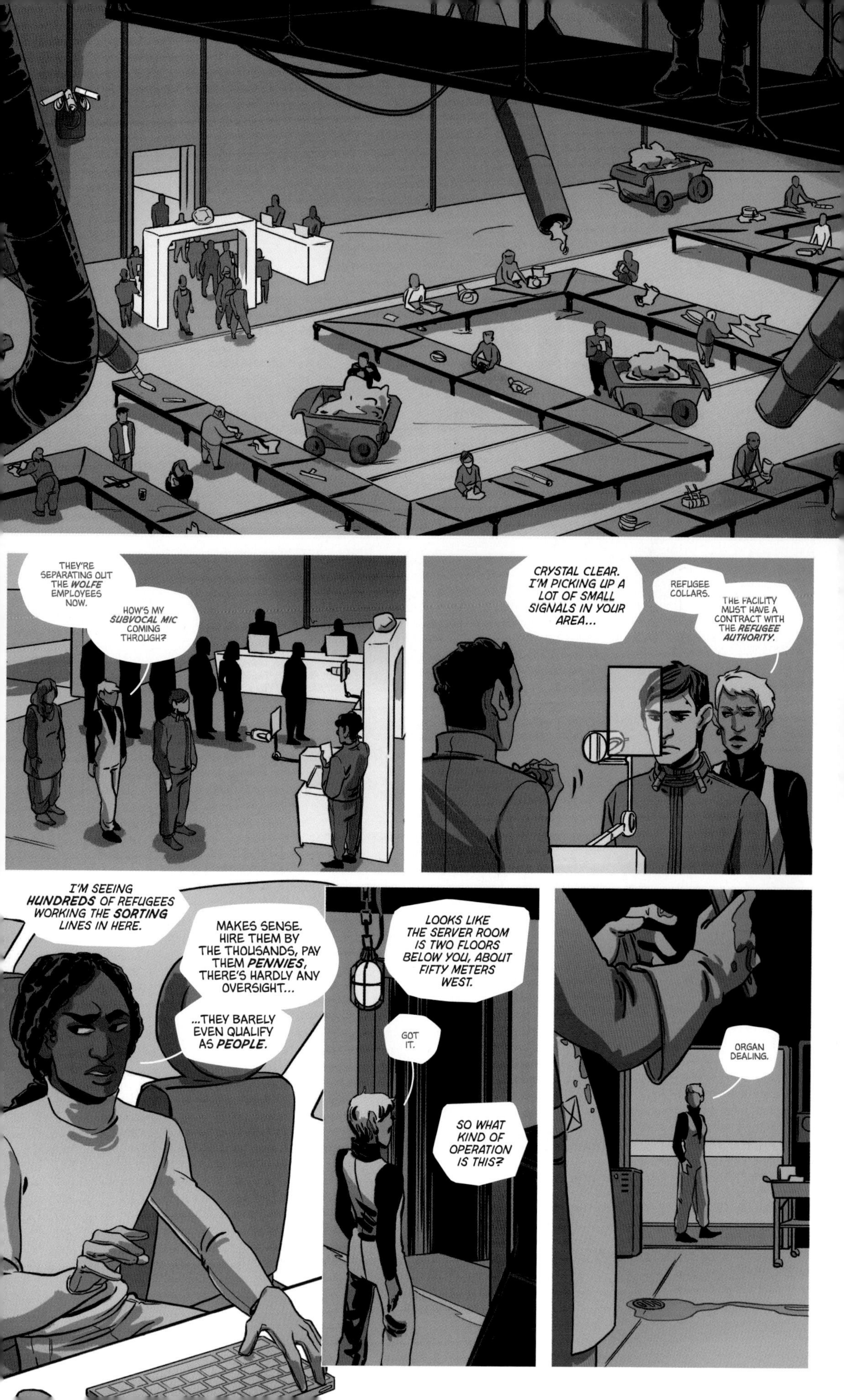
THEY'RE SEPARATING OUT THE *WOLFE* EMPLOYEES NOW.
HOW'S MY *SUBVOCAL MIC* COMING THROUGH?
CRYSTAL CLEAR. I'M PICKING UP A LOT OF SMALL SIGNALS IN YOUR AREA...
REFUGEE COLLARS.
THE FACILITY MUST HAVE A CONTRACT WITH THE *REFUGEE AUTHORITY*.
I'M SEEING *HUNDREDS* OF REFUGEES WORKING THE *SORTING* LINES IN HERE.
MAKES SENSE. HIRE THEM BY THE THOUSANDS, PAY THEM *PENNIES*, THERE'S HARDLY ANY OVERSIGHT...
...THEY BARELY EVEN QUALIFY AS *PEOPLE*.
LOOKS LIKE THE SERVER ROOM IS TWO FLOORS BELOW YOU, ABOUT FIFTY METERS WEST.
GOT IT.
SO WHAT KIND OF OPERATION IS THIS?
ORGAN DEALING.

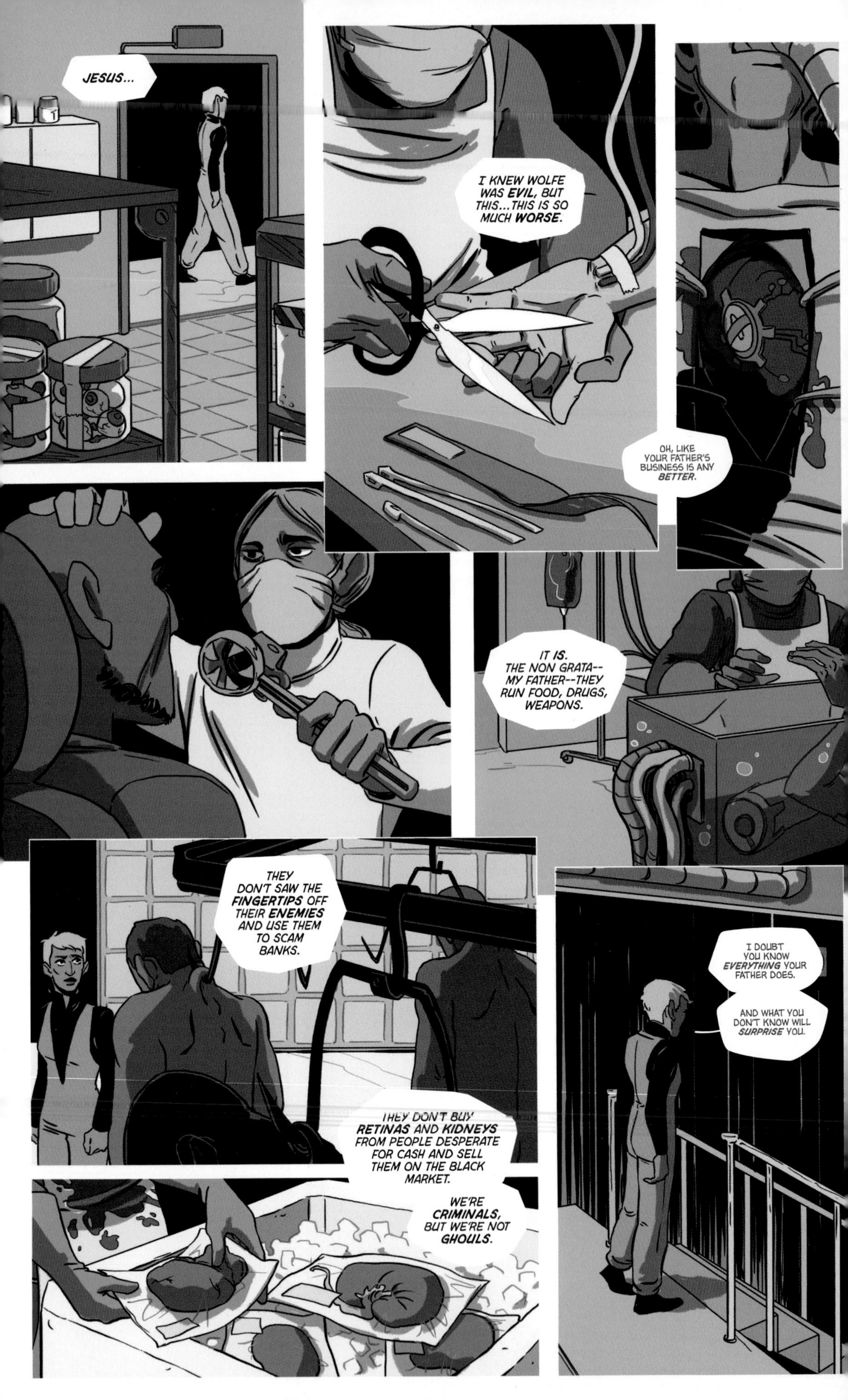
JESUS...
I KNEW WOLFE WAS EVIL, BUT THIS...THIS IS SO MUCH WORSE.
OH, LIKE YOUR FATHER'S BUSINESS IS ANY BETTER.
IT IS. THE NON GRATA-- MY FATHER--THEY RUN FOOD, DRUGS, WEAPONS.
THEY DON'T SAW THE FINGERTIPS OFF THEIR ENEMIES AND USE THEM TO SCAM BANKS.
THEY DON'T BUY RETINAS AND KIDNEYS FROM PEOPLE DESPERATE FOR CASH AND SELL THEM ON THE BLACK MARKET.
WE'RE CRIMINALS, BUT WE'RE NOT GHOULS.
I DOUBT YOU KNOW EVERYTHING YOUR FATHER DOES.
AND WHAT YOU DON'T KNOW WILL SURPRISE YOU.

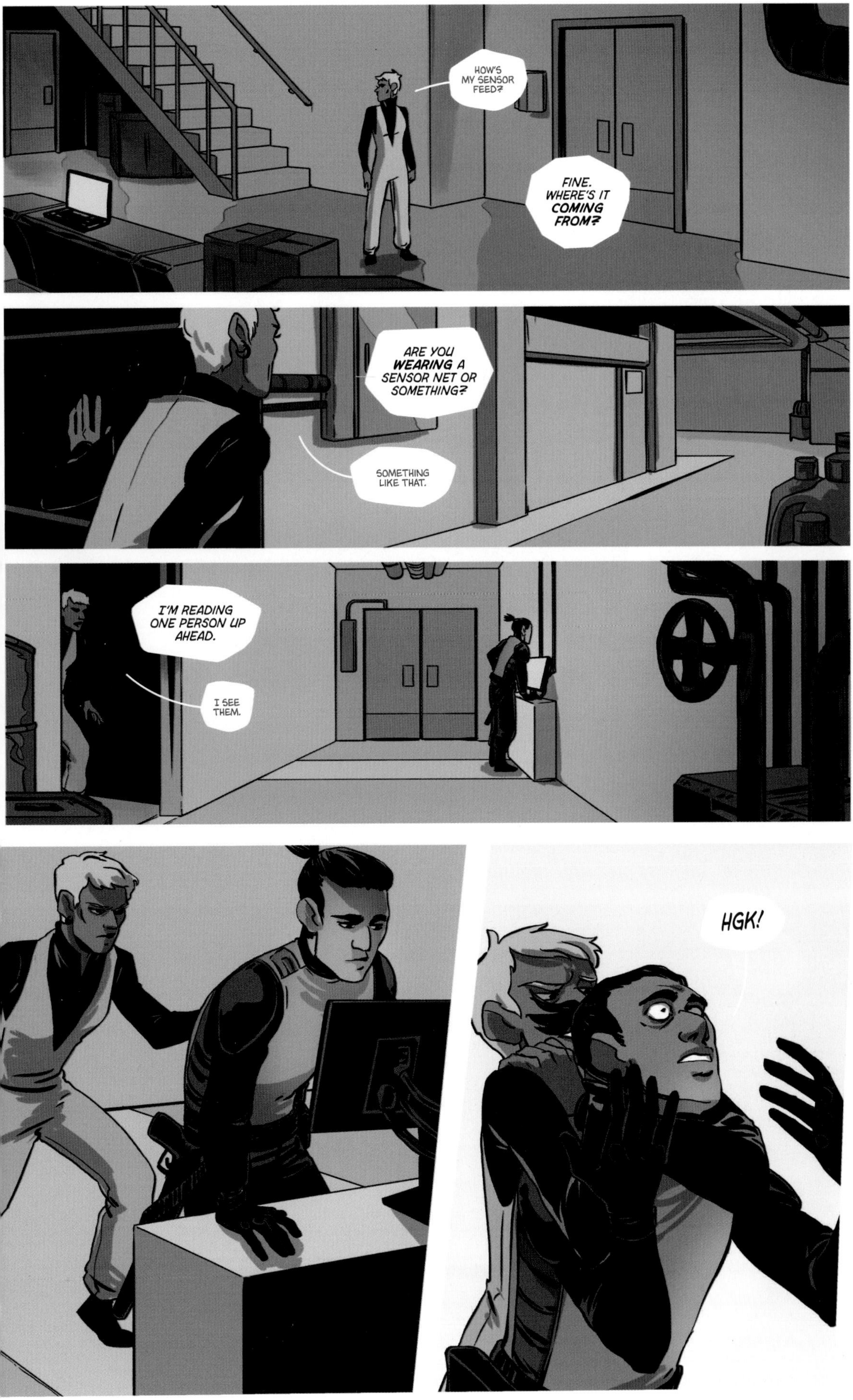
HOW'S MY SENSOR FEED?
FINE. WHERE'S IT COMING FROM?
ARE YOU WEARING A SENSOR NET OR SOMETHING?
SOMETHING LIKE THAT.
I'M READING ONE PERSON UP AHEAD.
I SEE THEM.
HGK!

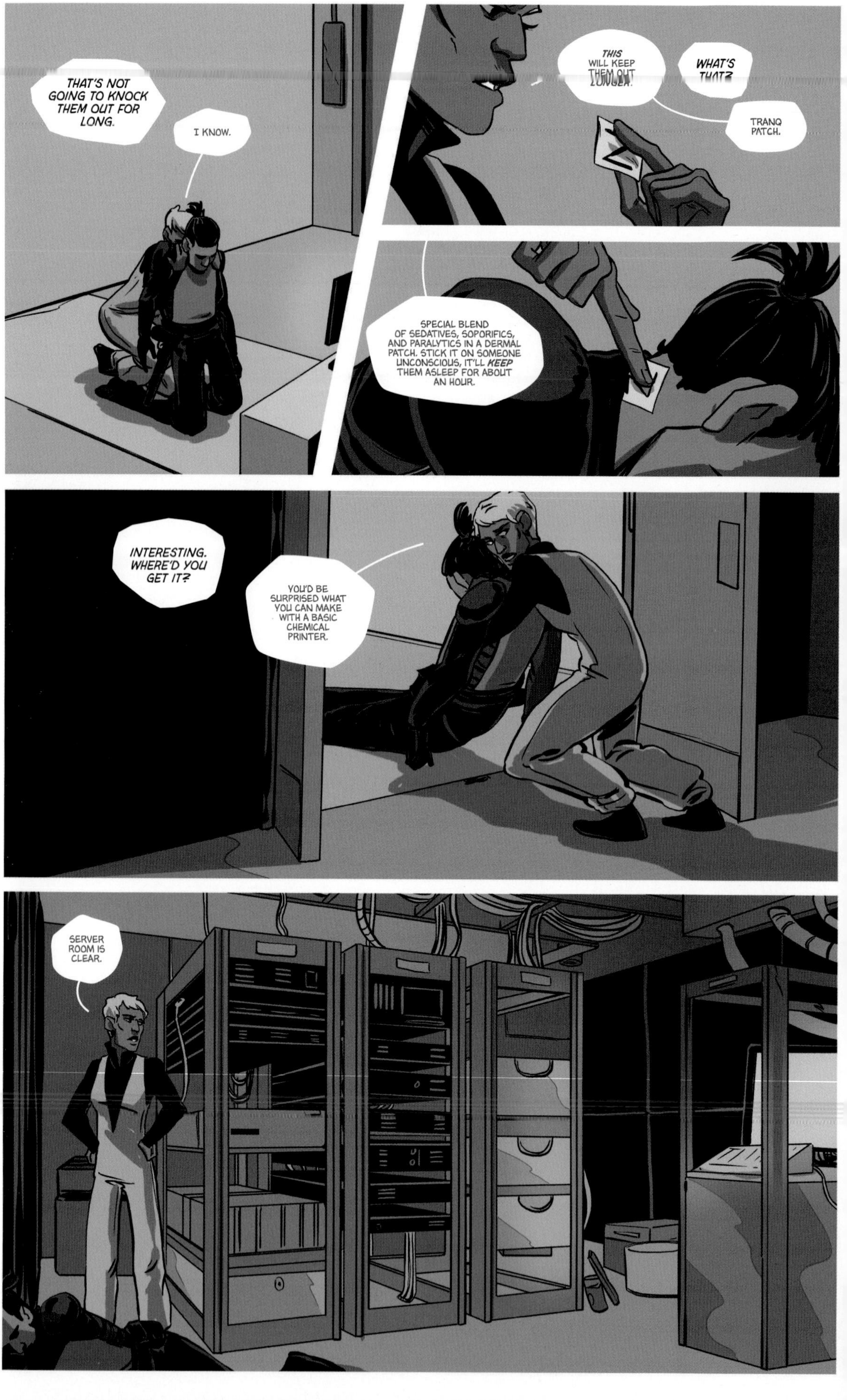
THAT'S NOT GOING TO KNOCK THEM OUT FOR LONG.
I KNOW.
THIS WILL KEEP THEM OUT LONGER.
WHAT'S THAT?
TRANQ PATCH.
SPECIAL BLEND OF SEDATIVES, SOPORIFICS, AND PARALYTICS IN A DERMAL PATCH. STICK IT ON SOMEONE UNCONSCIOUS, IT'LL KEEP THEM ASLEEP FOR ABOUT AN HOUR.
INTERESTING. WHERE'D YOU GET IT?
YOU'D BE SURPRISED WHAT YOU CAN MAKE WITH A BASIC CHEMICAL PRINTER.
SERVER ROOM IS CLEAR.

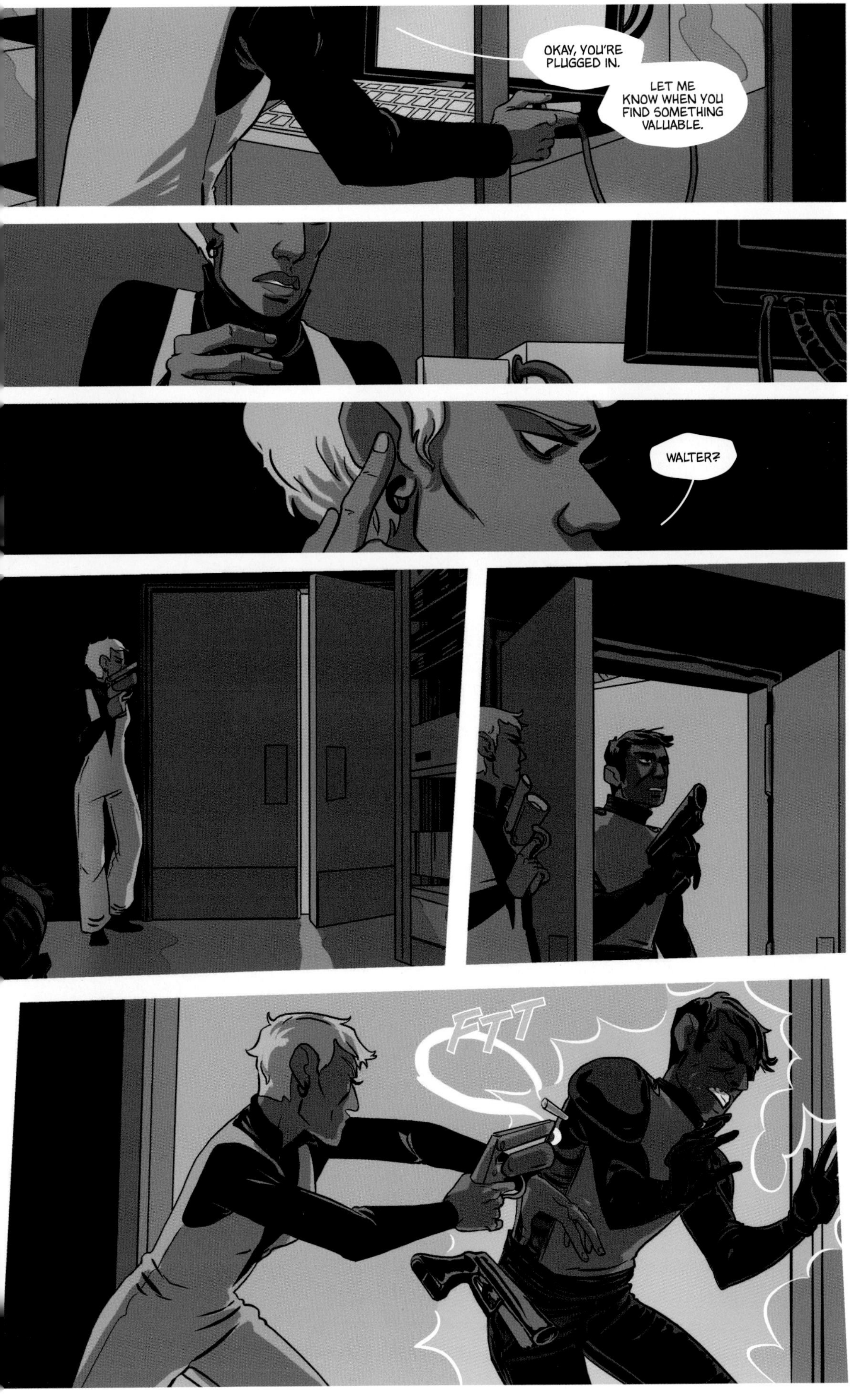

OKAY, YOU'RE PLUGGED IN.
LET ME KNOW WHEN YOU FIND SOMETHING VALUABLE.
WALTER?
FTT

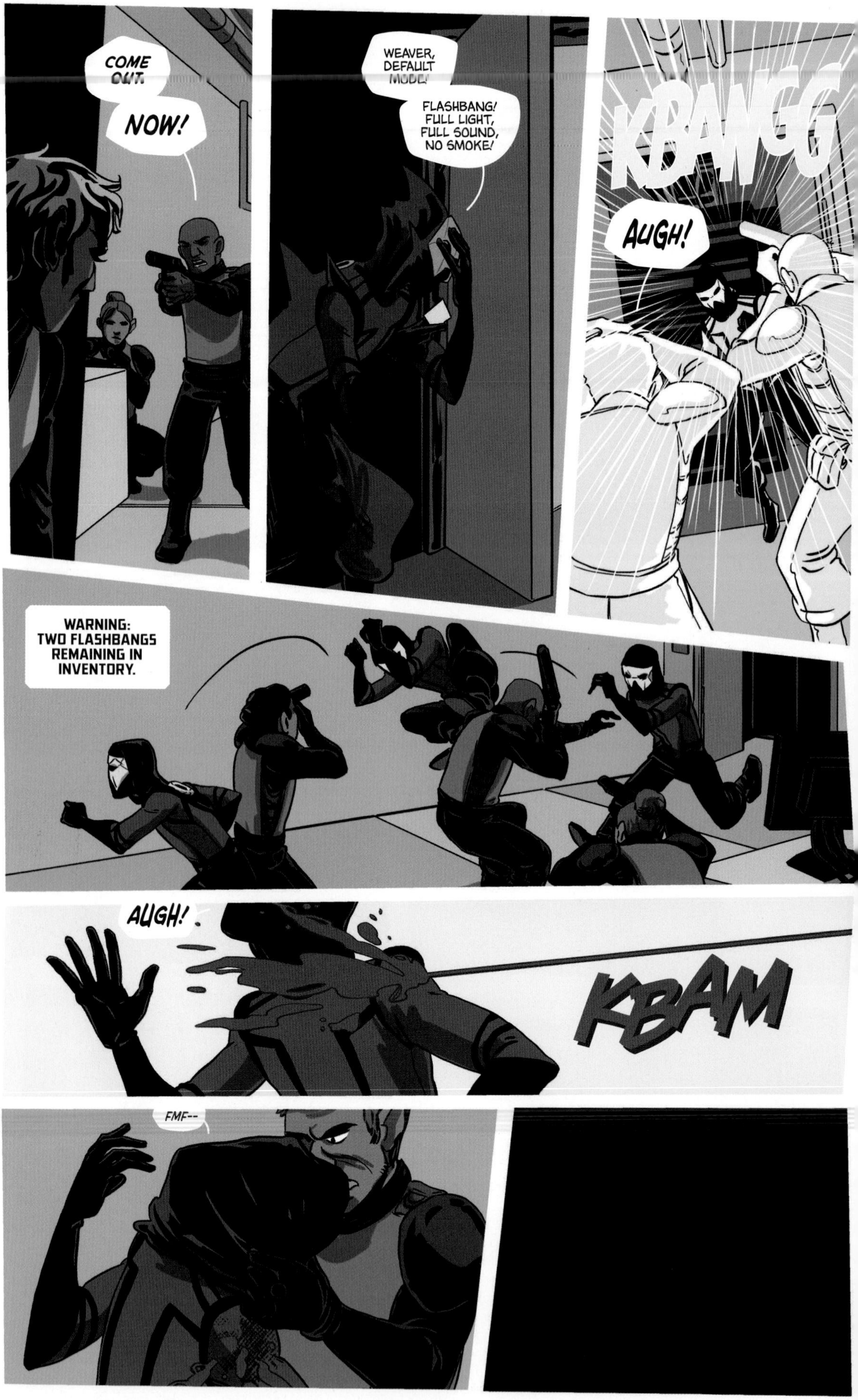
COME OUT.
NOW!
WEAVER, DEFAULT MODE!
FLASHBANG! FULL LIGHT, FULL SOUND, NO SMOKE!
KBANGG
AUGH!
WARNING: TWO FLASHBANGS REMAINING IN INVENTORY.
AUGH!
KBAM
FMF--

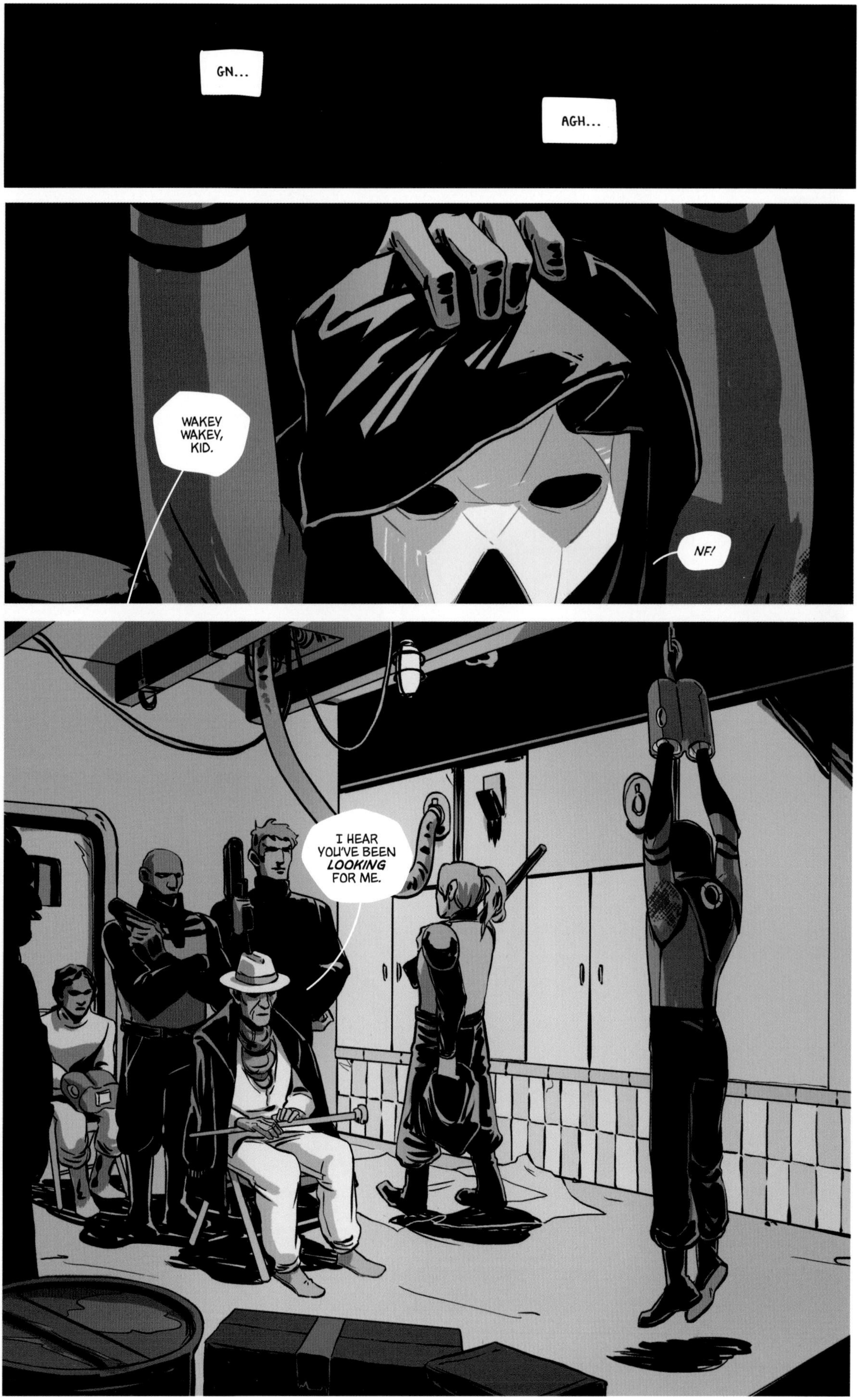
GN...
AGH...
WAKEY WAKEY, KID.
NF!
I HEAR YOU'VE BEEN *LOOKING* FOR ME.

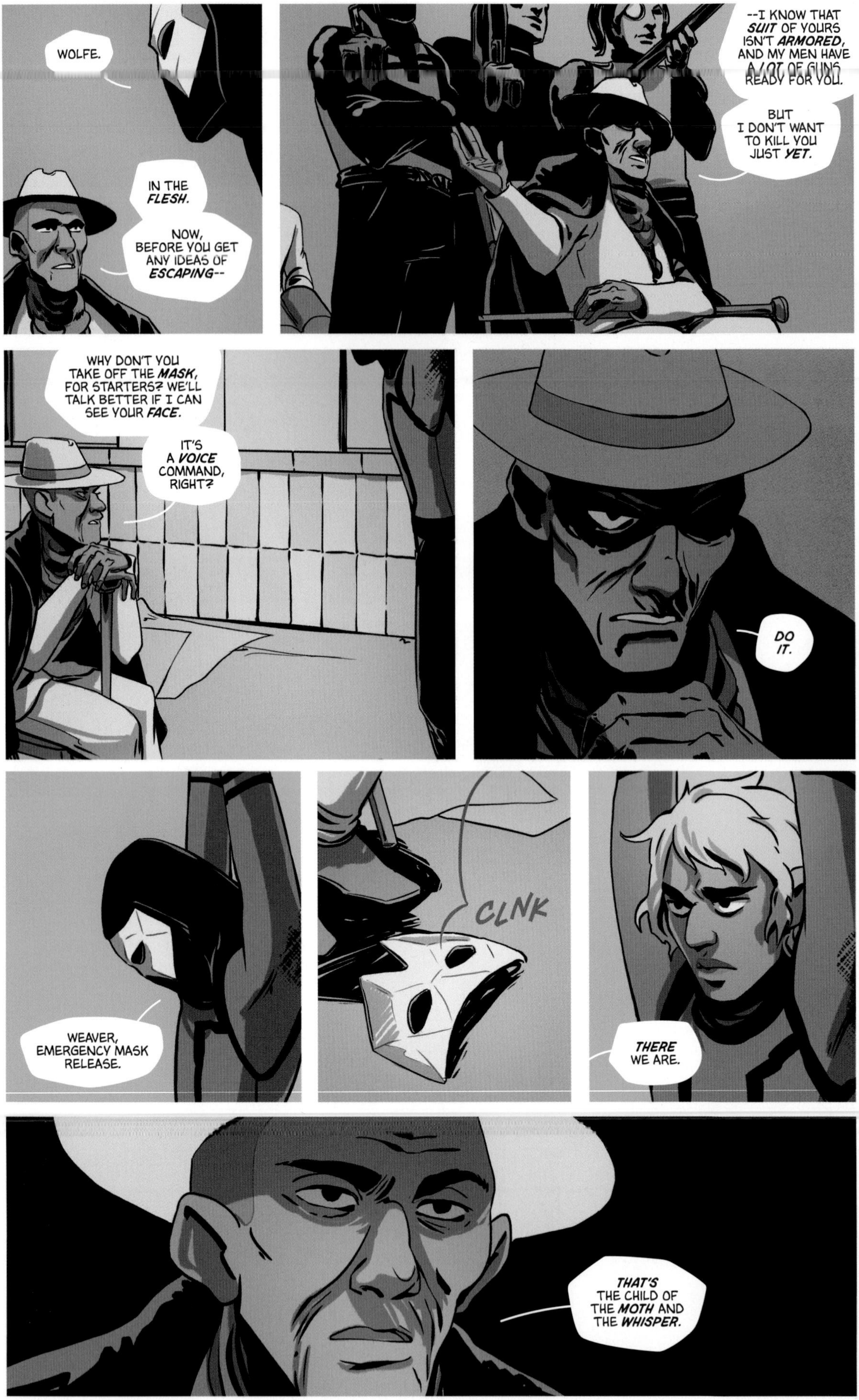
WOLFE.
IN THE FLESH.
NOW, BEFORE YOU GET ANY IDEAS OF ESCAPING--
--I KNOW THAT SUIT OF YOURS ISN'T ARMORED, AND MY MEN HAVE A LOT OF GUNS READY FOR YOU.
BUT I DON'T WANT TO KILL YOU JUST YET.
WHY DON'T YOU TAKE OFF THE MASK, FOR STARTERS? WE'LL TALK BETTER IF I CAN SEE YOUR FACE.
IT'S A VOICE COMMAND, RIGHT?
DO IT.
WEAVER, EMERGENCY MASK RELEASE.
CLNK
THERE WE ARE.
THAT'S THE CHILD OF THE MOTH AND THE WHISPER.

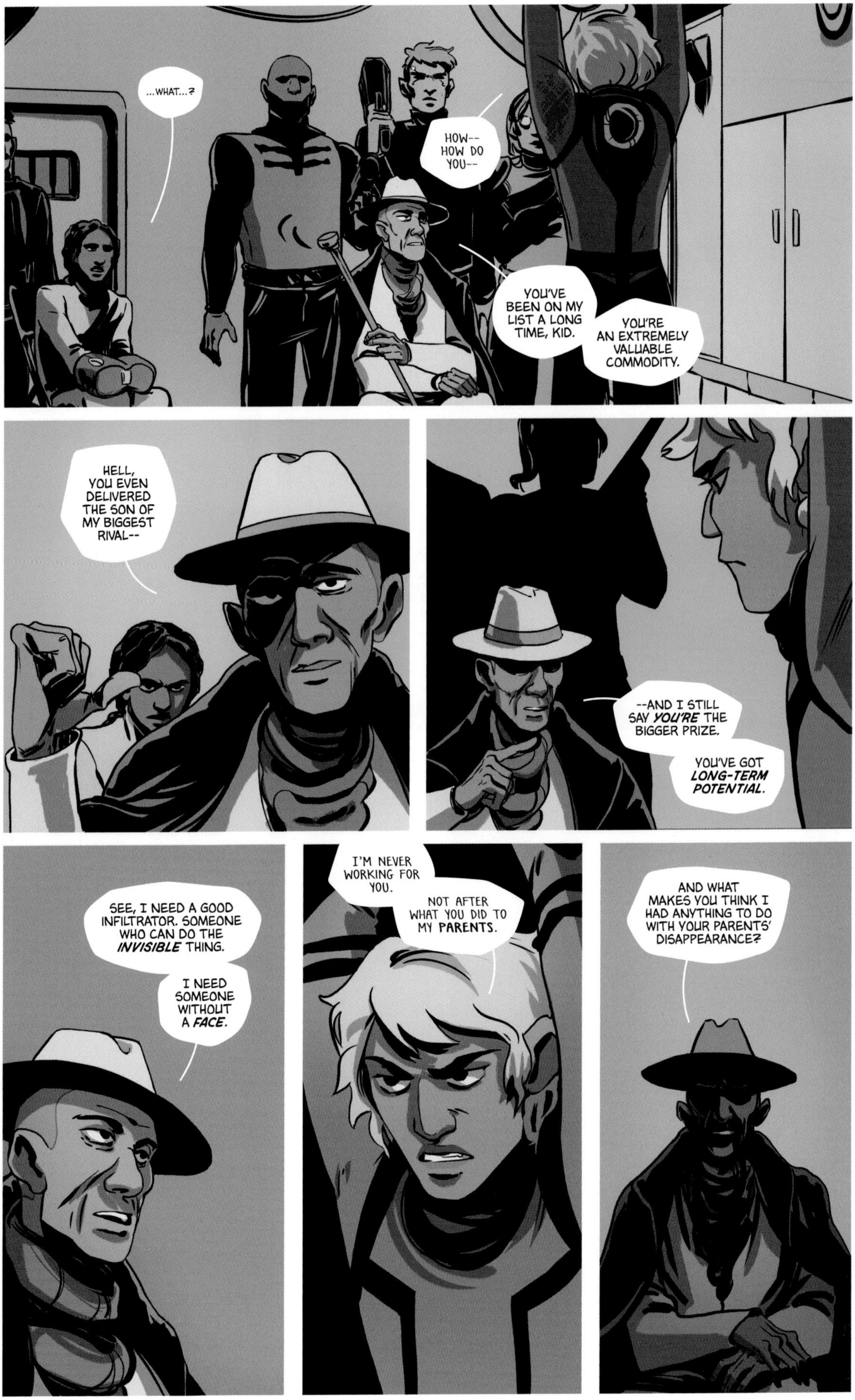
...WHAT...?
HOW-- HOW DO YOU--
YOU'VE BEEN ON MY LIST A LONG TIME, KID.
YOU'RE AN EXTREMELY VALUABLE COMMODITY.
HELL, YOU EVEN DELIVERED THE SON OF MY BIGGEST RIVAL--
--AND I STILL SAY *YOU'RE* THE BIGGER PRIZE.
YOU'VE GOT ***LONG-TERM POTENTIAL.***
SEE, I NEED A GOOD INFILTRATOR. SOMEONE WHO CAN DO THE ***INVISIBLE*** THING.
I NEED SOMEONE WITHOUT A ***FACE.***
I'M NEVER WORKING FOR YOU.
NOT AFTER WHAT YOU DID TO MY **PARENTS.**
AND WHAT MAKES YOU THINK I HAD ANYTHING TO DO WITH YOUR PARENTS' DISAPPEARANCE?

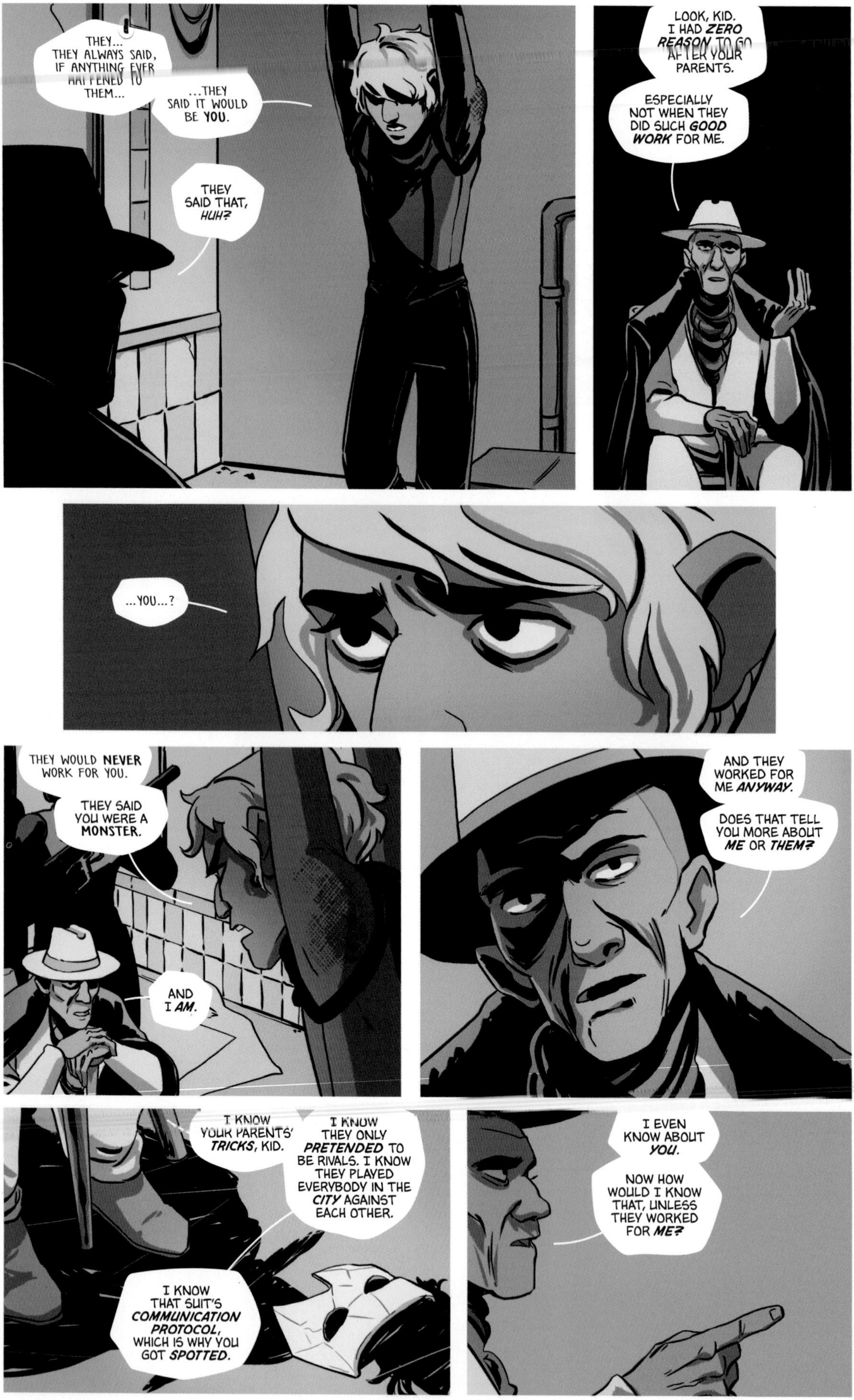
THEY... THEY ALWAYS SAID, IF ANYTHING EVER HAPPENED TO THEM...
...THEY SAID IT WOULD BE YOU.
THEY SAID THAT, HUH?
LOOK, KID. I HAD ZERO REASON TO GO AFTER YOUR PARENTS.
ESPECIALLY NOT WHEN THEY DID SUCH GOOD WORK FOR ME.
...YOU...?
THEY WOULD NEVER WORK FOR YOU.
THEY SAID YOU WERE A MONSTER.
AND I AM.
AND THEY WORKED FOR ME ANYWAY.
DOES THAT TELL YOU MORE ABOUT ME OR THEM?
I KNOW YOUR PARENTS' TRICKS, KID.
I KNOW THEY ONLY PRETENDED TO BE RIVALS. I KNOW THEY PLAYED EVERYBODY IN THE CITY AGAINST EACH OTHER.
I KNOW THAT SUIT'S COMMUNICATION PROTOCOL, WHICH IS WHY YOU GOT SPOTTED.
I EVEN KNOW ABOUT YOU.
NOW HOW WOULD I KNOW THAT, UNLESS THEY WORKED FOR ME?

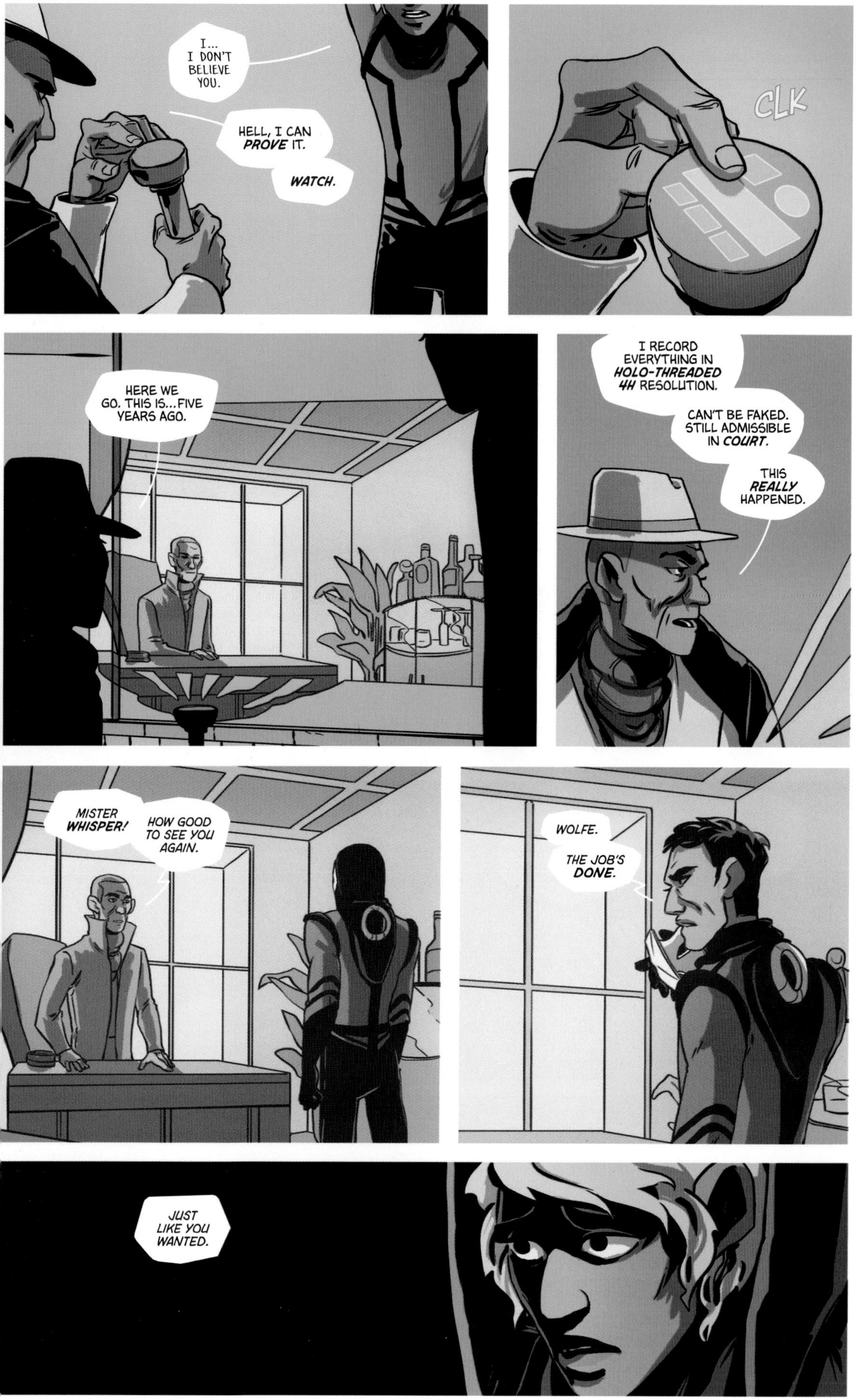
I... I DON'T BELIEVE YOU.
HELL, I CAN *PROVE* IT.
WATCH.
CLK
HERE WE GO. THIS IS...FIVE YEARS AGO.
I RECORD EVERYTHING IN *HOLO-THREADED 4H* RESOLUTION.
CAN'T BE FAKED. STILL ADMISSIBLE IN *COURT.*
THIS *REALLY* HAPPENED.
MISTER *WHISPER!*
HOW GOOD TO SEE YOU AGAIN.
WOLFE.
THE JOB'S *DONE.*
JUST LIKE YOU WANTED.

RELIABLE AS ALWAYS, MISTER WHISPER.

HAVE A DRINK?

NO. IS MY PAYMENT READY?

ALREADY DELIVERED.

YOU SEE?

YOUR DAD, YOUR MOM--THEY *BOTH* PULLED JOBS FOR ME, BACK IN THE DAY.

THEY TOOK MY MONEY AND DID MY DIRTY WORK.

OF COURSE, THEY *HATED* ME.

I'M NOT SURPRISED THEY TOLD YOU I WAS A *THREAT*.

BUT LIKE YOUR DADDY SAID:

IF YOU WANT TO *KNOW* A PERSON, TALK TO THEIR *ENEMIES*.

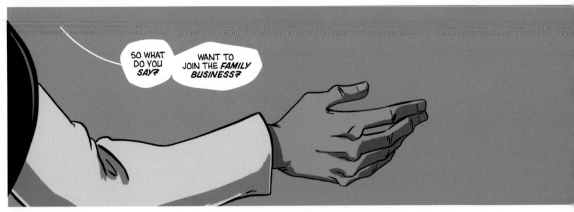

SO WHAT DO YOU *SAY*?

WANT TO JOIN THE *FAMILY BUSINESS*?

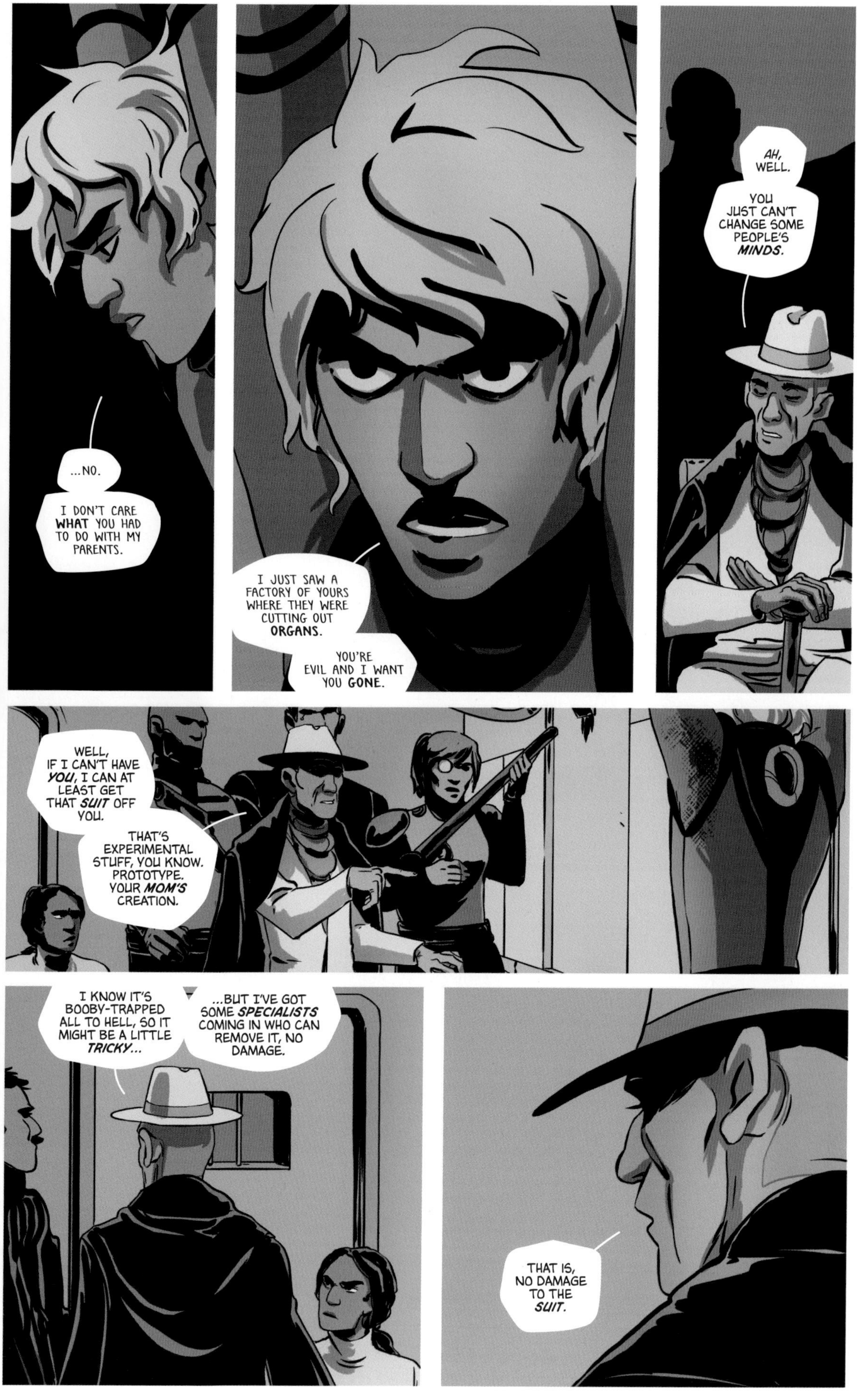
...NO.
I DON'T CARE WHAT YOU HAD TO DO WITH MY PARENTS.
I JUST SAW A FACTORY OF YOURS WHERE THEY WERE CUTTING OUT ORGANS.
YOU'RE EVIL AND I WANT YOU GONE.
AH, WELL.
YOU JUST CAN'T CHANGE SOME PEOPLE'S MINDS.
WELL, IF I CAN'T HAVE YOU, I CAN AT LEAST GET THAT SUIT OFF YOU.
THAT'S EXPERIMENTAL STUFF, YOU KNOW. PROTOTYPE. YOUR MOM'S CREATION.
I KNOW IT'S BOOBY-TRAPPED ALL TO HELL, SO IT MIGHT BE A LITTLE TRICKY...
...BUT I'VE GOT SOME SPECIALISTS COMING IN WHO CAN REMOVE IT, NO DAMAGE.
THAT IS, NO DAMAGE TO THE SUIT.

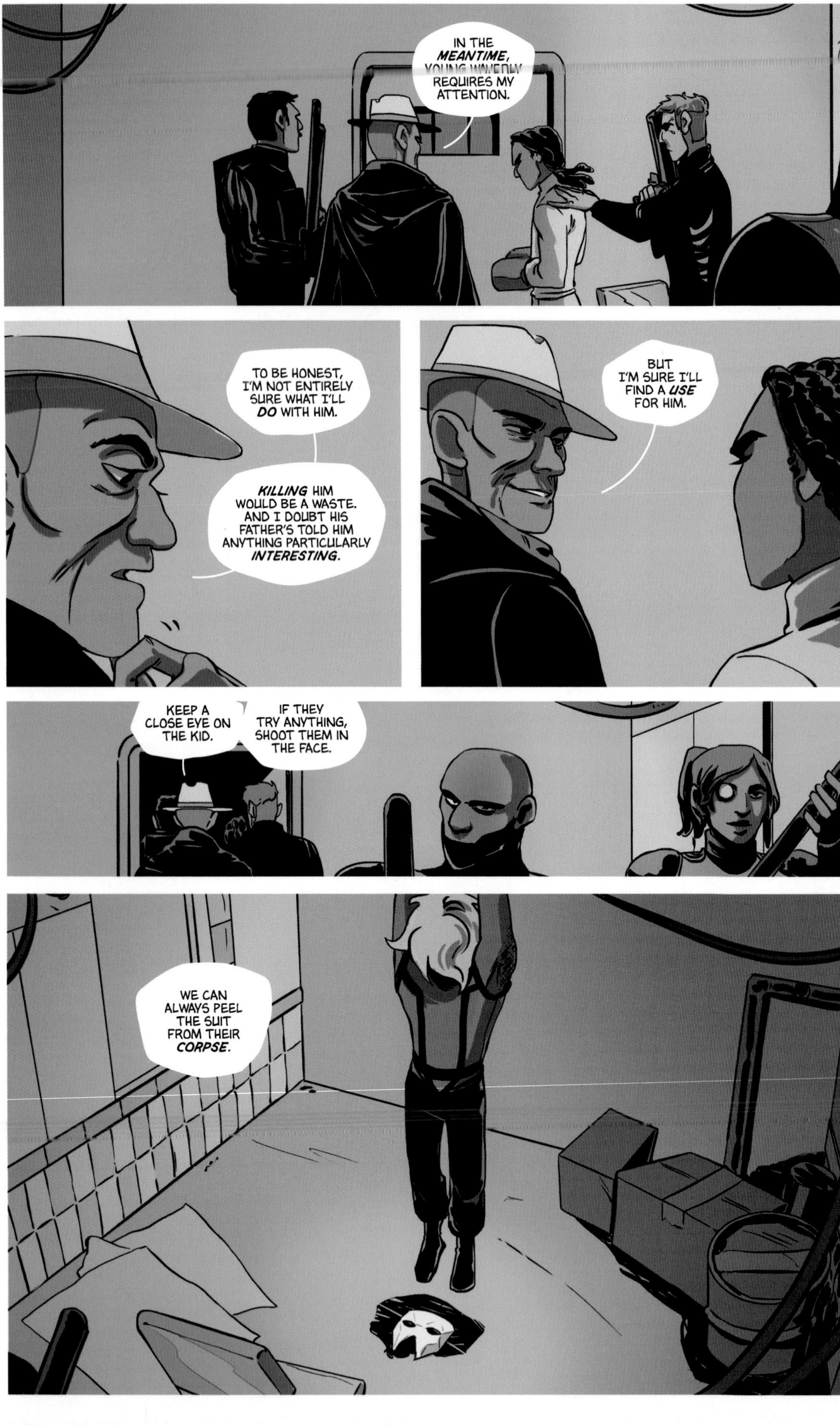
IN THE *MEANTIME*, YOUNG WAVERLY REQUIRES MY ATTENTION.
TO BE HONEST, I'M NOT ENTIRELY SURE WHAT I'LL *DO* WITH HIM.
KILLING HIM WOULD BE A WASTE. AND I DOUBT HIS FATHER'S TOLD HIM ANYTHING PARTICULARLY *INTERESTING*.
BUT I'M SURE I'LL FIND A *USE* FOR HIM.
KEEP A CLOSE EYE ON THE KID.
IF THEY TRY ANYTHING, SHOOT THEM IN THE FACE.
WE CAN ALWAYS PEEL THE SUIT FROM THEIR *CORPSE*.

Municipal Data Network
Data usage will be
monitored

CRIME PROBABILITY LEV
IN THIS AREA: MODERAT
AKE NECESSARY PRECAUT

YOUR FACE
WILL BE SEEN

FACIAL RECOGNITI
WARE IN US

DO NOT

RECOGN
WARE I

NO
DO

YOUR FACE
WILL BE SEE

ELECTRO
FIELDS IN E
300 HZ ARE PRESEN

O RELIGIOUS
YMBO DO NOT
COVER
FACE

NOT SHAR
ITH REFUGEES

YOU
WILL BE S

4

HIDDEN ASSETS

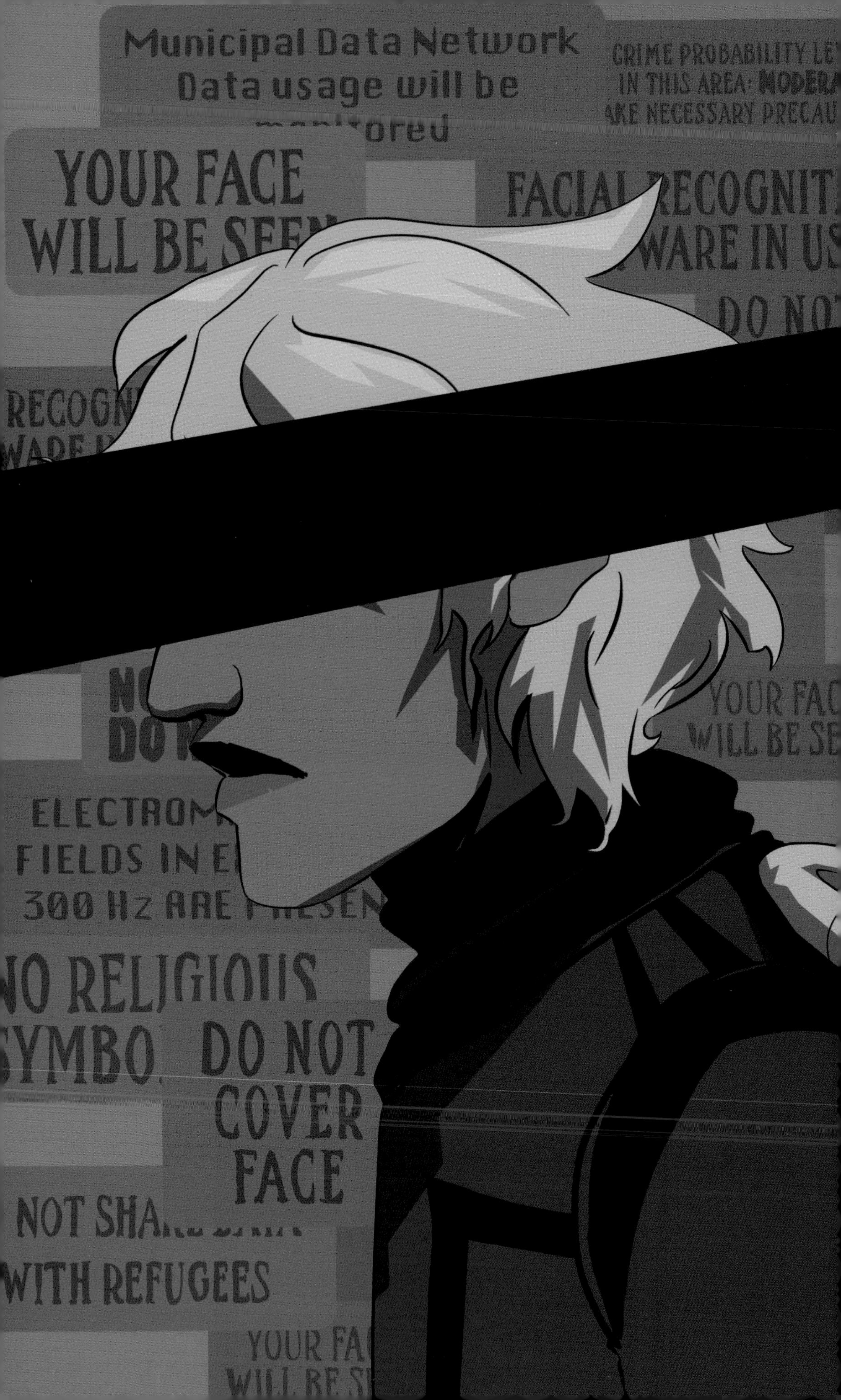
Municipal Data Network
Data usage will be
CRIME PROBABILITY
IN THIS AREA:
NECESSARY
YOUR FACE
WILL BE
FACIAL
WARE IN
ELECTRO
FIELDS IN
300 Hz ARE
RELIGIOUS
DO NOT
COVER
FACE
NOT
WITH REFUGEES
YOUR
WILL BE

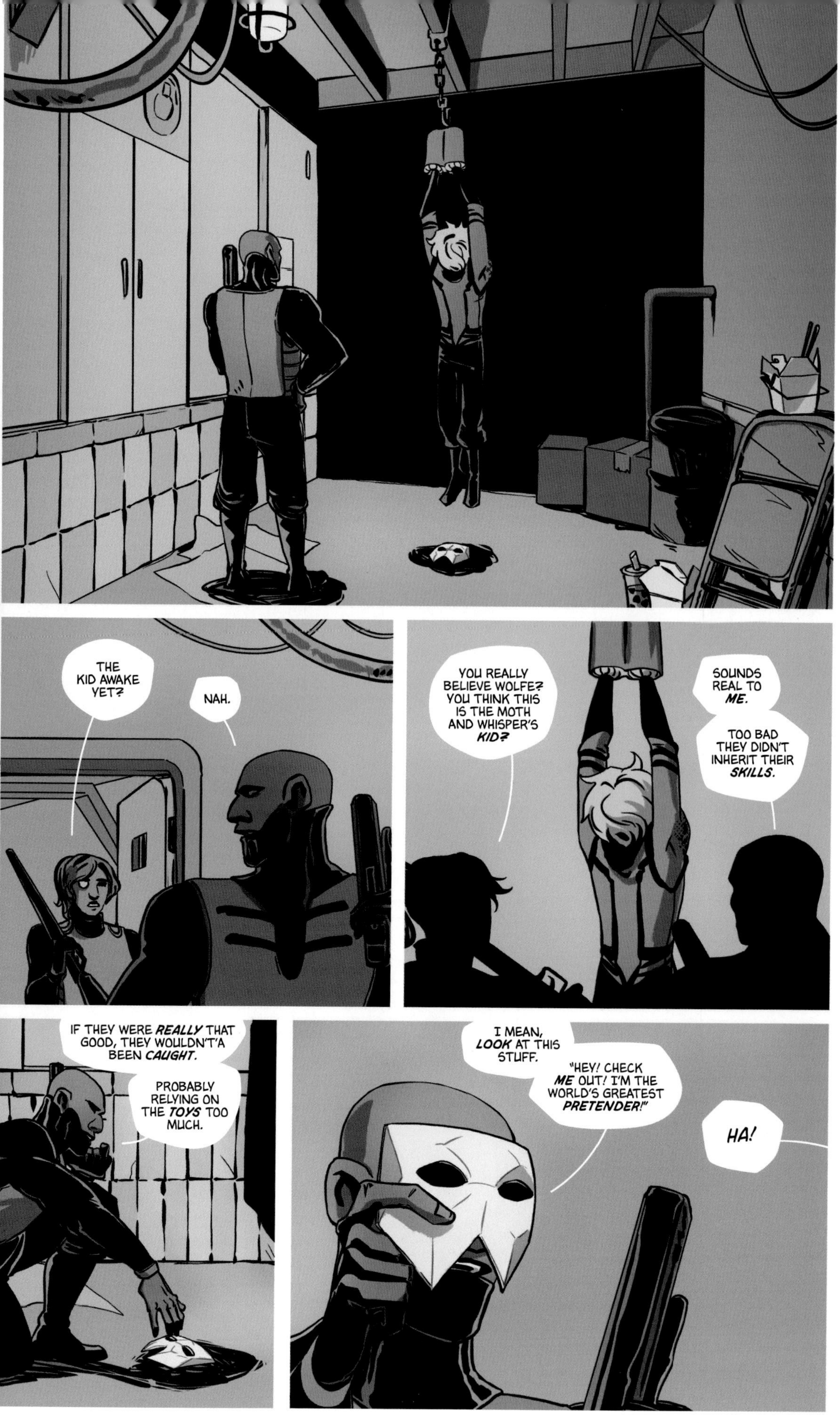
THE KID AWAKE YET?
NAH.
YOU REALLY BELIEVE WOLFE? YOU THINK THIS IS THE MOTH AND WHISPER'S KID?
SOUNDS REAL TO ME.
TOO BAD THEY DIDN'T INHERIT THEIR SKILLS.
IF THEY WERE REALLY THAT GOOD, THEY WOULDN'T'A BEEN CAUGHT.
PROBABLY RELYING ON THE TOYS TOO MUCH.
I MEAN, LOOK AT THIS STUFF.
"HEY! CHECK ME OUT! I'M THE WORLD'S GREATEST PRETENDER!"
HA!

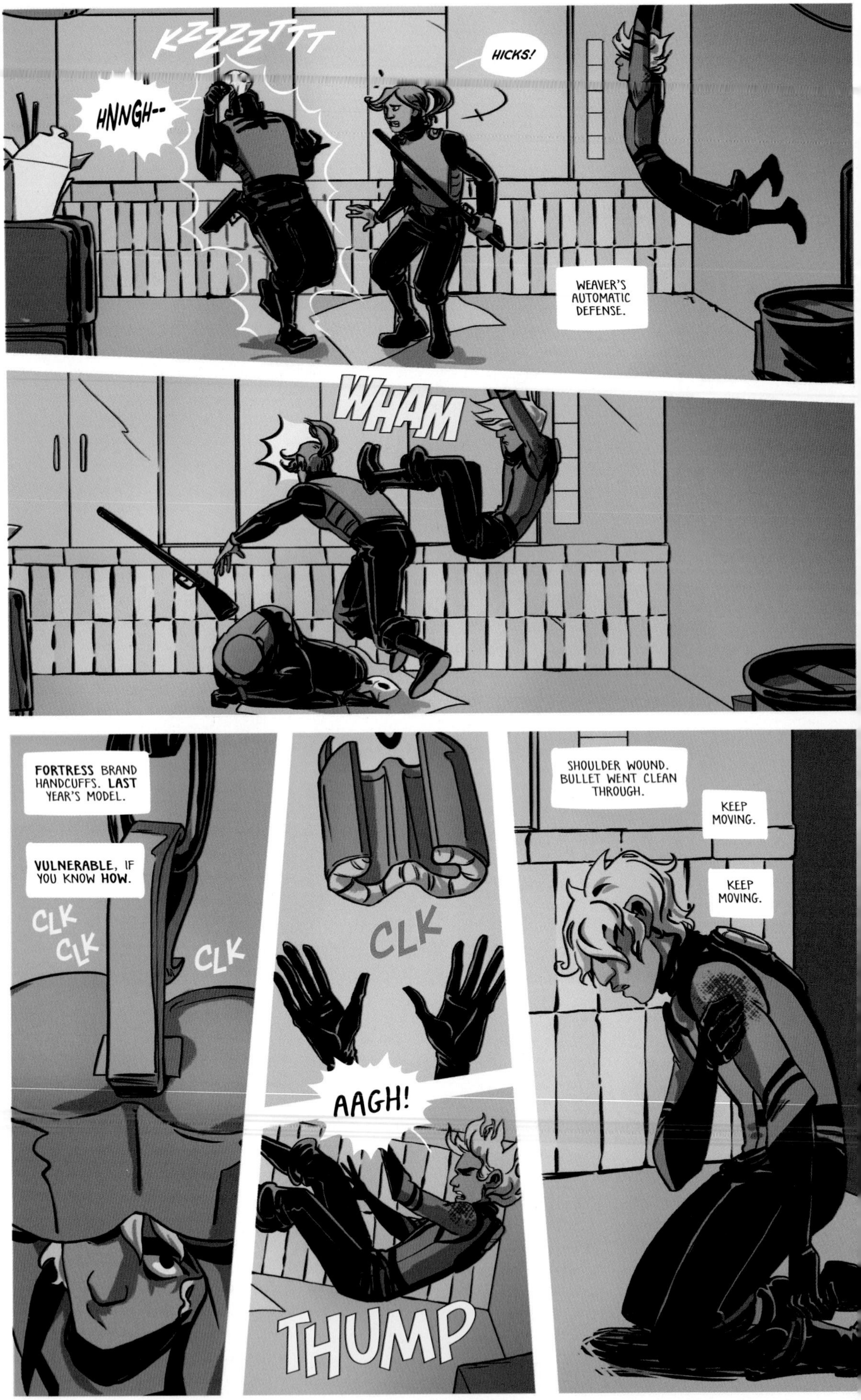
KZZZZZTTTT
HNNGH--
HICKS!
WEAVER'S AUTOMATIC DEFENSE.
WHAM
FORTRESS BRAND HANDCUFFS. LAST YEAR'S MODEL.
VULNERABLE, IF YOU KNOW HOW.
CLK
CLK
CLK
CLK
AAGH!
THUMP
SHOULDER WOUND. BULLET WENT CLEAN THROUGH.
KEEP MOVING.
KEEP MOVING.

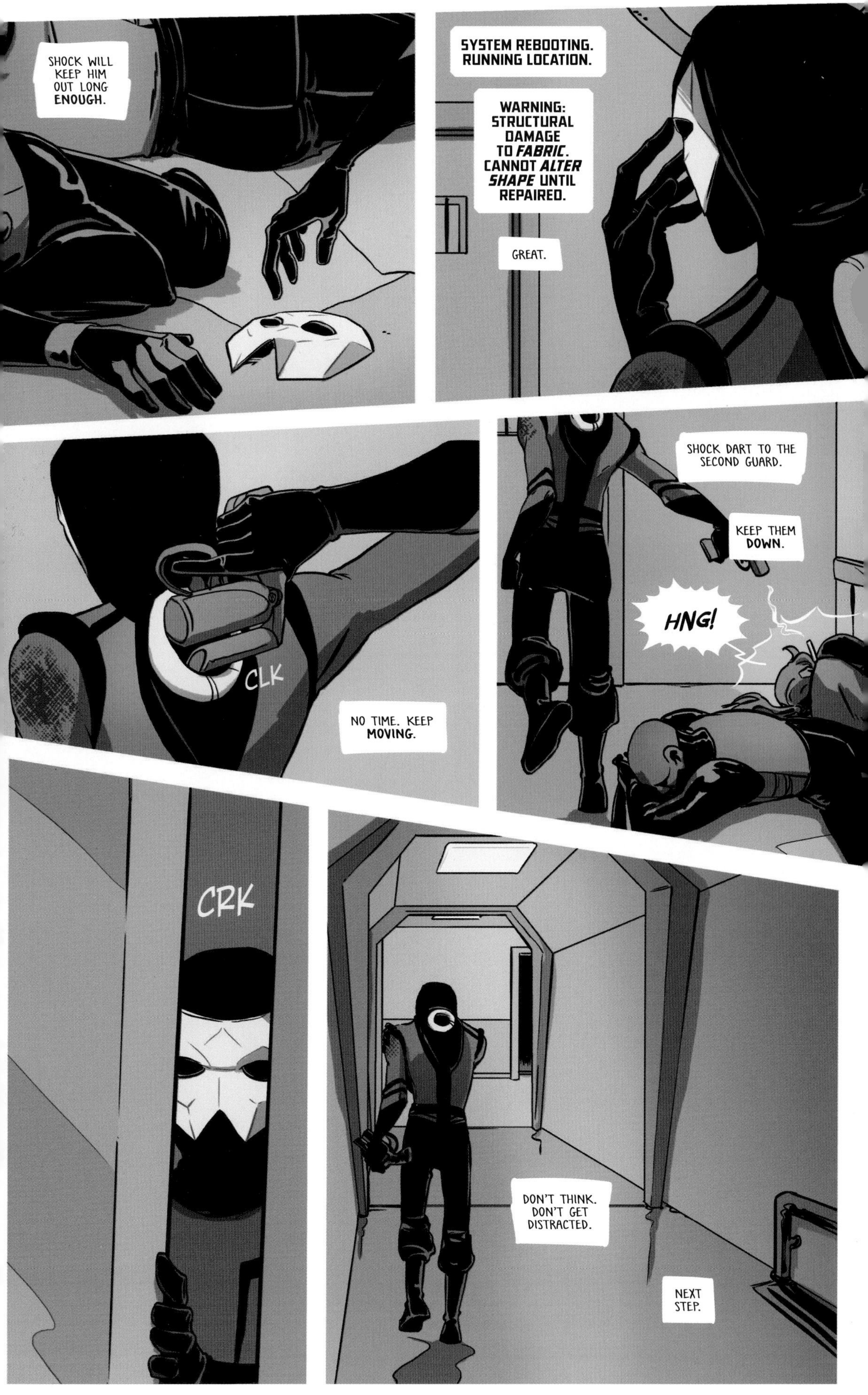
SHOCK WILL KEEP HIM OUT LONG **ENOUGH**.
SYSTEM REBOOTING. RUNNING LOCATION.
WARNING: STRUCTURAL DAMAGE TO *FABRIC*. CANNOT *ALTER SHAPE* UNTIL REPAIRED.
GREAT.
CLK
NO TIME. KEEP **MOVING**.
SHOCK DART TO THE SECOND GUARD.
KEEP THEM **DOWN**.
HNG!
CRK
DON'T THINK. DON'T GET DISTRACTED.
NEXT STEP.

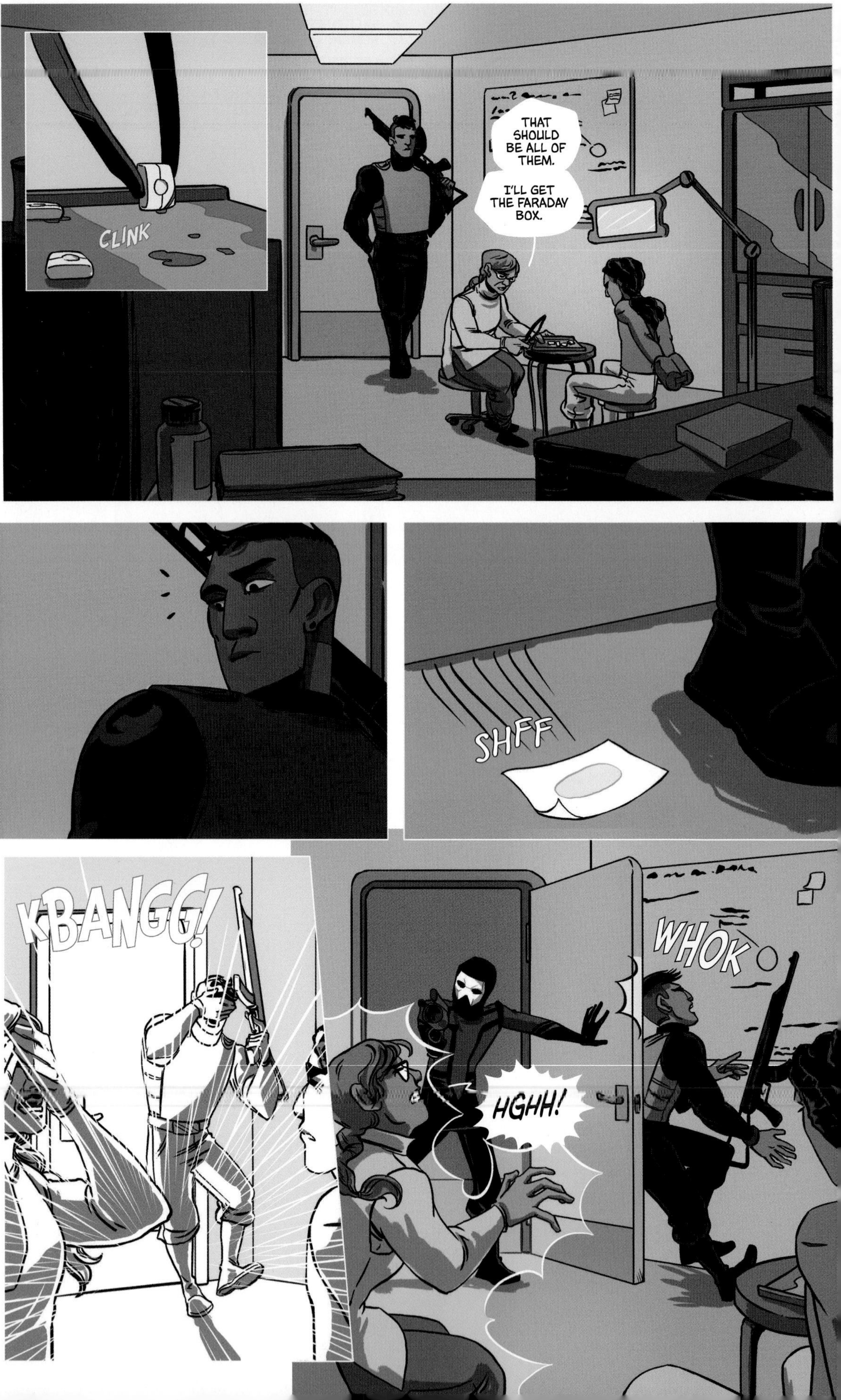
CLINK
THAT SHOULD BE ALL OF THEM.
I'LL GET THE FARADAY BOX.
SHFF
KBANGG!
WHOK
HGHH!

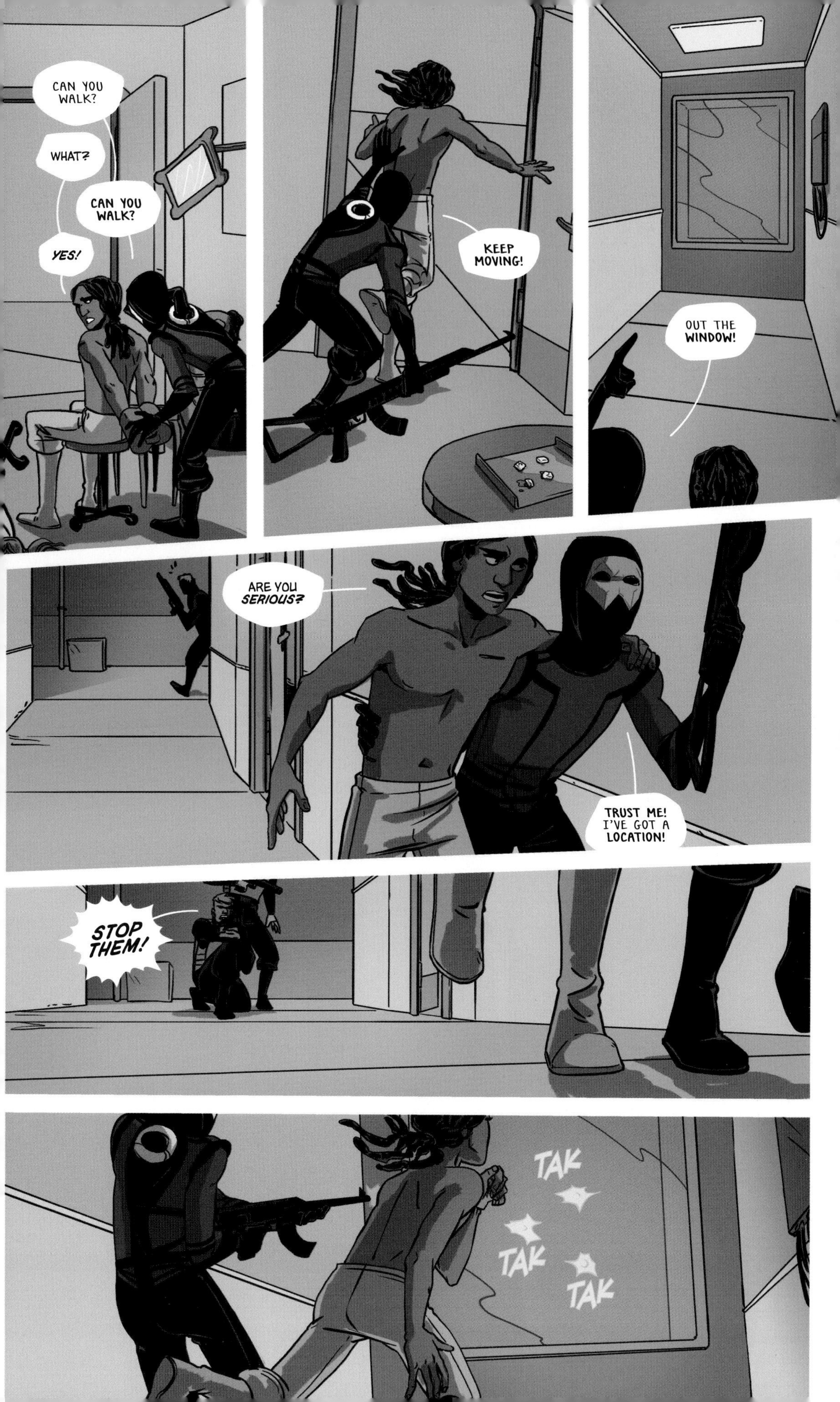
CAN YOU WALK?
WHAT?
CAN YOU WALK?
YES!
KEEP MOVING!
OUT THE WINDOW!
ARE YOU SERIOUS?
TRUST ME! I'VE GOT A LOCATION!
STOP THEM!
TAK
TAK
TAK

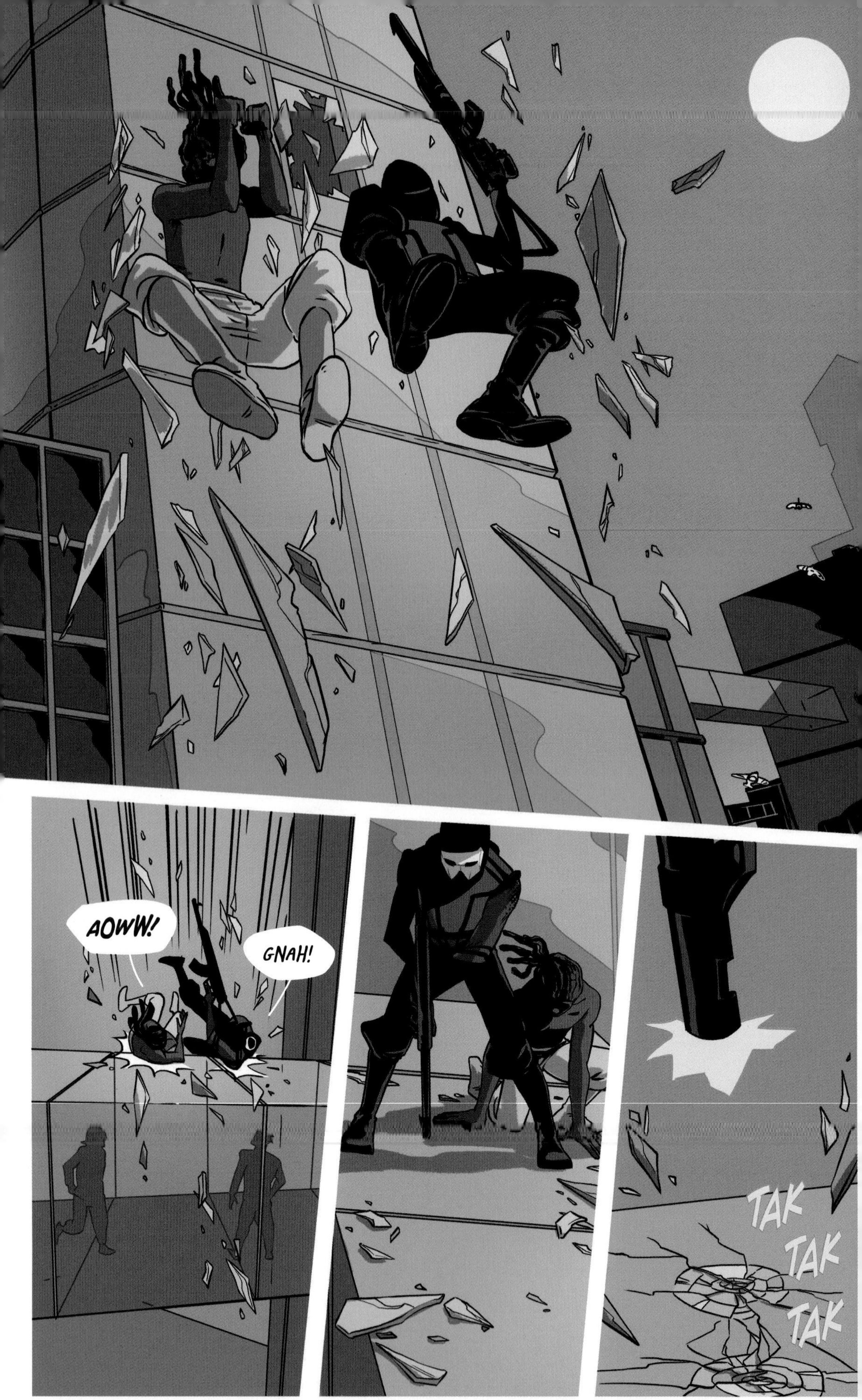
AOWW!
GNAH!
TAK
TAK
TAK

SKASH

NGH!

KEEP MOVING!

WHERE *ARE* WE?

GOVERNMENT DISTRICT! CENTER OF THE CITY!

WE SHOULD GET LOST IN THE *CROWD*.

WOLFE WON'T BE ABLE TO *TRACK* US--

YES, HE CAN.

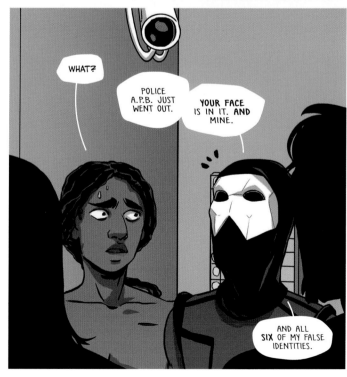

WHAT?

POLICE A.P.B. JUST WENT OUT.

YOUR FACE IS IN IT. **AND** MINE.

AND ALL **SIX** OF MY FALSE IDENTITIES.

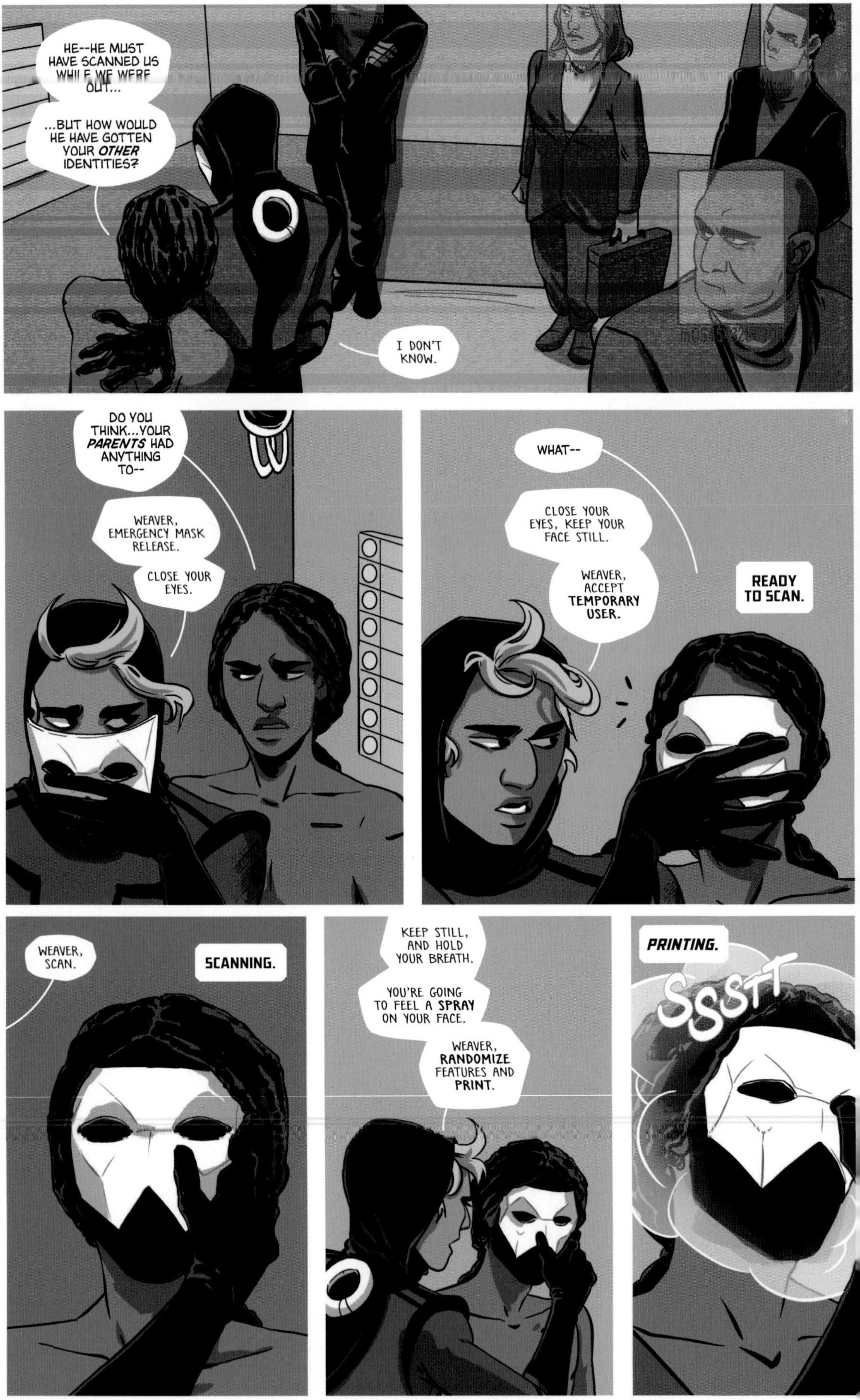
HE--HE MUST HAVE SCANNED US WHILE WE WERE OUT...
...BUT HOW WOULD HE HAVE GOTTEN YOUR OTHER IDENTITIES?
I DON'T KNOW.
DO YOU THINK...YOUR PARENTS HAD ANYTHING TO--
WEAVER, EMERGENCY MASK RELEASE.
CLOSE YOUR EYES.
WHAT--
CLOSE YOUR EYES, KEEP YOUR FACE STILL.
WEAVER, ACCEPT TEMPORARY USER.
READY TO SCAN.
WEAVER, SCAN.
SCANNING.
KEEP STILL, AND HOLD YOUR BREATH.
YOU'RE GOING TO FEEL A SPRAY ON YOUR FACE.
WEAVER, RANDOMIZE FEATURES AND PRINT.
PRINTING.
SSSTT

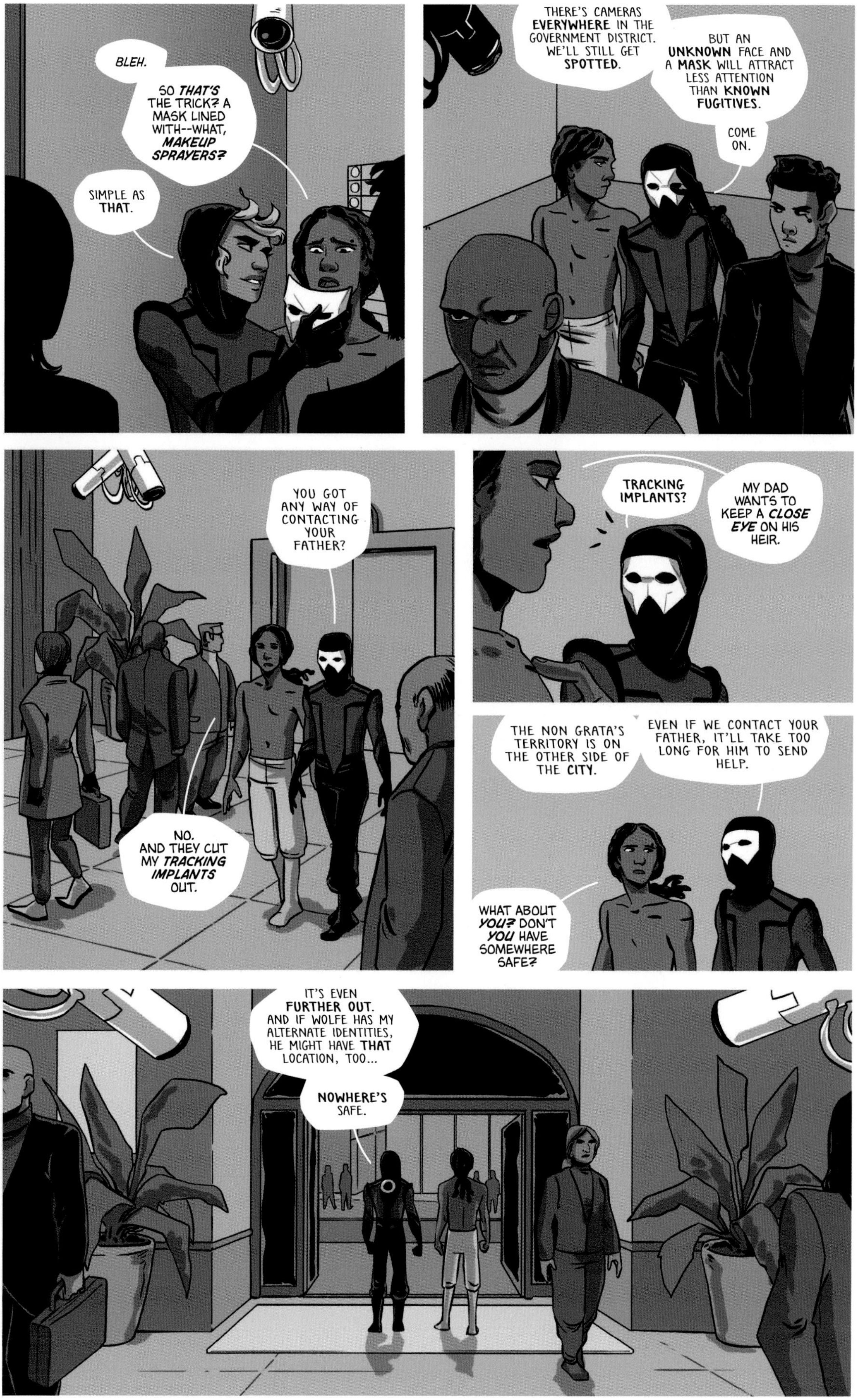
BLEH.
SO *THAT'S* THE TRICK? A MASK LINED WITH--WHAT, ***MAKEUP SPRAYERS?***
SIMPLE AS **THAT.**
THERE'S CAMERAS **EVERYWHERE** IN THE GOVERNMENT DISTRICT. WE'LL STILL GET **SPOTTED.**
BUT AN **UNKNOWN** FACE AND A **MASK** WILL ATTRACT LESS ATTENTION THAN **KNOWN FUGITIVES.**
COME ON.
YOU GOT ANY WAY OF CONTACTING YOUR FATHER?
NO. AND THEY CUT MY ***TRACKING IMPLANTS*** OUT.
TRACKING IMPLANTS?
MY DAD WANTS TO KEEP A ***CLOSE EYE*** ON HIS HEIR.
THE NON GRATA'S TERRITORY IS ON THE OTHER SIDE OF THE **CITY.**
EVEN IF WE CONTACT YOUR FATHER, IT'LL TAKE TOO LONG FOR HIM TO SEND HELP.
WHAT ABOUT ***YOU?*** DON'T ***YOU*** HAVE SOMEWHERE SAFE?
IT'S EVEN **FURTHER OUT.** AND IF WOLFE HAS MY ALTERNATE IDENTITIES, HE MIGHT HAVE **THAT** LOCATION, TOO...
NOWHERE'S SAFE.

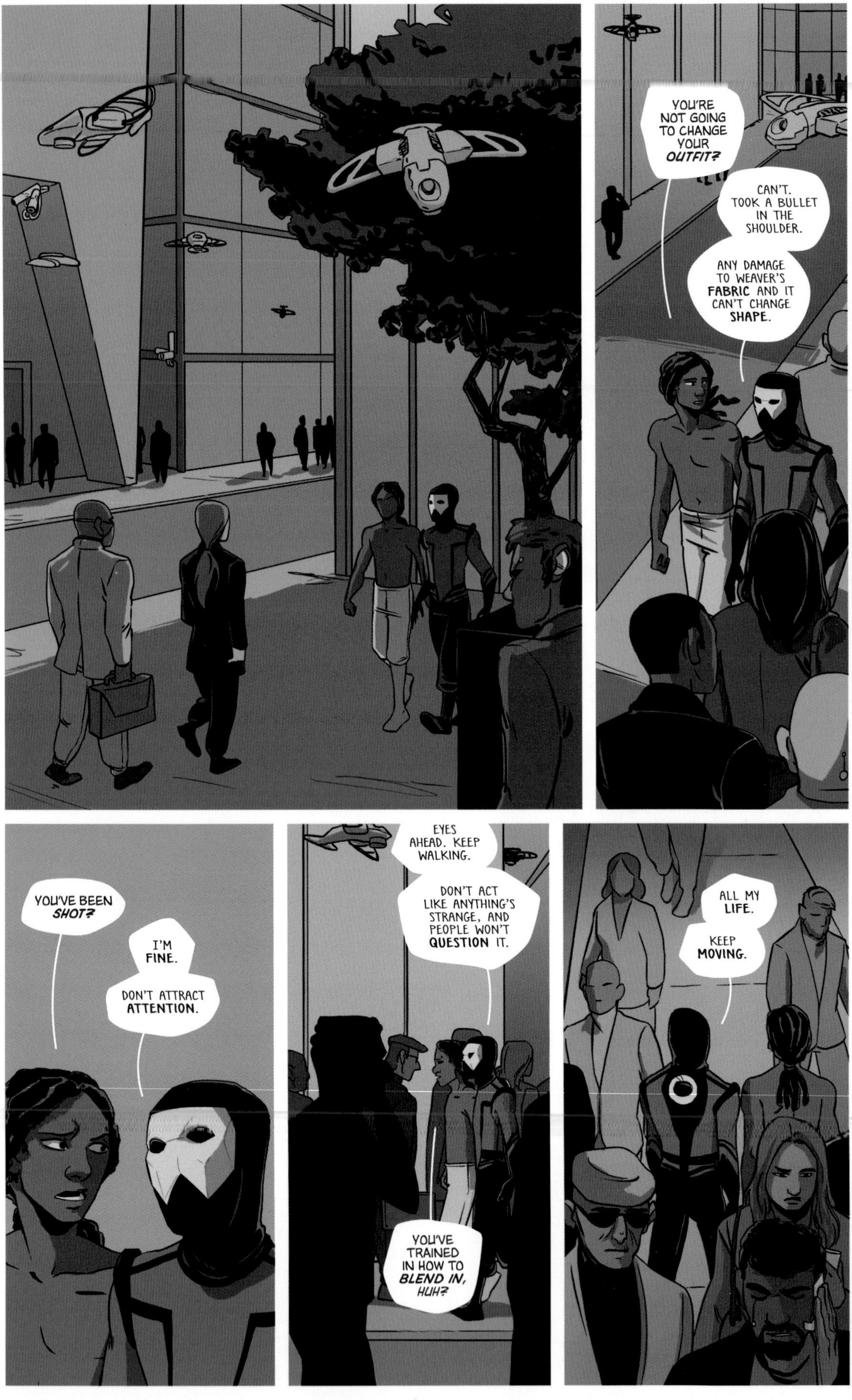
YOU'RE NOT GOING TO CHANGE YOUR *OUTFIT?*
CAN'T. TOOK A BULLET IN THE SHOULDER.
ANY DAMAGE TO WEAVER'S **FABRIC** AND IT CAN'T CHANGE **SHAPE**.
YOU'VE BEEN *SHOT?*
I'M **FINE**.
DON'T ATTRACT **ATTENTION**.
EYES AHEAD. KEEP WALKING.
DON'T ACT LIKE ANYTHING'S STRANGE, AND PEOPLE WON'T **QUESTION** IT.
YOU'VE TRAINED IN HOW TO *BLEND IN*, HUH?
ALL MY **LIFE**.
KEEP **MOVING**.

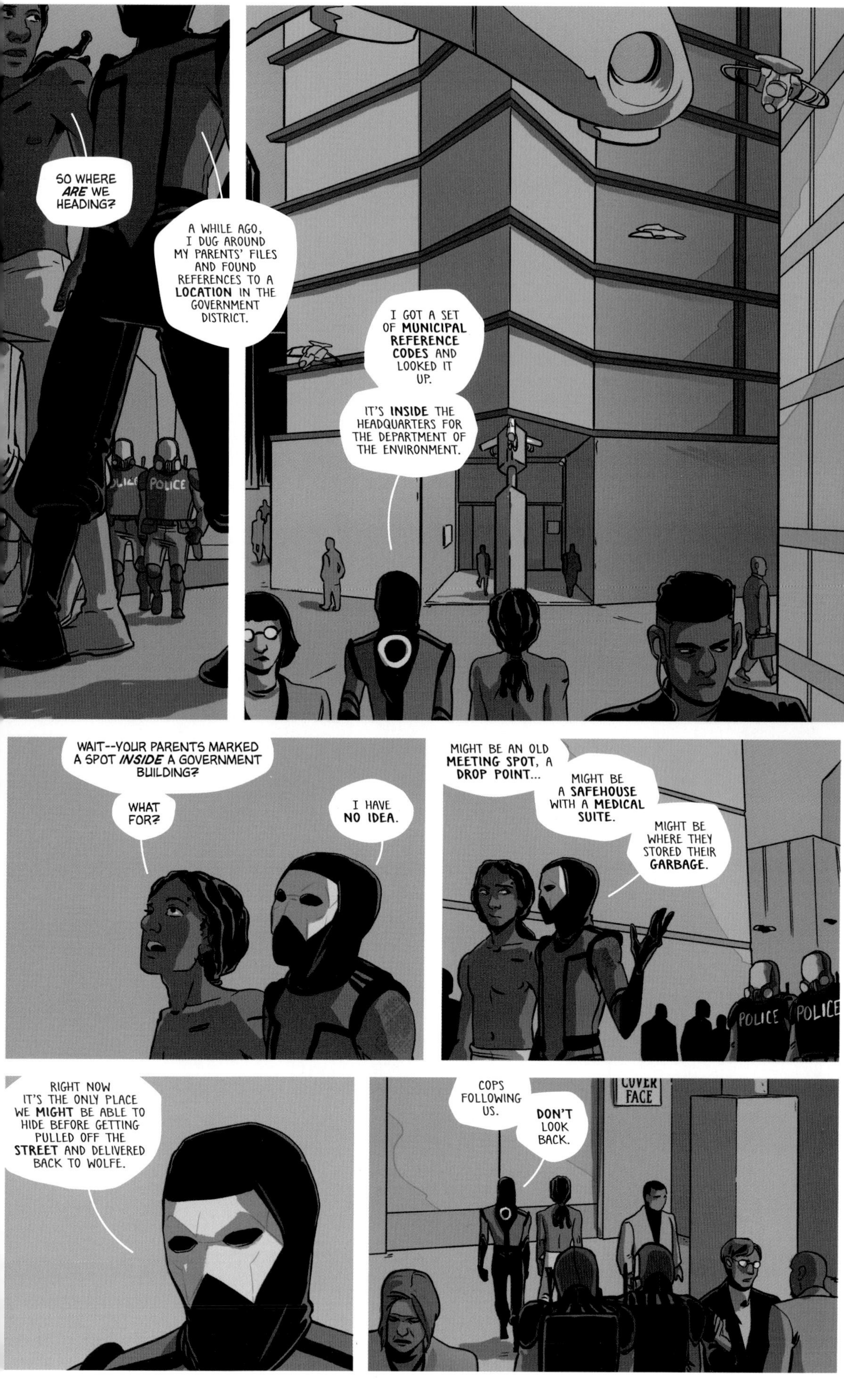

SO WHERE *ARE* WE HEADING?
A WHILE AGO, I DUG AROUND MY PARENTS' FILES AND FOUND REFERENCES TO A **LOCATION** IN THE GOVERNMENT DISTRICT.
POLICE
POLICE
I GOT A SET OF **MUNICIPAL REFERENCE CODES** AND LOOKED IT UP.
IT'S **INSIDE** THE HEADQUARTERS FOR THE DEPARTMENT OF THE ENVIRONMENT.
WAIT--YOUR PARENTS MARKED A SPOT *INSIDE* A GOVERNMENT BUILDING?
WHAT FOR?
I HAVE **NO IDEA**.
MIGHT BE AN OLD **MEETING SPOT**, A **DROP POINT**...
MIGHT BE A **SAFEHOUSE** WITH A **MEDICAL SUITE**.
MIGHT BE WHERE THEY STORED THEIR **GARBAGE**.
POLICE
POLICE
RIGHT NOW IT'S THE ONLY PLACE WE **MIGHT** BE ABLE TO HIDE BEFORE GETTING PULLED OFF THE **STREET** AND DELIVERED BACK TO WOLFE.
COVER FACE
COPS FOLLOWING US.
DON'T LOOK BACK.

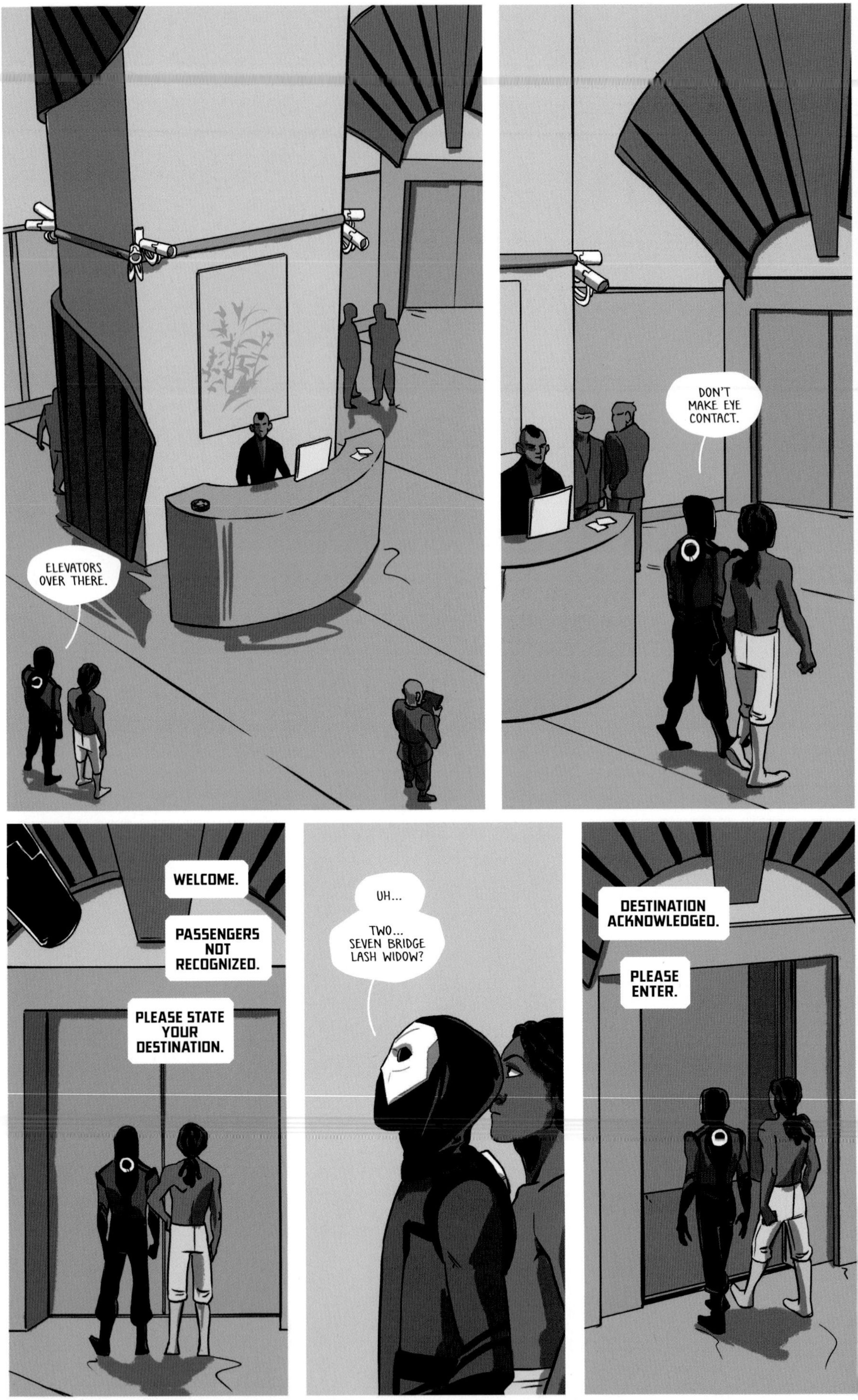
ELEVATORS OVER THERE.
DON'T MAKE EYE CONTACT.
WELCOME.
PASSENGERS NOT RECOGNIZED.
PLEASE STATE YOUR DESTINATION.
UH...
TWO... SEVEN BRIDGE LASH WIDOW?
DESTINATION ACKNOWLEDGED.
PLEASE ENTER.

SO YOUR PARENTS DIDN'T *TELL* YOU ABOUT THIS? YOU HAD TO DIG IT *UP?*

...YEAH.

THEY TAUGHT ME JUST ABOUT *EVERYTHING,* BUT...

...THEY KEPT SOME STUFF TO THEMSELVES.

A *LOT* OF STUFF, APPARENTLY.

DESTINATION REACHED. HAVE A PLEASANT DAY.

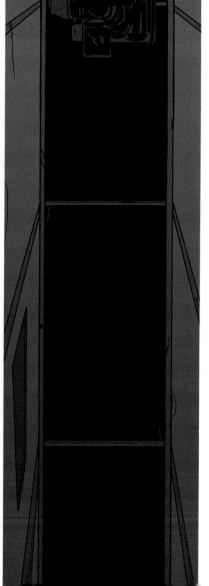

DON'T MOVE.

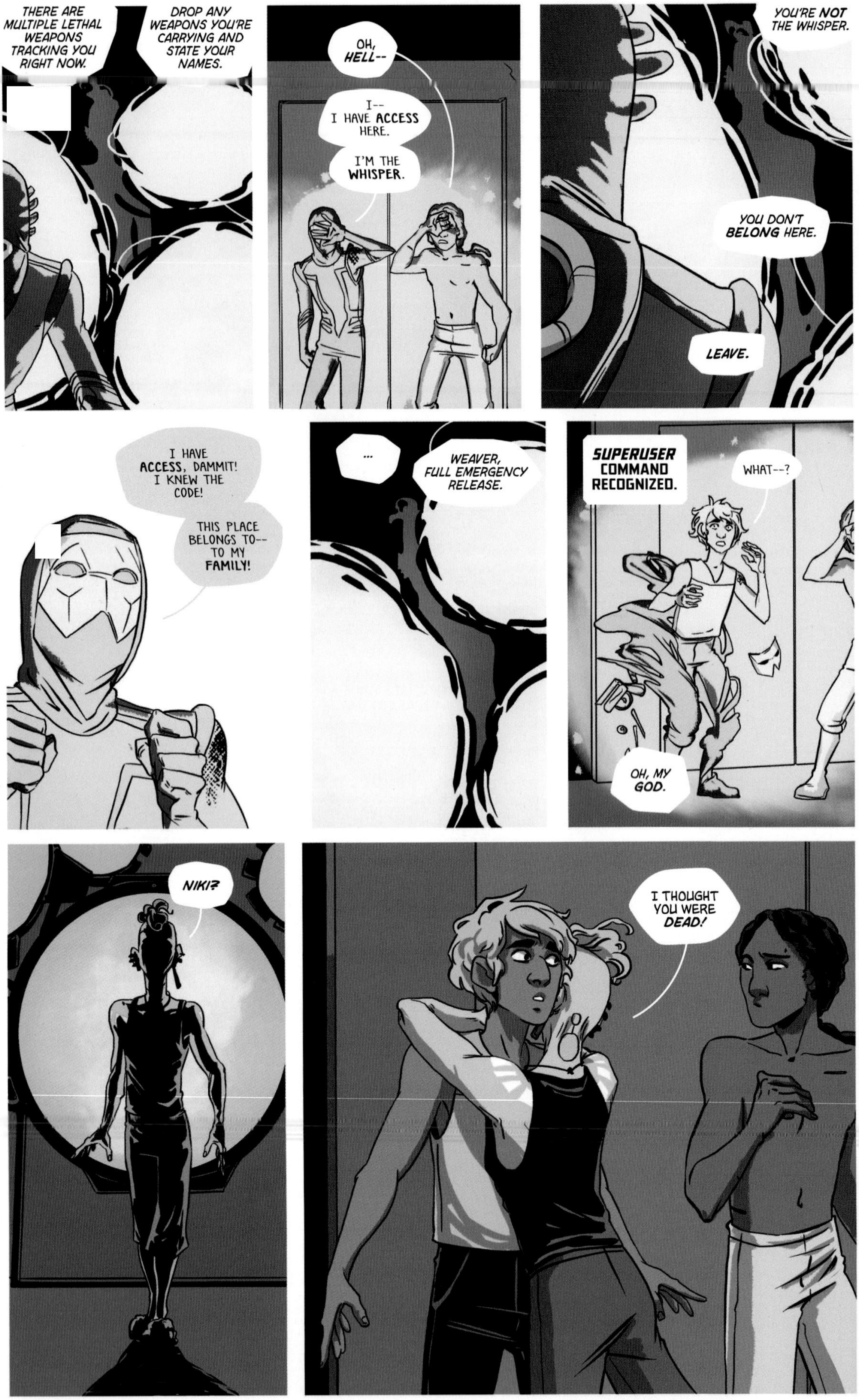
THERE ARE MULTIPLE LETHAL WEAPONS TRACKING YOU RIGHT NOW.
DROP ANY WEAPONS YOU'RE CARRYING AND STATE YOUR NAMES.
OH, HELL--
I-- I HAVE ACCESS HERE.
I'M THE WHISPER.
YOU'RE NOT THE WHISPER.
YOU DON'T BELONG HERE.
LEAVE.
I HAVE ACCESS, DAMMIT! I KNEW THE CODE!
THIS PLACE BELONGS TO-- TO MY FAMILY!
...
WEAVER, FULL EMERGENCY RELEASE.
SUPERUSER COMMAND RECOGNIZED.
WHAT--?
OH, MY GOD.
NIKI?
I THOUGHT YOU WERE DEAD!

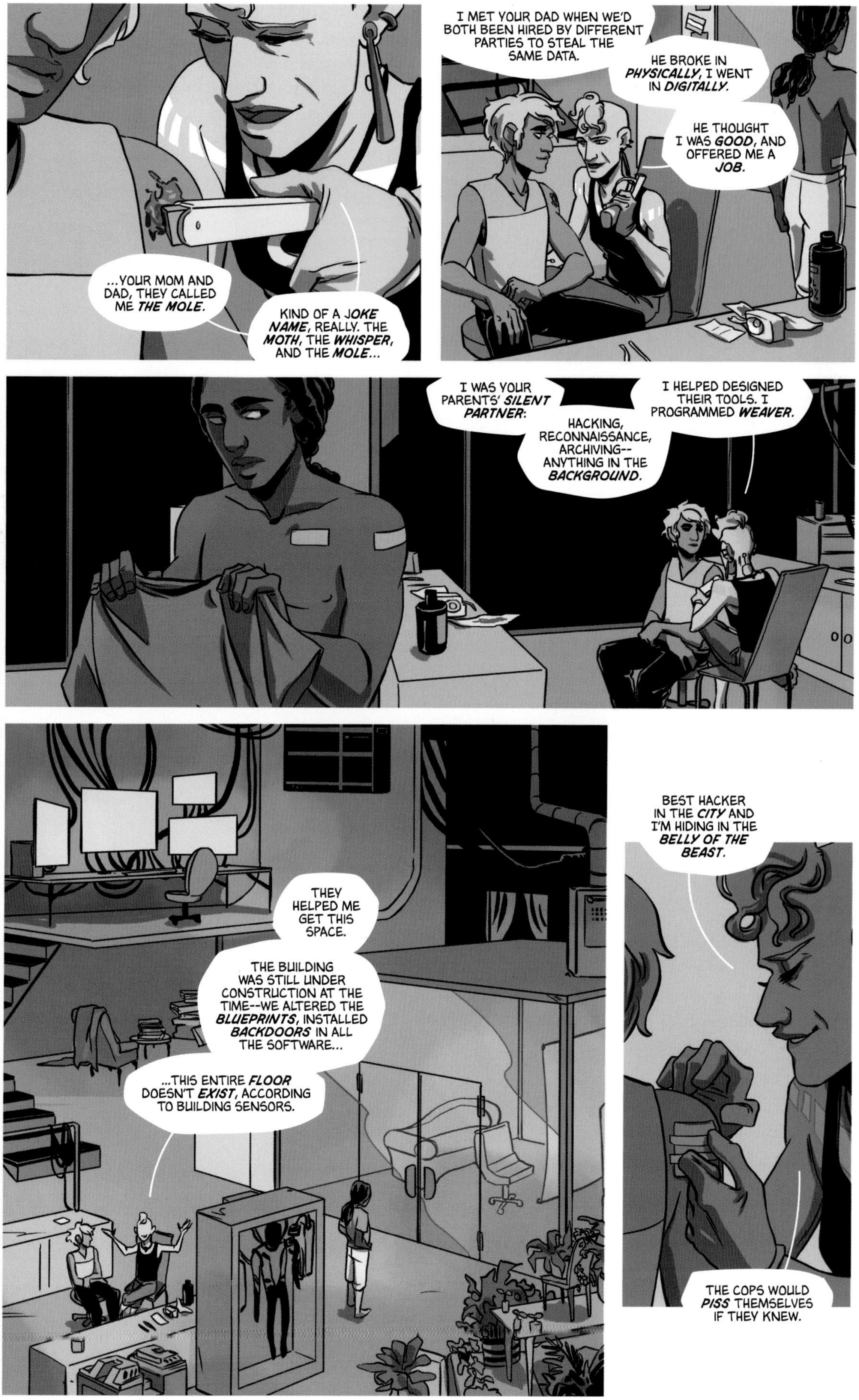
...YOUR MOM AND DAD, THEY CALLED ME THE MOLE.
KIND OF A JOKE NAME, REALLY. THE MOTH, THE WHISPER, AND THE MOLE...
I MET YOUR DAD WHEN WE'D BOTH BEEN HIRED BY DIFFERENT PARTIES TO STEAL THE SAME DATA.
HE BROKE IN PHYSICALLY, I WENT IN DIGITALLY.
HE THOUGHT I WAS GOOD, AND OFFERED ME A JOB.
I WAS YOUR PARENTS' SILENT PARTNER:
HACKING, RECONNAISSANCE, ARCHIVING--ANYTHING IN THE BACKGROUND.
I HELPED DESIGNED THEIR TOOLS. I PROGRAMMED WEAVER.
THEY HELPED ME GET THIS SPACE.
THE BUILDING WAS STILL UNDER CONSTRUCTION AT THE TIME--WE ALTERED THE BLUEPRINTS, INSTALLED BACKDOORS IN ALL THE SOFTWARE...
...THIS ENTIRE FLOOR DOESN'T EXIST, ACCORDING TO BUILDING SENSORS.
BEST HACKER IN THE CITY AND I'M HIDING IN THE BELLY OF THE BEAST.
THE COPS WOULD PISS THEMSELVES IF THEY KNEW.

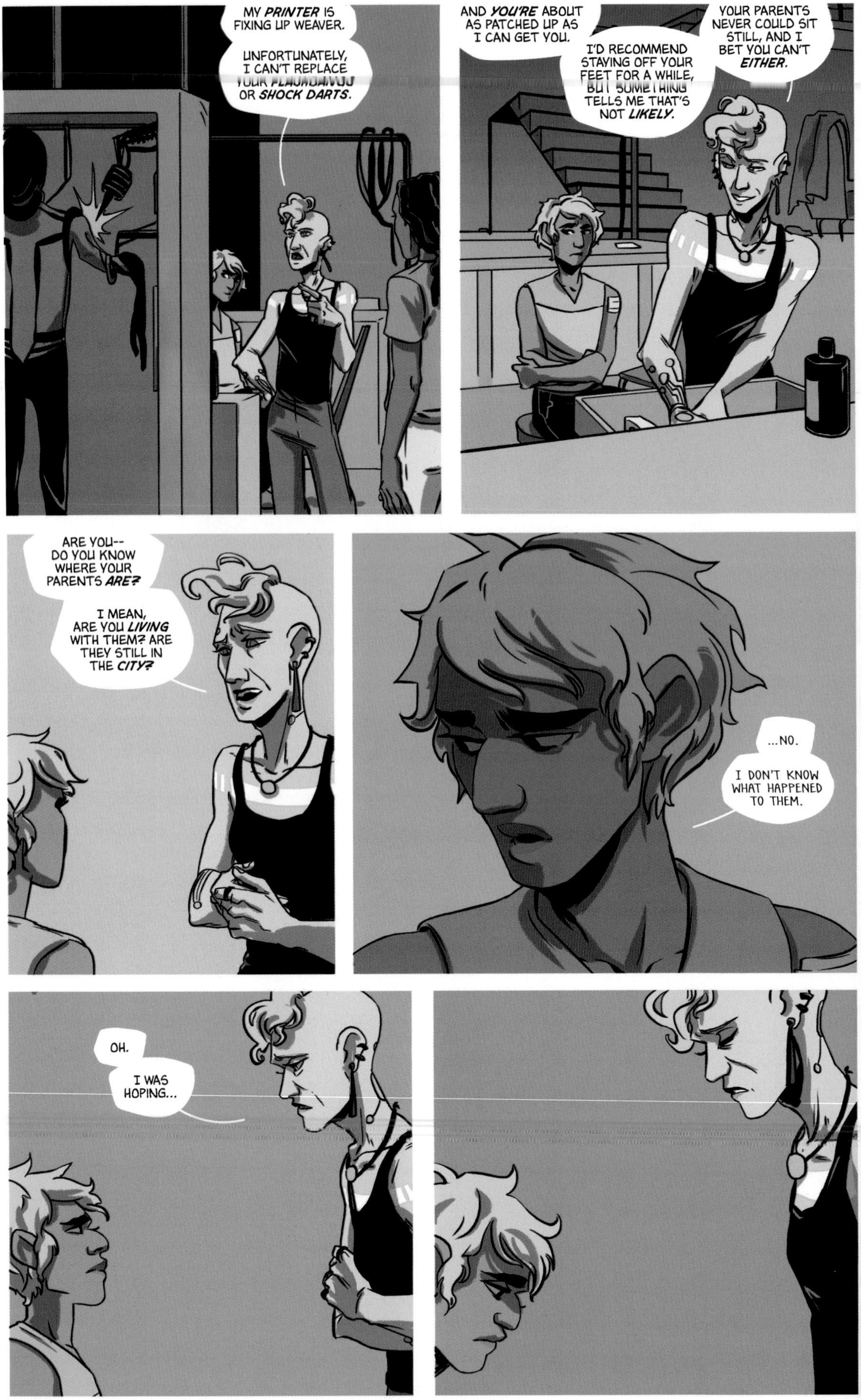
MY PRINTER IS FIXING UP WEAVER.
UNFORTUNATELY, I CAN'T REPLACE
OR SHOCK DARTS.
AND YOU'RE ABOUT AS PATCHED UP AS I CAN GET YOU.
I'D RECOMMEND STAYING OFF YOUR FEET FOR A WHILE, BUT SOMETHING TELLS ME THAT'S NOT LIKELY.
YOUR PARENTS NEVER COULD SIT STILL, AND I BET YOU CAN'T EITHER.
ARE YOU-- DO YOU KNOW WHERE YOUR PARENTS ARE?
I MEAN, ARE YOU LIVING WITH THEM? ARE THEY STILL IN THE CITY?
...NO.
I DON'T KNOW WHAT HAPPENED TO THEM.
OH.
I WAS HOPING...

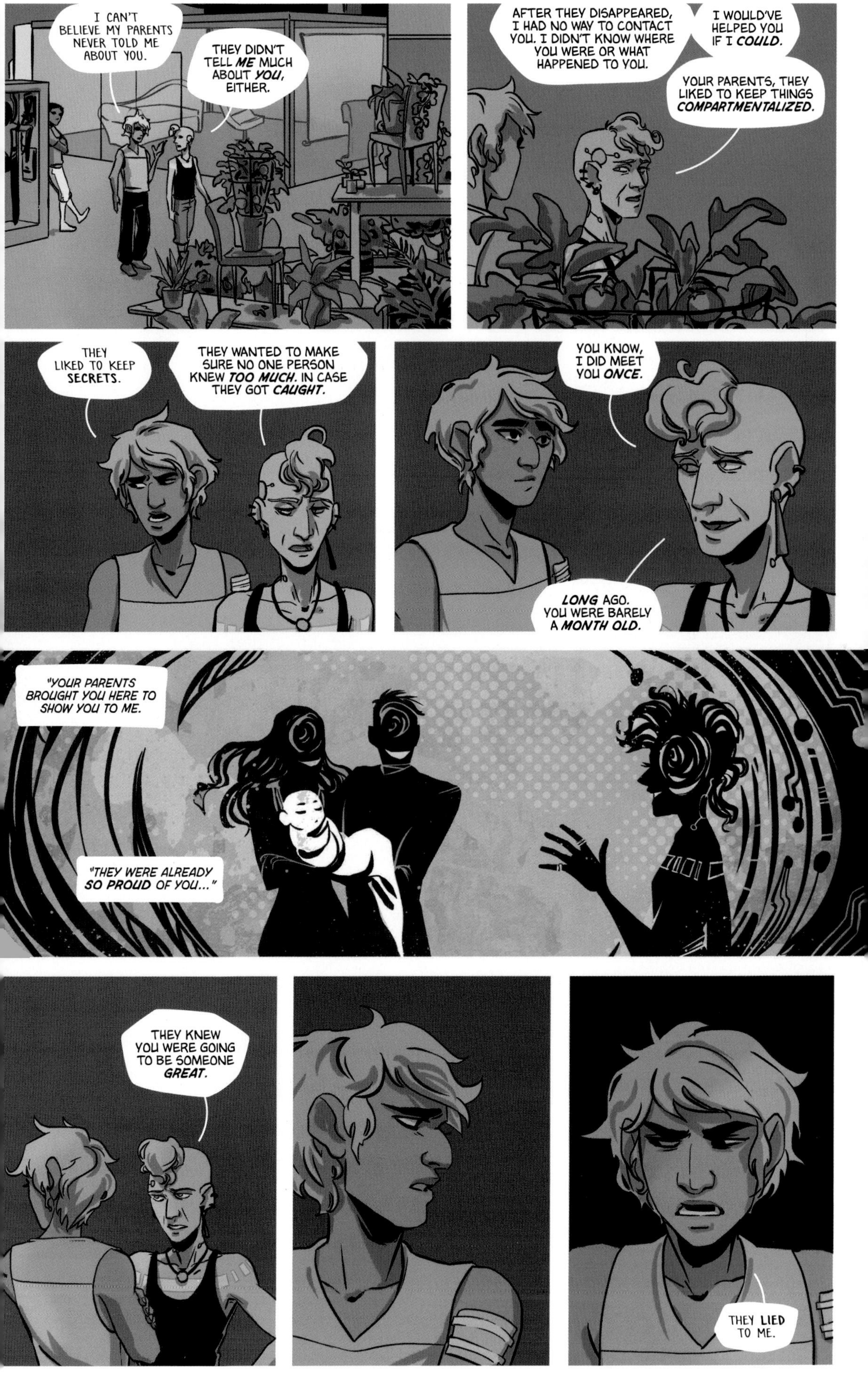
I CAN'T BELIEVE MY PARENTS NEVER TOLD ME ABOUT YOU.
THEY DIDN'T TELL *ME* MUCH ABOUT *YOU*, EITHER.
AFTER THEY DISAPPEARED, I HAD NO WAY TO CONTACT YOU. I DIDN'T KNOW WHERE YOU WERE OR WHAT HAPPENED TO YOU.
I WOULD'VE HELPED YOU IF I *COULD*.
YOUR PARENTS, THEY LIKED TO KEEP THINGS ***COMPARTMENTALIZED***.
THEY LIKED TO KEEP **SECRETS**.
THEY WANTED TO MAKE SURE NO ONE PERSON KNEW *TOO MUCH*. IN CASE THEY GOT *CAUGHT*.
YOU KNOW, I DID MEET YOU *ONCE*.
LONG AGO. YOU WERE BARELY A *MONTH OLD*.
"YOUR PARENTS BROUGHT YOU HERE TO SHOW YOU TO ME.
"THEY WERE ALREADY **SO PROUD** OF YOU..."
THEY KNEW YOU WERE GOING TO BE SOMEONE *GREAT*.
THEY **LIED** TO ME.

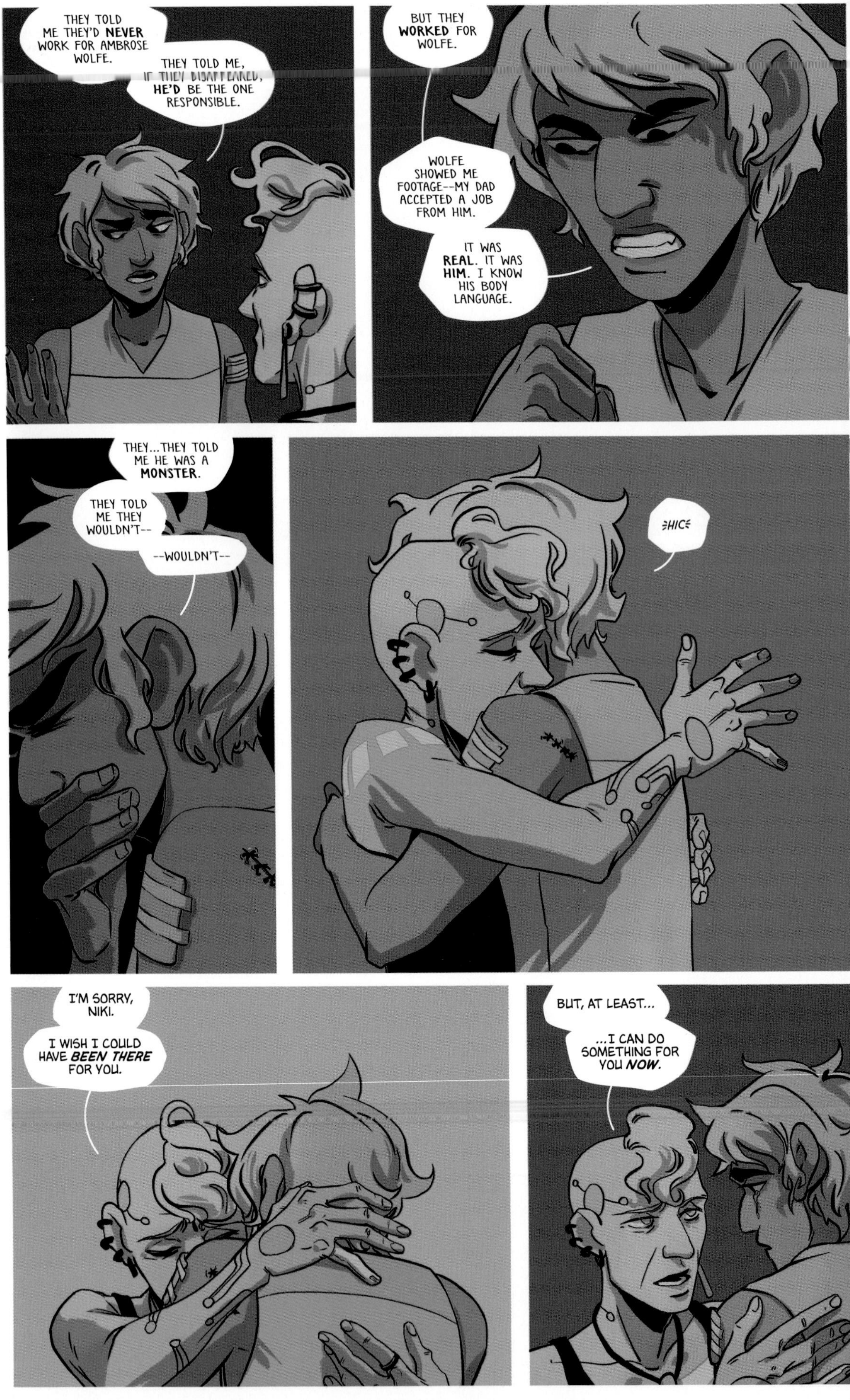
THEY TOLD ME THEY'D **NEVER** WORK FOR AMBROSE WOLFE.
THEY TOLD ME, IF THEY DISAPPEARED, **HE'D** BE THE ONE RESPONSIBLE.
BUT THEY **WORKED** FOR WOLFE.
WOLFE SHOWED ME FOOTAGE--MY DAD ACCEPTED A JOB FROM HIM.
IT WAS **REAL**. IT WAS **HIM**. I KNOW HIS BODY LANGUAGE.
THEY...THEY TOLD ME HE WAS A **MONSTER**.
THEY TOLD ME THEY WOULDN'T--
--WOULDN'T--
HIC
I'M SORRY, NIKI.
I WISH I COULD HAVE ***BEEN THERE*** FOR YOU.
BUT, AT LEAST...
...I CAN DO SOMETHING FOR YOU ***NOW***.

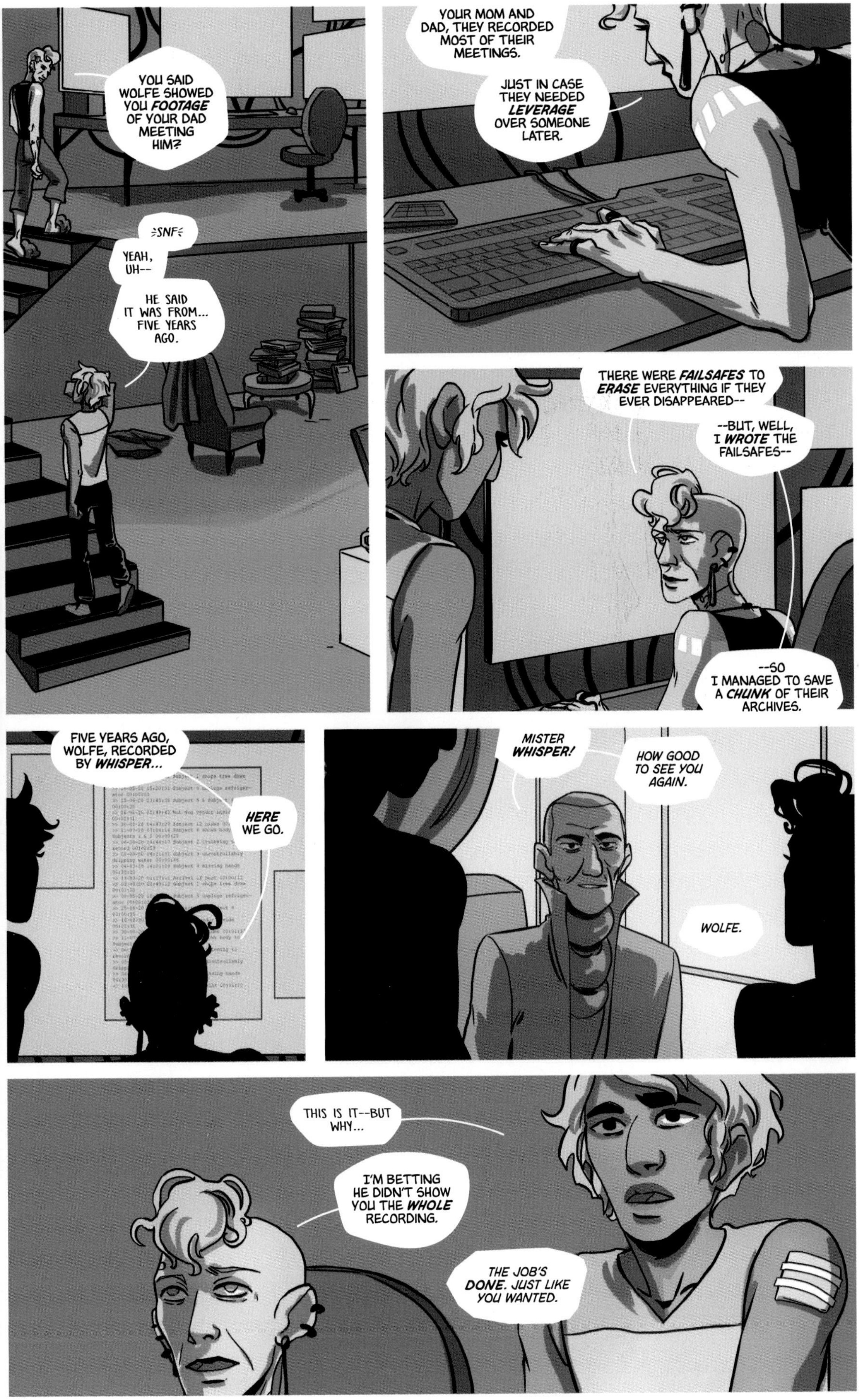

YOU SAID WOLFE SHOWED YOU *FOOTAGE* OF YOUR DAD MEETING HIM?
≶SNF≶
YEAH, UH--
HE SAID IT WAS FROM... FIVE YEARS AGO.
YOUR MOM AND DAD, THEY RECORDED MOST OF THEIR MEETINGS.
JUST IN CASE THEY NEEDED *LEVERAGE* OVER SOMEONE LATER.
THERE WERE *FAILSAFES* TO *ERASE* EVERYTHING IF THEY EVER DISAPPEARED--
--BUT, WELL, I *WROTE* THE FAILSAFES--
--SO I MANAGED TO SAVE A *CHUNK* OF THEIR ARCHIVES.
FIVE YEARS AGO, WOLFE, RECORDED BY *WHISPER*...
HERE WE GO.
MISTER *WHISPER!*
HOW GOOD TO SEE YOU AGAIN.
WOLFE.
THIS IS IT--BUT WHY...
I'M BETTING HE DIDN'T SHOW YOU THE *WHOLE* RECORDING.
THE JOB'S *DONE*. JUST LIKE YOU WANTED.

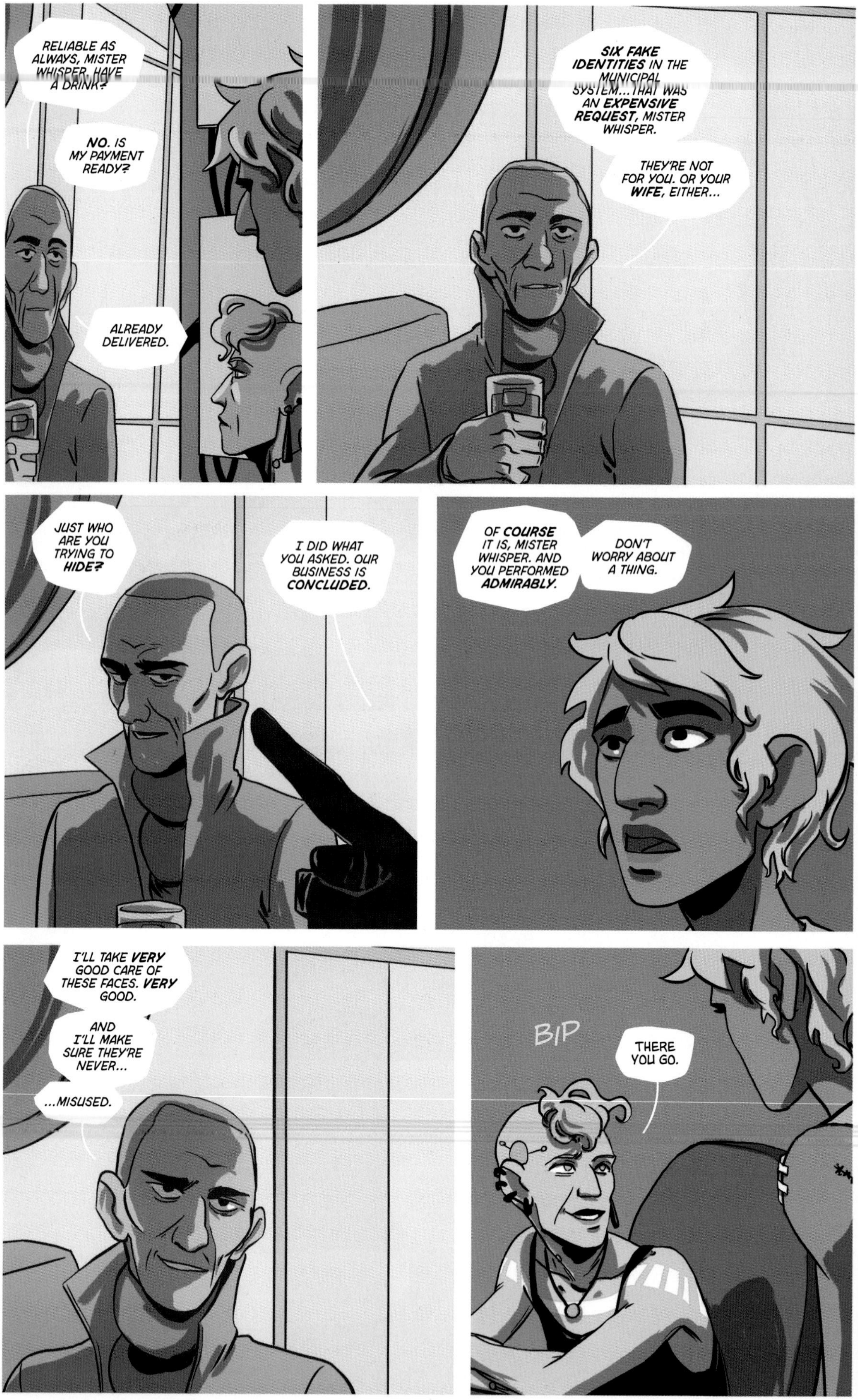
RELIABLE AS ALWAYS, MISTER WHISPER. HAVE A DRINK?
NO. IS MY PAYMENT READY?
ALREADY DELIVERED.
SIX FAKE IDENTITIES IN THE MUNICIPAL SYSTEM... THAT WAS AN EXPENSIVE REQUEST, MISTER WHISPER.
THEY'RE NOT FOR YOU. OR YOUR WIFE, EITHER...
JUST WHO ARE YOU TRYING TO HIDE?
I DID WHAT YOU ASKED. OUR BUSINESS IS CONCLUDED.
OF COURSE IT IS, MISTER WHISPER. AND YOU PERFORMED ADMIRABLY.
DON'T WORRY ABOUT A THING.
I'LL TAKE VERY GOOD CARE OF THESE FACES. VERY GOOD.
AND I'LL MAKE SURE THEY'RE NEVER...
...MISUSED.
BIP
THERE YOU GO.

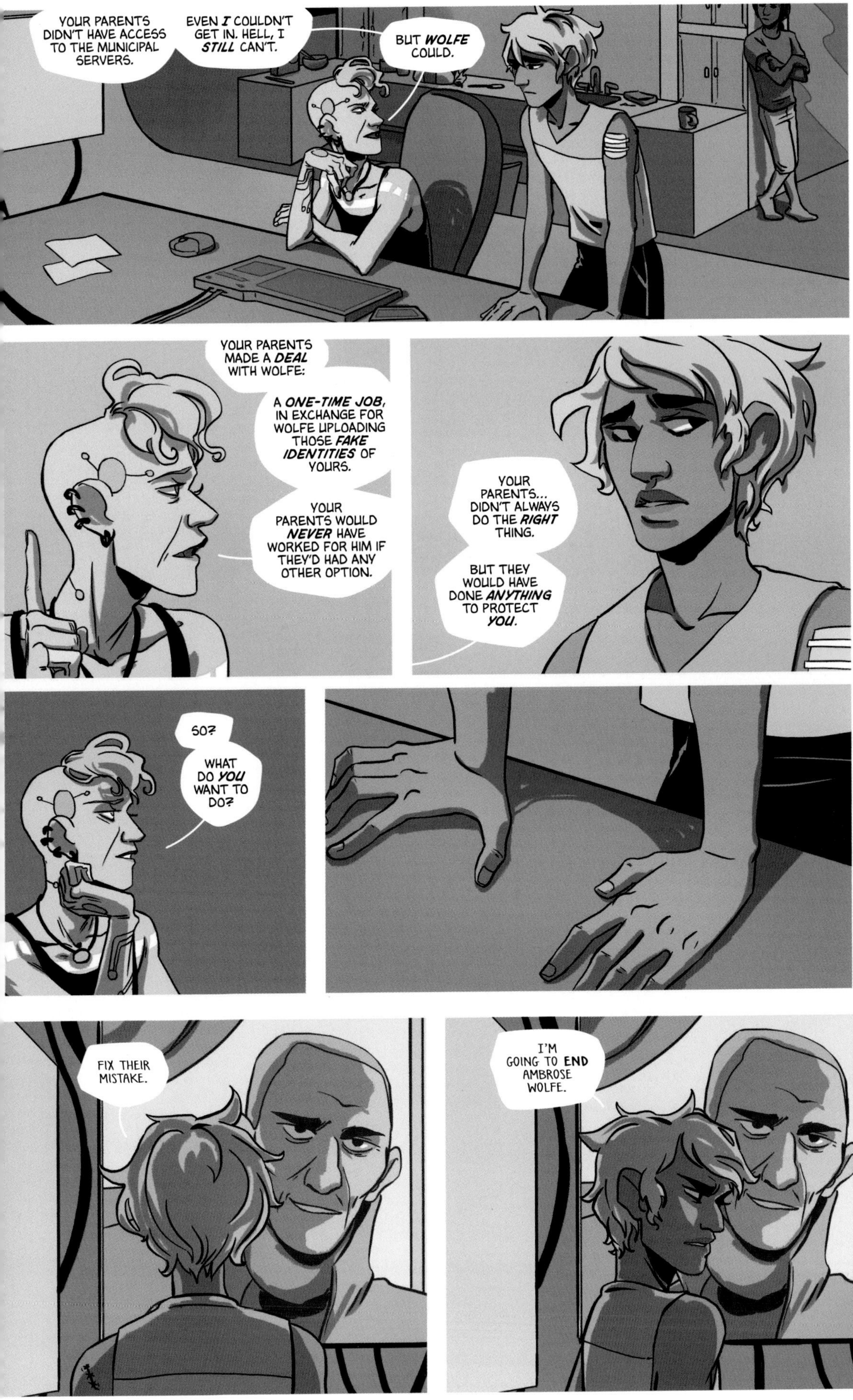
YOUR PARENTS DIDN'T HAVE ACCESS TO THE MUNICIPAL SERVERS.
EVEN I COULDN'T GET IN. HELL, I STILL CAN'T.
BUT WOLFE COULD.
YOUR PARENTS MADE A DEAL WITH WOLFE:
A ONE-TIME JOB, IN EXCHANGE FOR WOLFE UPLOADING THOSE FAKE IDENTITIES OF YOURS.
YOUR PARENTS WOULD NEVER HAVE WORKED FOR HIM IF THEY'D HAD ANY OTHER OPTION.
YOUR PARENTS... DIDN'T ALWAYS DO THE RIGHT THING.
BUT THEY WOULD HAVE DONE ANYTHING TO PROTECT YOU.
SO?
WHAT DO YOU WANT TO DO?
FIX THEIR MISTAKE.
I'M GOING TO END AMBROSE WOLFE.

5

PARENTAL GUIDANCE

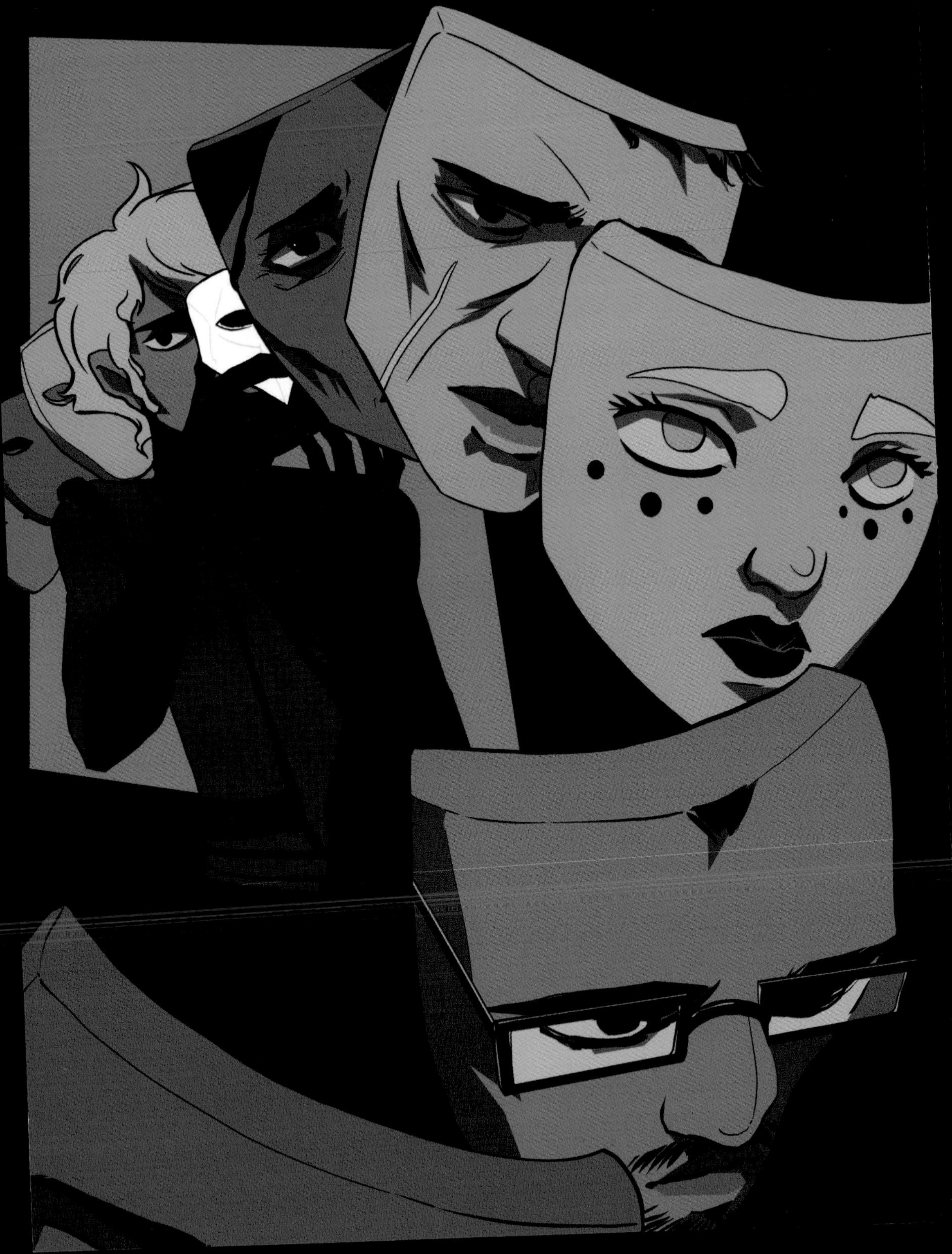

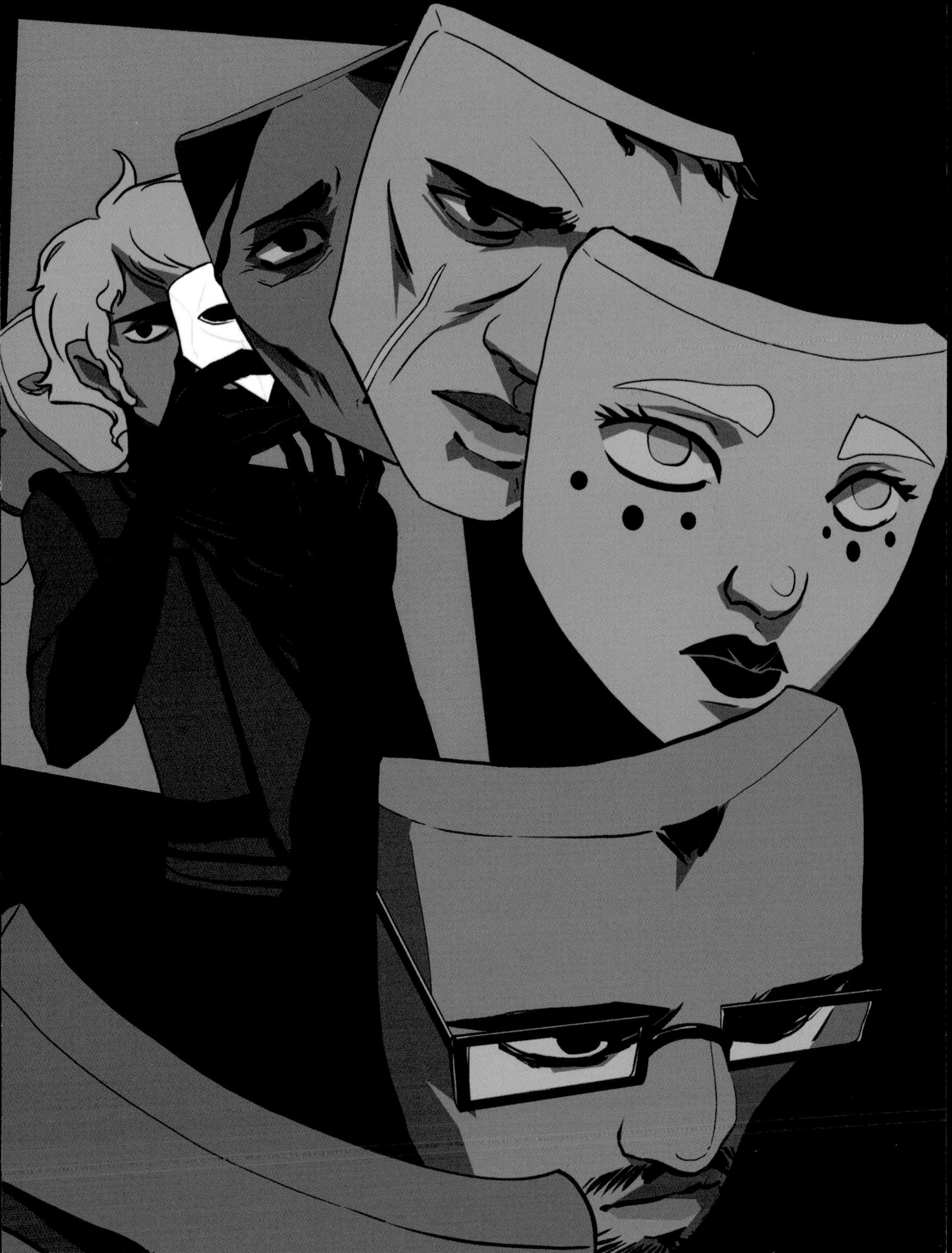

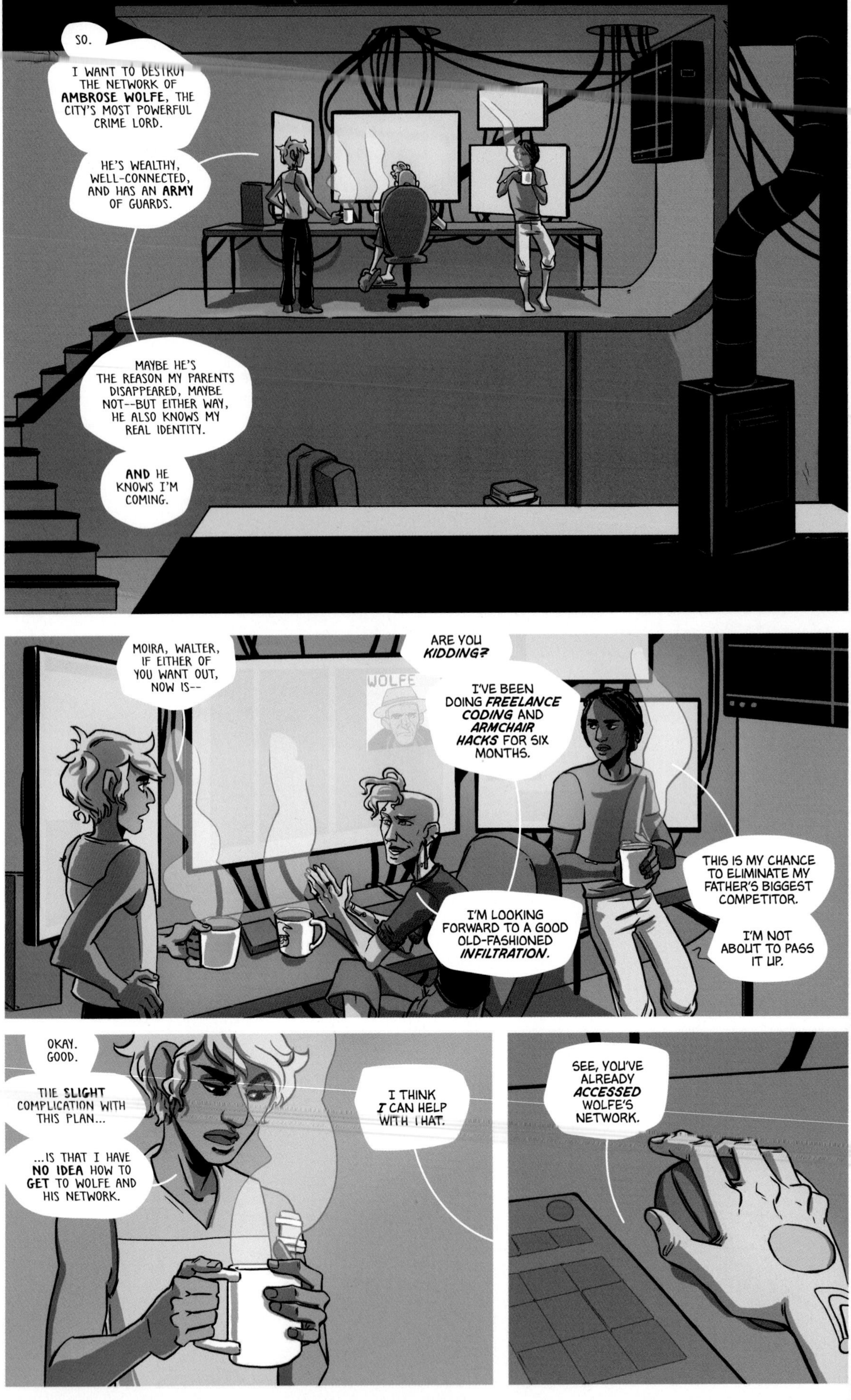

SO.
I WANT TO DESTROY THE NETWORK OF AMBROSE WOLFE, THE CITY'S MOST POWERFUL CRIME LORD.
HE'S WEALTHY, WELL-CONNECTED, AND HAS AN ARMY OF GUARDS.
MAYBE HE'S THE REASON MY PARENTS DISAPPEARED, MAYBE NOT--BUT EITHER WAY, HE ALSO KNOWS MY REAL IDENTITY.
AND HE KNOWS I'M COMING.
MOIRA, WALTER, IF EITHER OF YOU WANT OUT, NOW IS--
ARE YOU KIDDING?
WOLFE
I'VE BEEN DOING FREELANCE CODING AND ARMCHAIR HACKS FOR SIX MONTHS.
I'M LOOKING FORWARD TO A GOOD OLD-FASHIONED INFILTRATION.
THIS IS MY CHANCE TO ELIMINATE MY FATHER'S BIGGEST COMPETITOR.
I'M NOT ABOUT TO PASS IT UP.
OKAY. GOOD.
THE SLIGHT COMPLICATION WITH THIS PLAN...
...IS THAT I HAVE NO IDEA HOW TO GET TO WOLFE AND HIS NETWORK.
I THINK I CAN HELP WITH THAT.
SEE, YOU'VE ALREADY ACCESSED WOLFE'S NETWORK.

HUH?

WELL, *WEAVER* DID.

WEAVER PASSIVELY PROBES EVERY NETWORK NODE WITHIN ITS RANGE...

...INCLUDING WOLFE'S *CANE*.

WEAVER DIDN'T GET VERY DEEP INTO WOLFE'S NETWORK, BUT IT GOT *DEEP* ENOUGH TO TELL ME WHAT WE'RE UP AGAINST.

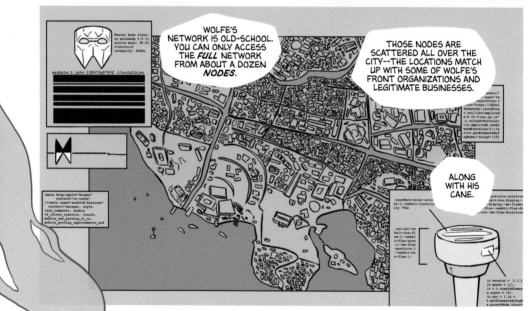

WOLFE'S NETWORK IS OLD-SCHOOL. YOU CAN ONLY ACCESS THE *FULL* NETWORK FROM ABOUT A DOZEN *NODES*.

THOSE NODES ARE SCATTERED ALL OVER THE CITY--THE LOCATIONS MATCH UP WITH SOME OF WOLFE'S FRONT ORGANIZATIONS AND LEGITIMATE BUSINESSES.

ALONG WITH HIS CANE.

IF YOU WANT ACCESS TO *ALL* OF WOLFE'S DATA, YOU NEED TO DO IT FROM ONE OF THESE LOCATIONS.

BUT LIKE I SAID:

HE'S *OLD-SCHOOL.*

HIS NETWORK SECURITY IS *LATTICE-BASED*--HARD TO CRACK, BUT THERE'S A WEAKNESS.

IF YOU CAN ACCESS *TWO* OF THE NODES *SIMULTANEOUSLY*, I CAN OVERLAP THEIR MATRICES AND *CRACK* THE SECURITY *WIDE OPEN*.

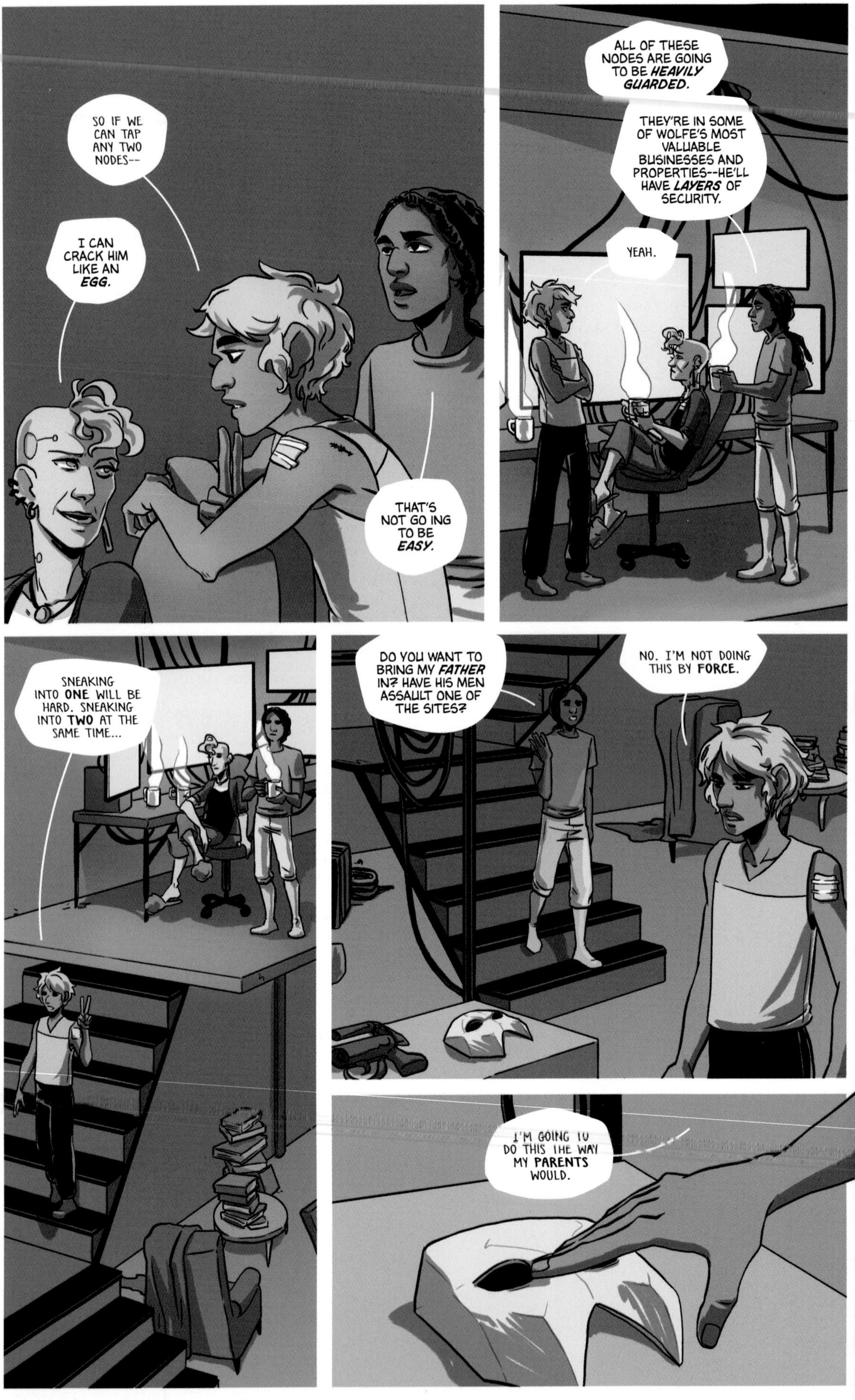
SO IF WE CAN TAP ANY TWO NODES--
I CAN CRACK HIM LIKE AN *EGG.*
THAT'S NOT GO ING TO BE *EASY.*
ALL OF THESE NODES ARE GOING TO BE *HEAVILY GUARDED.*
THEY'RE IN SOME OF WOLFE'S MOST VALUABLE BUSINESSES AND PROPERTIES--HE'LL HAVE *LAYERS* OF SECURITY.
YEAH.
SNEAKING INTO **ONE** WILL BE HARD. SNEAKING INTO **TWO** AT THE SAME TIME...
DO YOU WANT TO BRING MY *FATHER* IN? HAVE HIS MEN ASSAULT ONE OF THE SITES?
NO. I'M NOT DOING THIS BY **FORCE.**
I'M GOING TO DO THIS THE WAY MY **PARENTS** WOULD.

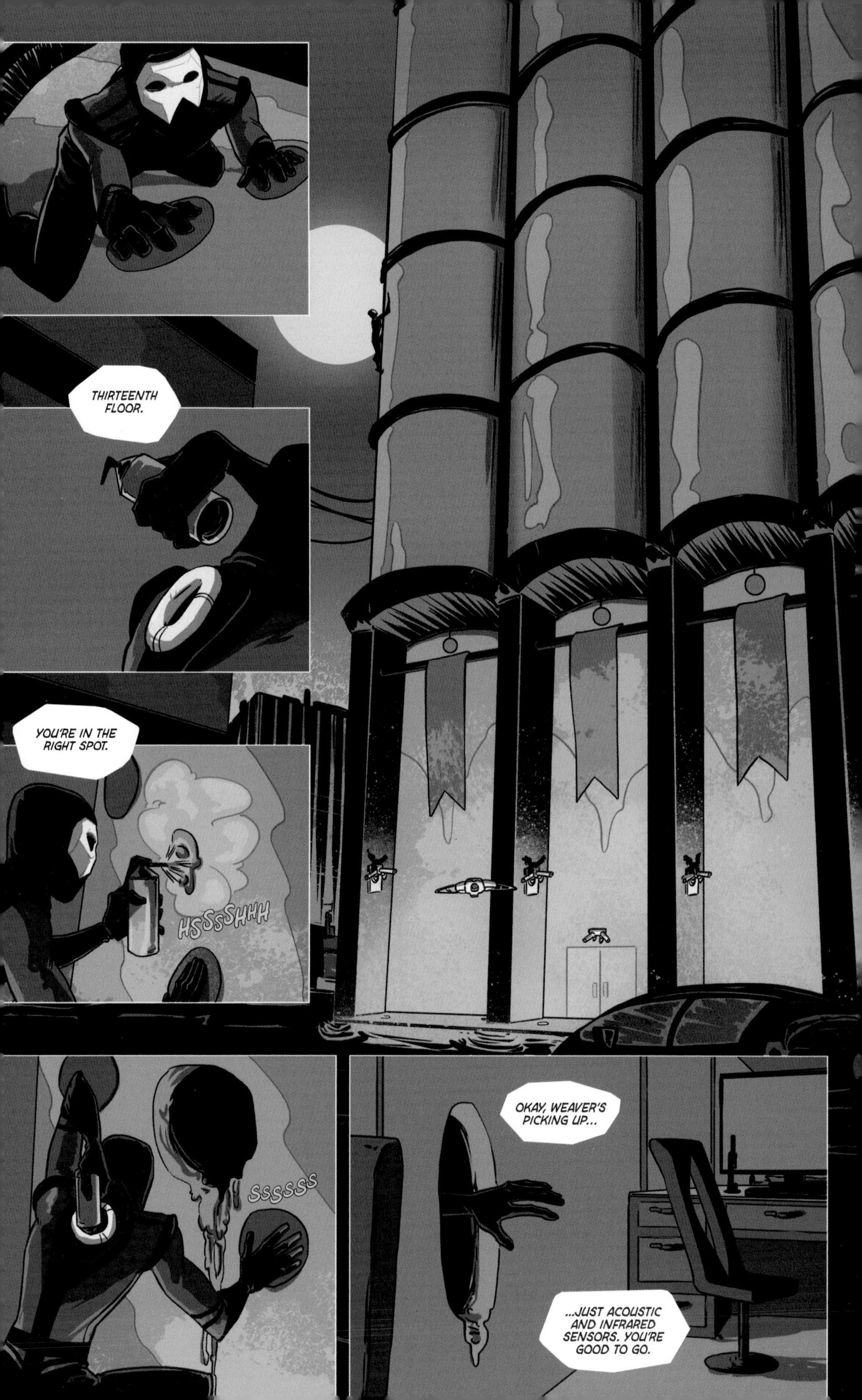
THIRTEENTH FLOOR.
YOU'RE IN THE RIGHT SPOT.
HSSSSHHH
SSSSSS
OKAY, WEAVER'S PICKING UP...
...JUST ACOUSTIC AND INFRARED SENSORS. YOU'RE GOOD TO GO.

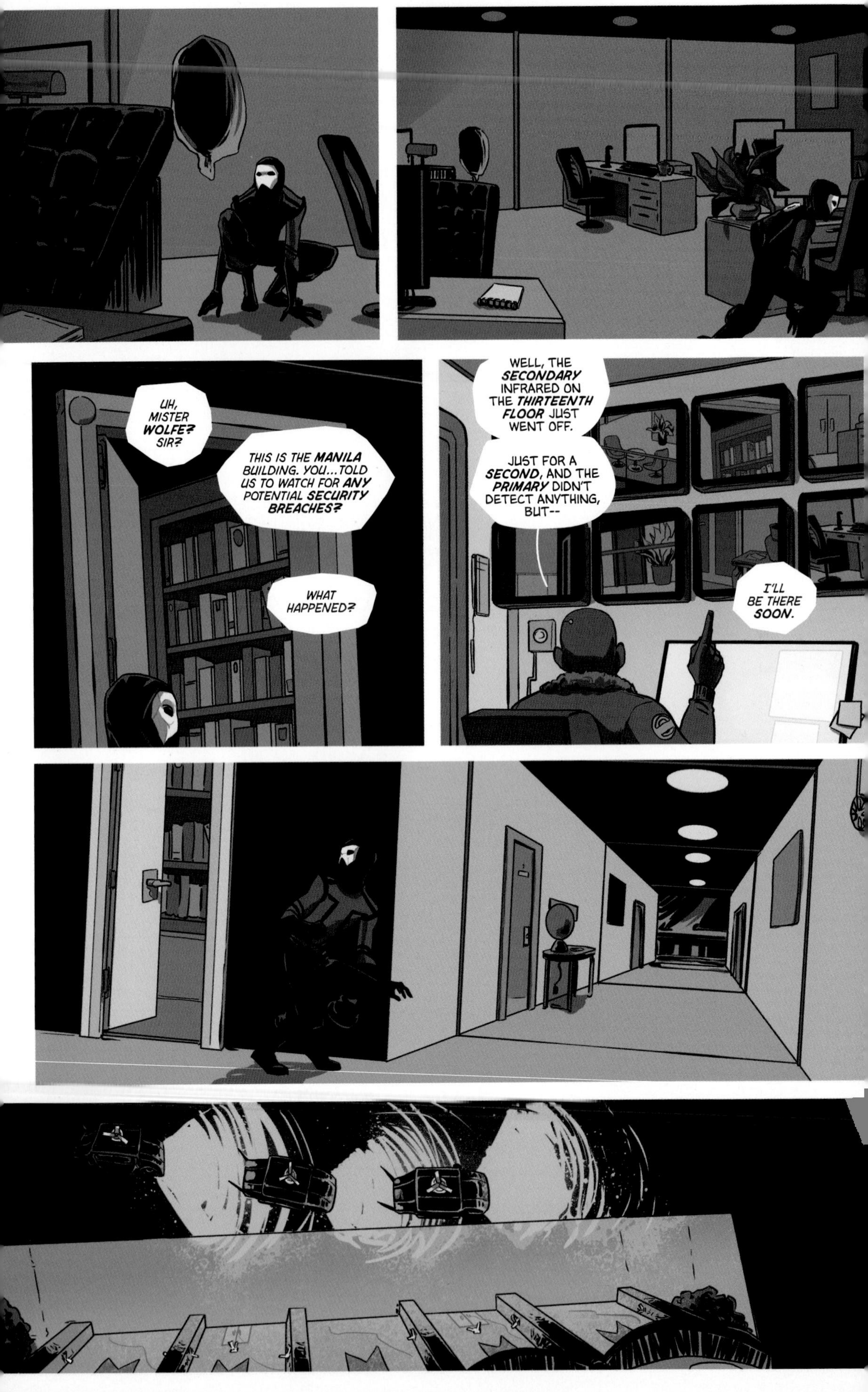
UH, MISTER WOLFE? SIR?
THIS IS THE MANILA BUILDING. YOU...TOLD US TO WATCH FOR ANY POTENTIAL SECURITY BREACHES?
WHAT HAPPENED?
WELL, THE SECONDARY INFRARED ON THE THIRTEENTH FLOOR JUST WENT OFF.
JUST FOR A SECOND, AND THE PRIMARY DIDN'T DETECT ANYTHING, BUT--
I'LL BE THERE SOON.

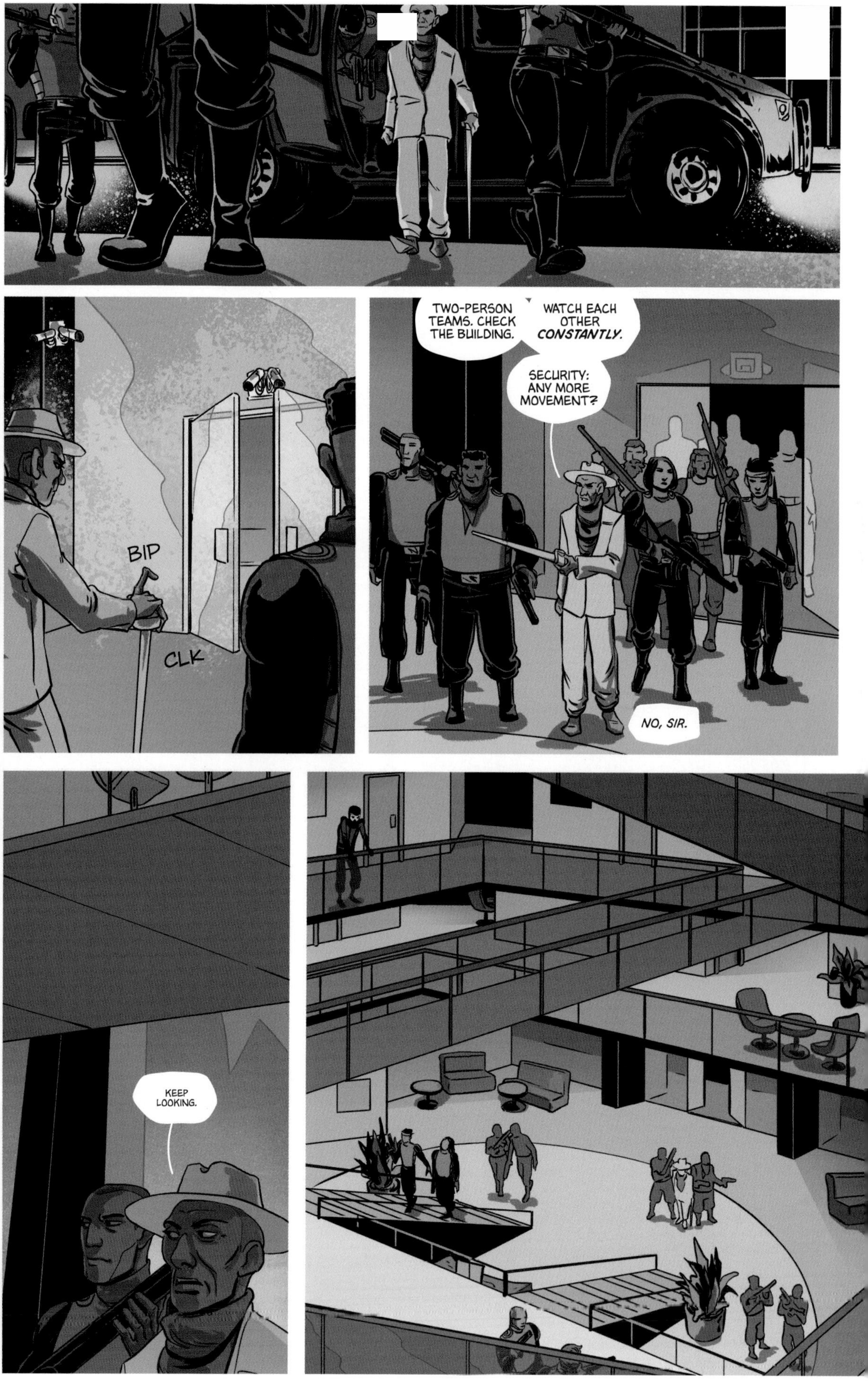

BIP
CLK
TWO-PERSON TEAMS. CHECK THE BUILDING.
WATCH EACH OTHER *CONSTANTLY*.
SECURITY: ANY MORE MOVEMENT?
NO, SIR.
KEEP LOOKING.

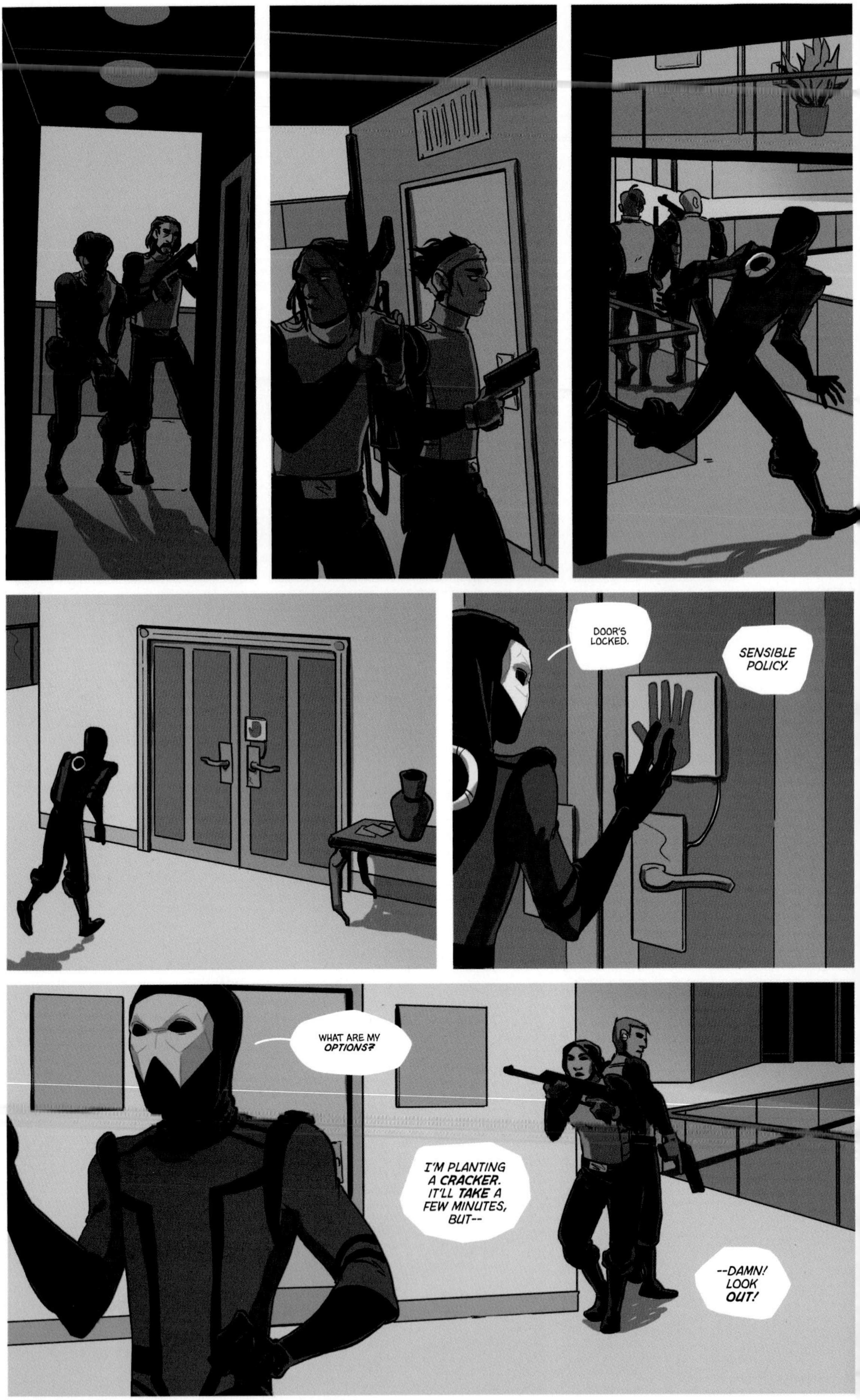
DOOR'S LOCKED.
SENSIBLE POLICY.
WHAT ARE MY OPTIONS?
I'M PLANTING A CRACKER. IT'LL TAKE A FEW MINUTES, BUT--
--DAMN! LOOK OUT!

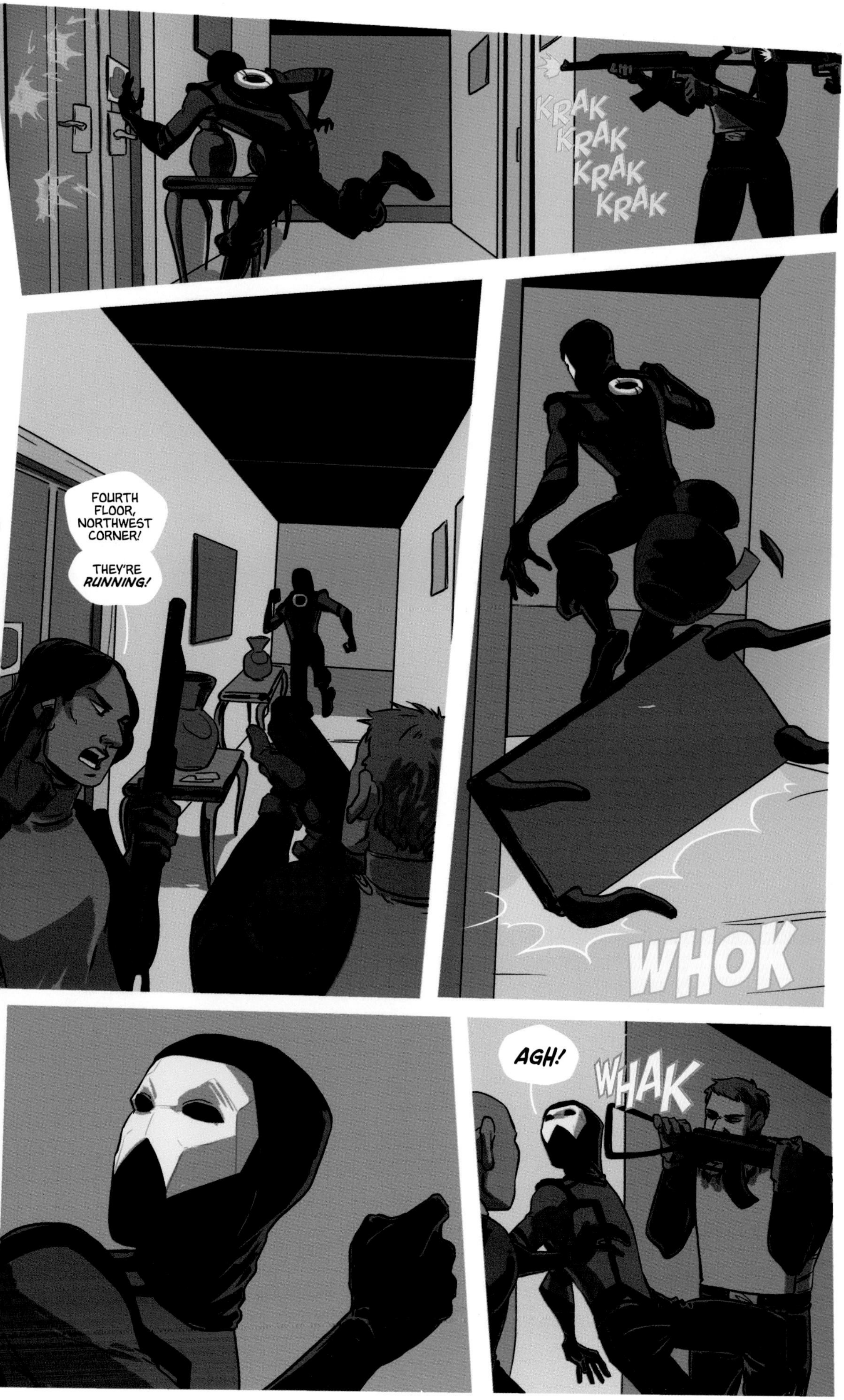
KRAK
KRAK
KRAK
KRAK
FOURTH FLOOR, NORTHWEST CORNER!
THEY'RE *RUNNING!*
WHOK
AGH!
WHAK

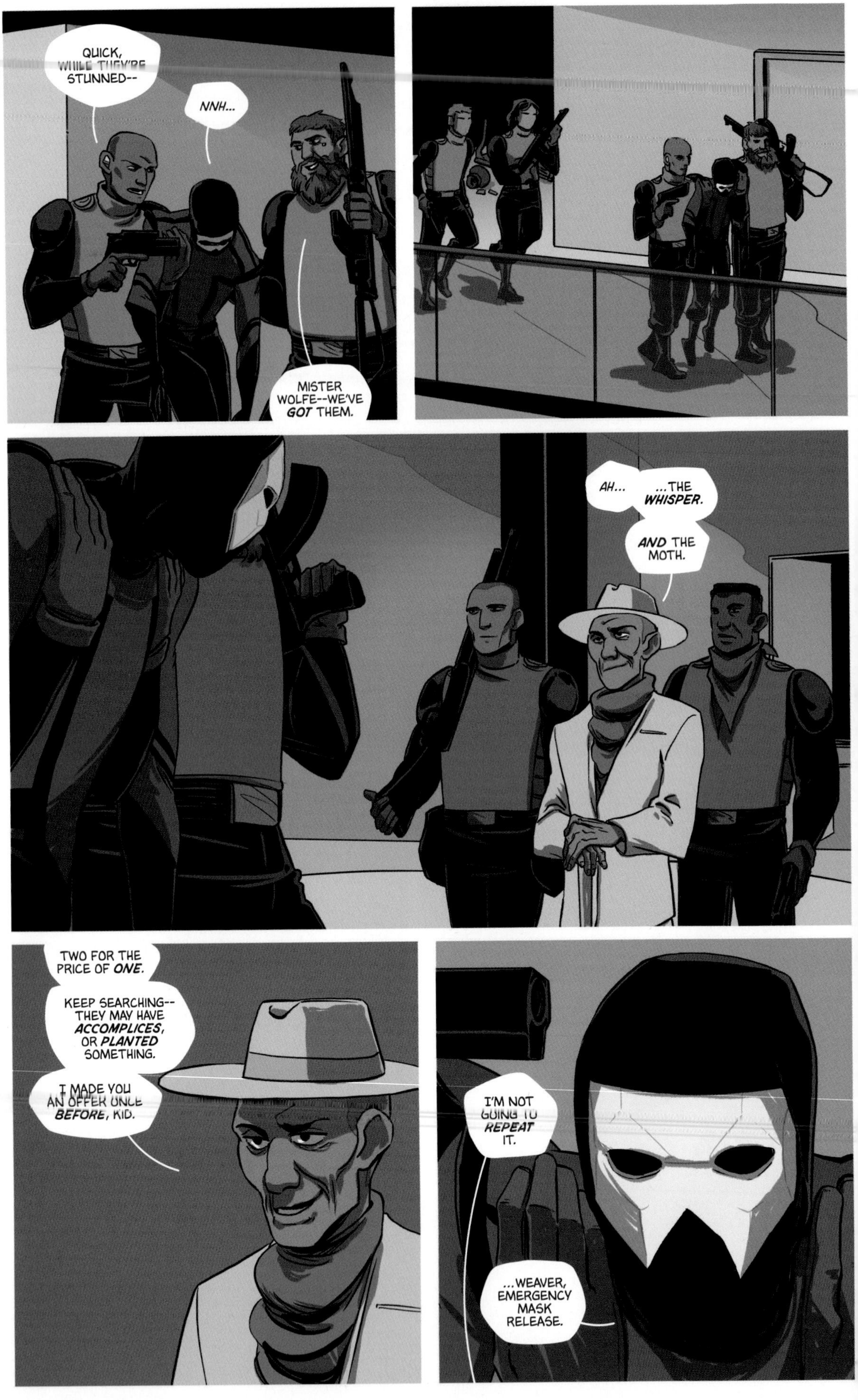
QUICK, WHILE THEY'RE STUNNED--
NNH...
MISTER WOLFE--WE'VE GOT THEM.
AH...
...THE WHISPER.
AND THE MOTH.
TWO FOR THE PRICE OF ONE.
KEEP SEARCHING--THEY MAY HAVE ACCOMPLICES, OR PLANTED SOMETHING.
I MADE YOU AN OFFER ONCE BEFORE, KID.
I'M NOT GOING TO REPEAT IT.
...WEAVER, EMERGENCY MASK RELEASE.

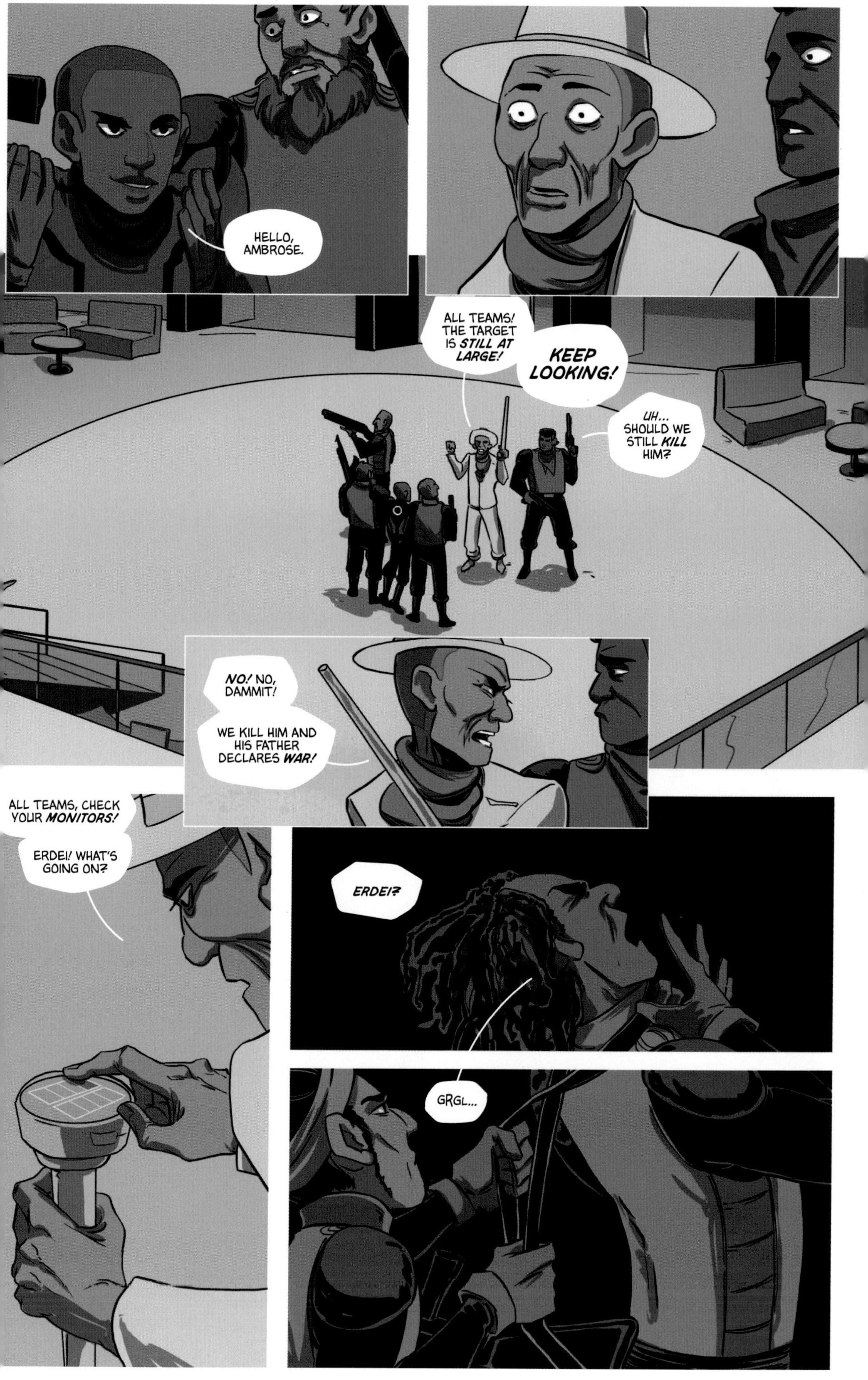
HELLO, AMBROSE.
ALL TEAMS! THE TARGET IS STILL AT LARGE!
KEEP LOOKING!
UH... SHOULD WE STILL KILL HIM?
NO! NO, DAMMIT!
WE KILL HIM AND HIS FATHER DECLARES WAR!
ALL TEAMS, CHECK YOUR MONITORS!
ERDEI! WHAT'S GOING ON?
ERDEI?
GRGL...

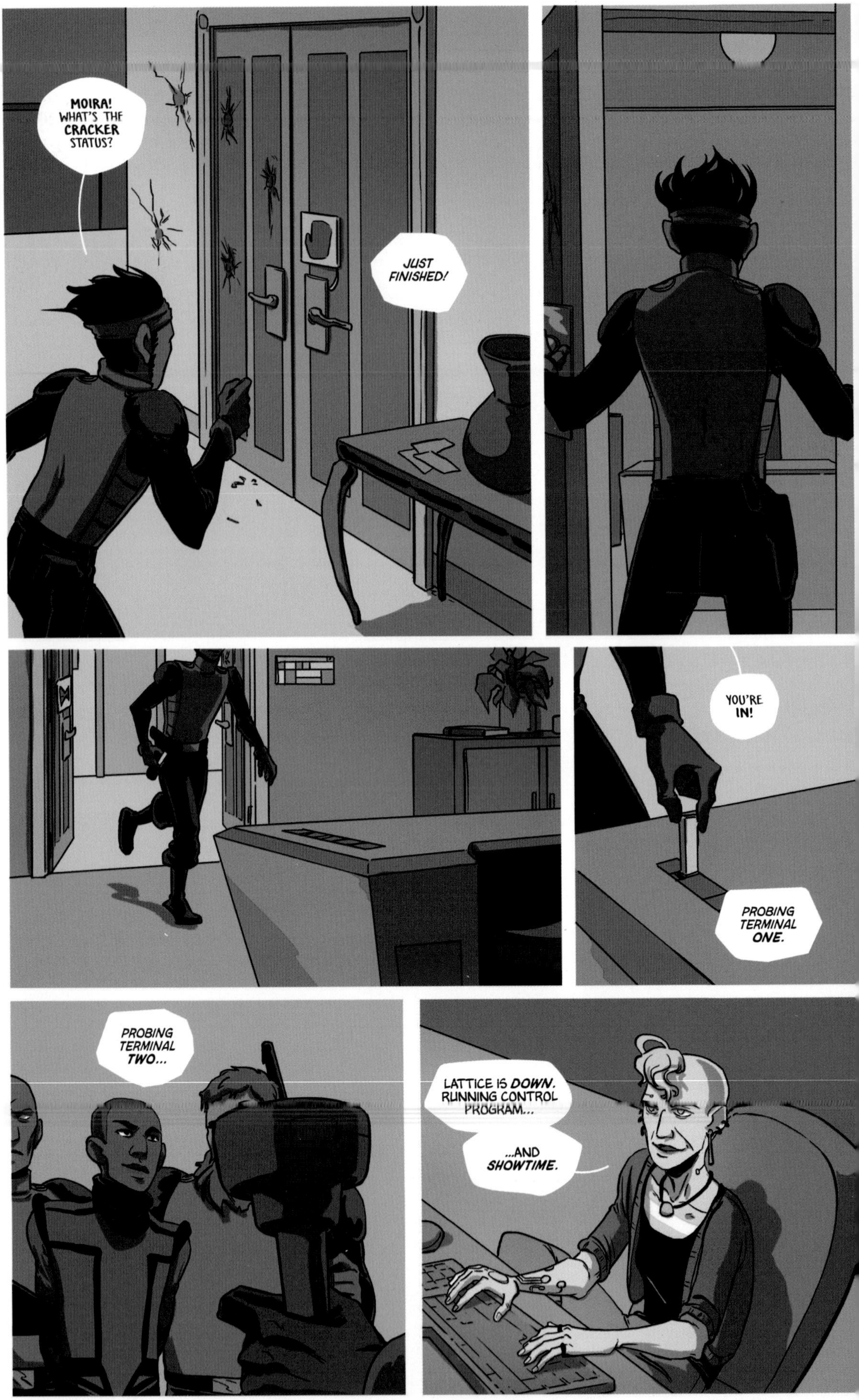
MOIRA! WHAT'S THE CRACKER STATUS?
JUST FINISHED!
YOU'RE IN!
PROBING TERMINAL ONE.
PROBING TERMINAL TWO...
LATTICE IS DOWN. RUNNING CONTROL PROGRAM...
...AND SHOWTIME.

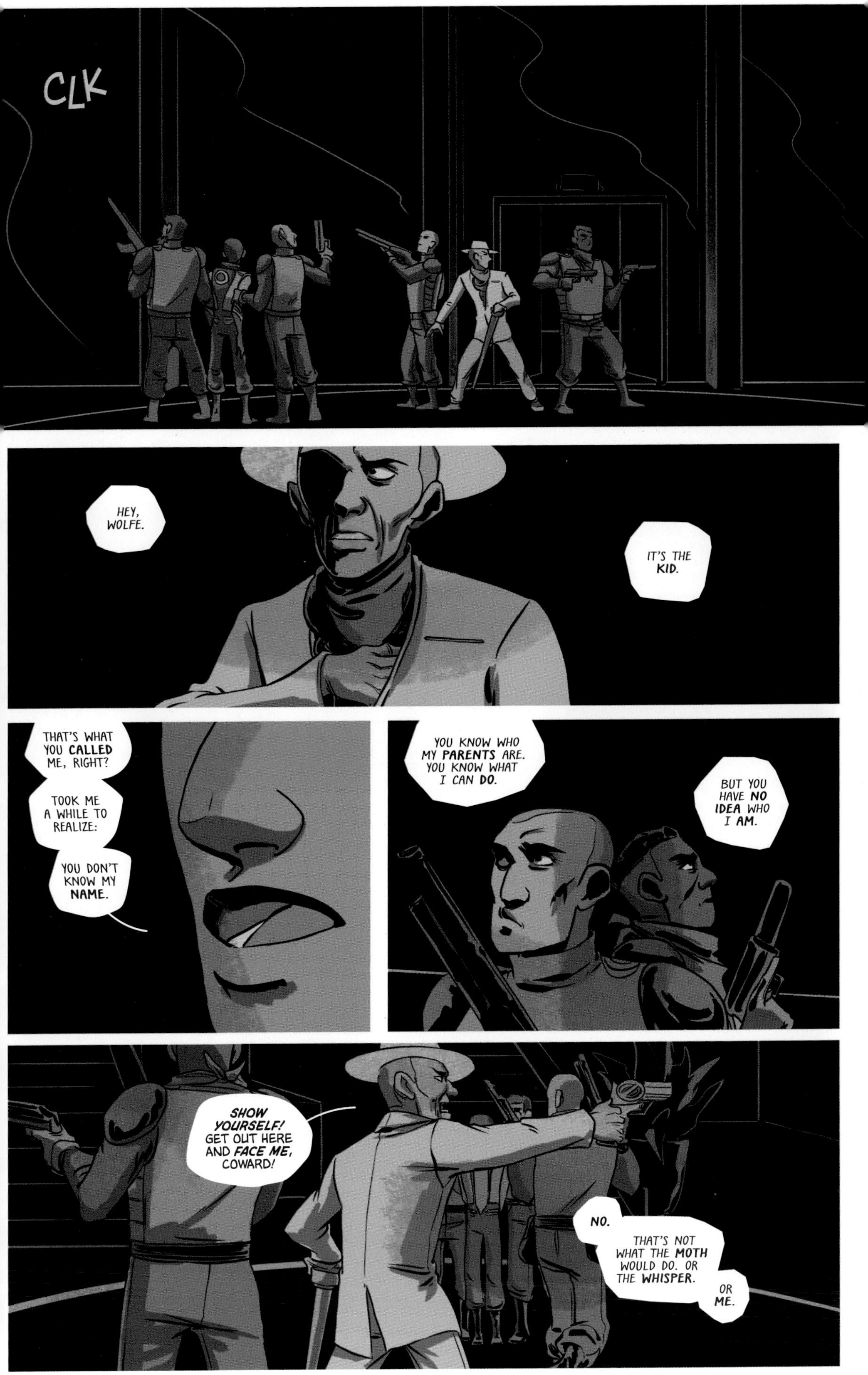
CLK
HEY, WOLFE.
IT'S THE KID.
THAT'S WHAT YOU CALLED ME, RIGHT?
TOOK ME A WHILE TO REALIZE:
YOU DON'T KNOW MY NAME.
YOU KNOW WHO MY PARENTS ARE. YOU KNOW WHAT I CAN DO.
BUT YOU HAVE NO IDEA WHO I AM.
SHOW YOURSELF! GET OUT HERE AND FACE ME, COWARD!
NO.
THAT'S NOT WHAT THE MOTH WOULD DO. OR THE WHISPER.
OR ME.

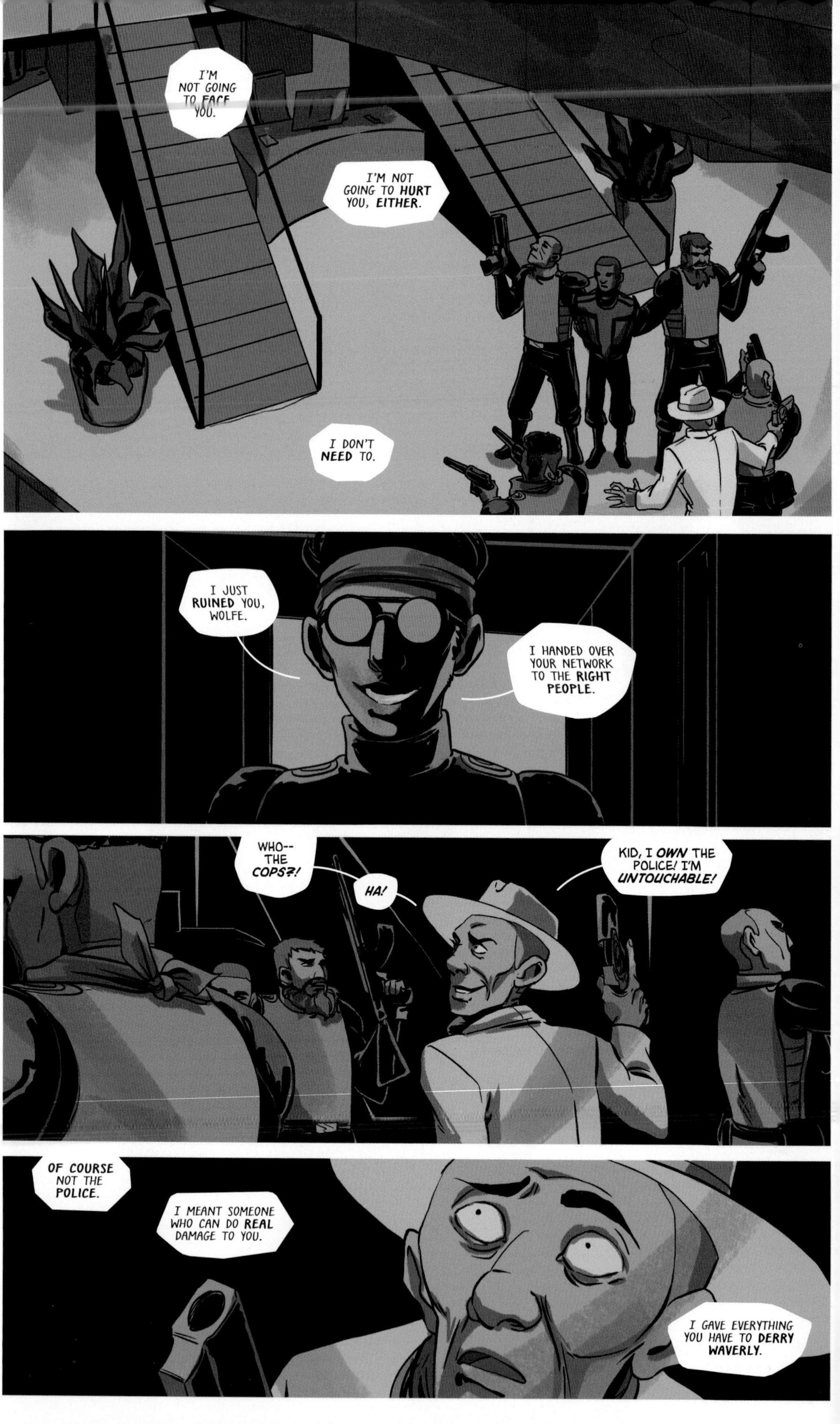

I'M NOT GOING TO FACE YOU.
I'M NOT GOING TO HURT YOU, EITHER.
I DON'T NEED TO.
I JUST RUINED YOU, WOLFE.
I HANDED OVER YOUR NETWORK TO THE RIGHT PEOPLE.
WHO-- THE COPS?!
HA!
KID, I OWN THE POLICE! I'M UNTOUCHABLE!
OF COURSE NOT THE POLICE.
I MEANT SOMEONE WHO CAN DO REAL DAMAGE TO YOU.
I GAVE EVERYTHING YOU HAVE TO DERRY WAVERLY.

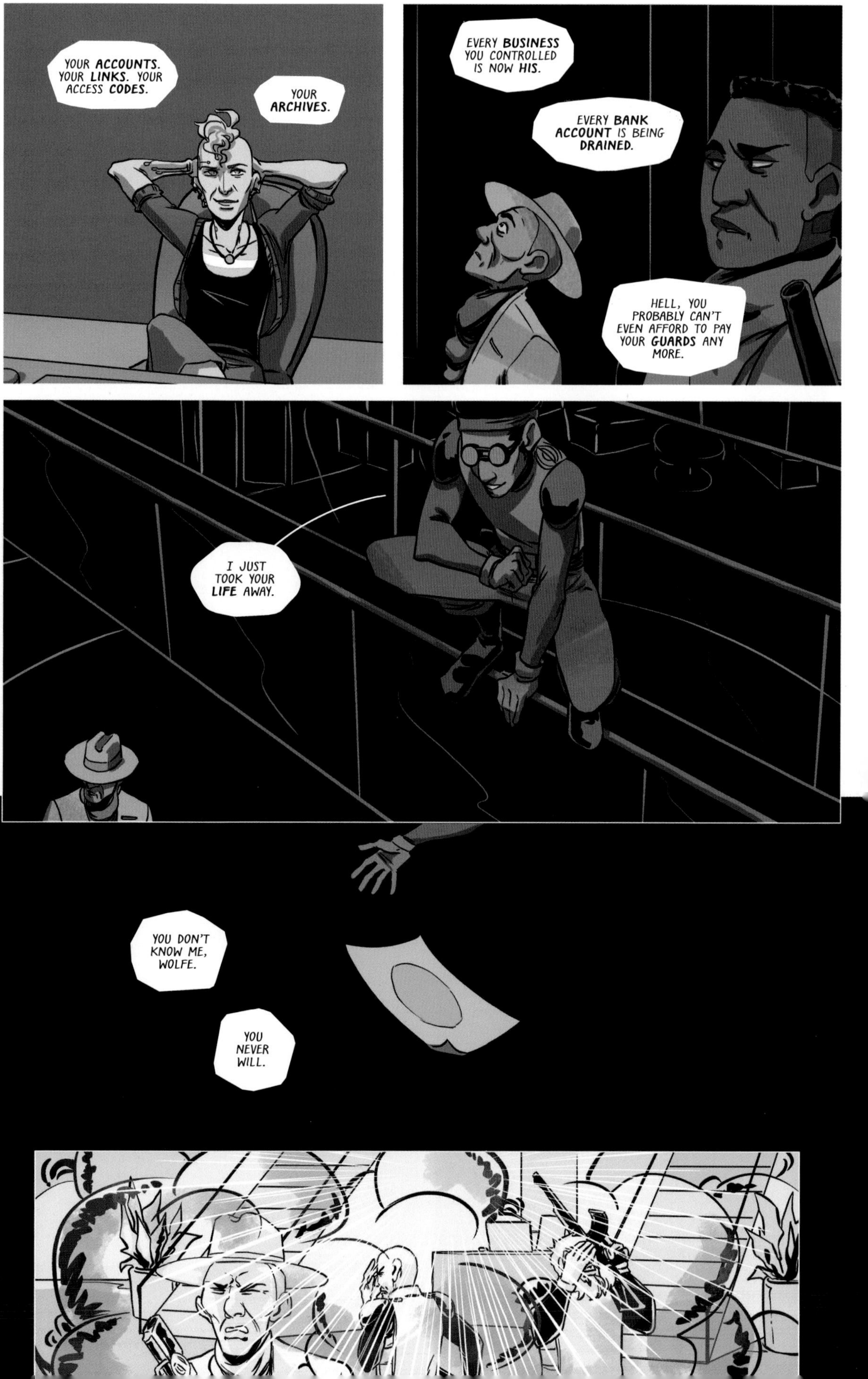
YOUR ACCOUNTS. YOUR LINKS. YOUR ACCESS CODES.
YOUR ARCHIVES.
EVERY BUSINESS YOU CONTROLLED IS NOW HIS.
EVERY BANK ACCOUNT IS BEING DRAINED.
HELL, YOU PROBABLY CAN'T EVEN AFFORD TO PAY YOUR GUARDS ANY MORE.
I JUST TOOK YOUR LIFE AWAY.
YOU DON'T KNOW ME, WOLFE.
YOU NEVER WILL.

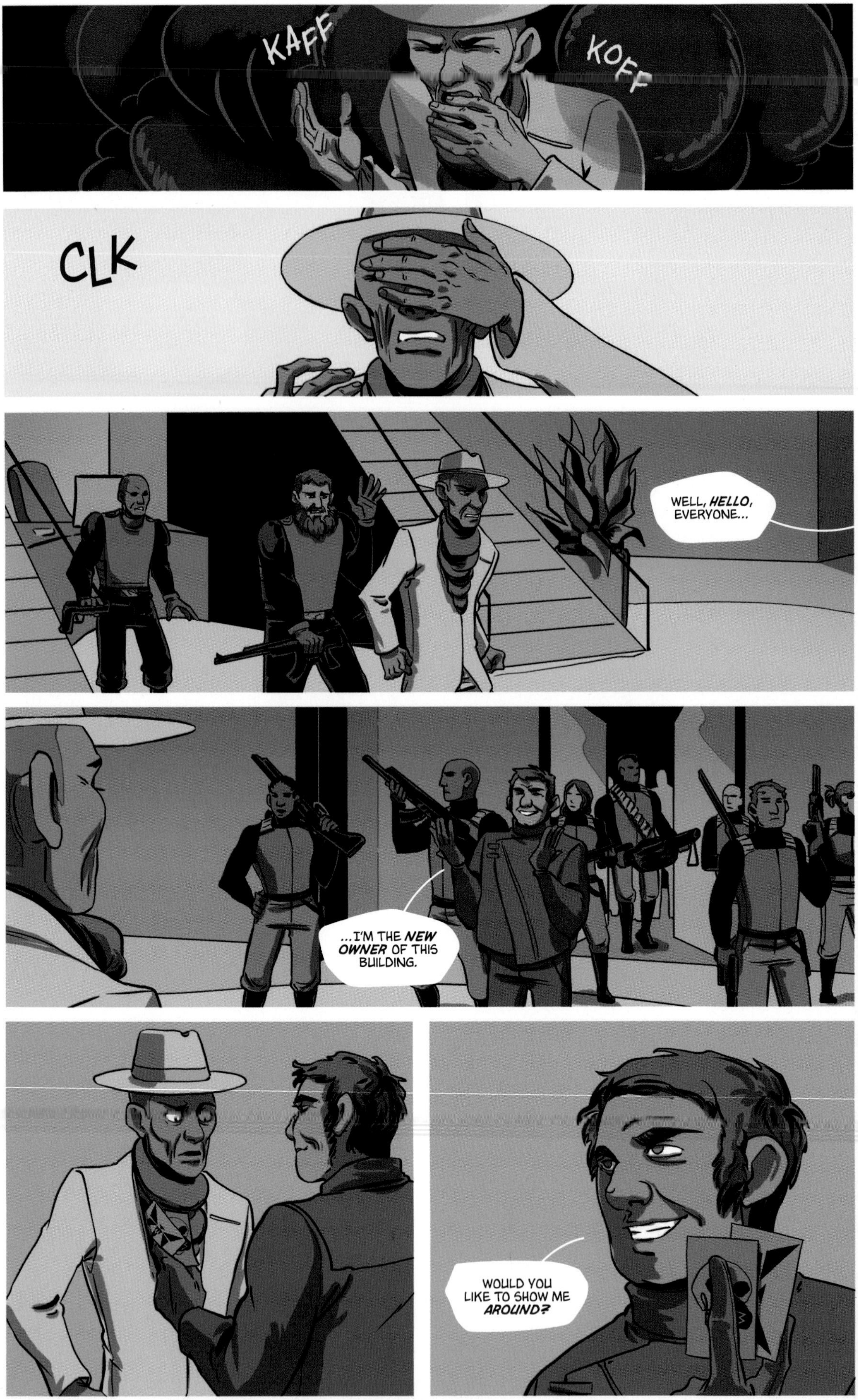
KAFF
KOFF
CLK
WELL, *HELLO*, EVERYONE...
...I'M THE *NEW OWNER* OF THIS BUILDING.
WOULD YOU LIKE TO SHOW ME *AROUND?*

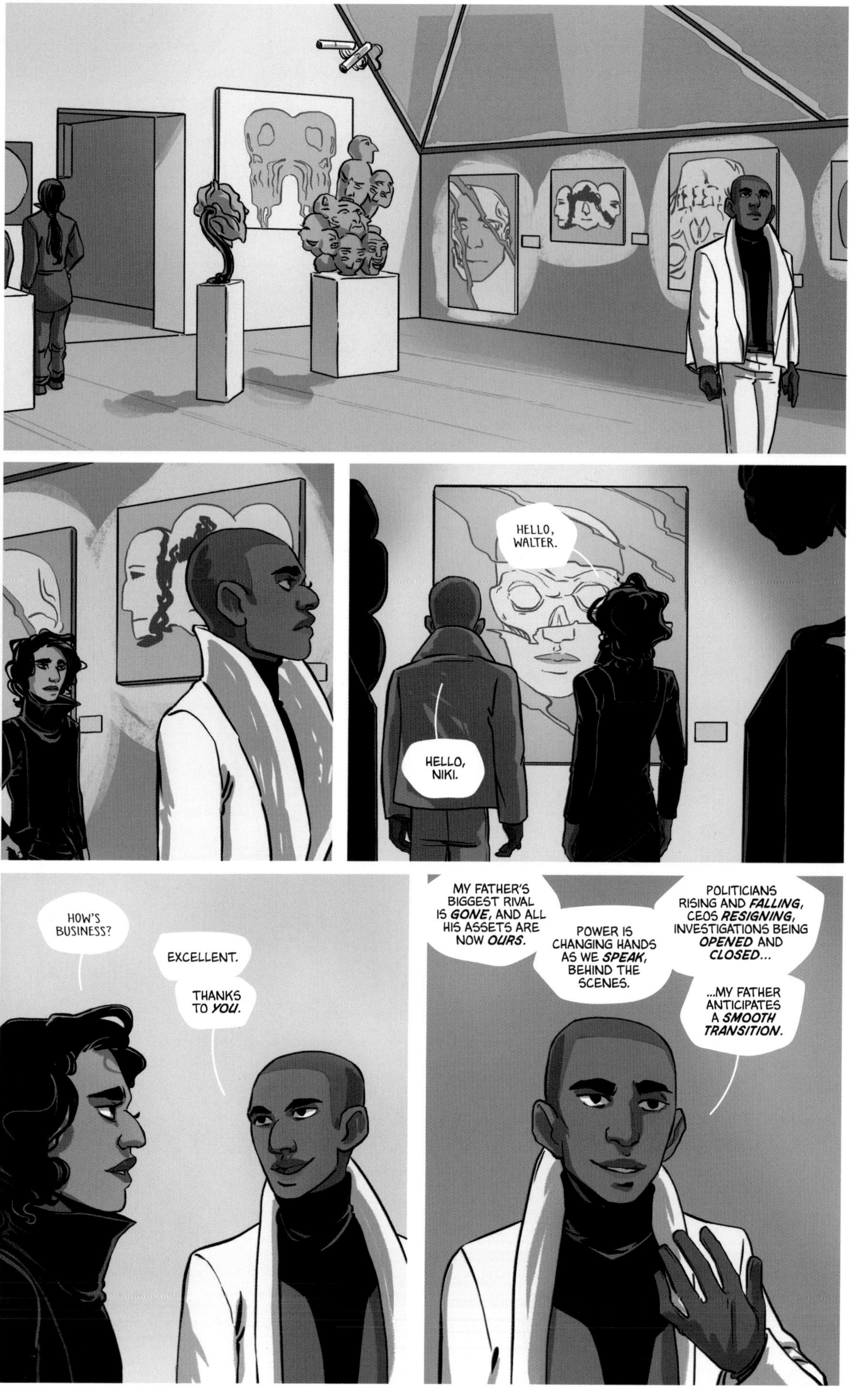
HELLO, WALTER.
HELLO, NIKI.
HOW'S BUSINESS?
EXCELLENT.
THANKS TO *YOU*.
MY FATHER'S BIGGEST RIVAL IS *GONE*, AND ALL HIS ASSETS ARE NOW *OURS*.
POWER IS CHANGING HANDS AS WE *SPEAK*, BEHIND THE SCENES.
POLITICIANS RISING AND *FALLING*, CEOS *RESIGNING*, INVESTIGATIONS BEING *OPENED* AND *CLOSED*...
...MY FATHER ANTICIPATES A *SMOOTH TRANSITION*.

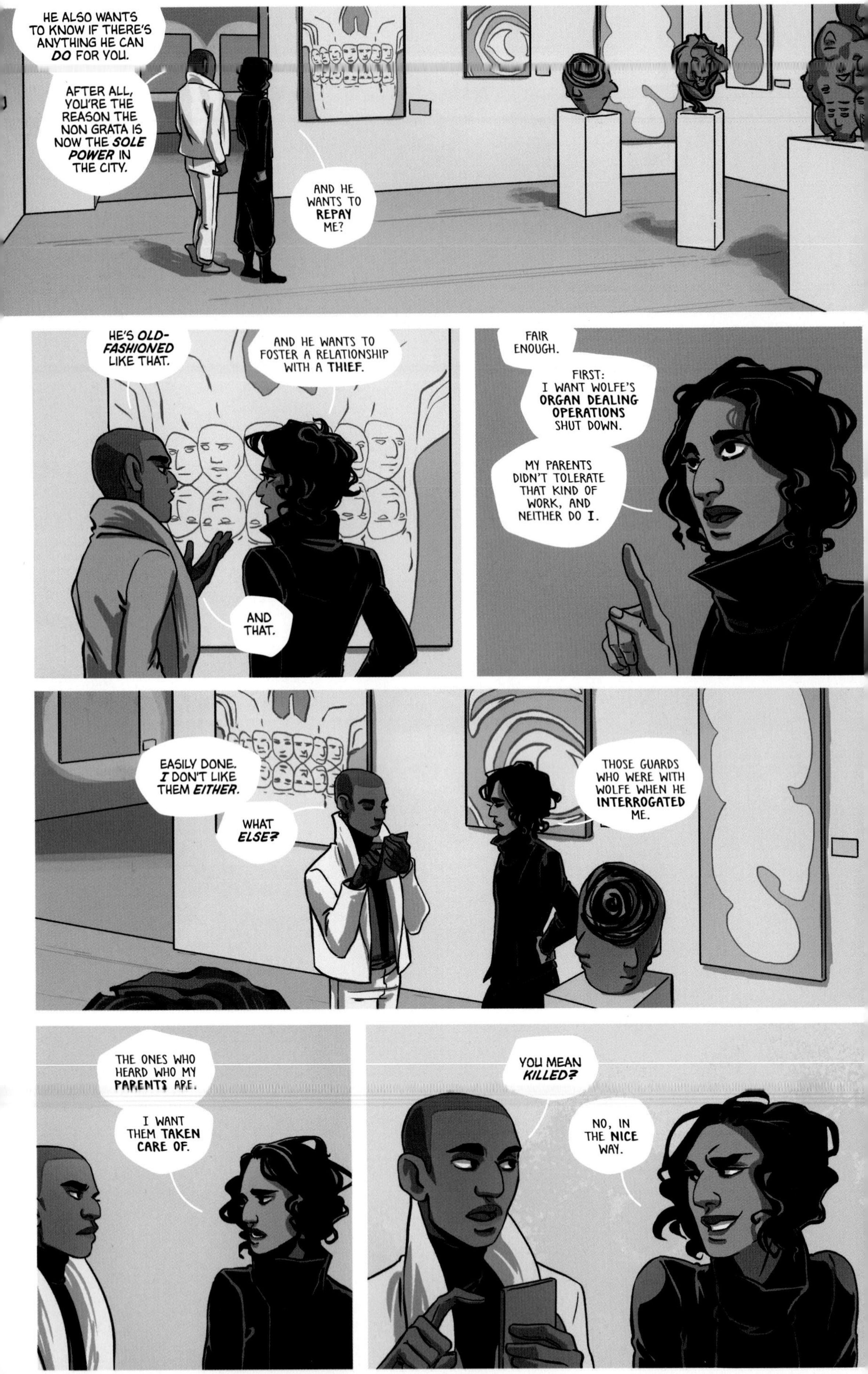

HE ALSO WANTS TO KNOW IF THERE'S ANYTHING HE CAN DO FOR YOU.
AFTER ALL, YOU'RE THE REASON THE NON GRATA IS NOW THE SOLE POWER IN THE CITY.
AND HE WANTS TO REPAY ME?
HE'S OLD-FASHIONED LIKE THAT.
AND HE WANTS TO FOSTER A RELATIONSHIP WITH A THIEF.
AND THAT.
FAIR ENOUGH.
FIRST: I WANT WOLFE'S ORGAN DEALING OPERATIONS SHUT DOWN.
MY PARENTS DIDN'T TOLERATE THAT KIND OF WORK, AND NEITHER DO I.
EASILY DONE. I DON'T LIKE THEM EITHER.
WHAT ELSE?
THOSE GUARDS WHO WERE WITH WOLFE WHEN HE INTERROGATED ME.
THE ONES WHO HEARD WHO MY PARENTS ARE.
I WANT THEM TAKEN CARE OF.
YOU MEAN KILLED?
NO, IN THE NICE WAY.

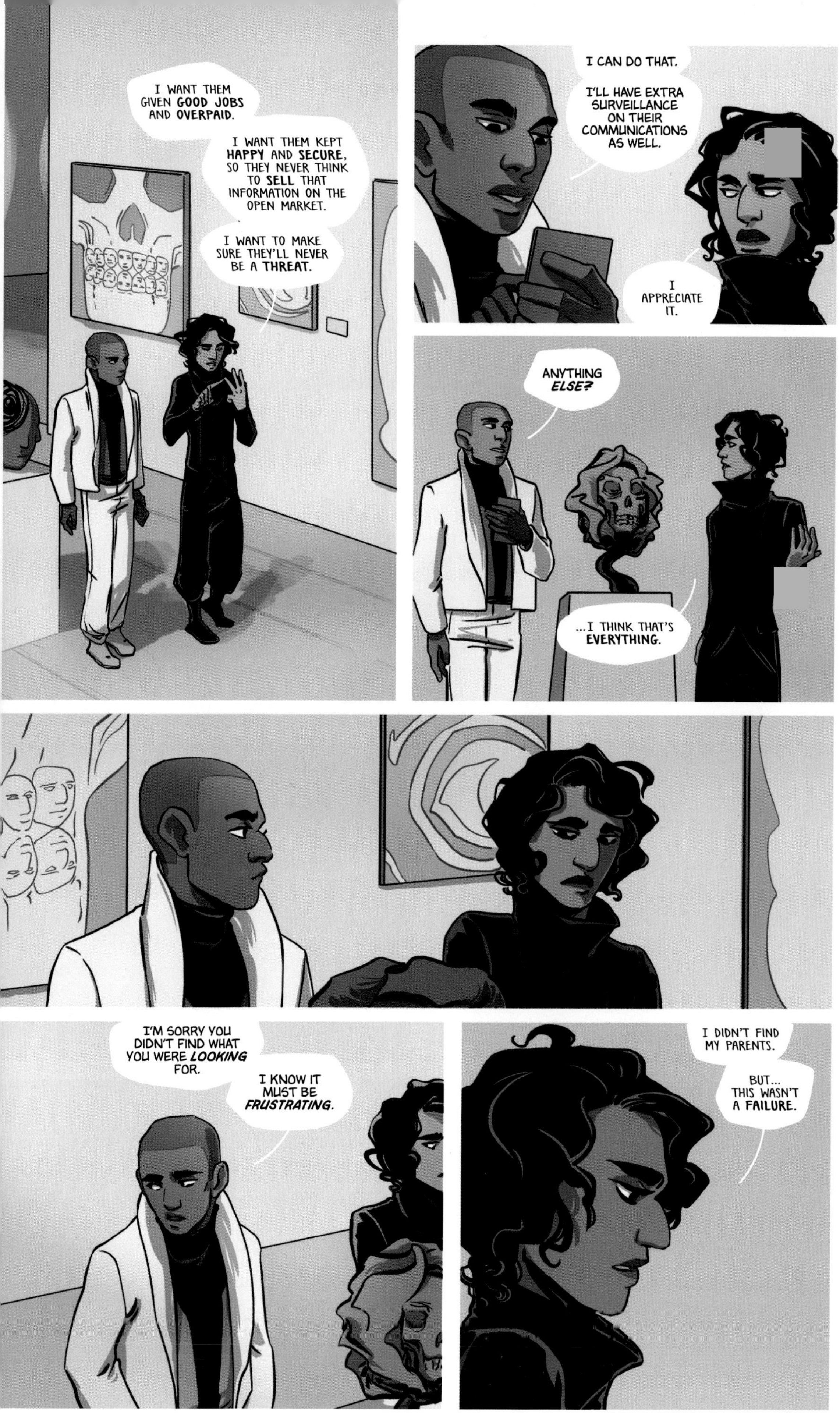
I WANT THEM GIVEN **GOOD JOBS** AND **OVERPAID**.
I WANT THEM KEPT **HAPPY** AND **SECURE**, SO THEY NEVER THINK TO **SELL** THAT INFORMATION ON THE OPEN MARKET.
I WANT TO MAKE SURE THEY'LL NEVER BE A **THREAT**.
I CAN DO THAT.
I'LL HAVE EXTRA SURVEILLANCE ON THEIR COMMUNICATIONS AS WELL.
I APPRECIATE IT.
ANYTHING ***ELSE?***
...I THINK THAT'S **EVERYTHING**.
I'M SORRY YOU DIDN'T FIND WHAT YOU WERE ***LOOKING*** FOR.
I KNOW IT MUST BE ***FRUSTRATING***.
I DIDN'T FIND MY PARENTS.
BUT... THIS WASN'T A **FAILURE**.

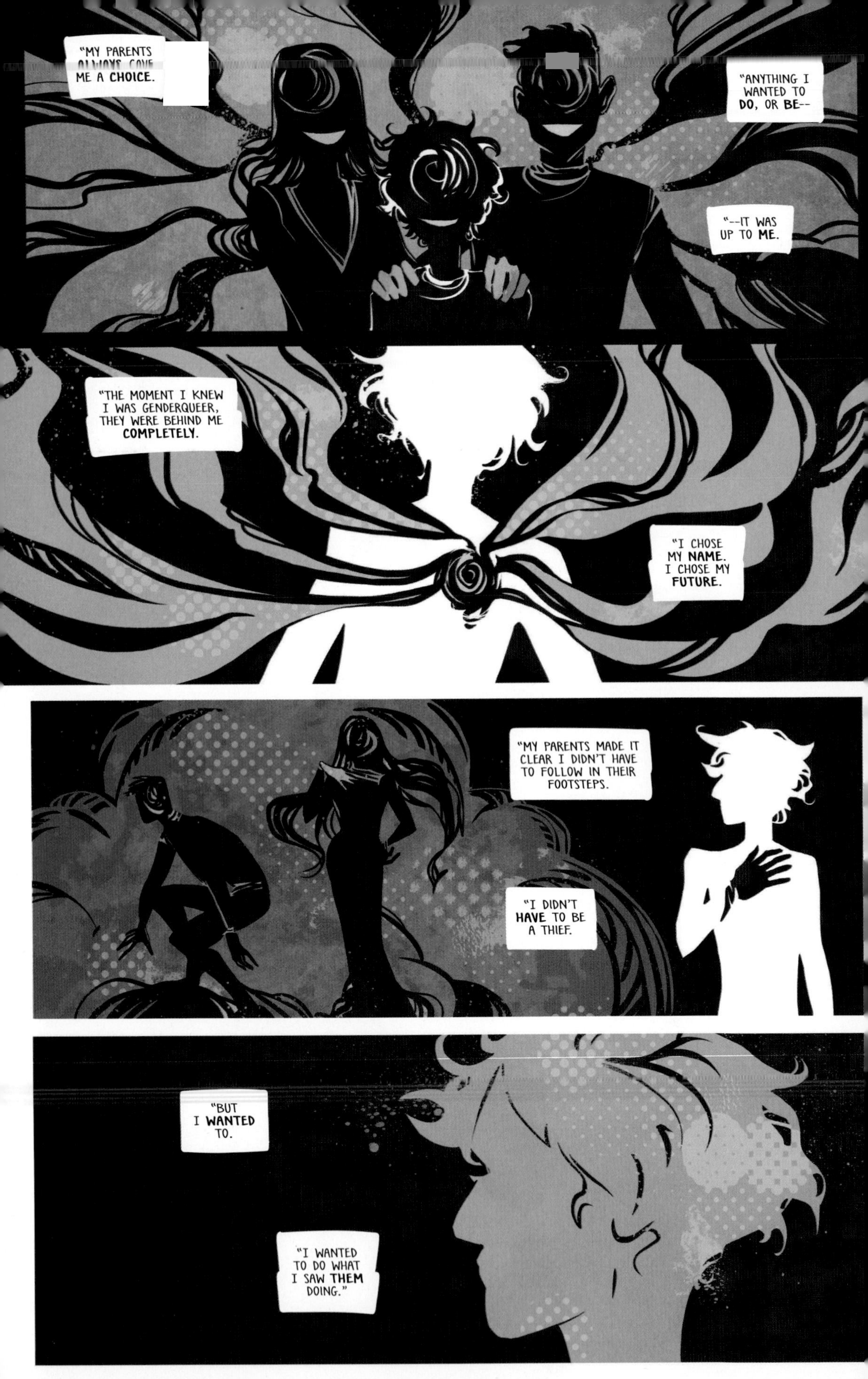
"MY PARENTS ALWAYS GAVE ME A CHOICE.
"ANYTHING I WANTED TO DO, OR BE--
"--IT WAS UP TO ME.
"THE MOMENT I KNEW I WAS GENDERQUEER, THEY WERE BEHIND ME COMPLETELY.
"I CHOSE MY NAME. I CHOSE MY FUTURE.
"MY PARENTS MADE IT CLEAR I DIDN'T HAVE TO FOLLOW IN THEIR FOOTSTEPS.
"I DIDN'T HAVE TO BE A THIEF.
"BUT I WANTED TO.
"I WANTED TO DO WHAT I SAW THEM DOING."

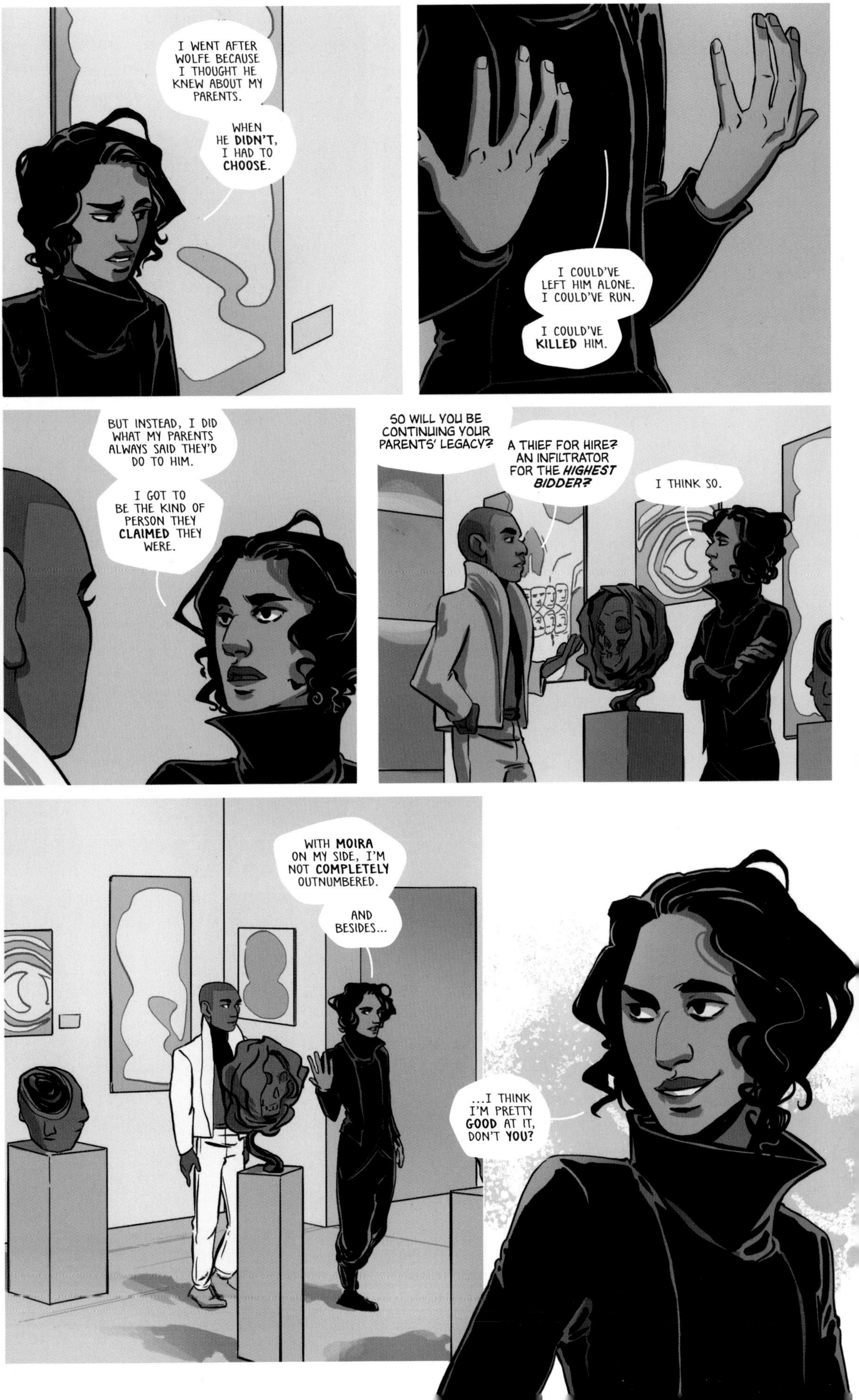
I WENT AFTER WOLFE BECAUSE I THOUGHT HE KNEW ABOUT MY PARENTS.
WHEN HE DIDN'T, I HAD TO CHOOSE.
I COULD'VE LEFT HIM ALONE. I COULD'VE RUN.
I COULD'VE KILLED HIM.
BUT INSTEAD, I DID WHAT MY PARENTS ALWAYS SAID THEY'D DO TO HIM.
I GOT TO BE THE KIND OF PERSON THEY CLAIMED THEY WERE.
SO WILL YOU BE CONTINUING YOUR PARENTS' LEGACY?
A THIEF FOR HIRE? AN INFILTRATOR FOR THE HIGHEST BIDDER?
I THINK SO.
WITH MOIRA ON MY SIDE, I'M NOT COMPLETELY OUTNUMBERED.
AND BESIDES...
...I THINK I'M PRETTY GOOD AT IT, DON'T YOU?

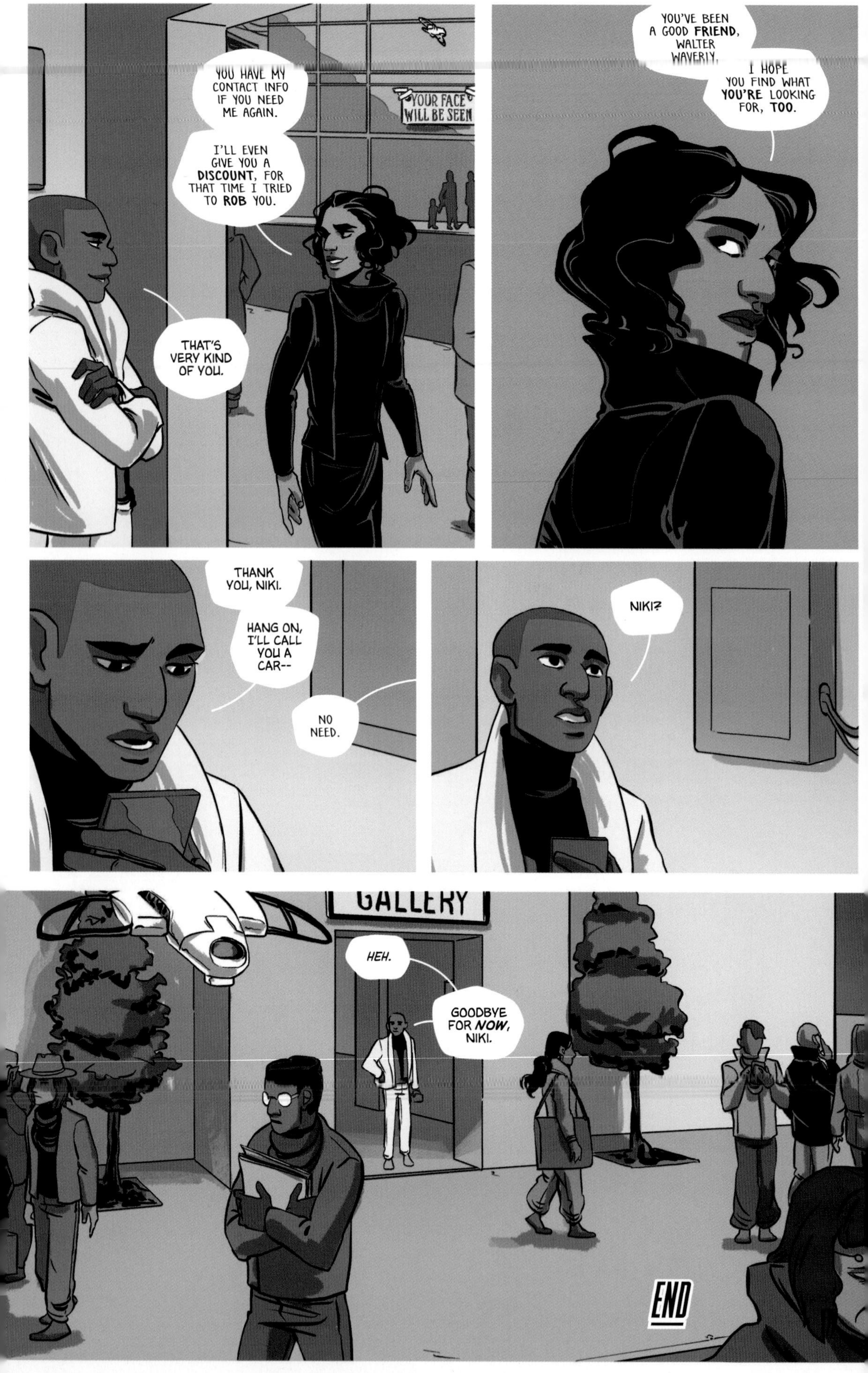
YOUR FACE WILL BE SEEN
YOU HAVE MY CONTACT INFO IF YOU NEED ME AGAIN.
I'LL EVEN GIVE YOU A DISCOUNT, FOR THAT TIME I TRIED TO ROB YOU.
THAT'S VERY KIND OF YOU.
YOU'VE BEEN A GOOD FRIEND, WALTER WAVERLY.
I HOPE YOU FIND WHAT YOU'RE LOOKING FOR, TOO.
THANK YOU, NIKI.
HANG ON, I'LL CALL YOU A CAR--
NO NEED.
NIKI?
GALLERY
HEH.
GOODBYE FOR NOW, NIKI.
END

Issue 1
JORGE CORONA
variant cover

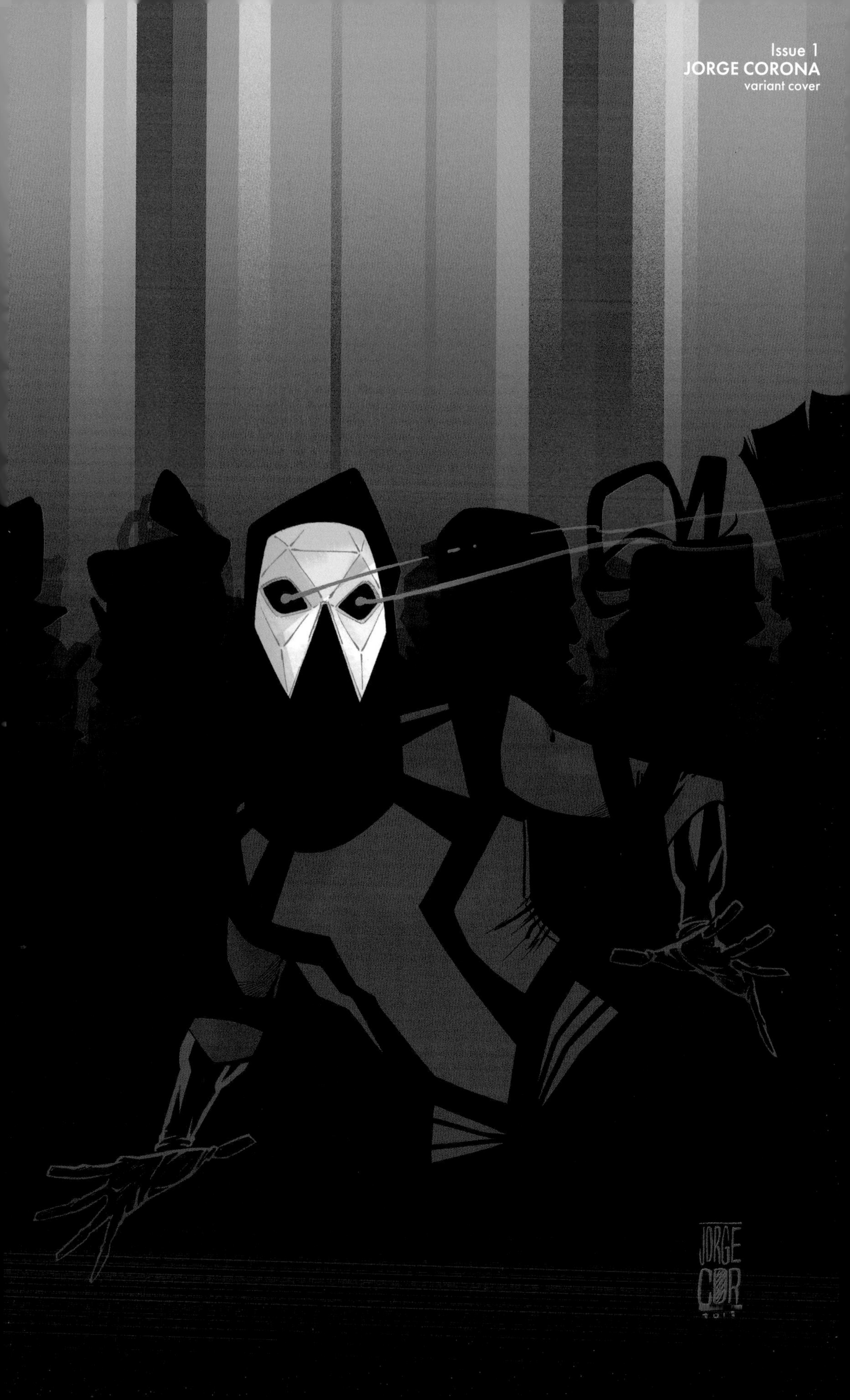
JORGE
COR

W O R L D B U I L D I N G

As part of the worldbuilding process, Jen and I came up with a number of signs that could appear in the background of various scenes. We talked extensively about how the world currently works, what issues are important, how technology has shaped this society, and these signs are more details that help establish this future history. We didn't get to use all of them, but check the backgrounds in the city scenes, and especially the cover of this trade paperback.

TED ANDERSON

YOUR FACE WILL BE SEEN - FACIAL RECOGNITION SOFTWARE IN THIS AREA

MUNICIPAL DATA NETWORK - DATA USAGE WILL BE MONITORED

[on a water source] FOR BATHING ONLY - NOT POTABLE - DO NOT INGEST

NO PRIVATE WATER - USE PUBLIC WATER SOURCES

ELECTROMAGNETIC FIELDS IN EXCESS OF 300 Hz ARE PRESENT

FACIAL RECOGNITION SOFTWARE IN USE - DO NOT COVER FACE

GERM-AWARE SPACE - PLEASE COVER HANDS AND MOUTH

DO NOT INTERACT WITH REFUGEES [display image of refugee collar]

[in a bathroom] YOUR WASTE MAY BE SAMPLED FOR ANONYMOUS PUBLIC HEALTH DATA

NO VISIBLE RELIGIOUS SYMBOLS IN THIS AREA

ALLERGENS PRESENT - PLEASE CHECK LOCAL ALLERGEN ALERTS

THIS CHARGING STATION PROVIDED BY [company] - NON-[company] USERS MAY USE THIS STATION FOR AN EXTRA SURCHARGE

MOTH & WHISPER sketchbook

art & words by JEN HICKMAN

For MOTH & WHISPER, I wanted to use character design to tell a story about the world. Clear face masks, implants, glasses, gloves—these little details help the reader understand the world without having to sit them down and saying "the air in the city is pretty bad" or "many people incorporate their tech into their bodies" or "the rich wear gloves to protect their identities" and therefore keep the plot moving.

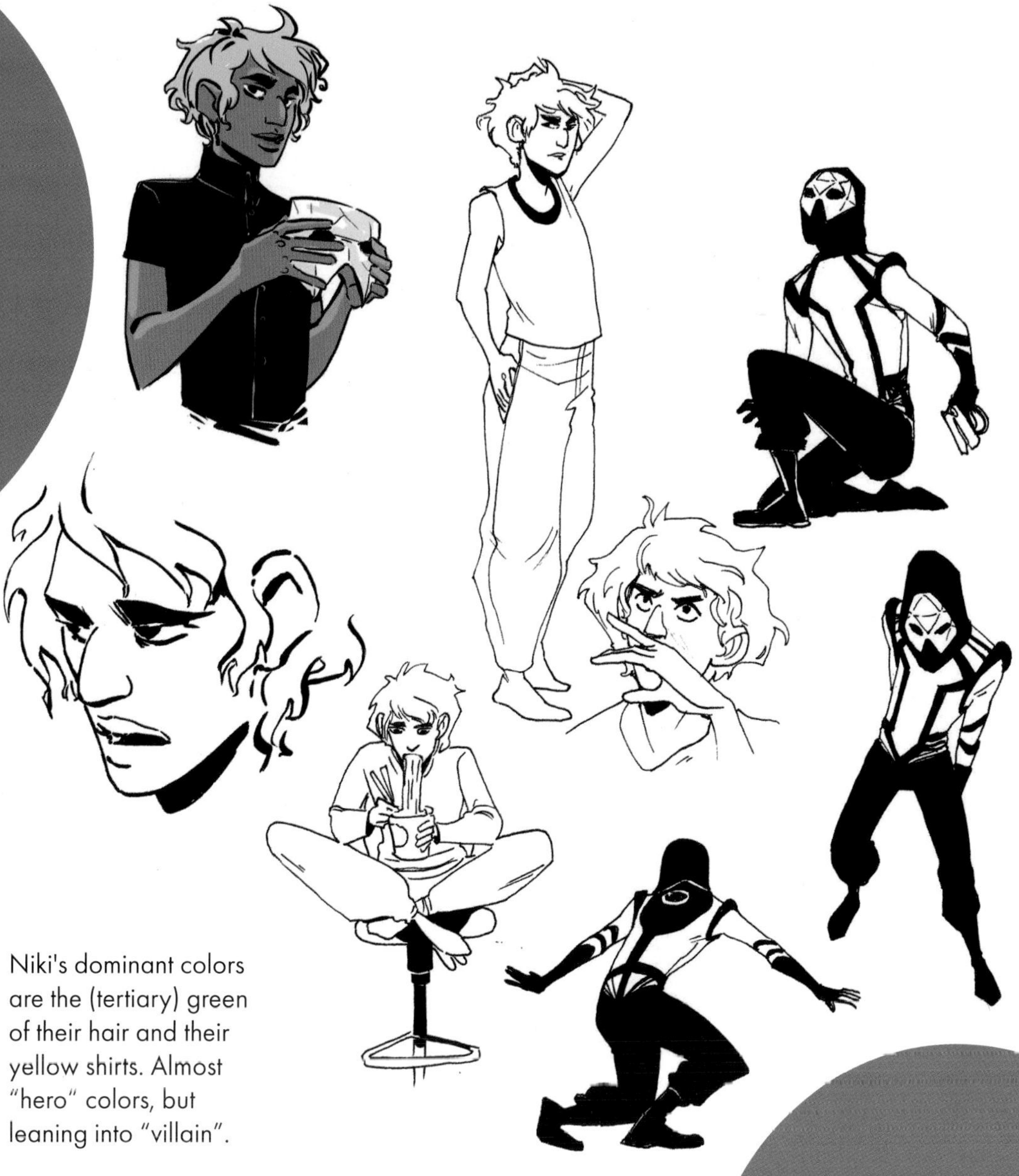

Niki's dominant colors are the (tertiary) green of their hair and their yellow shirts. Almost "hero" colors, but leaning into "villain".

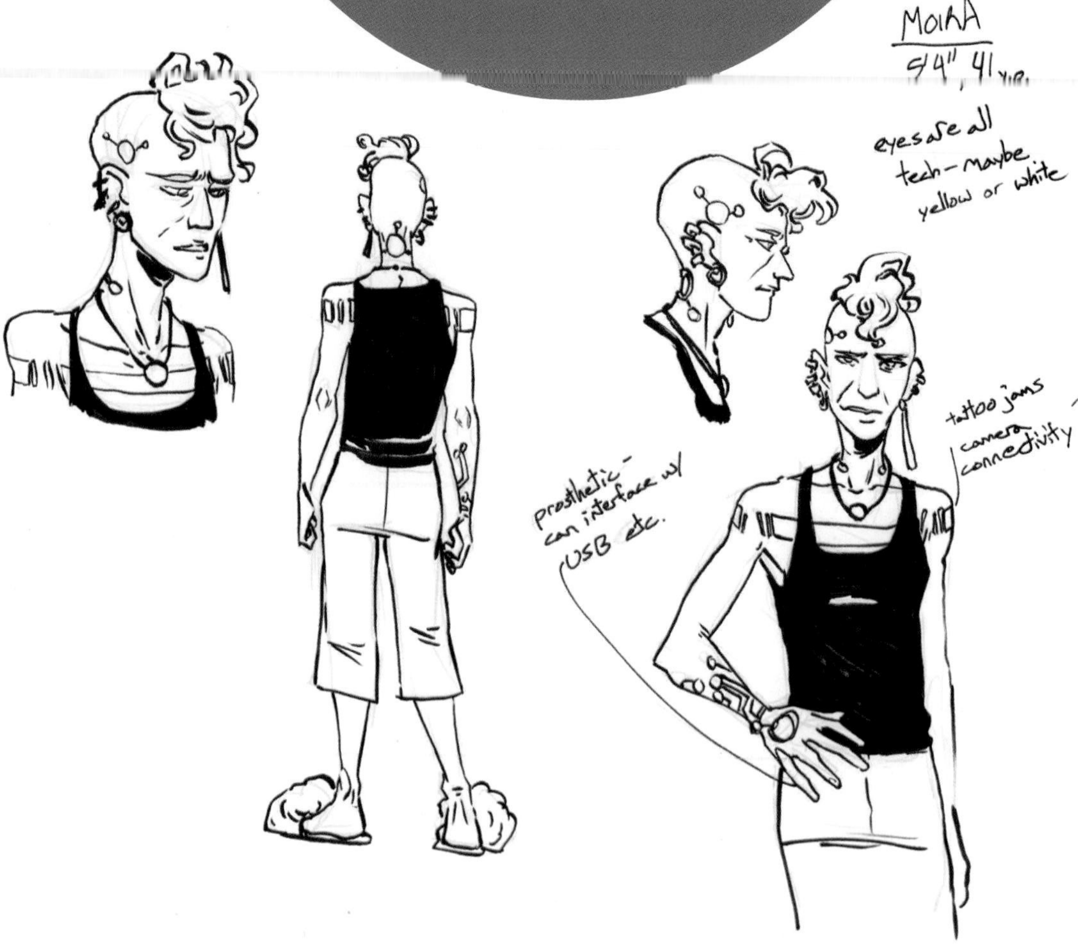
MOIRA
5'4", 41 yrs.
eyes are all tech - maybe yellow or white
tattoo jams camera connectivity?
prosthetic - can interface w/ USB etc.

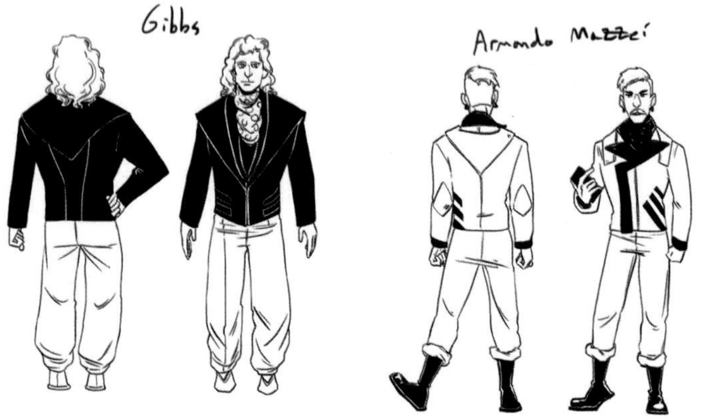
Gibbs
Armando Mazzei

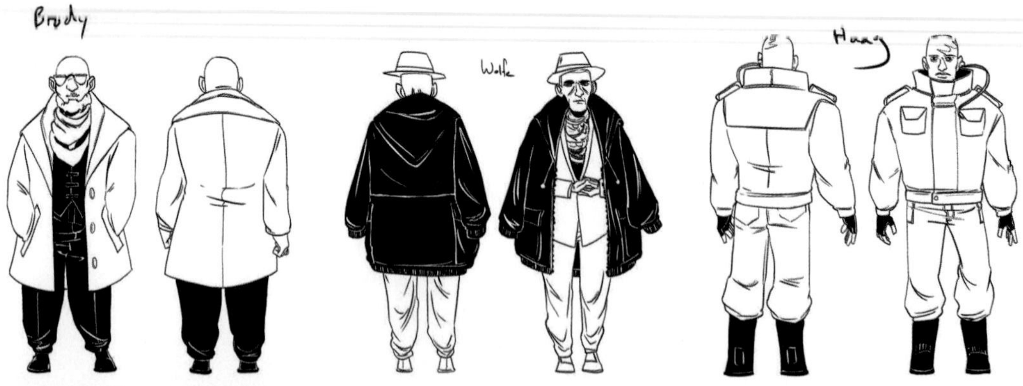
Brody
Wolfe
Haag

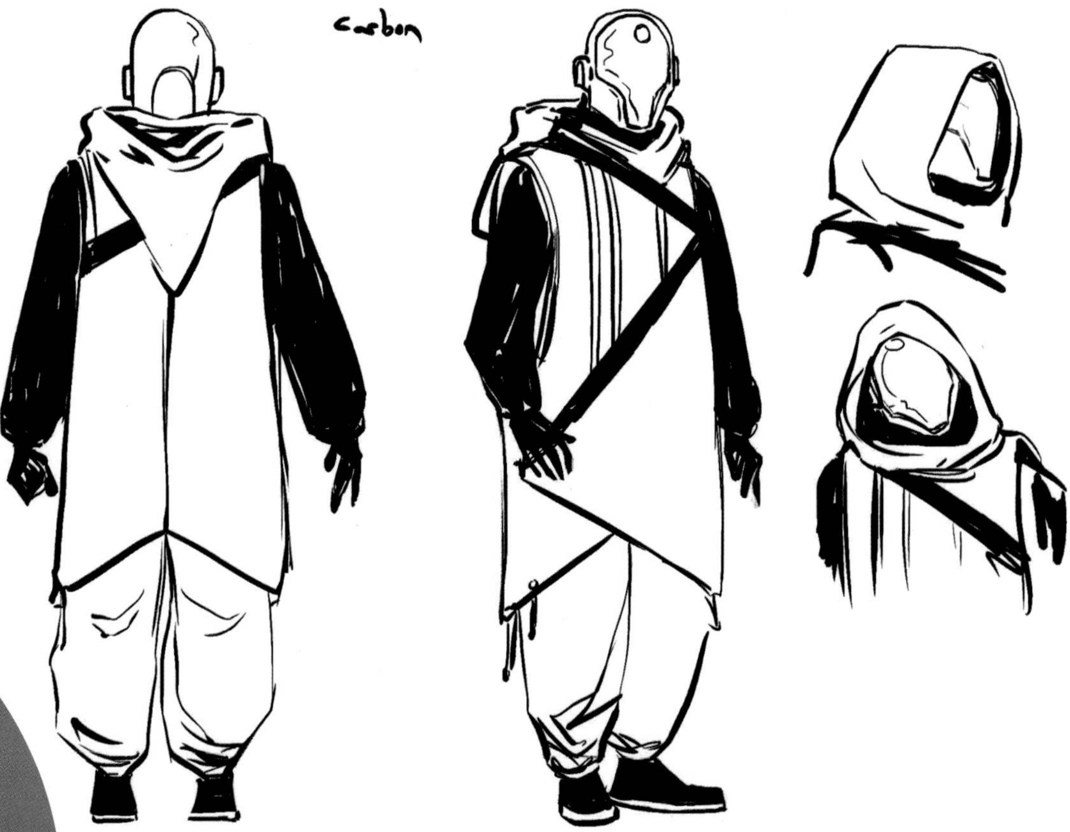
Carbon

For me, a character's design begins with their silhouette: how much space do they take up, where are their big shapes, are they round or angular, filled with fiddly details or simple lines, etc. There's a lot of information I can give the reader that will (if I'm doing it right!) subconsciously tell them about the character's personality, their place in the world, and what their actions might be—just through their shapes.

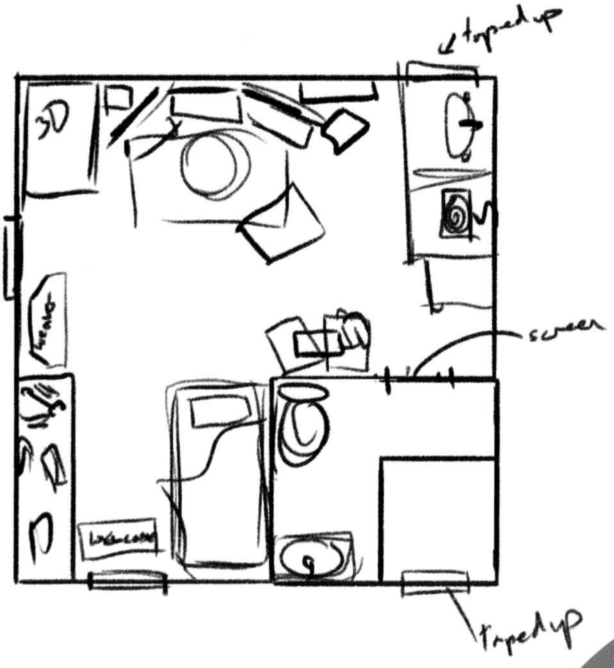
taped up
3D
screen
taped up

I prefer character designs where a character has one or two dominant colors that are always incorporated into their looks—it gives me something to use as shorthand for the character if I need it, plus it helps readers identify characters quickly.

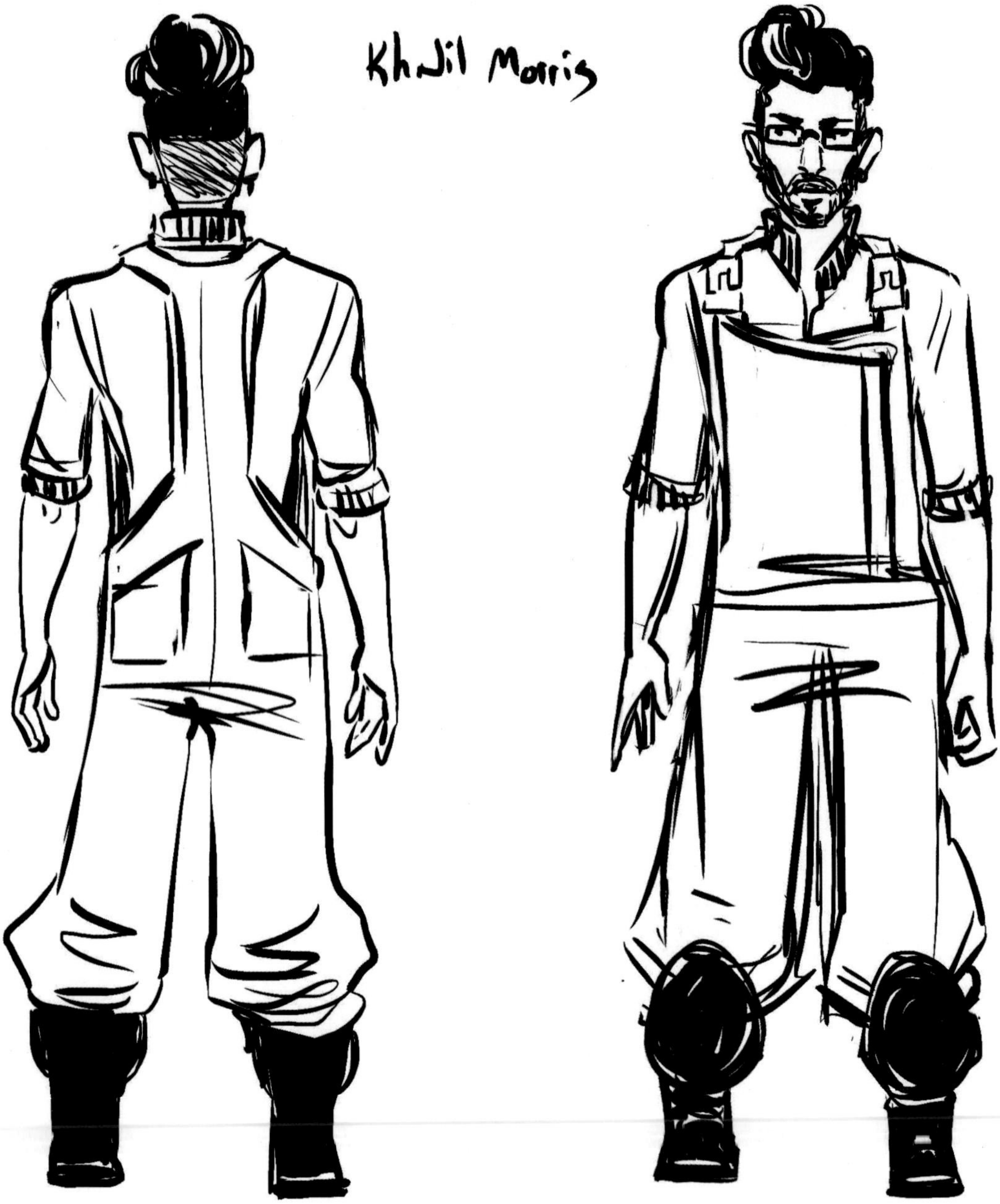
Khalil Morris

When I was in school, my amazing concept professor, Mia Goodwin, did a great lecture on color choices and the way we've coded some of them in our culture (primary colors for protagonists, tertiary colors for villains, etc.). I draw on what I learned from her every time I design a character, but more often than not to subvert expectations rather than uphold them.

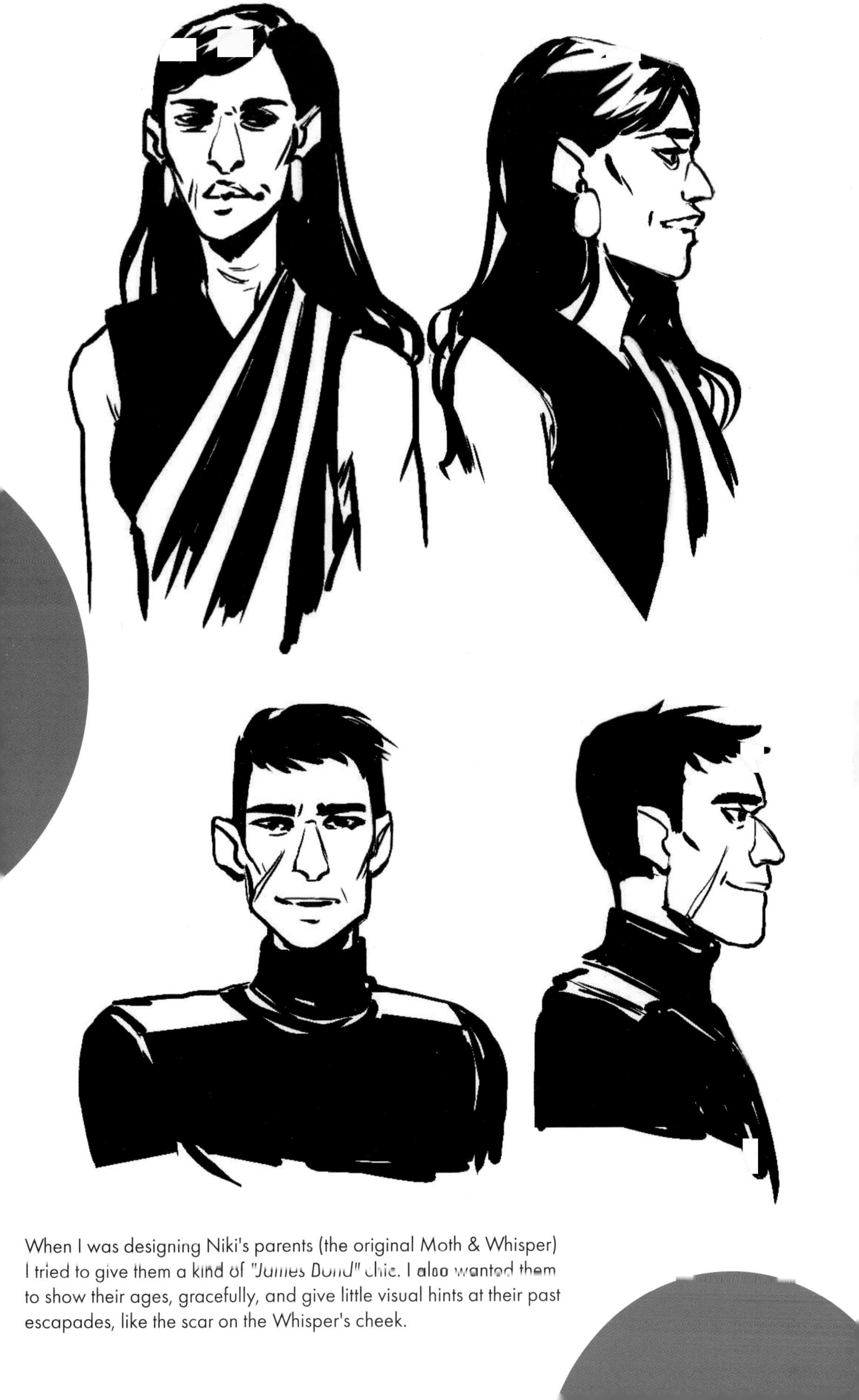

When I was designing Niki's parents (the original Moth & Whisper) I tried to give them a kind of *"James Bond"* chic. I also wanted them to show their ages, gracefully, and give little visual hints at their past escapades, like the scar on the Whisper's cheek.

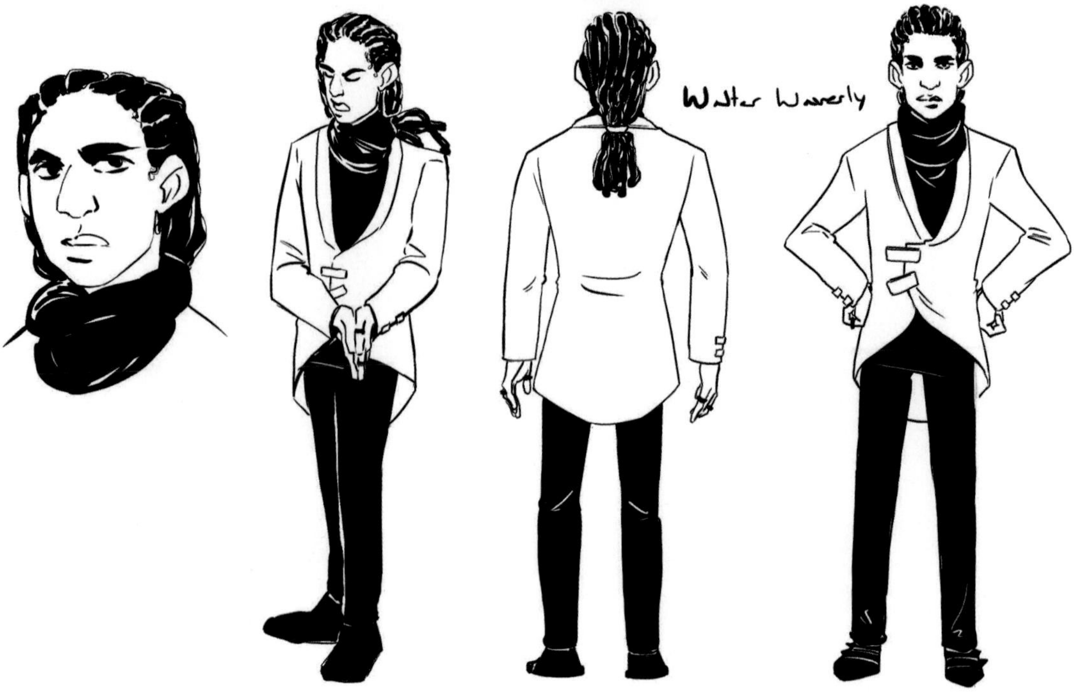
Walter Waverly

Walter took me a while to pin down. He needed to be Very Serious, but also a kid, and extremely meticulous and fashionable. I forget at what point Ted mentioned gloves as the height of fashion, but I loved the idea. It totally fit the world and was perfect for the character—so on the actual pages Walter wears gloves.

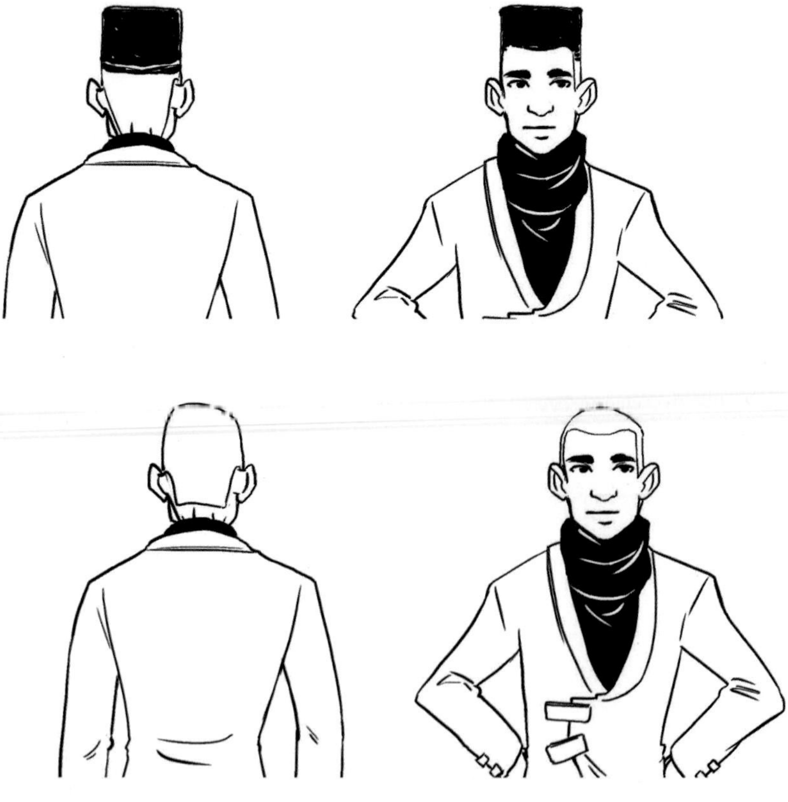

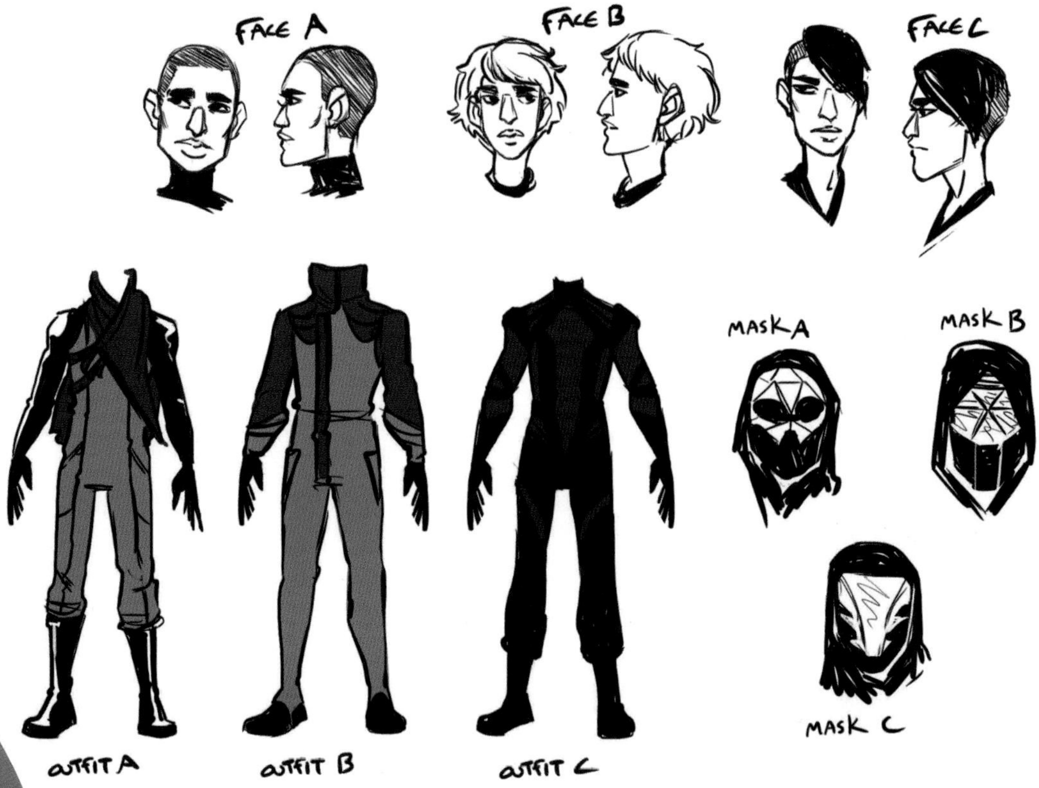
FACE A
FACE B
FACE C
MASK A
MASK B
MASK C
OUTFIT A
OUTFIT B
OUTFIT C

I get very fixated on designs being plausible/practical, so designing Weaver meant designing tons of little pockets and storage space so that Niki could carry tools easily. I think the little backpack is my favorite.

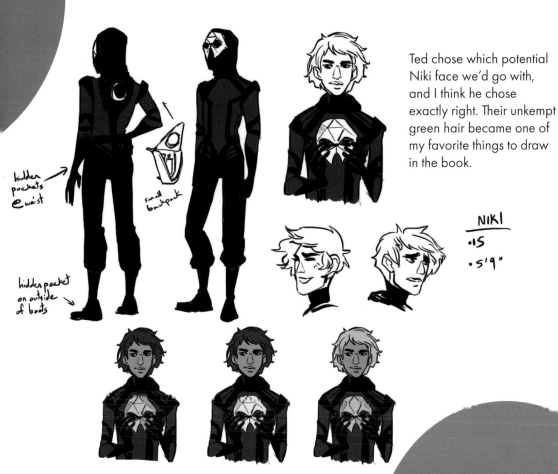

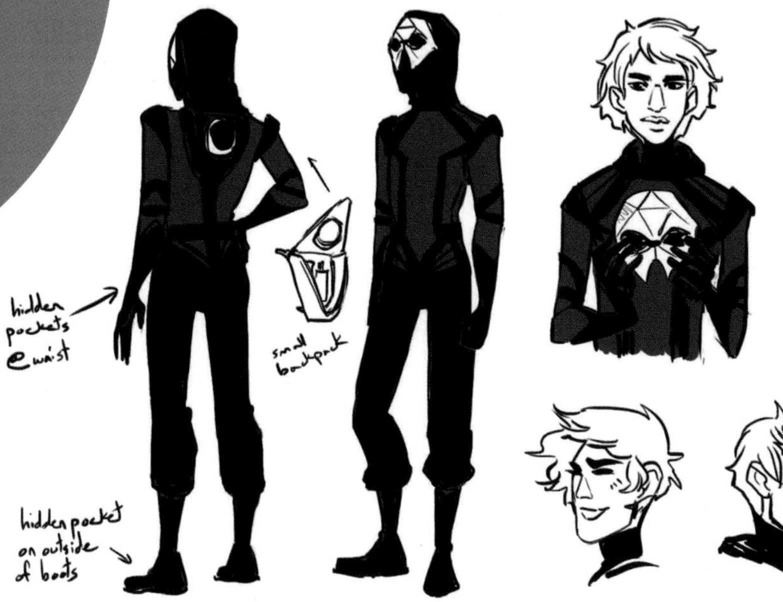
hidden pockets @ waist
small backpack
hidden pocket on outside of boots

Ted chose which potential Niki face we'd go with, and I think he chose exactly right. Their unkempt green hair became one of my favorite things to draw in the book.

NIKI
•15
•5'9"

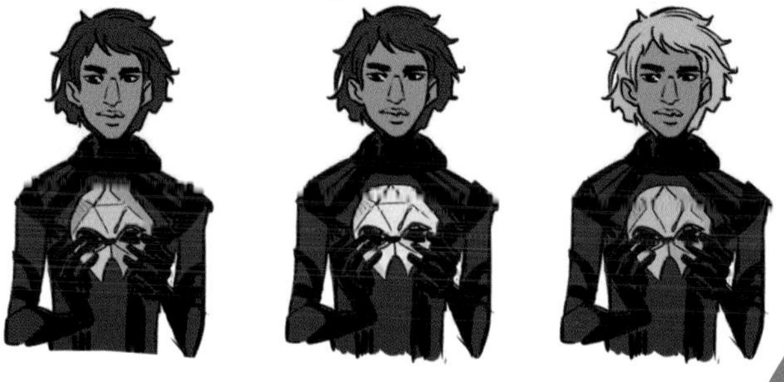

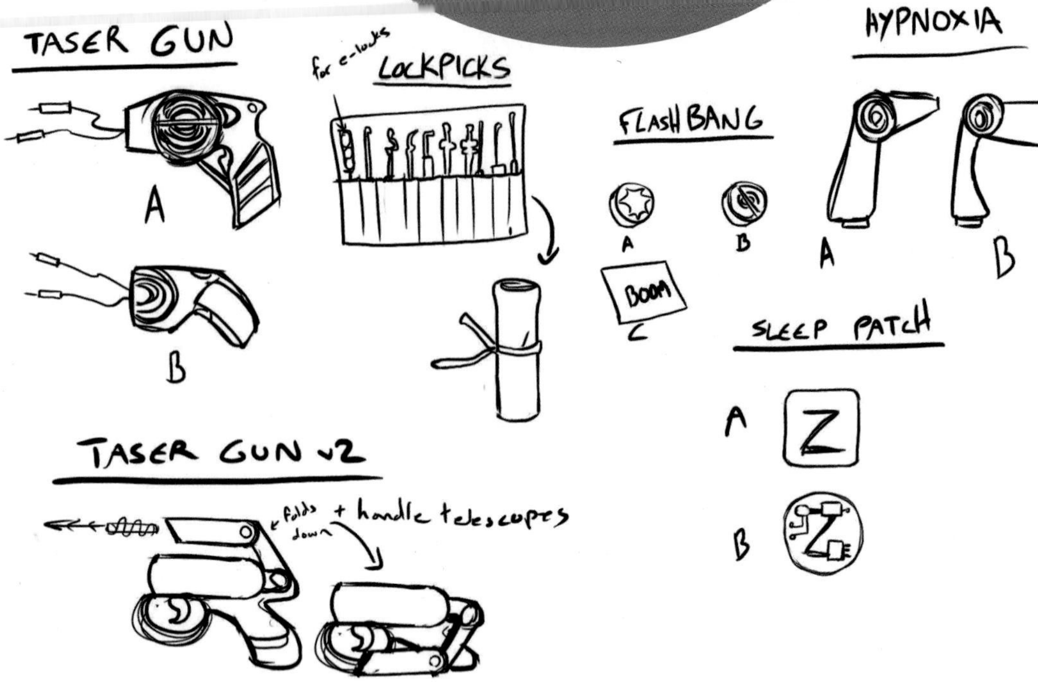
TASER GUN
A
B
for e-locks
LOCKPICKS
FLASHBANG
A
B
BOOM
C
HYPNOXIA
A
B
SLEEP PATCH
A
B
TASER GUN v2
folds down
+ handle telescopes

The mole's lair is completely, 100% me. Ted had some ideas, but I had this idea and he very kindly let me have it.

Before I drew comics, I worked in a corporate environment and used to spend boring meeting-hours daydreaming about some kind of apocalypse that would demand I take over the entire office as a home base. How would I fortify it? How would I get food, water? Which cubicles would I immediately destroy, which fishbowl-with-an-unbearably-clever-name would I choose for experiments and projects? What purpose would I use the bullpen for?

More or less that's Moira's home. It's probably the least realistic thing in the book (well, Weaver maybe...) but I love it.

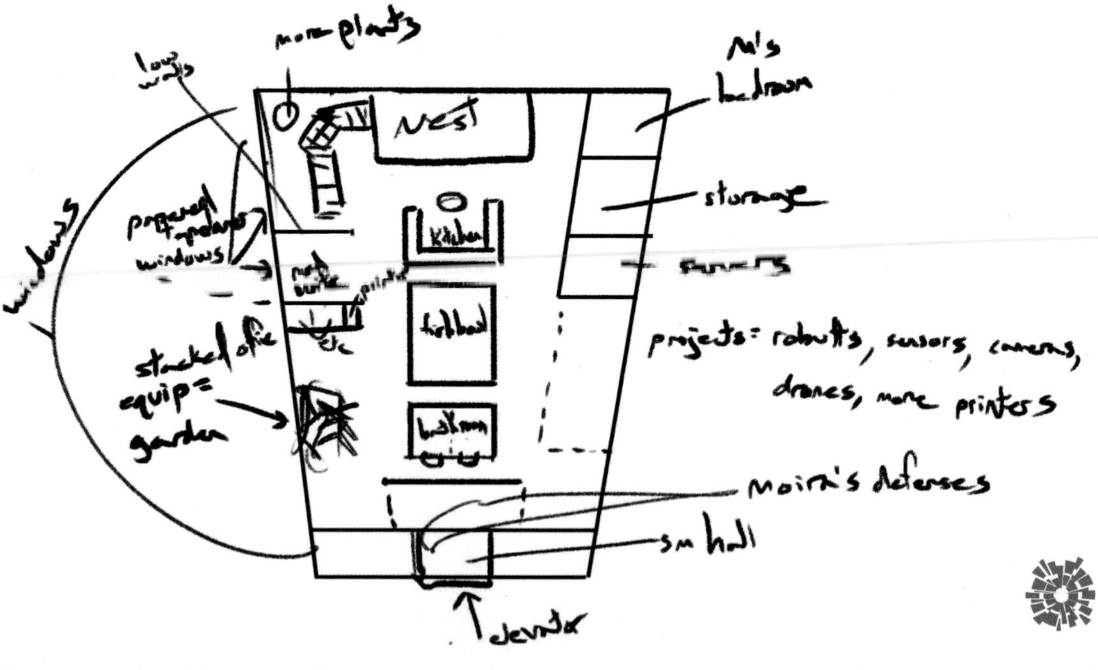
more plants
low walls
M's bedroom
Nest
storage
kitchen
windows
fishbowl
stacked office equip = garden
bathroom
projects: robots, sensors, cameras, drones, more printers
Moira's defenses
sm hall
elevator

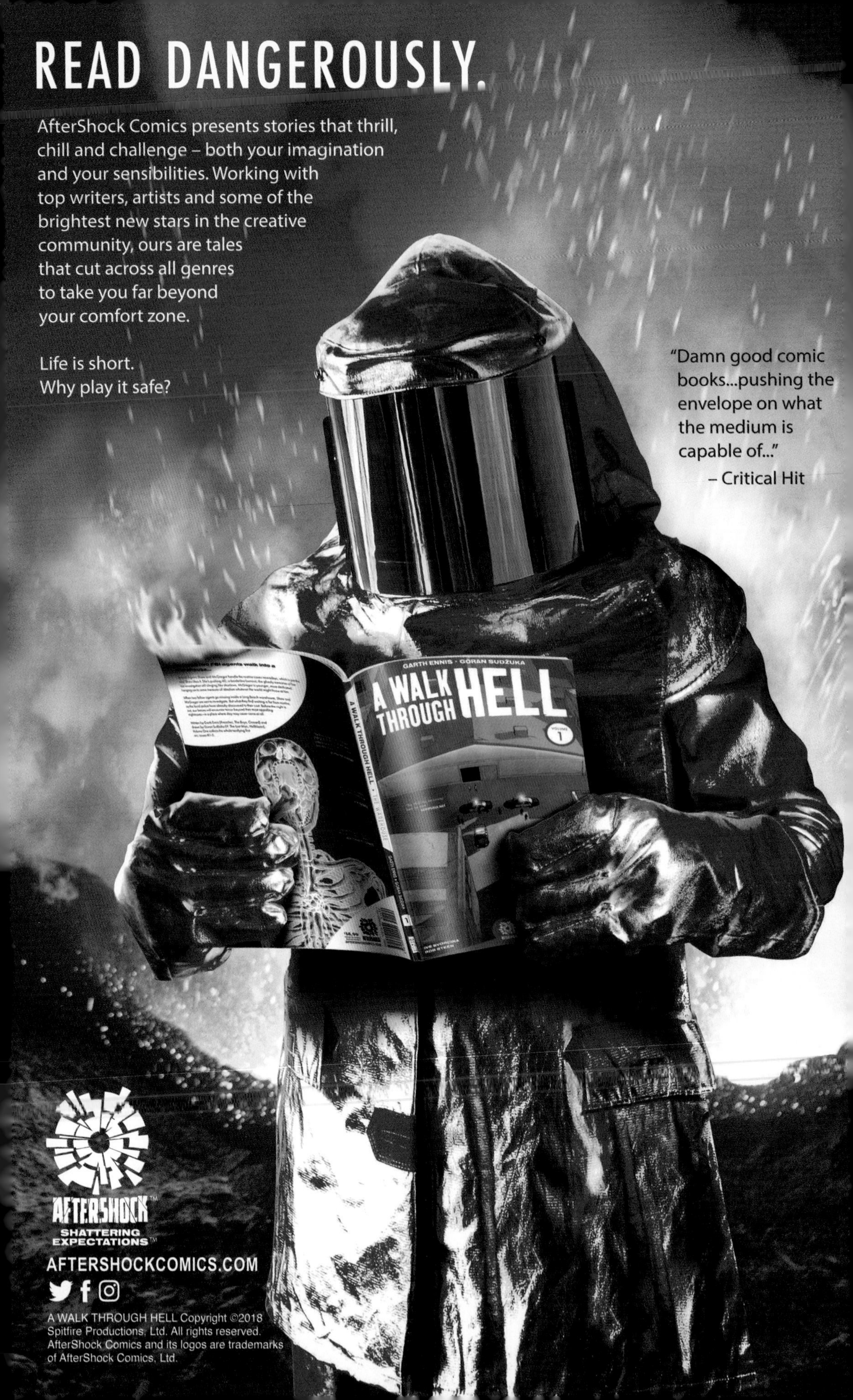
READ DANGEROUSLY.
AfterShock Comics presents stories that thrill, chill and challenge – both your imagination and your sensibilities. Working with top writers, artists and some of the brightest new stars in the creative community, ours are tales that cut across all genres to take you far beyond your comfort zone.
Life is short. Why play it safe?
"Damn good comic books...pushing the envelope on what the medium is capable of..."
– Critical Hit
GARTH ENNIS · GORAN SUDŽUKA
A WALK THROUGH HELL
VOLUME 1
AFTERSHOCK™
SHATTERING EXPECTATIONS™
AFTERSHOCKCOMICS.COM
A WALK THROUGH HELL Copyright ©2018 Spitfire Productions, Ltd. All rights reserved. AfterShock Comics and its logos are trademarks of AfterShock Comics, Ltd.

STOCK UP ON THESE GREAT AFTERSHOCK COLLECTIONS!

A WALK THROUGH HELL VOL 1
GARTH ENNIS / GORAN SUDZUKA
SEP181388

ALTERS VOL 1 & VOL 2
PAUL JENKINS / LEILA LEIZ
MAR171244 & APR181239

AMERICAN MONSTER VOL 1
BRIAN AZZARELLO / JUAN DOE
SEP161213

ANIMOSITY YEAR ONE, VOL 1, VOL 2 & VOL 3
MARGUERITE BENNETT / RAFAEL DE LATORRE
FEB181034, JAN171219, AUG171130 & MAY181314

ANIMOSITY: EVOLUTION VOL 1 & VOL 2
MARGUERITE BENNETT / ERIC GAPSTUR
MAR181079 & FEB188089

ANIMOSITY: THE RISE HARDCOVER
MARGUERITE BENNETT / JUAN DOE
AUG178324

ART OF JIM STARLIN HARDCOVER
JIM STARLIN
MAR181077

BABYTEETH YEAR ONE, VOL 1 & VOL 2
DONNY CATES / GARRY BROWN
OCT181328, OCT171087 & APR181225

BETROTHED VOL 1
SEAN LEWIS / STEVE UY
DEC181449161115

BEYONDERS VOL 1
PAUL JENKINS / WESLEY ST. CLAIRE
JAN191468

BLACK-EYED KIDS VOL 1, VOL 2 & VOL 3
JOE PRUETT / SZYMON KUDRANSKI
AUG161115, FEB171100 & JAN181152

BROTHERS DRACUL VOL 1
CULLEN BUNN / MIRKO COLAK
SEP181404

CAPTAIN KID VOL 1
MARK WAID / TOM PEYER / WILFREDO TORRES
APR171231

CLAN KILLERS VOL 1
SEAN LEWIS / ANTONIO FUSO
JAN191469

COLD WAR VOL 1
CHRISTOPHER SEBELA / HAYDEN SHERMAN
JUL181518

DARK ARK VOL 1 & VOL 2
CULLEN BUNN / JUAN DOE
FEB181035 & SEP181394

DREAMING EAGLES HARDCOVER
GARTH ENNIS / SIMON COLEBY
AUG161114

ELEANOR & THE EGRET VOL 1
JOHN LAYMAN / SAM KIETH
DEC171041

FU JITSU VOL 1
JAI NITZ / WESLEY ST. CLAIRE
APR181241

HER INFERNAL DESCENT VOL 1
LONNIE NADLER / ZAC THOMPSON /
KYLE CHARLES / EOIN MARRON
OCT181341

HOT LUNCH SPECIAL VOl 1
ELIOT RAHAL / JORGE FORNES
DEC181449

INSEXTS YEAR ONE, VOL 1 & VOL 2
MARGUERITE BENNETT / ARIELA KRISTANTINA
APR181228, JUN161072 & SEP171098

JIMMY'S BASTARDS VOL & VOL 2
GARTH ENNIS / RUSS BRAUN
DEC171040 & JUN181333

MONSTRO MECHANICA VOL 1
PAUL ALLOR / CHRIS EVENHUIS
JUL181517

OUT OF THE BLUE VOL 1
GARTH ENNIS / KEITH BURNS
JAN191460

PESTILENCE VOL 1 & VOL 2
FRANK TIERI / OLEG OKUNEV
NOV171154, OCT181340

REPLICA VOL 1
PAUL JENKINS / ANDY CLARKE
MAY161030

ROUGH RIDERS VOL 1, VOL 2 & VOL 3
ADAM GLASS / PATRICK OLLIFFE
OCT161101, SEP171097 & AUG181474

SECOND SIGHT VOL 1
DAVID HINE / ALBERTO PONTICELL
DEC161186

SHIPWRECK VOL 1
WARREN ELLIS / PHIL HESTER
MAR181078

SHOCK HARDCOVER
VARIOUS
JAN181139

SUPERZERO VOL 1
AMANDA CONNER / JIMMY PALMIOTTI / RAFAEL DE LATORRE
MAY161029

THE LOST CITY EXPLORERS VOL 1
ZACHARY KAPLAN / ALVARO SARRASECA
NOV181434

THE NORMALS VOL 1
ADAM GLASS / DENNIS CALERO
SEP181391

UNHOLY GRAIL VOL 1
CULLEN BUNN / MIRKO COLAK
JAN181151

WITCH HAMMER OGN
CULLEN BUNN / DALIBOR TALAJIC
SEP181387

WORLD READER VOL 1
JEFF LOVENESS / JUAN DOE
SEP171096

www.aftershockcomics.com/collections

ABOUT THE CREATORS OF

MOTH & WHISPER™

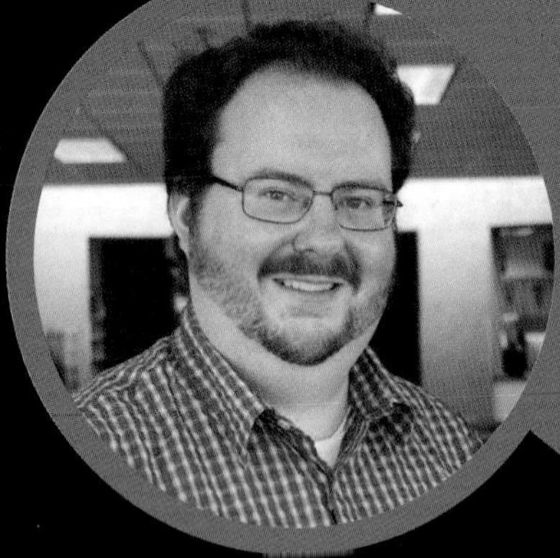

TED ANDERSON

writer

@TedlyAnderson

Ted Anderson is a librarian, writer and mammal. He has written for properties including *My Little Pony* and *Adventure Time*, and has never successfully defrauded a major corporation. He lives in Minneapolis with no regrets.

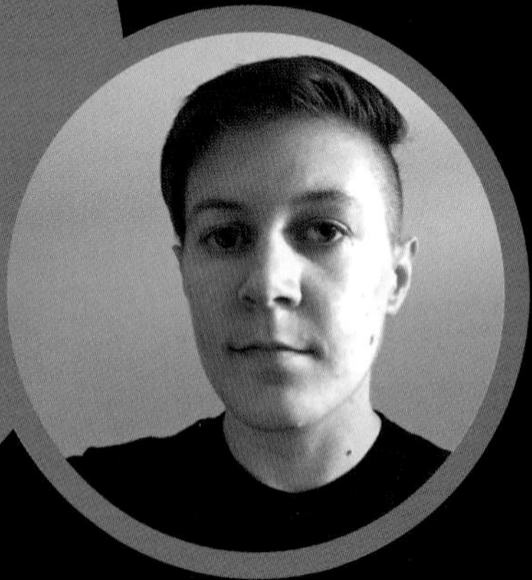

JEN HICKMAN

artist

@Umicorms

Jen Hickman is a visual storyteller and a graduate of the Savannah College of Art and Design's Sequential Art Program. Their primary passions are exciting narratives, good coffee and exceptional grammar.

MARSHALL DILLON

letterer

@MarshallDillon

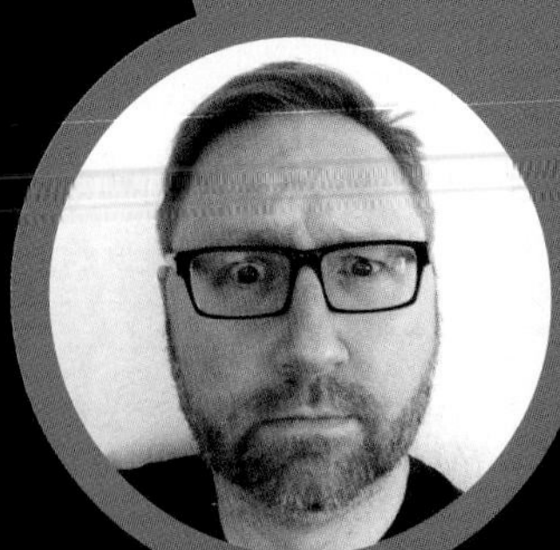

A comic book industry veteran, Marshall got his start in 1994, in the midst of the Indie comic boom. Over the years, he's been everything from an independent self-published writer to an associate publisher working on properties like *G.I. Joe, Voltron,* and *Street Fighter*. He's done just about everything except draw a comic book, and worked for just about every publisher except the "big two." Primarily a father and letterer these days, he also dabbles in old-school paper and dice RPG game design. You can catch up with Marshall at firstdraftpress.net.